LAYOVER
IN
DUBAI

LAYOVER
IN
DUBAI

DAN FESPERMAN

ALFRED A. KNOPF   NEW YORK   2010

THIS IS A BORZOI BOOK
PUBLISHED BY ALFRED A. KNOPF

All rights reserved. Published in the United States by
Alfred A. Knopf, a division of Random House, Inc., New York, and in
Canada by Random House of Canada Limited, Toronto.
www.aaknopf.com

Knopf, Borzoi Books, and the colophon are registered trademarks of
Random House, Inc.

Library of Congress Cataloging-in-Publication Data
Fesperman, Dan, [date]
Layover in Dubai / by Dan Fesperman.—1st ed.
p. cm.
"This is a Borzoi book."
ISBN 978-0-307-26838-9 (alk. paper)
1. Dubai (United Arab Emirates)—Fiction. I. Title.
PS3556.E778L39 2010
813'.54—dc22   2010006363

Manufactured in the United States of America
First Edition

LAYOVER

IN

DUBAI

1

April 2008

Sam Keller, still jet-lagged and still keeping a hand on his wallet, wondered how anyone could actually think of sex in a dump like this. There were at least three hundred people here, crammed beneath a low ceiling on a floor no bigger than a tennis court—slippery bodies wedged as tightly as the day's catch in the hold of a trawler. They stank of sweat, cigarettes, cheap whiskey, and spilled beer. Amber lights made every face queasy, and you had to shout to be heard over the din of a talentless rock band.

All in all, about as erotic as rush hour on the Jersey Turnpike. Pay the toll, roll up your window, and keep moving.

On the other hand, seeing as how everyone here was either a prostitute or a potential customer, how could you *not* think of sex, especially when each passing female rubbed against you like a cat on a trouser leg. It was enough to get the juice flowing in almost any male, and Sam, being twenty-eight, still had plenty of juice.

This chamber of squalors on the rim of the Persian Gulf was a brothel bar called the York Club. Sam still wasn't quite sure what he was doing there, other than gamely trying to enjoy the second and final night of what his business colleague, Charlie Hatcher, had billed as a free-spirited layover in Dubai. Ten hours from now he would be on his way to Hong Kong, but for the moment Sam was woozily laboring to make sense of this bizarre place seven thousand miles from home and eight hours ahead of Eastern Daylight Time.

His head for numbers told him that the cover charge of fifty dirhams—nearly fourteen dollars—was outrageous. His eye for documentation was amused by the entry ticket, with its official stamp from the Dubai Ministry of Tourism. Maybe it would pass muster for reimbursement.

The women's looks didn't wow him, but their variety was stunning. They were from India, Ethiopia, Indonesia, Thailand, Iraq, and seemingly each of the former Soviet republics, although their relentless sales pitch was always in English:

"You want nice time?"

"You want friendly date?"

"You like we go somewhere, have fun?"

Sam found it all a bit glum, sensing that for each of them the York Club was the last lonely bus stop on a long ride of despair. Yet onward they came, even more persistent than the merchants Sam had encountered that afternoon in Dubai's fabled Gold Souk, where brusque young Punjabi males had kept accosting him to ask: "You want fake Rolex? Nice copy watch? I give you good deal!"

Here it was the smiles that were fakes and copies, and as the 3 a.m. closing time approached, the salesmanship was turning desperate, with customers taking full advantage. Sam watched, appalled, as a drunken Brit in a smudged polo negotiated down the cost of a blow job to less than what he had paid for dinner that night at the Burj Al Arab, the famous hotel that looked like a giant blue sail. At this rate you'd soon be able to get laid for the cost of a crème brûlée and an espresso, tip not included.

Flesh was about the only bargain to be found in this eerie insta-city. Of the many places Sam had visited in his corporate travels for Pfluger Klaxon, none had been as well attuned to the quick-buck rhythms of runaway commerce as Dubai. Everything between the desert and the deep blue sea was for sale, and all of it was either going fast or being paved over to make way for more. The city's drumbeat was like the precision throb of an artificial heart, clicking and insistent, yet cool to the touch. Expats partied until dawn, and by the time they crawled out of bed the worth of their real estate portfolios had doubled. Sam couldn't help but wonder what would become of all the giddiness if the market ever collapsed beneath the weight of speculation. Suicide and depression, or more revelry? He was betting on some outlandish, oversized combination of the two, with a steep cover charge and a two-drink minimum.

Strange how a city so full of sun and sensation could leave him so cold. But that was Sam all over—the soul of a bohemian caged by the mind of an auditor. He yearned for new experiences, but couldn't resist the urge to analyze them as he went along. The sort of fellow, in other words, who while being lured onto a nude beach by a daring girlfriend would be calculating how much bottled water and sunblock they would need to last until sunset.

He sometimes wondered how it had come to this. As a boy he had been a neighborhood adventurer, a ringleader of elaborate pranks, even a daredevil. At age ten, to his mother's horror, he single-handed an eight-foot sailing dinghy the length of Lake Leland—a man-made lake, granted, and only six miles long, but the closest you could get to the high seas in the heart of rural Iowa. By the time he graduated with an MBA from the University of Chicago he had spent his previous three summers bicycling the California coast, backpacking the Pyrenees, and vagabonding the coast of Turkey.

Nor did he look particularly white-bread, thanks to a Greek grandmother on his mother's side, who lent the bloodline just enough Mediterranean spice to at least let him *pretend* to feel at home in the world's sultrier latitudes. That, plus an inquisitive gleam of mischief in his liquid brown eyes, left even his soberest observers convinced that he might yet act spontaneously.

But, alas, he was also the son of an accountant, with bean counting in his genes. And his employer, pharmaceutical giant Pfluger Klaxon, had little tolerance for stuff and nonsense, particularly among auditors, who were supposed to keep everyone else in line. Thus had four years on the corporate fast track subdued nearly all youthful impulse. Whenever opportunity knocked nowadays, Sam checked first through the peephole.

A moist dark hand squeezed his left forearm.

"You want date? Nice happy time?"

A second hand, pale as the snows of the Caucasus, took his right arm. Slavic vowels cooed into his ear.

"You want maybe two of us? Special deal just for you?"

Sam pulled free, smiled politely, and shook his head.

"No, thank you."

A third woman—Indonesian? Malaysian?—slid close on his right, moving sinuously against his hip.

"No, thank you. *Really.*"

The offers multiplied anyway, and his head-wagging refusals became pleasantly hypnotic. Too many air miles and too little sleep. The music, so irritating moments ago, now seemed to insist that he at least *consider* a proposal, if only as a pretext for human conversation, a touch of warmth. Perhaps he could take one of the more hopeless cases aside and slip her a twenty. Or would that set off a feeding frenzy? In these waters, hard currency would be like a bucket of chum.

Maybe the $9 Scotch was getting to him. Watered or not, it was his fifth drink of the night. Only his continuing concern for his wallet tethered him to reality. The tourist guidebooks had warned severely about pickpockets in joints like this, and Sam's job had trained him to never ignore sensible advice.

Frankly, he was also beginning to worry about the whereabouts of his traveling companion, Charlie Hatcher. Twenty minutes earlier, raffish old Charlie had flashed a lurid grin and vanished down a corridor, hand in hand with a husky-voiced Slav. Charlie was in his forties, and Sam guessed the woman was, too. Up close she had looked far older than her hairstyle and makeup, although the swaying of her sequined rump had produced the one flash of genuine eroticism Sam had experienced since arriving.

He brushed aside yet another arm hold and checked his watch—a real Rolex, to the best of his knowledge. It had now been twenty-seven minutes since Charlie disappeared. Did you really get that much time for your money in a place like this? And where had they gone? The way Charlie explained it in the cab, these women took you to a nearby apartment, or upstairs to a room in the dreary old York International Hotel. Charlie's had led him straight down a hallway toward what looked like a bank of offices. Were they humping on a fax machine? Squirming atop a pile of interoffice memos that rustled like autumn leaves? Did that cost extra?

The day had been building toward this so-called climax for twenty-one wearying hours, ever since Sam had risen at dawn for a walk on the beach in Jumeirah, a short drive from his hotel. Dazed and blinking, he had stared at the shimmer of the dredge boats as they labored in the sunrise, throwing high jets of sand. They were creating new waterfront real estate for resort islands being built offshore.

He had seen these grandiose projects from the jet on the approach the day before. One was a massive archipelago in the shape of a palm tree, miles across, each frond bearing the spiky fruit of luxury villas and posh hotels. Another mass of islands resembled a map of the world, spanning four miles from pole to pole. The in-flight magazine said it would be reachable only by boat—unless your house came with a helipad. Some rock star had purchased all of Great Britain, and Trump was building a nearby hotel—partially underwater, like the lost city of Atlantis. In fact, that was its name.

It all sounded pretty exciting. Could you really build paradise from scratch? Or was it all a mirage, an elaborate sand castle?

Sam then waded into the surf, only to find that even at 6 a.m. in mid-April the water was bathtub warm. Charlie later told him that by July, when air temperatures reached 120 degrees Fahrenheit, the sea would feel like a lobster boil. No wonder the wealthier visitors came by private jet. Only the possibility of a quick getaway could make such a place bearable.

Maybe Sam was just road-weary. Pfluger Klaxon had now sent him to twenty countries, nineteen more than his parents had ever visited (their lone foreign adventure: a one-hour crossing to Canada at Niagara Falls).

In the early going, he had exulted in his travels, using off days for treks and exploration. But things began to go wrong during a visit to the company's most important Asian supplier. Clueless about local customs, he alarmed his guides on a day-long kayaking trip, first by indiscriminately using the unlucky number four and then by scribbling in his travel diary in red ink, a signifier that the writer was on his last legs. The guides became convinced he was either suicidal or terminally ill, a conclusion they dutifully passed along to his local business host, who in turn asked Pfluger Klaxon why a walking dead man had been dispatched to do business with them.

Sam's boss, Gary Grimshaw, fired off an e-mail reminding him that an auditor "was supposed to clean up messes, not make them." But the whole thing would have blown over if Sam hadn't then proceeded to lose a company laptop, stolen while he sipped coffee in one of the city's dicier cafés. The rattled hosts nearly canceled their contract, and Sam's next scolding came from a far higher floor in Manhattan.

Since then, he had traveled only by taxi. He often ordered room service, and he did his drinking at the hotel bar. Forever arriving on the scene in suit and tie, he was now resigned to envying those adventure-some types he always saw at the baggage carousels—tanned fellows in bandannas and cargo shorts who would soon be bashing dunes, diving reefs, and breaking bread with the locals. Their dusty backpacks and bundled skis made his own gray garment bag loom like a sooty iceberg.

That was why Charlie's plans for the layover had appealed to him—finally, a fleeting chance to rebuild his more dashing persona, a fresh start on old aspirations.

"We'll cross you over to the wild side," Charlie promised. "Forty hours of Business Class hedonism." Although this latest stop at the York felt like a downgrade to Economy.

The fundamental flaw with this plan was that accompanying Charlie hadn't actually been Sam's idea. Nor even Charlie's. Their pairing had originated in a meeting the week before, when Gary Grimshaw had called him in for a chat.

Gary was the type of boss who lived for meetings, even if they were one-on-one. Sam stepped into his office to find Gary poring over a proposed itinerary, which must have just arrived from the corporate travel office. Gary motioned for him to take a seat.

"This trip of yours to Hong Kong. I see you've got a short layover in Dubai."

"I wouldn't call six hours short."

"Then stay overnight. Some of our eastbound guys do that, you know. Fun place."

"If you like duty-free shopping."

"Or beaches and good restaurants. Not to mention a little sunshine after this sack-of-shit weather we're having." It was snowing out Gary's window—big, grim flakes on the fifth day of spring, looking gray even before they reached the street, forty-seven stories below. "Nice club scene, too."

"What are you getting at, Gary?"

"Arnie Bettman's in Dubai, setting up our new regional office for Africa and the Middle East. He won't have it up and running until May, but in the meantime you could pay him a courtesy call for the department."

"I can handle that. I'll just leave a day earlier."

"Make it two. That way you can rest up and hit the ground running in Hong Kong. And stay somewhere nice. You've earned it. You're our top man in redlining stuff that saves bucks. And, frankly . . ." Gary cleared his throat and looked down at his papers. "It's not exactly news that you're always low man for travel per diem. By a lot."

"You're saying I'm making the rest of the department look bad?"

"Not intentionally. It's just that—"

"You think I'm a grind. It's okay, Gary. You're not the only one."

The timing for this brand of criticism was unfortunate. Deborah Kearns, Sam's girlfriend of the past two months, had dumped him the previous week for much the same reason, saying he was too careful, too cautious, a predictable drone on whom the opportunities of an international lifestyle were sadly wasted.

Nor was it the first time he had heard this sort of grumbling at Pfluger Klaxon. The longer Sam walked the straight and narrow, the more some of the older hands resented his brand of diligence. Although he easily made amends once they discovered his knack for picking apart the company's rosy quarterly reports and damage-control press releases. Still closer to their hearts, he was an expert at spotting holes in compensation packages.

That was the corporate risk of hiring a good auditor with a healthy curiosity—an honest one, anyway. Yes, he can save you millions. But let him wander off into the margins, and the slightest whiff of funny business will reek to him like a rotting corpse. All the more reason to keep shuttling him from one country to the next, with the strictest of marching orders.

Yet, here was Gary Grimshaw telling Sam to loosen up for a change. To slow down and enjoy the scenery. So why not give it a try?

"It's all set, then," Gary said. "A two-night layover in Dubai."

That was the moment when Nanette Weaver arrived.

"Got a minute, Gary?"

"Soon as I finish with Sam."

"No rush. It's just that I heard from the travel office that one of your people might be passing through Dubai, and I wanted to ask a favor."

"Sam's your man. Perfect timing!"

Too perfect, Sam thought—although Gary did seem genuinely ecstatic at the prospect of expanding his meeting into a threesome, especially with a figure as lofty as Nanette Weaver. As Pfluger Klaxon's executive vice president for corporate security and investigations, she was known throughout the building as a rising star. Sharp and canny, she was even more of a stickler for rules than Sam. She was a relentless enforcer, not only in combating international drug counterfeiters, but also in her more personal campaign to maintain decorum among company employees, both at home and abroad.

The previous year she had famously reeled in a vice president for finance after discovering that he had received Nubian antiquities in exchange for helping a West African foreign minister cook the books. Just last month her quick footwork had freed a Pfluger Klaxon executive who had been jailed in Singapore merely for whistling at a woman on the sidewalk.

Not that she always got her way. Rumor had it that on a few occasions she'd been forced to back down, supposedly when her targets had more clout in the boardroom than she did. But for frequent international travelers at Sam's level, rarely a week passed when she didn't stuff their in-boxes with some reminder about ethical dealings abroad, or the importance of cultural sensitivity (including a pointed warning against the perils of using red ink in a certain Asian country). And when she was consulted for opinions on whether one might properly do this or that, she so frequently ruled in the negative that one of the older hands dredged up an old Broadway title to dub her "No No Nanette." One didn't dare utter the name to her face, and only the foolhardy used it in e-mail, since, technically, she had access to every message that came and went from Pfluger Klaxon.

Sam learned all this only after he had developed a bit of a—well, not really a crush, more of a detached lusting, even though she was at least eight years his senior. Because for all her preaching on modest behavior abroad, while in Manhattan she notably favored clingy blouses in bold colors, skirts above the knee, and form-fitting suits. Her eyes were striking—a blue-green shimmer from the deep end of a swimming pool—set off nicely by auburn hair. Her figure was admirable, and she could be seen working on it several times a week during her lunch hour at the health club around the corner. As a representative of a pharmaceutical firm, she told colleagues, she felt obligated to project a healthy image. Sam certainly approved, and he doubted it cost her any points in the boardroom, where the predominant image was that of flabby white males.

So, by the time Sam had heard enough about No No Nanette to

realize that he ought to keep his distance, he had developed a habit of watching keenly from the lunch table as she arrived in the office cafeteria, fresh from her shower at the gym. He could never quite take his eyes off her as she briskly negotiated the salad bar, still flushed from her exertions. Her title, and even her age, only seemed to heighten her appeal, lending a stern air of risky authority.

For all those reasons, Sam was a little disconcerted as she stepped into Gary's office wearing a tapered black skirt and a green silk blouse, which stood out against the white walls like jade on bare skin. She took a seat directly across from him and crossed her legs with a swish of black nylons.

"So tell me about this trip of yours."

Gary began laying out the proposed itinerary. Nanette produced a small tape recorder, seemingly from nowhere. She stood it on Gary's desk and pressed RECORD.

"You're taping this?" Sam asked.

"Tapes all her meetings," Gary said briskly, as if he regularly attended.

Nanette frowned apologetically.

"A necessary evil for the head of corporate security, I'm afraid."

Sam had never heard of such a policy. Gary soon wrapped things up.

"Sounds like an excellent plan," Nanette said. "And as long as you're headed that way, Sam, I have a small assignment. Provided you're interested."

She recrossed her legs. The chair creaked like a mattress. She looked quite good, though he wasn't usually attracted to older women, especially ones in a position to ruin him.

"Sure," he said, his mouth dry.

"How well do you know Charlie Hatcher?"

Her tone was casual, but neither she nor Gary moved a muscle.

"Charlie in quality control? The older guy?"

"He's forty-four. But, yes, that Charlie."

"Can't say I know him well, but we worked together on the Brussels job last fall."

The job had been conventional, even routine, a three-day fixer-upper carried out in New York for one of their operations in Europe. Charlie and he had meshed easily enough, relating to each other in the usual way of older and younger colleagues. Sam deferred to Charlie's experience, while Charlie patiently humored Sam's hunger for fresh approaches. Things went so smoothly that Sam mildly regretted having to decline Charlie's offer of a drink after they wrapped things up on Friday. He had other plans, but might have squeezed in at least one round, and since then there had been no occasion to renew the acquaintance.

"He seemed like a good guy. Easy to work with."

"Any other impressions?" Nanette asked.

There were, in fact, but Sam wasn't inclined to offer them, not with his questioners looking so eager—particularly Gary. And it wasn't as if he had anything profound to say. It was just that Charlie had struck him as a man who, even within the rigid hierarchies of Pfluger Klaxon, had grown comfortable with the idea of going his own way. The solutions they worked out that week had fallen well within company practice, but in implementing them Charlie had bypassed the chain of command and contacted the European office directly.

"It's okay," Charlie had reassured him. "When you're out there in the provinces, old son, the leash grows very long and very slack. By the time our folks here think to give it a tug, those guys will have everything tidied up."

Charlie was a man who had come to terms with the arc of his career, and that was especially refreshing when compared to the burnouts and buttoned-up types Sam usually encountered in the older ranks. Still, he could see how such habits might eventually catch the attention of a corporate security officer, especially one as exactingly proper as Nanette Weaver.

"Well?" Gary prompted.

"He was a straight shooter. With me, at least. And a nice guy."

"Oh, he's plenty friendly," Gary said. "That's the least of our worries."

"You're worried about him?" Sam directed the question at Nanette. "He's very competent."

"I agree," Nanette said. "He's a valuable associate. Especially when he's home and behaving himself. It's when he gets out in the world that he becomes a concern. An embarrassment, even."

"Doing what?"

"The usual male transgressions. Women, booze. Not that all you fellows don't indulge in some of that. But Charlie crosses the line.

That's why I'd like you to travel with him, be his friend for the weekend. At least until he's well beyond the temptations of Dubai."

"Spy on him, you mean."

"Not at all. You'll simply be along for the ride, keeping his nose clean. I'm not asking for a single report on his behavior, or his movements, and I won't be badgering you for updates along the way. That would be unseemly, even improper. It's not like we expect saintly behavior. I just want you to, well, keep him from going off the deep end."

"Like a chaperone."

"If you prefer."

"For a man sixteen years older than me. Will you be telling Charlie about this?"

"In a manner of speaking. He'll be told it's you who needs a chaperone—because you're a little shy, unseasoned, especially in the Arab world. So he's supposed to take good care of you. Even show you a good time, within reason. To sweeten the pot, you'll be staying at Charlie's usual hotel, the Shangri-La, which is a regular, well, Shangri-La."

"What if he ditches me?"

"Then you're to let me know. Only as a precaution. By using this."

She slid a black cell phone across Gary's white desktop. The mere idea of it seemed to raise the stakes, and Sam's first inclination was to avoid it.

"I have my own."

"This one's better. It's already got a SIM card for Dubai's server, and the battery's good for a full week. You're to keep it switched on 24/7, in case I need you."

Sam still didn't pick it up.

"I'm not sure I'm comfortable with this. Maybe I'm not the right guy for the job."

Gary frowned.

"Do me a favor, Sam. Do the *department* a favor. Just play along."

"No, no. It's all right." Nanette smiled benevolently. "I don't want him doing something he's not comfortable with. But, Sam, I would like you to consider that Charlie has a family. A wife and three children, two in college. And if he runs off the rails again I'm not sure we can hush it up a second time. Much less keep him on the payroll."

"You'd fire him? What has he done?"

Gary spoke again.

" 'Whoremonger' would be the indelicate term."

Nanette frowned.

"Ever heard of the Cyclone?" she asked.

"Vaguely. Some nightclub in Dubai?"

"A brothel bar, in the local parlance. Or used to be. There was a big write-up about it in *Vanity Fair*. The government was so embarrassed they raided the place. Loads of cops. And, as luck would have it, our Charlie was there. That wouldn't have been so bad if he hadn't started railing drunkenly at the police. He told so many of them to fuck off that they dragged him to the station, where he said some even more unpardonable things."

"Like what?"

"Do you really need to ask that, Sam?" Gary said.

"It's all right. He's an auditor. It's his nature to ask. It's a *good* thing, Gary. One of the reasons you keep promoting him. What Charlie said was words to the effect of how Dubai was led by, and I'm quoting from the police report, 'a bunch of towel-headed hypocrites, stupid killjoys who need to get their own house in order before they start policing everybody else's.' "

"Oh."

"Yes, 'Oh.' It all got back to the royal family, of course. To the supreme ruler for the emirate, Sheikh Mohammed. His dad, Sheikh Rashid, was the one who built the place up from nothing. Not exactly good for business to offend them, especially when we're opening a new regional office there. If Charlie's experience and contacts weren't indispensable to our plans in that part of the world, we would just make Dubai off-limits. As it is, we have fences to mend, and with your help we can mend them. As you may know, Dubai is our most important transportation hub. The port at Jebel Ali handles everything we ship to points east, not to mention all the raw materials we receive in return. It's also the biggest transshipment point for pharmaceutical counterfeits, and the government has finally agreed to let us start training their customs inspectors on how to crack down. So these are people we can't afford to alienate, much less infuriate. As for Charlie, well, look at it this way. Your work just might save his career."

Which is why, after a little more nudging from Nanette, Sam ultimately agreed to play along. Although he wished he hadn't almost the moment Charlie and he landed, when Nanette, breaking a promise, phoned him for an update as he stood in the passport line. It was the first of three such calls she had made so far.

Charlie, at least, had softened the blow by dropping several hints that he knew the real reason they'd been paired. And up until an hour ago the man had been virtually trouble free, not to mention so companionable that Sam had finally turned off his phone while they were riding across town to the York, a small act of rebellion that he was already regretting now that Charlie had disappeared.

Sam checked his watch. Thirty-four minutes and counting. A few people were heading toward the exits. He decided he had better turn his special phone back on, just in case. He watched the screen come to life. Two messages from Nanette were waiting, but before he could check them the phone rang.

"You turned off your phone. Why?"

Nanette sounded furious. Sam calculated that it was nearly 7 p.m. in Manhattan. He imagined her seated by the window in her office on the fiftieth floor, bathed in the dusky light of early evening, her legs crossing with a dangerous hiss.

"I, uh, needed a recharge."

"Bullshit. But we'll deal with that later. Where's Charlie?"

"The two of us are at the York Club. It's—"

"A notorious fleshpot." Same words Charlie had used. "How long have you been there?"

"Maybe an hour?"

"Damn it, Sam. And where, exactly, is Charlie?"

"He seems to have disappeared. Maybe fifteen minutes ago. Or closer to thirty-five, I guess."

"With a whore?"

"Apparently."

"Russian?"

"Maybe. I'm not sure." Did she really know Charlie's tastes that well? "If it's any comfort, there aren't any police."

"You've dropped the ball, Sam. Dropped it and kicked it clear down the block into the gutter, along with your career and Charlie's, too. I'll take over."

"But I could—"

She hung up.

He sighed, shut the phone, and swallowed hard. Then he glanced nervously down the darkened hallway. Still no Charlie. Someone announced from the bandstand that it was closing time. A collective groan went up from the women. One brushed past on his left, practically in tears. Sam could sympathize. He, too, would soon be answering to an angry pimp. He was in a hell of a mess, and he feared Charlie was in a bigger one.

Ten minutes passed as he nervously cooled his heels, glancing every few seconds toward the empty corridor. By then the York was half empty, with a knot of departing men and women clogging the exit. A sudden commotion drew his attention toward two beefy fellows in black T-shirts and tight sport coats who were bulldozing in against the flow. They burst into the clear, headed for the corridor, and disappeared into the gloom where Sam had last seen Charlie.

Sam decided to find out what was up, but he had taken only a few steps when a woman emerged from the shadows at top speed. It was Charlie's whore, the one in blue sequins. She was wild-eyed and barefoot, and her dress was torn at the shoulder and wet across the front. Had gentle old Charlie done that? She recognized Sam and rushed toward him, tumbling into his arms—all musk and perfume. She blurted something unintelligible, then switched to English.

"Your friend! You must come now! Hurry!"

She tugged his hand. The sound of slamming doors echoed from the corridor, except the noise was louder, sharper. The two big guys stepped out into the light and headed for the exit. They weren't running, but they weren't strolling, either. It was a businesslike pace, assuming your business was trouble. One had a hand in his jacket. The other scanned the floor and locked eyes with Sam, a glance that dropped the temperature to Siberian levels. Gray eyes, buzz cut, Slavic cheekbones. Features sharp enough to break ice all the way to the Arctic Circle. Russian, Sam guessed, like the woman. Her angry pimp, or maybe the pimp's enforcer. What on earth had Charlie done, and what had become of him?

He followed the frantic woman down the hallway to an open door at the far end. Charlie lay a few feet inside, faceup in a spreading pool of blood. His midsection was a meaty red blotch torn at the edges like the tip of an exploded cigar. Viscera and pulp, blood and intestines. Sam had failed him, had failed everyone, and Charlie was dead, practically blown in half. Switch off your phone in a single moment of independence, and this was what happened.

Sam bent forward. Then he retched and heaved. Five drinks and an overpriced dinner streamed hotly up his throat and onto the bloody floor.

Poor dead Charlie. He deserved better.

2

Sam heard the first wave of cops approaching down the hallway—the clank of gun belts and nightsticks, excited shouting in Arabic, the heavy tread of boots. He sat exhausted and distraught in a swivel chair. Charlie's body lay at his feet, fully clothed but crudely disemboweled, as if clumsy surgeons had hacked the man open and then abandoned the operation. The room smelled like gunfire, blood, vomit, and new carpeting.

Charlie's face was a pale grimace, a trace of righteous anger seeming to linger even as his corneas filmed over like the eyes of a beached fish. His arms were spread wide, as if his last words had been a question: "Why here, and why now?"

At least the pool of blood was no longer spreading. Sam had already vomited a second time, into a trash can. A few minutes ago he had phoned Nanette to break the news. Her anger turned instantly to shock.

"Oh, my God!" she said. "How?"

"Someone shot him. Two men, I think, but I didn't see it happen, and they ran off. I'm with him now. It's horrible. They blew him apart."

"Have you alerted the police?"

"They're on the way."

"Stay with the body, if you can bear it. And Sam?"

"Yes?"

"I know this is awkward, but can you check for his BlackBerry? It's a terrible thing to ask of you, but we can't risk having it fall into the wrong hands, not in Charlie's line of work."

"Quality control?"

"You'd be surprised."

Sam squeezed his eyes shut, already bracing for the grisly task. Good God, but she was coldly efficient. Or maybe it was simply the difference between sitting in a spotless office in Manhattan and being in a bloody room with a dead body. And it was her job. She'd probably handled this sort of thing before.

"I—I'll try. It's a pretty big mess."

"I understand. Just do what you can. I'll phone the embassy, they'll want to know. At some point there will be forms to fill out, procedures to follow, but leave all that to me. I'm coming on the next flight. Leaving tonight, probably."

"You're coming here?"

"We've lost one of our own, Sam. In the line of duty. Of course I'm coming. Just stay there until help arrives. And whatever else you do, cooperate fully with the authorities. We have lawyers there on retainer if you need one. In fact, I'll round one up now."

"Why would I—?"

"You probably won't. It's only a precaution. Police aren't always the best in places like Dubai. Another reason to get his BlackBerry before they arrive. Otherwise, do what they ask and get some rest. I should arrive in the evening, your time, and I'll take it from there. Better cancel your appointments in Hong Kong when you get a chance. There are usually a few loose ends in these situations, and I might need your help tying them up."

"Sure. See you tomorrow, then. Or later today, I guess. It's three thirty here."

"I'm sorry, Sam. I know this wasn't what you bargained for. I never should have asked."

"If I'd only—"

"Please. Save it for later. I'll call the lawyer. Stay strong, Sam."

"Right."

After hanging up he felt lonelier than ever, and faced the grim prospect of poking around in Charlie's pockets for BlackBerrys, or phones, or whatever else needed salvaging. He found himself hoping that the bullets had destroyed any hardware so he could just leave everything in place. It was sticky and glistening down there, a slaughterhouse.

He peeled back a lapel of Charlie's suit jacket, wondering vaguely why the man was fully dressed. Maybe he and the whore had finished their business and Charlie was preparing to leave. There was no Black-Berry, no phone. Next he checked the side pockets of Charlie's trousers, finding a handkerchief, the entry ticket for the York, a silver Cross pen, and nothing more. That left the rear pockets. Sam wasn't sure he could bear the idea of trying to roll the big man over in all this blood. The mere thought of rooting beneath the body made him gag. His fingertips were bloody, so he wiped them clean on the base of Charlie's trousers. Then, carefully avoiding the pool of blood, he got down on his knees and poked his right hand beneath Charlie until he felt the bulge of a wallet in the right rear pocket.

No BlackBerry or phone there, either. But there was something tucked behind the wallet. Sam withdrew a thin datebook with a black vinyl cover and alphabetized tabs, the old-fashioned kind that no one carried anymore. Fortunately, it was clean. It was the closet thing to what Nanette had wanted him to look for, so Sam slipped it into his own lapel pocket for safekeeping. Then he stood, checked for blood-stains on his clothes, and slumped back into the chair. His stomach was heaving like a ship at sea.

That was when he heard the police. He wondered if the woman in blue sequins was with them. He hadn't seen her since she hurried off to phone for help.

The first three cops shouldered noisily through the door. At first glance they looked as multinational as the York's selection of prosti-tutes. The tall one in front was almost certainly Sudanese, and Sam was guessing the second was Egyptian from his noble Pharaonic face. Bringing up the rear was a possible local. All three wore khaki uni-forms with berets.

The Egyptian took one look at the scene and flew into a rage. He grabbed Sam's shirtfront, pulled him up from the chair, and shoved him against the desk.

"Why you do it?" he shouted. "Why you do it, huh?"

The Sudanese quickly restored order, prying them apart with a sur-prisingly gentle manner. He offered a few words of incomprehensible

Arabic, presumably an apology on behalf of his colleague. The third one, who Sam would later learn was Jordanian, was already taking notes as he scanned the room.

A fourth cop entered, and the atmosphere changed immediately. He was older, early thirties perhaps. Unlike the others he was clean-shaven, and his uniform was lettuce green. He must have outranked them, because they stepped aside to offer clear access to both Charlie and Sam.

"Are you the witness?" he asked. He spoke English with a British accent.

"No. I'm his friend. And colleague. The woman who reported it might have seen it, but I don't know where she's gone. I did see two men running from the room. They were big guys, foreigners. Maybe Russian, but I'm not sure."

The words came out in a rush, an outburst of dammed-up nerves, rage, sorrow, and probably some guilt as well. Jolly, reckless Charlie, dead on the floor in a mess of his own fluids, all of it happening while Sam stood in the bar, willfully ignorant, his phone switched off. He collapsed back into the chair. The officer placed a hand on his shoulder.

"I am Lieutenant Assad," he said gently. "I know this has been a shock. Why don't we go across the hall, where we can talk quietly."

Sam nodded, temporarily emptied of words and emotions. Mostly what he wanted to do was take a long, hot shower, then collapse on a clean bed in a silent room. But at least now he could leave behind this horrible scene, although it felt like another act of abandonment. Another failure in a night filled with them.

"Lead the way," he said.

The other office was almost identical, minus the body. Desk, chair, computer, printer, filing cabinet. Sam wondered anew why Charlie and the woman had gone there.

"Better?" Lieutenant Assad asked.

"Yes. Thank you."

"My condolences for the loss of your friend." He opened a small notebook and clicked a pen. "But the first thing I must ask you is what you were doing in the York Club?"

"Charlie was looking for a woman," Sam said, deciding to be blunt about it.

"A particular woman? Or just any woman?"

"I don't know. Whoever she was, he found her in a hurry. She's the one who went for help. Where is she, anyway? I'd like to talk to her."

"Sometime later, perhaps. When did you first realize he was in trouble?"

"About half an hour later. They'd just announced closing time, and the woman came running out to get me. Her dress was torn, and she looked scared, told me to hurry. Then we heard shots, or I guess they were shots. The two big guys came running out of the room, and that's where we found him."

"They were big? Tall, you mean?"

"Stocky, like weight lifters. But not that tall."

"Describe them. Their faces, what they were wearing."

Sam did so. The lieutenant nodded as he wrote it all down.

"Your friend, was he carrying a cell phone, or a BlackBerry?"

Sam looked down at his feet.

"No. Or if he was, somebody took them. I checked."

Assad raised his eyebrows. Maybe Sam shouldn't have mentioned that. He supposed he had better keep Nanette's name out of this.

"Did you find anything else?"

"A handkerchief. A pen. His wallet. I left them in his pockets." He decided not to mention the datebook, and immediately wondered if it was the right move.

"I'm surprised you had the stomach for it."

Sam shrugged and looked away. He knew he must look guilty, and the detective was eyeing him closely. Maybe he'd need that lawyer, after all.

Mercifully, Assad flipped a page in his notebook and moved on.

"Have the two of you been together since your arrival in Dubai?"

"Pretty much. He slept later than me this morning, but I saw him downstairs at breakfast."

"At your hotel?"

"Yes. The Shangri-La."

"And how long have the two of you been in the country?"

"Two nights now. About . . ." Sam checked his watch. "Thirty-six hours."

Assad paused in his note taking and snapped to attention at the sound of a new voice from the corridor. The voice mentioned the lieutenant's name, and Assad squinted, tilting his head like a dog who has just heard a disagreeable noise.

"Excuse me a moment," he said, rising from the chair. He crossed the room and opened the door. It was clear from his face that he didn't like what he saw.

3

When he was a boy, diving for pearls among sharks, and gambling with smugglers three times his age, Anwar Sharaf was rarely underestimated by his peers. Nowadays, in his fifties, people did it all the time. Especially Westerners, who needed only one look before writing him off as either incompetent or inconsequential.

Sharaf's police uniform was part of the problem—green with epaulets and red piping, a canvas military belt, laced boots, a silly beret—a getup that would have been right at home in some banana republic far across the waves. He accentuated the effect with a potbelly, a sloppy mustache, and the hangdog jowls of the long-suffering family man.

Glimpse him hunched over paperwork at his undersized desk and the word "beleaguered" came instantly to mind. So did "inept" and, possibly, "corrupt." Because surely here was an underpaid fellow who would soon have his hand out, sighing and grumbling about this rule and that until you bribed him and were merrily on your way. A harmless nuisance, in other words. A scrap of local color to liven up your texts and postcards home: *Dumbest cop ever, LOL!*

The moment Sharaf opened his mouth, impressions began to change. Fluent in English and Russian (his father, hiring tutors at the height of the Cold War, had hedged his bets), Sharaf had also picked up Hindi from the streets and Persian from the wharves. That left him in command of four of Dubai's main languages of commerce, with his native Arabic murmuring beneath them like an underground stream. His tutors had also schooled him in literature, economics, biology, philosophy—the works. Throw in his seasons of instruction on the high seas at the age of thirteen—a summer of pearling, an autumn of smuggling—and he was arguably better equipped for intellectual combat than many of his contemporaries who had gone abroad to university.

Yet Sharaf usually held his fire. For one thing, why blow his cover? Enemies were more easily disarmed when they underestimated you. For another, he was accustomed to dismissive treatment, having endured it since the age of twenty-two, when he enraged his father by refusing to take a second wife even though his first one hadn't yet produced a child in two years of marriage. Thus did he break with a family tradition of Sharaf males taking multiple wives. Sharaf's father refused to acknowledge the move for what it was—a gesture of rebellion by a young man determined to be "modern." He instead scorned it as a craven surrender to foreign values and a domineering wife, and the berating continued without letup until his death six years later.

At that point, Sharaf's wife, Amina, took up the cudgel, even though by then she was producing offspring as bountifully as Dubai's new offshore wells were spouting oil. It wasn't out of malice. It was part of her job as an Emirati wife, which in those days included running a household with the tyrannical rigor of a ship's captain.

Little surprise, then, that as we join Sharaf late one weeknight he is stoically fending off the latest blow, grimacing as Amina says, "You really can be a heartless imbecile, you know, when it comes to the welfare of your sons."

Amina had chosen a vulnerable moment for her new offensive. It was right before bedtime, when she knew that what Sharaf cherished most was a cool glass of camel's milk before climbing into bed with a book.

He was a man of uncomplicated tastes. Whereas Dubai's new elite favored art auctions, horse breeding, and an eclectic cuisine of, say, creamed leeks with shaved truffles, followed by poached Dover sole (which happened to be exactly what Sharaf's top boss, Brigadier Razzaq, had ordered that very night on the tab of a British banker), Sharaf preferred shopping malls, domino parlors, greasy mutton kebabs, and, his most recent discovery, sushi bars, which he treasured for their elemental taste of the sea.

In his reading he was far more adventuresome, a seeker of exotic riches from every hemisphere. He was particularly relishing tonight's offering—Dostoevsky's *Crime and Punishment*, in the original Russian. A copy had arrived in the afternoon mail and awaited him on the bedside table. Sharaf was hungry for its insights, especially since certain Russians had lately been much on his mind. But now he would have to fight his way to sanctuary.

He set down his glass of milk with deliberation. He knew better than to answer hastily to such a skilled opponent. Early in their marriage Sharaf had enjoyed a clear advantage in these verbal contests, mostly because Amina's all-girl school had valued piety and deportment over rhetoric and quick thinking. But she had a sharp mind, and in raising their five children she had honed it on the whetstone of their daily stratagems and evasions. Sharaf, meanwhile, had steadily dulled his by going up against oafish criminals and sleepy desk sergeants, to the point that on the home front he was now sometimes overmatched.

"So suddenly it's a hardship if Yousef can't fly business class to Paris?" he answered.

"It's seven hours. He needs the legroom."

"He's five-eight. He only wants it for the free booze."

"Anwar!"

"He drinks, you know. Ali said his son told him. Saw him in London once, in a pub. Maybe we should start checking his credit card receipts."

"As if you didn't already. And Ali's a shameless gossip. Yousef doesn't go near that sort of thing, and you know it."

"Not here, at least. I'm not saying he's a fool, just a profane opportunist."

"Says the Muslim who loves bacon and spareribs."

The pork story again. A mistake to have told her. It had slipped out the week before, while he was sharing fond memories of a boyhood tutor: Gregor, half bear and half man, a roaring Muscovite who had served bountiful lunches with his verb conjugations and Euclidean geometry. The best part of those meals was the most succulent goat meat Sharaf had ever eaten. Deliciously fatty, redolent of smoke. Gregor had explained that it was an exotic breed, imported from the motherland. The feasts continued until the day Sharaf described the pleasures of this "imported goat" to his skeptical father, who quickly got to the bottom of things. The boy got a beating for his gullibility, not to mention a skinny new tutor who served only bread, olives, and hummus. But his memories of the flavor were still so vivid that he sometimes slipped into the forbidden pork sections of the local Spinneys supermarket, justifying his unauthorized presence among the foreigners with a furtive wave of police credentials, as if he might be checking for narcotics among the slab-cut bacon and inch-thick chops. He never bought any. A glance was sufficient. Even now his mouth was watering, so he conceded the point and moved on.

"Okay, let him fly first class. But where's he staying, and for how long?"

"He didn't say."

"Some five-star hotel, no doubt. Four hundred euros a night if it's a franc."

"They don't use francs anymore."

"I know, dear. It's a figure of speech. I just wonder if our son knows, since he never pays the bill, even though he's twenty-five."

"Twenty-six. And he's a student."

"Now and forevermore. What he *ought* to be is someone's employee."

"See? Next you'll start in on Hassan."

He wouldn't actually, even though at age twenty-three Hassan also ought to have a job but instead was studying overseas. Nor would he mention their third son, Rahim, who was living in the house next door, scandalously single at the age of twenty-nine. Or even Salim, the eldest, who also made his home within the high stucco walls of the Sharaf family compound. Salim inhabited the largest of the family's houses, yet he was constantly agitating for a bigger one. Salim needed more room because during the previous year he had symbolically joined forces with Sharaf's dead father by taking a second wife. You could now hear the family arguments from the street. Salim's growing brood had become as noisy and chaotic as a clan of Bedouins and all their goats.

Only on the subject of their daughter, Laleh, were Amina and Sharaf generally in agreement, mostly because she still lived under their roof. Right down the hall, in fact, where she was probably eavesdropping at this very moment.

Even when Amina was inclined to take her daughter's side, she generally didn't need to, because Laleh could hold her own. Father-daughter arguments almost always concerned issues of personal freedom, such as Laleh's scandalous wardrobe—business casual, she was now calling it, even though she supposedly covered everything with a black abaya—or her longest-running grievance, that as a single woman of twenty-four who ran her own business, she was somehow entitled to live in her own apartment. Fat chance of that, even if she did operate a small marketing firm in the shimmer and sprawl of Media City, one of Dubai's newest office parks.

"Please, Amina," Sharaf said, bidding to de-escalate. "You know our schedule. We argue about Hassan on Tuesdays, Rahim on Thursdays."

He smiled to make it seem more like a concession. Fortunately Amina smiled back. The creases on her forehead eased. With any luck he'd be reading in five minutes.

"What about Wednesdays?" she replied. "Don't tell me that's an off night."

"That slot is reserved for Laleh. She's been asking again about traveling by herself to New York."

Amina rolled her eyes. "Out of the question."

"That's what I said."

"Then you can fight that one on my behalf. Single combat, weapon of your choice."

She pinched his belly, which she had been doing since the days when he didn't have one. He reciprocated with a quick kiss, and then retreated behind the kitchen table for the final swallow of milk. Rich stuff, camel's milk. Too rich for bedtime. But repetition had trained his stomach to handle it.

"What will we ever do if she marries?" Amina said, following him to the bedroom. "She's our last frontier."

"I fear we'll never have to worry about that."

"Don't say that! She'll hear you. Besides, I don't want to think about it."

He knew now he was in the clear. Amina never wanted to probe too deeply into the subject of Laleh's marriage prospects. It had been that way since their daughter had turned eighteen and they had bowed to her wishes by not arranging a match. Their break with tradition hadn't seemed momentous at the time—plenty of families were doing it—but six years later it was beginning to feel like a miscalculation. A husband would have kept her in line far better than they could.

Sharaf switched on the bedside lamp, puffed his pillows, and settled in, propping himself against the headboard in a comforting pool of light. He opened the book, enjoying the pulpy smell of the new pages. He flipped past the scholarly introduction, which would have told him all the things he wanted to figure out for himself, and began acquainting himself with the tormented young Raskolnikov. A real piece of work. Not at all like the Russians he had come across here. Sharaf could have spotted Raskolnikov's brand of guilt from a block away. Remorse was wonderful that way, although in Dubai it was in short supply. Criminals of the new breed didn't have an ounce of it. Nor were they poor, like the threadbare Raskolnikov. Wrong place, wrong century, he supposed.

Sharaf turned the page and sighed, resigning himself to the prospect that the book might not hold any lessons for him, after all. Literary enjoyment would have to be its own reward. But twenty minutes later a paragraph jumped from the page that made him reconsider. It was a cryptic flash of insight from Raskolnikov at the end of chapter 2: *What if man is not really a scoundrel, man in general, I mean, the whole race of mankind—then all the rest is prejudice, simply artificial terrors and there are no barriers and it's all as it should be.*

This was more like it. Disturbing. Baffling, too. Was he saying that man was his own God, setting his own rules, and therefore even our crimes and self-made disasters were according to plan, if only because we were making up the plan as we went along?

It was an intriguing concept, because this was how Sharaf was beginning to feel about his latest assignment, a puzzle in its own right. He had been commissioned to quietly look into the activities of a few of his fellow officers and their possible relations with certain Russians about town. Scoundrels, indeed.

One of the job's most daunting aspects was the lofty rank of the assigning officer. Not Brigadier Razzaq, who ran their department, nor even the brigadier's boss, who ran the entire police force and had a seaside villa the size of a castle. It was one of the ministers in the royal cabinet, who technically wasn't supposed to be in touch with a mere detective inspector. Yet, Sharaf and the person he called "the Minister" now conversed regularly, although never on a landline and never when Sharaf was in his office or the Minister was in his.

This meant Sharaf had to work on his own time and his own dime, while still meeting his official obligations. It was new ground, and it already felt alien and unsafe. No rules other than the ones he made up along the way.

Oddly appropriate, Sharaf supposed, because that was how Dubai's newest criminals operated. Except their rules were backed by more money and muscle. The Minister had implied from the beginning that he had backing from the very top, but who could say for sure when Sharaf wasn't allowed to ask, and when all their conversations occurred in the shadows?

Such worries were part and parcel of Sharaf's bewilderment over the booming new Dubai. As a young man he had embraced all of the change and modernization, even relished it. But in recent years he'd felt overwhelmed. It wasn't just the construction binge, with a new Manhattan rising on the skyline every year, or the horrendous traffic with its cataclysmic accidents, or the profligate use of water, or even the prevailing idea that Big was the new normal, and today's Big would be tomorrow's Tiny. Nor did he have a particular grudge against any of the new bars and restaurants, with their free-flowing alcohol and their rules against entry for anyone in traditional local dress. It was all of those things, he supposed, plus the fresh hordes of outsiders who had flocked here to build, sell, develop, consume, and party 'til dawn.

Just the other day he had read in the paper that a million and a half people were now living in Dubai, and 90 percent were foreigners. In the workplace, the percentage was even higher, no thanks to the lazy sense of entitlement held by so many local males, his sons included. Sharaf felt as if his country was slowly being pried from his grasp, with full permission and a regal bow. Not that he had ever complained about the free land that the rulers provided, or the giveaway villas, or the manner in which the royal family had so assiduously shared the wealth—first from the oil, before it ran dry, and now from real estate— spreading it generously among the 150,000 Emiratis who could genuinely call themselves natives of Dubai.

Yet, for Sharaf, even prosperity now seemed fragile, threatened by a hovering sense of doom that grew stronger every time he saw another of those SOLD OUT! signs go up at the latest development. In this mood of floating anxiety, nothing seemed the same from one day to the next. Look at his daughter, for example, yearning to dress and act like an outsider. At times he hardly knew her. Modernizing a culture was one thing. Letting it be overgrown by an invasive species was quite another, especially when it was happening at the pace of a time-lapse nature video. Oversleep and you might awaken covered in vines. And now, with this risky new assignment, Sharaf was having to climb the beanstalk of change even as it grew to farther, more dizzying heights. Surely any slip would be disastrous.

The camel's milk grumbled in his stomach, as ornery as the beast that had produced it. Sharaf's palms sweated onto the pages. God in heaven. If a cryptic passage of Dostoevsky could upset him this much, then it must be time to sleep.

He shut the book and turned out the light. Amina was snoring, but the sound was reassuring, as familiar as the call of frogs along Dubai Creek when he was a boy. He massaged his belly and sought out a calming memory—his summer on the pearl boat, working alongside his good friend Ali al-Futtaim, that was a good place to start.

Amina was right. Ali was a shameless gossip. Always had been. It was part of his charm, and as an executive at the Dubai Land Office Ali was at the nexus of everything worth knowing. This had always been the nature of their friendship—Ali supplying insider knowledge and Sharaf using it to their mutual advantage. The pattern was established on the pearl boat, when Ali was fifteen and had two years of experience and Sharaf was a newcomer of thirteen.

The pearling fleet put to sea every May, and harvested the reefs and shoals until mid-September, when the skipper of the head boat hoisted a red-and-white flag to signal it was time to return home. During those four months on the water the daily routine never varied. Everyone slept on the deck and rose before dawn for prayers, performing their ablutions with seawater. Each diver gulped coffee and dates for breakfast. Then he plugged his nose with a pin of carved bone, placed a bucket around his neck, tied twenty pounds of India zinc to his ankles, and dropped feetfirst into the sea. He sank ten or even twenty feet while a *saib*, or helper, tended his rope at the gunwale, and he collected as many oysters as he could before tugging the rope to signal the *saib* to haul him back to the surface. Up and down he went for three hours, eyes stinging from the salt. Then came lunch—more dates and coffee, another round of prayer—followed by a second shift of diving broken only by a pause for afternoon prayer. Dinner was rice and fish, washed down with a dipperful of barreled well water.

In the evenings everyone pried open their shells, piling them in the middle of the deck while the captain collected pearls in a wooden lock-box that he slept on. Afterward, the divers rubbed themselves with the ooze of a gum tree to keep their skin from cracking. Then they finally relaxed by smoking plugs of *shisha* tobacco in a water pipe built from a hollowed coconut. Everyone said the evening and late prayers back-to-back so they could go directly to sleep.

It was grueling work, but with Ali's help Sharaf fared reasonably well, at least until the fleet reached the waters of Al Qarat Island, where the oyster beds were a daunting thirty and even forty feet deep. Sharaf was terrified. With each extra foot of descent, the tropical light faded. Pressure built against his ears and chest, and the creatures of the sea turned spooky and wraithlike, peering from crevices and cracks in the rocks and coral, or casting long shadows from above. In a panic, he nearly drowned during his first dive, after underestimating how long it would take his *saib* to pull him up. Ali, surfacing next to him, saw right away that Sharaf was quivering like a speared fish. He reacted by breaking into a grin, lips cracked.

"Scary, isn't it?" the older boy said, smiling hugely, as if the experience had been wildly entertaining. "That's why the oysters are bigger and the pearls are better. That's why you must embrace it, make love to it, like a dangerous woman who won't let you go even when her husband is coming through the front door. Befriend the danger, the same way that an eel learns to love the shadows in his cave. Watch me."

Ali drew a deep breath and slipped back beneath the waves. Sharaf saw his friend disappear in a trail of bubbles, and he began counting off the seconds. Four minutes passed. Then five. Then six. The captain shouted angrily from the deck at the idling Sharaf.

"Get to work, you lazy slug, or I'll cut your share!"

But Sharaf had to see this through. Finally, after another agonizing minute, and more taunts from above, something seemed to burst loose in his chest, like a pigeon fluttering free from a cage. Ali's rope was still taut in the water next to him. Then it shook twice. The *saib* began to haul it upward. A few seconds later Ali burst to the surface, laughing as he exulted in his saving gasp.

"Forty feet!" he exclaimed breathlessly. "Look at the size of them!"

His bucket overflowed with huge, encrusted shells. The lesson was like a tonic, and from then on Sharaf was never quite as fearful.

And so, as he slid into sleep with his newest doubts and concerns,

Sharaf allowed himself to be carried ever deeper, as if again towed by a load of India zinc, while searching the currents of his dreams for answers he might take back to the surface.

Just as he was reaching the limit of his tether, the telephone rang.

Sharaf slowly pulled himself upward, keeping pace with his bubbles until he opened his eyes to the glowing red digits of the bedside clock: 3:37 a.m.

The phone rang again.

His cell phone, he realized, clear across the room on the bureau. Amina, right on cue, grumbled about the terrible demands of his job and rolled onto her side.

He stood, walked slowly to the bureau, and answered in businesslike fashion.

"Sharaf."

It was the Minister. Not even Amina was privy to this new arrangement, and up to now Sharaf had always taken these calls from a room of his own at the center of the house, a windowless sanctum where he conducted family business and the affairs of his business investments. But the Minister sounded impatient. Sharaf would have to guard his language.

Amina folded her pillow around her ears, but still couldn't block out the sound. This was the one-way conversation she heard from her side of the bed:

"The York Club? Yes, of course. Nationality?"

Pause.

"If true, that will complicate things. Who's the attending officer?"

Pause.

"Yes, I am familiar with him."

Pause.

"He won't like it. But certainly, I'll do what's necessary."

Pause.

"Yes, I am on my way."

The phone snapped shut.

Twenty years earlier, Sharaf would have been off and running, forsaking coffee to hop immediately into his car. He would have buttoned his shirt as he drove, not bothering to even loop his belt or lace his boots until he reached the scene.

Nowadays he knew better. He dressed deliberately and marshaled his energy, standing by the bed for a moment to let gravity ease his sleepy joints back into place. The arches of his feet ached as he detoured to the toilet for a pee, a reluctant stream. Amina, despite her misgivings about his work, belted her robe and shuffled loyally to the kitchen to brew coffee. He lingered over his cup, chewing a wedge of bread to soak up the acid.

The Minister had expressed urgency, of course, but Sharaf was better acquainted with how these things worked. A dead body couldn't flee the scene, and in any event he would have to tread lightly, because another detective had already laid claim to the territory. It would be best to let the players get comfortable in their roles before he arrived. Of course, he would have to concoct an excuse for being there at all, one that didn't involve the Minister.

"Anwar, what is it?" Amina stood by the stove, frowning. "What's happening with your job? Something's changed, hasn't it? Who was on the phone just now?"

"No one you need to know about. Trust me. It should all be over in a few weeks."

"Well, don't wait too late to ask for help. Even if I'm the only one left to ask."

"Thank you."

She lingered in case there was more, and for a moment Sharaf considered telling her everything. It would have been a relief. But it would also have been a hazard, mostly for her, so he said nothing. She turned toward the bedroom, resigned to his secrecy. He swallowed the last of his coffee, grabbed his keys, and went out into the cool darkness of the wee hours.

Sharaf drove a Camry, same model as every taxi in town. Cheap and unassuming, but you could hit a hundred if necessary. Practical, like the old ways. Incredibly, after only a few miles he ran into a backup at an underpass, due to yet another cataclysmic accident. The previous week, twenty-one people had been killed on the roads in a span of only three days. This time a Ferrari F430 was wrapped in a fatal embrace with a concrete abutment. A crumpled Jaguar XKR, spun sideways, smoldered next to it. More than a million dirhams worth of rubble. Sharaf crept past with the window down. The traffic police were supervising, an all-Syrian crew as far as he could tell from their accents. From his familiarity with the courthouse schedule, he knew that any survivors would be arraigned later that morning before a Palestinian judge. Oh, well. Someone had to keep the damn country running.

When he arrived at the York, a nervous barmaid with circles under her eyes directed him to the corridor where all the action was. Sharaf looked through an open door and saw a sprawled pair of legs in dark trousers and black Italian loafers jutting from beneath a cluster of white-smocked evidence technicians. The opposite doorway was shut, but he heard voices behind it. One was unmistakably that of Lieutenant Hamad Assad, asking questions in his Exeter College English. The answers were barely audible, but from the accent Sharaf guessed it was an American with some polish and education, not a backpacker or some vagabond kid. And in the York, of all places. If the dead man across the hall met the same profile, then this case could be rife with complications, just as the Minister had guessed.

He entered the open door and shouldered past a technician. A flutter went through the group. They sensed immediately that he wasn't supposed to be there. Sharaf ignored them. The room smelled of blood and vomit, but he was focusing on the body, because he could already see that the Minister's suspicions had been realized. The cut of the suit and the make of the watch said this was a businessman, and a prosperous one. Some high-paying position that required him to sit in boardrooms and scurry through airports.

Just behind the man's head, arranged as neatly as a burial offering, was a pile containing his wallet and a stack of credit cards. An American driver's license from the state of New York was perched on top. No cell phone, smart phone, or BlackBerry. Curious omissions, unless Assad had already confiscated them.

Sharaf stooped forward and nimbly plucked a business card from the middle of the pile, like a magician whipping a tablecloth from beneath a crystal setting. The name, embossed in black ink, matched the one on the driver's license:

Charles R. Hatcher
Quality Control

It sounded familiar. Wasn't this the fellow who had made such a fuss at the Cyclone a few months back? A humorous story, if true, but nothing to suggest this sort of fate. Above the name, embossed in bloodred, was the well-known corporate logo of Pfluger Klaxon. That would also get the Minister's attention. Pfluger Klaxon meant lots of clout at the palace, and lots of backup from home. They'd be sending their own people, and soon.

He paused a moment to watch the forensics team do its work, while paying special attention to the chatter. Already he had picked up useful information, especially considering that Assad probably wouldn't share his report.

Scanning the room, Sharaf spotted something on the carpeted floor near the far wall, just to the left of the doorway. Stepping closer, he took a pen from his lapel pocket, leaned down and used the nib to pick up a 9-millimeter shell casing. Based on what he had already heard, he was guessing it had been ejected by a Makarov semiautomatic, a model favored by dubiously employed Russians with military backgrounds. A second casing lay nearby.

"Sir, I need to bag that."

A technician stood behind him. Sharaf rose, knees creaking, and tilted his pen to let the shell slide into the fellow's gloved hand.

"They eject to the right, so make sure to note the location," Sharaf said, knowing it would piss him off. "What more can you tell me about the two men in black sport jackets?"

The technician turned toward his supervisor, a Yemeni named al-Tayer, who shook his head with an expression of warning.

"You will have to ask the detective in charge," al-Tayer said.

"And that would be Lieutenant Assad?"

"If you already knew, then why did you—"

"Thanks for your help."

Sharaf eased into the corridor. He had shaken this hornet's nest enough, but was weighing the value of an additional poke when the door across the hall opened.

"Sharaf. Why are you here?"

As always, Lieutenant Assad was impeccably creased and starched. He was one of the few officers who actually made their uniforms look dignified. Or maybe it was that the lettuce green color complimented the chestnut brown of his eyes. Assad's reputation was exalted, especially among those who mattered. Prominent tribal family, well spoken. In recent years he had helped whip the waterfront customs police force into shape at the port of Jebel Ali as part of a crackdown on smuggling. Now he was making a name for himself as a detective specializing in vice and homicide. His clearance rate was the department's highest. Which meant he was either very good or very efficient—they weren't necessarily the same. He was one of those up-and-comers who, like Sharaf's sons, believed his natural calling was supervising dozens of others from behind a vast desk in a well-appointed office, dues paying be damned. He probably resented being called here at this hour, and would therefore be more prickly than usual.

"Same reason as you, I suppose," Sharaf answered. "Responding to a late-night summons. Obviously someone got his wires crossed and got the wrong man."

"A reference to yourself, I hope."

"Of course. But as long as I was here, I figured why not take a look? I should have realized you would have matters well in hand."

"Very well in hand, yes."

Sharaf peeked behind Assad at the second American, who had stood up and was edging forward for a better view. Definitely another specimen of the business breed, but younger, and minus the customary vulpine cast that made so many of them seem acquisitive and lurking. Or was the fellow simply in shock, having so recently discovered his colleague dead on a whorehouse floor? Except this wasn't really the whorehouse part of the operation. It was an office, a place where records were kept and deals were cut. To Sharaf that suggested complicity, involvement, in a way that a mere sexual tryst never would have. Innocent victim? Perhaps not.

The young man seemed on edge. His right hand kept straying protectively toward his wallet. Given what Sharaf knew of some of his police colleagues, maybe it wasn't a bad idea.

"Hello, sir. I am Lieutenant Anwar Sharaf. And your name is?"

"Sam Keller."

Lieutenant Assad's features darkened at this further intrusion.

"A pleasure to meet you. I only wish it could have been under better circumstances. The deceased was your friend?"

Assad tried to steer Keller back to the chair, but the young man held his ground.

"Yes. And a business colleague. We were traveling together."

"And he was showing you a good time?"

Keller's mouth dropped. He seemed affronted. Fine with Sharaf, who had hoped to make an impression, even if one of callousness. Lieutenant Assad again intervened. This time Keller let himself be herded back to the chair.

"I hope the rest of your stay in Dubai is not so unfortunate," Sharaf said.

The door shut in his face.

Any sort of run-in with Assad was potentially troublesome. But Sharaf supposed it was inevitable, because he was already thinking he wanted to pursue this case further. Unofficially, of course, just the way the Minister wanted it. This might well be the opening they had been seeking—a suitable spot for diving deeper, so to speak, to see if there was anything worth retrieving from the seabed. A few oysters, perhaps. Maybe even a pearl or two. And the Minister wouldn't exactly be sorry if Assad was involved, seeing as how they were from rival clans. That was an aspect of Dubai that outsiders never quite fathomed. They might all dress the same, and draw wealth from the same pools of oil and real estate, but deeper loyalties were still sometimes determined by long ago battles in the dunes.

Sharaf's only reservation had to do with whether he had the guts to take the plunge. Not only were the waters potentially deep but he already sensed fins breaking the surface, mostly due to the personalities involved. For every minister in his corner, surely there would be at least two on the other side. Perhaps he should simply embrace the danger, as Ali had once counseled. But that was not so easy for a man who had come to value contentment above all else.

Whatever was down there, Sharaf felt certain that the best secrets would be hiding in the trickiest locations, right there with the eel in his cave. Make a move now, and he might have to hold his breath for a very long time. He only hoped the Minister would remain steadfast up at the gunwale as the seas turned rough, prepared to haul Sharaf to safety at a moment's notice. Anything less, and he might never resurface.

Just thinking about it made him a little short of breath. Or maybe he was just tired. He sighed deeply, shut his notebook, and headed for the exit.

4

"Who the hell was that?" Sam asked after Lieutenant Assad shut the door.

"A nuisance. One you needn't worry about."

"Callous jerk is more like it."

Sam hadn't liked the look of him. Another officer in green, but his uniform had sagged like the skin of a toad, or a balloon losing its air. Hot air, at that.

"Will he be wanting to talk to me?"

"No," the lieutenant said. "It is not his case. If he tries to contact you, I want to know immediately."

Just what Sam needed, to get caught in a turf war between rival cops. For the moment at least, he seemed to have landed on the right side.

"Should I refuse to speak with him?"

"Yes. And you will be perfectly within your rights."

"I'll tell him you said so. I'd like to keep this as uncomplicated as possible, at least until our chief of corporate security arrives. She's due later today."

"She has already phoned." Assad consulted his notes. "Miss Weaver?"

Nanette had moved fast, and Sam was grateful for her efficiency. He supposed he should have expected no less.

"Where were we, then?" Assad asked.

Sam hoped to avoid revisiting the awkward subject of why he had searched through Charlie's pockets.

"I, uh, believe we were talking about how long we'd been in the country."

"Thirty-six hours, you said. Meaning you arrived Friday afternoon."

Assad flipped back a few pages in the notebook. Sam cleared his throat and wiped his palms on his trousers. Charlie's datebook was burning a hole in his pocket.

"What I'd like you to do now, Mr. Keller, is to take me back through everything you two have done since your arrival. People you met, things you saw, particularly with regard to Mr. Hatcher, even on occasions when you might not know a name. Physical descriptions, whatever you can tell us. I know you are tired, and much of this may seem trivial. But there are people in Dubai who prey on wealthy businessmen who come to places like the York. Someone may have been following you all evening, or even from yesterday. The sooner I have any sort of lead, the sooner I can find who is responsible."

Where to begin? Sam had seen quite a lot in a short time, and most of it had left a vivid impression, beginning with Charlie himself. Sam had been nervous about how the old boy would greet him. But when they met at JFK Charlie bounded forward with the easy warmth of a shaggy retriever, a little overweight and a little untrimmed, his eyebrows arching readily in good humor. It was as if the Brussels job they'd cooperated on had ended only the week before, and they were picking up where they'd left off. Sam spent a few minutes feeling guilty about the role he was about to play, then decided to relax and let Charlie set the tone.

It made for an easy passage, despite all the long hours on the plane, and from the moment they landed, Charlie had offered a running commentary on all things Dubai, beginning with the modernesque airport, which to Sam looked like a spaceport with palm trees and Armani billboards.

"Take a good look," Charlie said as they stood in the passport line. "But reserve final judgment 'til departure, when we run the gauntlet of Duty Free. Gold, caviar, Cuban cigars, shoppers in a frenzy. Last time I came through, a single planeload of Poles packed away sixty DVRs and eighty cases of Johnnie Walker Red. I just wish you could've been here for the arrival of one of those all-girl Aeroflot flights. Five a day, sometimes."

"All-girl?"

"Whores. Flew 'em in a hundred at a time, like mail-order brides on the Wells Fargo. But that was before the government started paying attention. Not so easy anymore, alas."

Good to hear, Sam thought. Maybe that meant Charlie would be keeping his nose clean. The old boy kept up his patter in the taxi through some of the worst traffic Sam had ever seen. They wound up on a clogged ten-lane thoroughfare, Sheikh Zayed Road, that led to their hotel.

"And you said you're staying at the Shangri-La?" Lieutenant Assad asked.

"Yes."

"Did you meet anyone there, you or Mr. Hatcher?"

"I was supposed to meet the head of our new regional office, Arnie Bettman. But he canceled. Otherwise, nobody, unless you count the bellhops and doormen. We pretty much kept to ourselves."

"Nice place, the Shangri-La."

An understatement. Even the lobby was a palace, with a ceiling four stories high.

"Eight hundred a night," Charlie had boasted as they stepped from the cab. "But if you let me handle the check-in, they might knock it down. I'm a regular. Give me your passport."

Someone whisked away their bags on a gilded cart. Still dazed from the flight, Sam wandered past the front desk toward the lobby bar, where a chef in a high hat was building an abstract tower of gourmet breads, cheeses, and swirled oil, none of it ever to be eaten. It looked like a place where you could spend a week's salary in ten minutes.

Sam wandered out the entrance facing onto Sheikh Zayed Road. A liveried Filipino doorman bowed as he approached.

"Good afternoon, sir!"

An Asian woman was waiting in the foyer to open the second set of doors. She, too, bowed and offered her regards. Sam stepped into a wall of heat and traffic noise. Maybe it was the jet lag, or the alien climate, but he again experienced the sensation of having arrived at a spaceport. He gazed upward, half expecting to see a glass bubble protecting the atmosphere. In every direction, tall, gleaming buildings were topped by spires, globes, and bizarre structures that resembled regal turbans and papal miters. It was as if the world's most playful architects had been lured here by blank checks and a huge box of toys.

At a glance he counted more than twenty towers under construction. The largest, off to the right, was the Burj Dubai, already the world's tallest at 160 stories and climbing. Two giant cranes swiveled atop it. From the ground they were tiny, like antennae on a gleaming cockroach that had reared up on its hind legs, begging for crumbs.

Directly across the way, a quadruple-width billboard advertised the next project: PENTOMINIUM: THE DEFINED HEIGHT OF LUXURY. 120 FLOORS OF ALL-PENTHOUSE LIVING. Good luck making it to your apartment in a power outage. Sam decided this was how the Emerald City must have looked after the Wizard flew off in his balloon, taking all the rules with him.

But he already noticed one problem with this Oz—a gritty breeze that stung his eyes. Sand was the source of the haze. Not pollution or exhaust, but the desert itself, airborne and hovering. It was piling up against the curbing and along the sidewalks. A hotel worker vacuumed the excess from the marble porch. It reminded Sam that somewhere beneath all this grandeur was still the sandy bed of past encampments and barest survival. The moment man let his guard down, the desert would reclaim it all.

A flurry of "Good afternoon, sirs" announced Charlie's arrival from behind.

"What do you think, old son?" He was grinning like a mischievous wolf.

"I was just wondering how you'd ever cross the street. Look at it. Ten lanes, four Jersey walls, a bunch of guardrails, and a fence. Plus the traffic."

"You'd need a commando team. Even then you'd take heavy casualties. See that restaurant, just across the highway? Ten-minute cab ride. But stop staring at the traffic—you're making the doorman nervous. Few months ago they had a rash of suicides. Desperate men throwing themselves in front of speeding cars, hoping to earn blood money for their families from whoever mowed 'em down. For whatever reason, this was their favorite spot, right here at the Shangri-La. Got so bad they posted a cop."

．　．　．

"Mr. Keller? Mr. Keller?"

It was Lieutenant Assad, snapping Sam out of his daydream. Or night dream. It was now 4 a.m., and the York Club had gone silent.

"Continue, please. So you arrived at the Shangri-La in late afternoon. Did you or Mr. Hatcher go anywhere that first evening?"

"Emirates Mall. To the ski slope."

"Ah, yes. Very popular with the tourists."

Pretty much what Charlie had said—but with gentle tolerance—when Sam suggested going.

"We could do that. We could do that, Sam. Of course the way I see it, if you want to ski, then go to goddamn Aspen." He laughed aloud. "But I can see the novelty appeal. Big hill of snow inside a shopping mall, smack in the middle of blazing Arabia. So, by God, let's buckle 'em on. Who knows, maybe with a little exercise we'll sleep better. More energy for the real action tomorrow."

It turned out to be like the rest of Dubai—surreal, an artful con, worthy successor to the mirages that must have once fooled thirsty caravans. Super-strength air-conditioning kept the temperature at 29 degrees Fahrenheit beneath a sky blue ceiling. You rented parkas and snow pants along with the skis and poles, and caught the lift straight for the top. Not exactly Aspen, but still fun in a discombobulating sort of way.

Sam, who slalomed down with an easy grace, waited for Charlie at the bottom. The older man descended like Laurel and Hardy, a slapstick of tumbles and splayed legs that ended with an ignoble roll at the bottom. But when he stood, snow in his stubble, his cigarette was still clamped in his lips and he wasn't at all embarrassed.

"Haven't done this in a while," he said. "I think I'll watch from the bar."

He nodded toward a big plate-glass window up high in the back. Everyone on the other side looked cozy, steaming drinks in hand, video fireplaces ablaze. A little like the Alps, as long as you didn't glance to the right, where another big window faced out from the mall's main concourse. A line of shoppers peered in, all in a row with their sunburns, their bags, and their ice cream cones.

. . .

"Did Mr. Hatcher meet anyone in the bar while you were skiing?" Assad asked. "Did anyone approach either of you?"

"No."

Sam's only conversation had been with Charlie, afterward in the Alpine bar:

"So how'd we end up traveling together, anyway, young Mr. Keller? Any insights you'd care to share?"

Obviously Charlie hadn't bought Nanette's rationale—the idea that Sam needed a chaperone. She had given him a cover story in case this subject came up—a lame one, but it was all he had.

"The travel office thought it would be a good way to save money."

"Some sort of package deal, you mean?" Charlie snorted. "They obviously don't know the way things work at the Shangri-La. But tell me something. You weren't summoned to meet with the lovely Nanette by any chance, were you?"

He had a story for this, too.

"I was. She wanted to update my security status, seeing as how I might be stopping in Pakistan on the way back from Hong Kong."

Charlie nodded, but didn't seem convinced.

"Tell me," he said. "This earlier departure of yours, the one that put you in sync with my schedule. Was that Nanette's idea as well?"

"Uh, no." He felt terrible lying. "The travel office handled everything."

Charlie smiled.

"Whatever you say, boss. But I do kind of like the idea of making her squirm. And I don't mean in the carnal sense."

He must have noticed Sam redden, judging from what he said next.

"So even you think she's kind of hot, huh?" He laughed. "Well, I guess we're always doing it, aren't we?"

"Doing what?"

"Sizing them up. Stripping them down in our heads, whether they're our waitress, our boss, or our second cousin. Wondering what it would be like. Or, if they're a little too old, what it might have been like ten years ago. Doesn't take much to set us off, really. A curve of the hip. A certain look in the eye. But let me tell you something about our Nanette. Put together nicely, I'll grant you, but she's cut from solid granite. Cold, hard, and sharp at every edge. Probably a little bitter for her own good, but very effective at pretty much everything she does."

"Why bitter?" Sam immediately wished he hadn't asked. Better to have let the subject die a natural death.

"Passed over for bigger and better things one too many times, I suspect. That tends to happen when you blow the whistle and no one listens. And, yes, I know all about that poor veep for finance she busted in Africa. But he was an easy mark. The stronger ones with better protection always survive. And after that happens a few times maybe the inclination is to say, hey, if you can't beat 'em, join 'em."

Or maybe, Sam thought, the inclination was to take out your frustrations on smaller fry, like a quality control officer with a penchant for randy behavior. Assuming that what Charlie said was even true. Obviously there was no love lost between the two of them.

"Well, if you think she's interested in me now," Charlie said, "just wait 'til a week from Monday, on the fourteenth. She'll get all of me she wants."

"Monday? In Hong Kong?"

"That's another thing. I won't be going to Hong Kong. I'm staying here through the week. Go ahead and tell her if she happens to ask. But it's strictly for business. Tell her that, too. The reckoning is coming, old son."

Sam told none of this to Lieutenant Assad, of course. Too much to explain. Nor did he even consider revealing his role as Nanette's spy, which would have raised unwarranted suspicion. But with Charlie now lying dead on the floor, the man's earlier words took on a new significance. What was supposed to be happening on Monday the 14th, and what was Charlie's "reckoning"? Or had he prematurely brought that on himself, tonight at the York?

"So, then," Assad asked, "where did you go next?"

Dinner, drinks in a few places he now barely remembered, followed by a fairly early bedtime. Sam then showered and crashed into a dreamless sleep, with the whine of the Emirates jet still roaring in his ears as he drifted off.

"And this was what time?"

"Maybe ten. No, later. I was pretty beat."

"So for all you know, Mr. Hatcher could have met someone downstairs. Or gone back out on the town."

"I suppose." The idea had occurred to him as he showered, but he had been too tired to stay out longer, and he had counted on Charlie's age to keep him grounded as well.

"What about the next day?"

"I was up pretty early. Caught a cab to the beach at Jumeirah to take a walk. Charlie slept in 'til noon."

"Yes. He almost definitely went back out without you."

Great, Sam thought. Just don't put that in your report, in case Nanette reads it.

"We had brunch, then took it easy in the afternoon around the hotel pool. We both did some business by phone."

"Local contacts?"

"Not for me. With Charlie, who knows?"

Assad scribbled a note.

"These calls. He would have been using a smart phone or BlackBerry, correct? Which you say you weren't able to find?"

"Yes."

It made Sam curious to see what was in the datebook. He wondered if he should hand it over. But that would be admitting he'd hidden it to begin with.

"And in the evening?"

"We had dinner at Al Mahara in the Burj Al Arab, the seafood place with the big aquarium."

Assad smiled wryly.

"Did you happen to see a fat local gentleman in a very ugly brown pin-striped suit?"

"Not that I recall."

"My boss, Brigadier Razzaq. He is there at least twice a week. His banker friends know it's his favorite. He has been observed drinking alcohol there."

"I wouldn't know."

"And you dined alone, just the two of you?"

Was it Sam's imagination, or was Assad beginning to leer, as if he suspected a homosexual relationship?

"Yes. Just the two of us."

"Very cozy. And then?"

"Barhopping for the next few hours. Except for a stop at the Palace

Hotel." Sam realized he actually had an item of possible interest for Assad. "Charlie had an appointment there. Someone I didn't know."

Assad sat up straighter and flipped a page.

"The Palace Hotel at the Royal Mirage? The big resort?"

"Yes."

"And you saw this person?"

"From across the room. I was waiting by the front desk."

He remembered the cab ride up a curving driveway beneath under-lit palms, the spooky feel of arriving at an oasis by night. They crossed a bridge over a man-made creek to enter a massive stone gate flanked by flaming torches. Facing them from the courtyard was a life-size sculpture of eight Bedouin camel riders, galloping straight toward them, as if guarding the hotel's marble entrance. The lobby featured a high domed ceiling painted in multicolored pastels, with enough room beneath it for a grand fountain and four towering palms.

Charlie made a call from the courtesy phone and crossed the room to wait by the elevators. Sam took a seat on the opposite side. A few minutes later a man came down. To Sam's surprise, it was not a colleague in Western business attire or resort clothing, nor even a local in a flowing white *kandoura*. It was a member of the hotel staff, looking a bit ridiculous in a white silk turban and a red satin robe embroidered in gold. Hollywood's idea of an Arab bellhop, or maybe a bouncer.

They stepped into a little alcove on the far side of lobby. The hotel man sat on an overstuffed couch, looking as if he wanted to hide beneath the cushions as he glanced this way and that. Charlie, for a change, seemed deadly earnest. He sat kitty-corner in a chair of carved wood and inlaid ivory. Sam was intrigued enough to stroll closer, hoping to catch the drift of their conversation. But the splashing fountain masked their words. Charlie spent most of the conversation nodding. He paused once to scribble briefly in a small black notebook. The datebook, Sam realized now. Maybe the fellow had been some sort of pimp, procuring women for later. He might even have phoned ahead to the woman in blue sequins. Sam must have voiced this thought, because Assad spoke up.

"A pimp? You may be right. Do you remember his name?"

"Charlie didn't say. But he was pretty big, built like a wrestler. Full brown beard, neatly trimmed."

"Yes. That will help. How long did they talk?"

"Maybe ten minutes."

"Did anything pass between them? Papers? Money, perhaps?"

"Now that you mention it, I think Charlie slipped him something just before they finished. Probably cash, some folded bills."

"You don't know how much?"

"No. But when the guy left, Charlie was all smiles. Then he took me around the corner to the hotel's private club. The Kasbar, it was called. There was a bouncer out front in the same kind of uniform. There was a guest book and a velvet rope, but when Charlie mentioned we were with Pfluger Klaxon he waved us through."

"Did he say anything about his meeting?"

"No." Sam hesitated. "But I asked."

"And?"

"He said it was personal. 'Personal business.' Those were his words."

"Anything else?"

"I didn't press him for more."

He hadn't needed to. In truth, Charlie had talked awhile longer, although none of it was anything Sam felt comfortable sharing.

"Wonder where they got *her* from?" Charlie had said, staring as their waitress departed in a skirt cut to the tops of her thighs. "Whatever. We'll be seeing plenty more of that later."

He enjoyed a laugh at Sam's expense.

"Don't worry, Sam. I know you've been told I'm a bad boy."

Sam looked down at his drink, tongue-tied. He was unwilling to lie anymore to maintain his cover.

"Well, Nanette's right. I *am* a bad boy. Unfortunately, I'm not the only one. We've got some real predators at Pfluger Klaxon, old son."

"You mean our pricing policies?"

"Oh, hell, don't come at me with any of that Big Pharma crap. Yes, we're profiteering bastards, but our products do save a few million lives. I made peace with all that ages ago. You either *do* business or you go *out* of business. What I'm talking about is personal. People who aren't bothered by any sort of behavior, no matter who it hurts."

Charlie made it sound like a confession, and then briefly lowered his head, as if seeking absolution. But when he looked back up he grinned widely.

"But why am I telling you, of all people? From what I hear you've got the opposite problem. Shortest leash in the building, and self-maintained. Saint Sam of Auditing."

Sam shrugged, embarrassed.

"True enough, I guess. But I screwed up early on. Nearly blew a whole account." He told Charlie about his debacle in Asia, and the ensuing crackdown from upstairs.

Charlie snorted.

"Hell, that's nothing. And all those warnings? Take 'em with a grain of salt. Learn from it, sure. But always remember, you're the one out in the field getting his boots muddy, so live like you want. Stretch yourself. Soak up a little atmosphere. They don't own you, you know."

The man had a point. There had to be a happy medium between running off the rails and chugging along in the same narrow-gauge track, around and around. Not that Charlie offered such a great example. Follow his path and someday maybe he, too, would be traveling with a correct little junior chaperone.

A similar thought must have occurred to Charlie, judging by his next remark.

"Just don't overdo it, old son. No matter what some misbehaving old fart like me tells you. Because once you do, atonement is damned near impossible. Only extraordinary measures will suffice. And that's what I'm all about these days, Sam. Atonement. You'll see."

For all his ogling and salacious remarks, Charlie was sounding more like a penitent than a whoremonger. What's more, Sam liked him, just as he had when they had worked together before. Charlie wasn't just fun, he was genuine. Flawed, yes, but he knew it, and even seemed determined to do something about it. That was one reason Sam decided then and there to turn off his cell phone, severing contact with Nanette. Anyone with this much need to make amends couldn't possibly go astray, at least not that night.

Wrong again, as it turned out. And given Charlie's statement, the murder now seemed like some sort of divine retribution for the old fellow's fall from grace.

"How long did you stay at the Kasbar?" Assad asked.

"We bought drinks, but Charlie seemed kind of preoccupied. The place was pretty empty. The only time he really perked up was when the guy in the beard came in."

"The same one? The employee Charlie talked to earlier?"

"Yes. He came to our table and whispered something in Charlie's ear. Charlie nodded, like it was pretty much what he'd expected. Then we finished our drinks and left."

"Did he say what the man had told him?"

"No. I figured it was none of my business."

"What time did you leave?"

"Must have been about nine thirty."

"Continue."

From there Charlie had led them eastward down Sheikh Zayed Road, through a procession of joyless bars and discotheques with lots of chrome and black plastic, smoke machines and strobe lights, huge cover charges, strict dress codes, and glacial air-conditioning. The final such stop was only a few blocks down from the Shangri-La, a techno-rave dance club called Zinc in the Crowne Plaza, where an obnoxious deejay created his own tunes—if you could call them that— on a mixing board. The throbbing bass made Sam's fillings ache. They left shortly after 2 a.m., and Sam figured Charlie was going to order the cab back to the Shangri-La. Instead he suddenly perked up, the liveliest he had been since dinner.

"Now for the main event," Charlie said. "Our descent into the notorious fleshpots of Bur Dubai. Driver, take us to Bank Street. My young friend here needs an education."

The cabbie nodded knowingly. Obviously it was a popular destination.

Bur Dubai was a revelation. Neither glitzy nor upscale, its sidewalks teemed with men, most of them dark faces from the Indian subcontinent, lit by neon and clouded by the greasy smoke of kebab shops. The cab reached a large and crowded traffic circle.

"So what'll it be?" Charlie asked, gesturing in two directions. "The York Club or the Regal Plaza?"

Men stood in long lines outside both places. A banner near the York's entrance advertised TV showings of English football, but Sam doubted everyone had come to watch Tottenham Hotspur play the Blackburn Rovers.

"How 'bout the Regal?" Sam said.

Charlie frowned.

"Sure. But if you want my advice . . ."

"All right, then. The York."

Lieutenant Assad seized on this right away.

"So your friend, *he* chose the York?"

"I guess you could say that."

The York Hotel's check-in desk was along the back wall. As with every other hotel in the city, from the poshest to the seediest, the lobby displayed a trio of portraits depicting Dubai's past and present ruling sheikhs, all in a row, as ubiquitous as Big Brother.

To the right was a small pub in which English football was indeed showing on a wide screen to a handful of customers. But the real action was just ahead on the left, where the crowd was lined up at a pay window by a stairwell.

"Spot me a C-note," Charlie said. "I'm afraid the York doesn't take plastic."

"Fifty dirhams apiece for this dump?"

"It's not the wrapping that's important. You'll see."

They waited ten minutes to buy their tickets, stamped by the Ministry of Tourism. Then they joined a second long line of men waiting to pass through a metal detector.

"The place must be mobbed," Sam said.

Charlie grinned widely.

"And to think, we have the end of the Cold War to thank for this fine commercial establishment."

Sam frowned, trying to establish the connection.

"The Russkies, old son! The moment the Iron Curtain fell, loose women from Poland to Hungary started lining up along the roads leading from every border crossing out of the West. Putting their best foot forward, so to speak, and showing plenty of leg. It didn't take long for a few enterprising old secret policemen and KGB types to figure out that this was their future, and within a year or two they'd franchised their operations worldwide. As a quality control officer I have to admit it's impressive. Even an auditor can probably appreciate its amazing efficiency."

"So this is a Mafia joint?"

"The York? Certainly not. I'm sure its ownership papers are in perfect order."

"The clientele, then?"

"Let's just say that your initial assessment—'The place must be mobbed'—was right on the money."

The line was moving faster now. A second bouncer had sprung into action with a security wand, doubling the intake of customers.

"Doesn't that bother you?" Sam asked.

"You sound like one of those scolds who won't shop in a Wal-Mart because they're mean to their cashiers." At this point Charlie had a manic gleam in his eye. Sam couldn't tell if he was serious or was having a little fun at his expense. It might even have been anger. "They're providing a service, Sam. In Dubai there are only two women for every three men, and heaven knows you'd certainly better not get caught slipping your hands up the veil of any Emirati woman. Let me put it this way. What's more valuable in that kind of demographic—making a nifty little pill to help the menfolk get horny, the way we do at Pfluger Klaxon, or actually providing the means for those fellows to get their rocks off? Between us and them, I'd say we've got supply and demand pretty well covered, wouldn't you?"

It was Sam's turn at the metal detector. He noticed a security goon taking stubs from darker men and stamping their hands, so he held out his own hand but was summarily waved upstairs.

"How come . . . ?"

"You're white, old son. Just the sort of customer they want more of."

"Tell me about the woman again," Lieutenant Assad said. "Did he pick her, or did she approach him?"

"I didn't see it happen. We got separated. He headed off into the crowd while I bought a Scotch. Next thing I knew he was coming back with her, hand in hand."

"But he found her quickly?"

"Yes. A few minutes at the most."

"Did he introduce you, or say her name?"

"No. Don't you have her in custody?"

"And your impression is that she was Russian?"

"Slavic, anyway. From her face, the accent."

"So she spoke to you?"

"Just said 'Hello,' or 'How are you,' something like that. Then they ran off."

"And you're sure you didn't go with them?"

Sam frowned.

"I'm not into that."

"I am not talking about sex, Mr. Keller, and I think you know it."

"Then what *are* you talking about? And where's the woman?"

"I suspect you know the answer to both those questions."

What was happening? Why had Assad turned on him? Or had that been the lieutenant's plan all along? Sam decided to say nothing.

"Tell me again about your earlier stop at the Palace Hotel. The one with the rendezvous with the member of the staff."

"I told you what I know. Charlie met someone in the lobby."

"Yes, but tell me what was said."

"I didn't hear it."

"Have you always had such poor hearing, Mr. Keller?"

"I wasn't privy to the conversation."

"Of course you were."

Sam shook his head. He was exhausted, upset, and now he was worried.

"Why are you doing this?"

"There are too many gaps in your story. Convenient lapses of hearing and memory."

Sam had nothing to gain by speaking further. His nervousness gave way to anger. First, the fat cop had taunted him. Now the smart, smooth one was practically accusing him of complicity. And poor Charlie was still dead on the floor in the room across the hall.

Assad snapped his notebook shut and leaned forward.

"What I ought to do, Mr. Keller, is take you down to the jail and let you consider these matters further until I can question you after breakfast, or maybe lunch, or even dinner. Instead I am going to let you return to your hotel. But once you have had time to rest, I will want to speak with you again. And when I do, you had better give me the full version. Do you understand?"

Sam was about to protest, but figured that might prompt a trip to jail. Besides, in one sense Assad was right. Sam was holding out on him. He'd been spying on Charlie and had confiscated the man's datebook. Not the sort of complicity Assad suspected, but complicity all the same. So he nodded and said nothing.

"Be ready after breakfast," Assad said. "I will come to your hotel."

As far as Sam was concerned, Nanette couldn't get here soon enough.

5

Sharaf slept fitfully until he was awakened by shouting from the kitchen—his wife and daughter, arguing yet again about Laleh's choice of clothes. Amina could not be worn down in these wars of attrition, a lesson that Laleh had yet to learn.

He heard Laleh retreat to her room. A door slammed, followed by the screech and slide of clothes hangers being moved with great fury along the bar of her closet. A moment later footsteps clomped back down the hallway. She must have passed inspection, because the next sound was that of her BMW backing out of the drive.

Good for Amina. Sharaf had seen some of the predatory males out in Media City. Lean and curious, stoked on caffeine or worse. Hungry for sensation, the very nature of their business. They would pursue Laleh the instant she offered the slightest hint of an invitation, such as a pair of exposed calves, or a plunging neckline. There were too many lonely men here in Dubai, hunting on their own. It was why you saw so many prostitutes, even in some of the better neighborhoods. After dark, a man in Western attire stood an even chance of being propositioned on his way to buy a quart of milk.

Not that Laleh was supposed to be showing *any* of herself outside the home. No matter what outfit she chose, she was supposed to cover everything with a black abaya, as almost every Emirati woman did when she was out in public. And that was indeed how Laleh always left the house, covered in black from head to toe.

Why, then, all the arguments over hemlines, necklines, and bare shoulders? Because, frankly, the Sharafs didn't trust their daughter not to throw off her abaya once she reached the office. Not that they ever actually accused her of this. That would have been too close to admitting its possibility, and they preferred to ignore the thought altogether. Better, instead, to fight over the garments themselves, as if the abaya was a moot point.

Sharaf got out of bed. He hadn't bothered to undress after returning from the York, so his uniform looked worse than usual. No time for Amina to iron it if he was going to make it to work on time, and he didn't want to arouse suspicion by arriving late.

Amina had gone by the time he reached the kitchen. She'd left a note: "I'll be at the nail salon at Mercato."

Mercato was her favorite little mall, down on Jumeirah Road. Sharaf could take it or leave it. Too cute by his standards, done up to resemble a Venetian piazza. Fairly tasteful as such things went, and the air-conditioning was top-notch. But the mall's compact size was stifling. Sharaf preferred the wide-open mega-spaces with four or even five levels. Mazelike floor plans where you could roam for miles at a time. In the summer it was the only sensible way to take a stroll, although you might have to endure an hour of traffic for the privilege.

Halfway to the office he realized he'd forgotten his notes from the night before. A few blocks after turning around he was stalled in a tie-up that stretched through most of Jumeirah. By the time he reached the house, Laleh's BMW was back in the driveway. Maybe she, too, had forgotten something.

She stepped out of the house as he pulled up the drive, and she stopped immediately, mouth open, caught in the act. Laleh had again changed clothes, and, worst of all, her abaya was still bunched in her right hand. She stood for all the world to see in a knee-length skirt of lustrous black silk, cinched tightly at the waist by a patent leather belt. The top button was undone on a crisp burgundy blouse. Black nylons shone in the sunlight. Her dark brown hair was shaken loose to her shoulders, with nothing at all to cover it.

Sharaf's voice caught in his throat as he stepped from the Camry. Before he could summon the energy to vent his outrage it occurred to him how beautiful and vulnerable she was, a mature young woman with a mind of her own, working every day among people her family scarcely knew.

By now she had recovered from her embarrassment and was moving briskly toward the BMW, keys out of her purse. She was hastily putting the abaya on, throwing it atop her shoulders and then shimmying as she walked. It dropped like a silk curtain, and she paused to poke her arms into the sleeves, a striptease in reverse. Sharaf stood by the Camry's open door, dumbfounded but enraged.

"Young lady!"

"I've been through this already with Mom. This outfit is a compromise. What she wanted me to wear was simply ridiculous. I couldn't have taken myself seriously."

"It didn't look like much of a compromise." His voice rose. "Especially when it *wasn't covered at all!*"

"Sorry, Father, but I'm late." Her face was sullen, unrepentant.

"We'll discuss it this evening. Be home by ten!"

"I'm *always* home by ten!"

He was about to admonish her disrespectful tone when his cell phone rang. A glance told him it was the Minister, and by the time he looked up again, Laleh was backing down the drive, zooming past his Camry in a dazzle of style and polish. Music throbbed through the rolled-up windows, radiating with her anger.

So what was he supposed to do now? Chase her halfway up Sheikh Zayed Road with all the other commuters? He leaned wearily on the Camry's door frame and watched until the BMW was out of sight. In her wake: a silent neighborhood of empty sidewalks and pale brown villas, curtains closed.

The phone rang again.

"Sharaf."

"The York. You went?"

"Of course."

"Well, what do you think? Is it a trap, or is it real?"

"Why can't it be both? The important thing is that it's an opening." Sharaf briefly outlined what he intended to do next.

"No," the Minister said. "Too risky."

"Of course it's risky. You hired me for results. You also told me to use unorthodox methods, keep everything off the books, and look for the first possible opening. This is our opening."

"How can you be sure?"

"He was killed by the Russians, for one thing."

"Assad has a suspect?"

"Of course not. And unless he arrests some patsy just to clear the case he never will. But everything fits: the location, two Slavic thugs, and the weapon, a Makarov semiautomatic."

"There is already a ballistics report?"

"I saw a shell casing."

"So you're guessing."

"An educated guess. Assad won't let me near the paperwork anytime soon, so that's the best I can do for now."

"If you haven't seen the report, then how do you know about the thugs?"

"The forensics team. They gossip like old women at a wedding."

"So even that's secondhand. Not good enough, not with these people."

"What people? The Russians? Or are you referring to Pfluger Klaxon, the victim's employer?"

"Merciful God, is that true?"

"He worked in quality control, meaning he was a natural troubleshooter. Or trouble*maker*, judging from what happened to him."

"All the more reason to avoid this one, even though that jackal Assad is involved."

"Pardon me, sir, but, as my daughter likes to say in English, 'Get real.' Because if anything out of the ordinary is involved, the mere proximity of a Pfluger Klaxon employee ensures that certain higher-ups will want to help clean up the mess. It's the kind of name that always draws the big boys out of the shadows. The very people you're interested in."

Your ministerial rivals, he could have added, but didn't.

For a moment the Minister said nothing. Sharaf imagined him cringing as he considered the various friends and associates he might alienate if things went wrong. Sharaf had seen it before—bosses who talked big about cleaning house, then blanched as the day of reckoning drew near. Fine by him. If the Minister backed out, so would Sharaf. But, somewhat to his surprise, Sharaf found himself hoping for the opposite. Having poked a toe in the water, he was now itching to make the dive. A last plunge for old times' sake. Or maybe he just relished the challenge.

The Minister sighed.

"Okay, then. But work it from our side only. And for the moment leave the Americans alone."

"You're already tying one hand behind my back."

"Those are my rules. If you're as good as everyone says, it shouldn't prevent you from achieving success."

Another reason Sharaf preferred to be underestimated. It kept expectations lower.

"Don't expect a miracle," he said.

And don't expect me to play by your rules, he thought after hanging up. Because the first thing he needed to do was to come up with some excuse for contacting the second American, rules be damned. Like father, like daughter, he supposed. No wonder Laleh was so defiant. Sharaf restarted the Camry and crept back into the maelstrom.

6

Someone was in Charlie's room.

You could hear the ruckus next door even through the Shangri-La's fortified walls—drawers opening, closets slamming, loud voices issuing orders. In English, no less.

Sam sat up in bed, wondering what the hell was happening. He must have finally dropped off to sleep at sunrise, not long after the first call to prayer. Now it was bright enough to be midday.

He had slept poorly. Charlie's face kept bobbing up in his dreams— laughing in one moment, dead in the next, eyes fixed and vacant, rigid skin gone fish-belly white. As Sam stumbled out of bed he wondered how old Charlie's kids were, what Charlie's wife would say, what he would tell her. He supposed he would face them all at the funeral, a convicted man before a firing squad. Deservedly so.

The banging from next door grew louder. Sam shrugged on a T-shirt and pulled up his trousers from a wrinkled pile at the foot of the bed. Then he wandered barefoot into the hallway, where an American in khakis and a navy polo looked up from a clipboard.

"You must be the friend. Sam Keller?"

"Who are you?"

"Hal Liffey, U.S. consular section. I'm sorry for your loss. My condolences."

Liffey extended a hand, but Sam was more interested in the doings next door, where there had just been a huge thud. Had they upended the mattress? The door was open, and Sam tried to move close enough for a look, but Liffey blocked his way.

"What's going on in there?"

"Collecting his belongings. Sorry about the noise."

"Sounds more like a search."

"Well, they don't want to miss anything. Standard procedure with an overseas death of a U.S. citizen. We collect the personal effects of the deceased and ship them home with the, uh, the body."

"Shouldn't the police be present?"

"They've been notified. They're okay with it. If we find anything relevant, we'll let them know, of course. We just figured it was in everybody's best interest to move fast, especially after your office called."

"Nanette Weaver?"

"She seems very efficient."

"She's due in at six. I'm meeting her at the airport."

Sam checked his wrist for the time, but he had left his watch on the nightstand.

"It's almost noon," Liffey offered.

"I should get dressed." He wondered vaguely why Lieutenant Assad hadn't already stopped by.

"I'll need you for a few minutes when we're done, if you don't mind. Some forms to sign, that kind of thing."

"Sure. You haven't spoken with a Lieutenant Assad this morning, have you?"

"No. I'll knock for you when we're done."

Sam showered while the thuds continued. A curious business. He wondered if it was really routine. As he dressed he noticed Charlie's black datebook on the nightstand next to his watch, out in plain view. He considered giving it to Liffey before Assad arrived, but he supposed that might also land him in trouble, or complicate the paperwork. Better to deliver it personally to Nanette. She'd know what to do. In the meantime he would hide it in a drawer, although his auditor's curiosity demanded that he first glance inside.

There was little to see. Every page was blank except for the one tabbed with the letter "D," where Charlie had written "Dubai" above a list of three names and phone numbers. The numbers were local. The first name was Rajpal Patel, the second was Tatiana Tereshkova, and the third one was merely Basma, a female Arabic name, but nothing more. None was familiar, and as far as Sam knew none worked for Pfluger Klaxon. There were no addresses, no job titles, and no other identifying information.

Below, in a sloppier hand, was "Monday, 4/14!" underlined twice, along with a two-line mishmash of letters and numbers: "50! IMO9016742, JA T2-G6, L17-R4."

None of it made sense. Probably a bunch of abbreviations, some personal shorthand that only Charlie could decipher. Sam remembered their conversation at the Alpine bar, and Charlie's promise of big doings on Monday the 14th. It was now Sunday the 6th. Charlie would never make it to his avowed day of reckoning, and his black book offered few clues as to what might have been in the works. Was this all or part of what Charlie had scribbled with such urgency during his rendezvous at the Palace Hotel?

Sam flipped through the rest of the book. Nothing. Maybe Charlie had been talking big only to toy with him, trying to goad him into reporting something back to Nanette.

A knock at the door made him flinch. He slid the datebook into a drawer.

"It's Liffey. We're done out here, so whenever you're ready."

Sam opened the door to find Liffey with forms in hand, pen at the ready. Whoever had been helping was gone, and the door to Charlie's room was shut.

Sam ordered a room service breakfast, then spent most of the next few hours pacing, first in his room and then in the lobby, while nervously wondering if and when Assad would make good on his threatened visit. At 3:30 he tried calming himself with a swim in the hotel pool, but it felt wrong to be among squealing children and luxuriating couples, people without a single care, so he returned to his room.

Shortly after 4:00 his curiosity about matters of consular policy got the best of him, so he fired up his laptop and poked around a State Department Web site long enough to discover that when an American died abroad, it was indeed a consular duty to "take possession of personal effects, such as: convertible assets, jewelry, apparel, and personal documents and papers." Although this was supposed to occur only "if the deceased has no legal representative in the country where the death occurred." Presumably Nanette had set the process in motion.

He had another hour to kill before going to the airport, so he sat on the end of the bed watching CNN International. There was nothing about a murdered American businessman in Dubai.

By 6 p.m. he was waiting outside the arrivals gate next to the limo drivers holding signs with their clients' names. Nanette spotted him right away as she burst through the door from customs, and she nodded in recognition. For someone who had just flown through an entire night from halfway around the world, she was crackling with energy. She rolled an overnight bag with a laptop strapped smartly to the top. Not a wrinkle on her suit, which featured a skirt cut well below the knee. She was dressed for the locals, although her lipstick and makeup were flawless. So was her hair. She might have just hopped out of a cab after a four-block ride through Manhattan. It was mildly unnerving.

To his relief, she smiled in greeting.

"We took the corporate jet," she said, as if to explain her polished appearance.

"We?"

"My assistant is back there somewhere. Stanley Woodard. He's along to help pick up the pieces."

"Am I one of the pieces?"

Sam hadn't meant to say anything so self-pitying. He realized he was still off balance from jet lag and a lack of sleep.

"I guess that depends on what happened after we talked. How'd it go with the police?"

He gave her a quick rundown, ending with Lieutenant Assad's threats.

"I doubt the lieutenant will be a problem. I phoned him while we were on the taxiway. Have the consular people been in touch?"

"They came by to clear out Charlie's room. It was kind of weird."

"It's routine. In fact, they're our first order of business. They're staying open after hours on our behalf, so we'll go straight there if it's all right with you."

"Sure. I'll hail a cab."

"No need. There should be a car waiting."

As if on cue, Stanley Woodard bustled through the doors with a cell phone tucked to his ear. He was younger than Sam, fresh out of college. He looked like he had slept in his clothes, and he seemed to be in a great hurry.

"Driver's on the line," he said. "Car's out front."

"Maybe you should follow in a taxi. Sam and I have some delicate business to discuss."

Woodard looked crestfallen but didn't protest. He pocketed the phone and nodded gamely at Sam. Nanette didn't seem inclined to introduce them, so Sam nodded back. He wondered what "delicate business" she was referring to.

The black Mercedes limo, technically a stretch, was far shorter than its huge American counterparts, which made it seem modest by comparison. The interior nonetheless had the feel of a swank private chamber, and when Sam sank deeply into the black leather upholstery he again realized how exhausted he was. Nanette slid toward him from the other door, coming closer than he would have expected on such a roomy seat. With the windows up, her perfume was noticeable. It seemed like ages since their previous meeting back in Gary's office. He wondered where he would have been right now if he had said no to her plan. Or had that really been an option?

She turned to face him from only a foot away. He noticed a small black dot in her left eye, against the green of her iris.

"So how are you holding up, Sam? It must have been terrible for you."

"All right, I guess. I keep thinking of Charlie. I go back and forth over everything that happened, wishing I'd done things differently. I'm sorry. I really did drop the ball, like you said. Although I guess it's Charlie's family I should apologize to."

"No, no, Sam. The whole thing is my fault. You're an auditor, a good one. But you're not a security operative, and I shouldn't have expected you to be one. I was only trying to make it a little easier for Charlie. A little less awkward, if that makes sense. Obviously I miscalculated. And, not to speak poorly of the dead, but Charlie didn't exactly help himself. He made his own bed, Sam."

"But I—"

"No. Not another word. Stop blaming yourself."

The car slowed, easing into what appeared to be a horrendous traffic jam. The driver gestured in exasperation toward a cordon of orange cones, where a backhoe was hefting a slab of broken pavement.

"They make new roundabout," he complained. "For only two days I not come here, and already they make new roundabout."

Without replying, Nanette reached forward to press a button. A smoked-glass window slid shut between them and the driver. Incredibly rude, but mildly thrilling. They were secluded in boudoir comfort. In Sam's sleep-deprived mind, aching for solace, almost anything seemed possible.

"I hope you'll have time for dinner later," she said.

"Sure. Absolutely."

He was too tongue-tied to say more.

To Sam's surprise, the U.S. Consulate was a Dubai anomaly—plain and unremarkable. He had once seen it portrayed in a movie as a palatial spread of marble and glass, with a luxurious courtyard of bubbling fountains and towering palms. Instead, it was a dreary block of offices on the twenty-first floor of the Dubai World Trade Centre, which was itself an uninspiring slab of concrete at the east end of Sheikh Zayed Road. The ambassador, the round-the-clock U.S. Marine guards, and the bulk of the diplomatic workforce for the Emirates were all based at the big embassy over in Abu Dhabi.

A green military truck from the Dubai Police was parked outside the building's ground-floor entrance, with a drowsy sentry at the wheel. Visitors had to pass through metal detectors in the downstairs lobby, and the elevator wouldn't stop on the twenty-first floor unless you punched in a numeric code, which Nanette seemed to know by heart. Sam watched out of the corner of his eye, unable to prevent himself from registering the sequence. Part of the auditor's curse, he supposed, forever filing away extraneous data, like a Web crawler that never slept. Stanley Woodard, whose taxi had fallen behind in traffic, barely made it aboard before the doors shut, and seemed none too pleased about it.

Hal Liffey welcomed them as the doors opened upstairs, except now he was dressed in a charcoal suit. To Sam's surprise, Nanette greeted him like an old pal.

"Hal's the commercial attaché," she told Sam.

"We've met," Liffey said, a little embarrassed.

"Is it always the commercial attaché's job to retrieve the personal effects of the deceased?" Sam asked.

"It is when he's the only person available. We're just an outpost here, and are staffed accordingly."

Liffey led them to a conference room where a gray-haired man and a slender young woman with a severe haircut waited at a long wood-grain table. Narrow windows offered a prime view of another tall building across the way. Its white sides were wrapped partially in a robe of brown marble. Perched atop it was a dimpled sphere that looked like a giant tan golf ball. With a good swing you could have swatted it up Dubai Creek, which shimmered beyond it on a dogleg left.

The gray-haired fellow at the head of the table stood. "Todd Mooney, consul general. I'm sorry for your loss." He turned toward the woman with the bad haircut. "Maura Steele, my assistant. I take it you've met Hal. We're here to do what we can to make everything go as smoothly as possible. We know this must be a trying time for you."

He sounded like a funeral director. Maybe that was the recommended demeanor in the Foreign Service manual. Sam wondered if their duties also involved interceding with the local police. He wished he had brought along Charlie's datebook. This would have been a good time and place to drop it off.

"Hal tells me he has taken possession of all personal effects of the deceased," Mooney said. "And, Ms. Weaver, am I correct in assuming that next of kin have been notified?"

"That is correct." Nanette offered a subdued smile.

"In that case, the next order of business is to obtain the death certificate from the UAE Ministry of Health. Then we'll proceed with the official Foreign Service Report of Death. Maura here will assist with that.

"And now, although Ms. Weaver is no doubt familiar with these logistics, I am nonetheless required to brief you on the various local laws and customs with a bearing on the disposition of Mr. Hatcher's remains, as well as the procedures for their subsequent shipment to the United States."

He continued in a similarly bureaucratic vein for several minutes more, repeating the words "disposition of remains" far too often. Woodard took copious notes. Sam tuned out when Mooney began discussing local embalming practices and the shipment costs of a loaded coffin. Nanette had already done so. She had retreated to a rear corner with Liffey, where she was whispering intently while he nodded with his head down.

Woodard tapped Sam's arm.

"He's asking you a question."

"Oh. Sorry. I'm a little out of it." He felt ready for a nap, and oddly vulnerable. He wished someone would just say, "Look, why don't you go on home and let us handle this?"

Instead, Mooney said, "I was just wondering if, once the death certificate is issued, you would be available to sign out the body from the refrigeration unit, in order to expedite transportation. Not that there's any monetary urgency. Refrigerated storage is provided free of charge."

"I, uh, don't know. Shouldn't there be an autopsy first?"

"That's not our understanding. According to Ms. Weaver, the family hasn't requested one."

It would have been an appropriate time for Nanette to jump in. But she was still conferring with Liffey, and Mooney seemed unwilling to interrupt. Instead he turned back toward Sam with an air of mild exasperation.

"I also gather that the cause of death isn't in dispute. I mean, well, you *saw* him, correct? Do you retain any doubts?"

"No. He was shot. That was pretty clear. But what about other factors?"

"Such as?"

"Well . . ." Sam fought hard to clear his mind, and he seized on a couple of stray thoughts that had occurred to him earlier. "Whether he'd been drugged in advance, for example. Or whether he'd engaged in any sexual activity before he was killed."

Maura Steele frowned disapprovingly.

"How could that possibly be relevant," she asked, "other than as a potential embarrassment to his family and colleagues?"

"Because if he *didn't* have sex, it could mean he was there for something else, which could have had a bearing on his death. So I would think that at the very least—"

"Sam?"

It was Nanette, who was back at the table. She didn't look or sound angry, or even disappointed. Her demeanor was closer to abiding, tolerant, as if she completely understood his concerns but nonetheless needed him to see things their way.

"It's the police who counseled this course of action," she said. "Apparently they're convinced they know what transpired beforehand, and from what little I've heard I trust their judgment."

"Okay. Good enough for me." Even though it wasn't. Or maybe he was just exhausted. Whatever the case, the weight of all his worries and what-ifs seemed to press him deeper into the chair. He resolved to say nothing further unless called upon.

The rest of the meeting passed in a blur. An hour later Nanette and he were again seated in the limo, this time with Woodard between them as they headed for the Shangri-La. The two new arrivals checked into their rooms while Sam went upstairs to crash. He drifted off to sleep before he could even remove his shoes. His cell phone woke him a half hour later. It was Nanette, offering to meet him in the lobby. She had reserved a table for dinner at Marrakech, one of the hotel's restaurants—that is, if he was still interested. Still in a fog, he figured he had better say yes. It was now dark outside. He had been in Dubai for barely forty-eight hours, but it felt like weeks.

He splashed his face in the bathroom sink, shaved, and changed into a fresh shirt and trousers, all of which left him feeling a little more alert. He wondered if he should also change into fresh briefs. That made him realize that at some level he was treating the evening like a date, which was downright silly, not to mention unwise. Fortunately, Woodard would be along to dispel any such illusion.

He reached the lobby to find Nanette alone on a couch, drink in hand. She had changed into a skirt far more accommodating of expat tastes. With her legs crossed it rode several inches above her knees.

"Where's Woodard?"

"Too busy. Consular paperwork, plus some other arrangements. I'm sorry that Mooney fellow ran on like that. I could have briefed you on pretty much all of that. He's new here, so I suppose he felt like he had to impress us. How 'bout a drink? You look like you could use one."

It was the same remark Charlie had made to start off their night on the town, and Sam was briefly disoriented, feeling as if Charlie might come bounding around the corner at any moment, raring to go.

"Are you all right, Sam?"

"Fine. Although maybe I should hold off any drinks until dinner."

No sooner had he said that than a waiter appeared with a gin and tonic, which Nanette must have ordered on his behalf. Why not? he figured.

.   .   .

Sam was hungrier than he had expected, and he ate his fill. The waiter brought dish after dish of North African *mezze*, plus plenty of wine. He hadn't realized they were drinking quite so much until the waiter uncorked the second bottle.

Between that and his lack of sleep, he felt like he was floating. It was a precarious sensation, but also quite pleasant considering everything he'd endured in the past twenty-four hours. An oud player calmly plucked his instrument in the corner of the restaurant, adding to the serene atmosphere. Sam was finally able to put his auditor's brain on idle, content to let Nanette dictate the flow of conversation. She blessedly steered clear of any mention of either Charlie or Pfluger Klaxon, and they might have avoided the subjects altogether if Sam hadn't blundered during a moment of relaxation, right after the waiter brought the coffee.

"One thing about all this that still bothers me," he said, the thought rising to the surface like a bubble. "Why was Charlie fully dressed when he was shot? I mean, considering what he was supposedly there for."

"Maybe he had, well, finished?"

"I thought that, too. But in an office? That's where they went, as far as I could tell. There was no bed, no couch. Nothing but a desk."

Nanette raised her eyebrows at the mention of the desk.

"A *small* desk," he clarified.

"You're blushing, Sam."

She reached across the table to touch his hand. Then she smiled. Or had he imagined the touch? Her hand was already back on her side of the table. He was wrung out. Sauced and marinated, too. Venturing back onto the subject of the murder was making his mind pop and buzz like neon, a jazzed condition that seemed likely to persist as long as Nanette kept looking at him so intently with those vivid green eyes. Her cheeks were flushed, the way they were after her workouts at the Manhattan health club.

"I hate to admit this," she said, "but it bothers me, too."

"Really?"

"Yes. Mostly because none of the possible explanations are very flattering."

For a briefly giddy moment he thought she was about to describe the various sexual positions that could be achieved atop a small desk.

He then realized from her downcast expression that it was something more serious.

"Charlie may have been more deeply involved in this whole thing than we'd like to admit," she said. "It's one reason we're not demanding an autopsy."

"By 'this whole thing,' you mean prostitution?"

She nodded gravely. Sam couldn't help but recall his conversation with Charlie as they'd waited in line at the York.

"He did seem to know a lot about how the business worked. Or at least its origins."

"I'm afraid we have to entertain the idea that he may have been more than just a customer. It's a thriving trade here, in case you hadn't noticed. Gobs of money. And, well, with all the places Charlie regularly travels—traveled, sorry—he certainly would have been well positioned to help with, shall we say, manpower procurement."

"You really think so?"

Then why the big lecture on atonement? Sam wondered. Unless Charlie had, once again, been toying with him. What a fool Sam had been.

"He mentioned something about next Monday."

"Monday?" Nanette seemed to perk up.

"Big doings, apparently. Or maybe he was baiting me. He said he'd canceled his flight to Hong Kong and was going to stick around."

"I suppose all this could explain why he got so upset when the police raided the Cyclone. If he was truly in the flesh trade, a crackdown would've been bad for business."

Sam's mind careened drunkenly back through everything Charlie and he had done, trying to see the events in a different light. It only made him dizzy.

"You know," he finally said, "this Lieutenant Assad was pretty interested in Charlie's movements. Especially his local contacts."

"Oh, dear. This could be embarrassing. What did you tell him?"

"All that I knew. I thought we wanted to help—"

"Of course we do. And you were right to be open and honest."

"Except about the datebook."

"The datebook?"

"I've been meaning to tell you. After you said to get his BlackBerry, well, it wasn't there. But he had a datebook in his pocket, so I took it."

"And you didn't turn it over to the police?"

He nodded.

"You should have told me sooner, Sam. This could have created a real problem."

"I guess it slipped my mind. And the consulate didn't seem like the right place to bring it up, since I didn't have it with me."

"Where is it now?"

"In my room. I stuck it in a drawer."

"You should get it for me, right after dinner. In case the police search your room."

"Why would they do that?"

"Why wouldn't they? In a place like Dubai you can never be sure who is working for whom. Especially with the police. They're staffed by foreigners, mostly, and the pay is terrible. Another reason we should move you back to Manhattan as soon as possible. They'll be looking for someone to pin this on. Besides, you'll want to attend the funeral."

"Of course." He swallowed hard, imagining a tearful widow. "So you won't be needing me here?"

"When I spoke with Lieutenant Assad, I gathered he had reassured himself on whatever doubts he had expressed earlier."

Sam supposed he should feel relieved, but he was oddly disappointed. Was it the wine, or was it that part of him had begun to enjoy participating in something a little reckless and unscripted for a change? Or maybe he felt he owed it to Charlie to see things through.

"Look, Sam. From here on out, matters are only likely to get more complicated. Apart from the personal tragedy, we have to worry about competitive considerations as well. Corporate secrets may have been compromised. I'm sure some policemen are only too happy to participate in that market."

It made him think of the second detective, the fat one called Sharaf. He'd certainly looked like the type who might try to cash in.

"Well, the datebook didn't seem to have any information like that."

"You looked through it?"

Was it his imagination, or did she disapprove?

"Only briefly. Last night before bed. Or this morning, I guess it was. I've sort of lost track of time."

"And?"

"He'd only written on one page. Three names with local numbers, and none of them were our people. Plus a bunch of numbers and letters. Maybe a code, maybe nothing."

"Then we'll forward the information to the authorities, of course. The same with his BlackBerry, once we've removed any proprietary information."

"You found it?"

"The consular people did, in his hotel room. I'll tell you what, Sam. How about if you retrieve that datebook while I pay the bill? Corporate account, of course, so it's my treat. Then you can bring it downstairs to my room. I have to take care of a few arrangements for tomorrow with the concierge, then I'll meet you there. Room 408."

"Now?"

"Sooner is better, don't you think? I'd have thought you'd be relieved to get rid of it."

"You're right."

He headed upstairs, tipsy in the elevator, then panicking when he couldn't find the datebook right away. But it was still in the drawer, hiding beneath the hotel directory. He flipped it open for a final glance. It was then that the meticulous side of him, the part that always demanded thoroughness, backups, and double-checking, kicked back into gear. Given what Nanette had said about the police, he decided to write down the information, in case they lost it or, worse, never followed up. The names might be Charlie's contacts in the flesh trade, the very people who had done him in. Even if the man was crooked, his killers deserved to be punished.

So, feeling a little sneaky, Sam took a sheet of hotel stationery and logged everything verbatim, even the gibberish Charlie had written at the bottom after the "Monday, 4/14!" reference. He folded the paper twice and stuffed it in his wallet.

He arrived at the doorway of 408 before Nanette, and had to wait for a few awkward minutes in the corridor until she rounded the corner from the elevators.

"Sorry it took me so long."

Sam reached into his pocket.

"I've got the—"

"Not here. Just bring it into the room. In fact, why don't you stay for a nightcap? I'm sure there's something suitable in the minibar."

"I, uh, sure."

He flushed at the possible implications of her invitation, and as he nervously followed her through the door she stopped abruptly, causing him to bump into her from behind, just across the threshold.

"Excuse me," she said, "but I've dropped my key card." She turned and gently nudged him backward, pushing her fingertips against his chest. "If you'll just back up a step so I can pick it up."

She stooped beneath him, her perfume reaching him on a heady updraft.

"There. Come on in. Gin and tonic, right?"

"Sure."

She mixed it strong, and they sat side by side on a love seat by the window—or small couch, he supposed. Thinking of it as a love seat seemed reckless. He sipped carefully, aroused but wary, while she asked him where he had grown up, what places he liked to travel—small talk that seemed to be leading nowhere until she moved closer and, with a look of great intensity, placed a hand on his knee.

"So tell me something, Sam."

"Yes?"

Her face was inches from his. Her lipstick looked very moist, like she had just applied a fresh coat. He found it a little hard to believe this was happening, but in his dreamlike state it somehow seemed perfectly plausible.

"You certainly seem like the type who doesn't like to let go of something once you've sunk your teeth into it. Am I right?"

"I do tend to chew things over, I guess."

"Which is an asset. You're steadfast, persistent. It's why Gary hired you."

"But?"

She smiled. Dazzling. He sipped his gin and tonic.

"See? You even anticipated the 'but.' But, as I was indeed about to say, this time I want you to let go, for your own mental health and well-being. Leave the mess for others to clean up for a change. And by all means stop torturing yourself over Charlie. The man was a natural-born charmer, so at some point you were bound to let him slip his leash. If there was ever a leash to begin with. Gary and I certainly weren't very clear in our marching orders."

Charlie. Just hearing the name made him think of the man's rakish grin, his sense of fun. Then he thought of how Charlie had looked at the end—the ragged hole in his chest, the blood-soaked suit.

"Sam?"

He looked up, startled to find Nanette still there, ever so close.

"See?" she said. "You're doing it now, aren't you? Going over everything again in your mind. It's a form of torture, really, for people like you."

He supposed it was true. Why else would he have taken down the names from the datebook unless, at some level, he was still replaying everything in his head. And he *did* want to find out what had really happened, and why.

"You're right," he said. "It's just how I'm wired, I guess."

"That's why you needed this drink, this moment of calm. And it's why I rather enjoy helping to, well, distract you for a while. You might even say it's my corporate duty."

She moved marginally closer and slid her hand a bit higher from his knee. Now he could *smell* her lipstick. He wondered how it would taste when mixed with the juniper sharpness of the gin.

"You're a very nice distraction," he said.

"Thank you. But we have to be careful, you know."

She retreated slightly, no more than an inch or two, just enough to make him wonder if he had said the wrong thing.

"Careful?"

"With appearances. In Dubai, I mean. They're very sensitive about these male-female arrangements. Unless you're married, it's practically a crime to even touch in public. And being in the same hotel room together like this, well . . ."

"Really?"

"Oh, yes. It's why I always advise male and female associates traveling together in this part of the world to stay on different floors, sometimes even in different hotels. And by all means never, ever look too cozy at the breakfast table. Or don't you ever read those little memos I send out?"

"Sure. Sometimes."

She smiled at his obvious discomfort. Then she removed her hand from his knee.

"It's all right. I know you're probably too busy. But the police do make a fuss about it here. That and drugs. One poor fellow was locked up for months when they found a poppy seed in the sole of his shoe."

"Wow."

"You've seen them in action. Do you trust them?"

He thought of Assad's threats, and the rudeness of the other one, Sharaf, plus the vibe that something hadn't been quite right between them.

"No. I don't."

"Nor do I. So we'll try to keep you insulated."

"But I want to help."

"Do that through me, then. It's my job. Not always the easiest job, I'll confess. Nor do I always get the support I need from our board-room. Another issue entirely, but it's why I can sympathize so easily with your feeling of helplessness. And this time you really do need to just let go. I don't want you to be too easily available for any mischief the police might try. Sometimes they'll file charges just to extort a bribe, knowing we'll pay. And the possibility that Charlie was up to his eyeballs in this mess certainly wouldn't strengthen our hand if something like that happened. So until you're safely aboard a flight home, lay low. And if all else fails there's always Hal Liffey at the consulate. They'd offer sanctuary, I'm sure, as long as I vouched for you."

"Thanks."

Her words, although intended to reassure, were a little unsettling. He also wondered vaguely what had become of the intimacy of a few moments ago. She seemed to have edged even farther away.

"Sam?"

"Yes?"

"You look exhausted. I should let you go."

It was an exit line, and fortunately he wasn't too addled to take the hint. How had he ever let himself believe that she was making a move on him? He supposed he had misread her completely, although as he rode the elevator back to his floor her signals still puzzled him. If he hadn't been so wiped out they might have kept him awake for quite a while. As it was, he slipped almost immediately into a deep and healing sleep, not stirring until well after sunrise, when he was awakened by an insistent knocking.

He threw on a hotel robe and opened the door.

Two policemen in khaki stood in the hallway. Neither was Lieu-tenant Assad. Perhaps there was news of an arrest.

"Are you Mr. Sam Keller?"

"Yes."

"You are pleased to get dressed and accompany to us."

"I'm what?"

"You are being in our custody with us, Mr. Keller. You are under our arrest."

"*Arrest?* On what charge?"

"You are pleased to get dressed, sir, and accompany to us. Now, sir, let us go. Unless we are forced to take evasive action."

The second cop, smaller and wirier, had apparently had enough of this ridiculous exchange. He gripped Sam's forearm with surprising strength and pulled him out the door.

"Arrest!" he shouted, thrusting his face within inches of Sam's. "You come! Arrest!"

"But I haven't done anything!" he said, pulling for all he was worth. Everything Nanette had said about the police came charging back, dark and frightening. It was a frame-up, and he was the victim.

"Let go!" he shouted.

The shorter cop struck him sharply across the jaw, a blow that tumbled him to the floor. Then the first cop handcuffed him and hauled him to his feet.

"You are pleased, sir, to get dressed and accompany to us!" he said again. "You are under our arrest."

7

Sharaf was just settling into the comfortable squalor of his desk after a late lunch when he heard the voice of the American, shouting in the next room. He was certain it was Keller, the fellow from the York. But why would a foreign businessman be out with the rabble in the main booking area?

Curious, Sharaf got up to look through the open doorway of his office. Sure enough, Keller was seated opposite Sergeant Habash, who was typing out a charging document.

As usual, the room was in chaos, the atmosphere of a bus station at rush hour. Its floor space, roughly that of a trailer home, was bisected lengthwise by a cordon of six desks, with the public on one side and the police on the other. Most of the public was confined to a few rows of chairs in a small waiting area, where everyone looked bored or impatient. Hanging from the ceiling above each desk was a numbered sign, but the numbers were out of sequence, proceeding 1-2-3-4-6-5. No one had ever explained why.

This was where you came to be charged, or fingerprinted, or to swear out a warrant, claim an impounded vehicle, ask for a file, or even request a good-conduct certificate, an indispensable document for any domestic employee seeking to return to his home country. And that was just for the men. Behind a privacy curtain down at the far end was an area where the needs of women were handled by officials of their own gender.

The low-slung building had once been the headquarters for the Criminal Investigations Division, but a few years ago most of the detectives had moved upward and onward to a new two-story building, where bigger and quieter offices were well removed from the prying eyes of the public.

Sharaf had chosen to stay behind, a move his colleagues viewed as akin to a soldier turning down a home leave in favor of more shelling at the front. To more ambitious types, such as Lieutenant Assad, it was yet another sign of Sharaf's lack of initiative.

But he had his reasons. For one thing, it was part of his disguise as someone of little consequence. It also kept him attuned to the rough-and-tumble of the criminal marketplace. The bookings, the complaints, even the stupid arguments over who was next in line—all of it gave him a better feel for the mood of the street in this fast-changing city. His colleagues were welcome to their peace and quiet. Bedlam was its own reward.

And here was a fresh case in point. Up in CID headquarters he never would have overheard the American, Keller, loudly protesting his arrest. Curious, indeed, to find him here. Fortunate, too, since Sharaf had just been trying to come up with an excuse for getting in touch, in spite of the Minister's orders to lay off.

Keller appeared to be in a bad way. He was unshaven, hair uncombed, and there was a bruise on his lower jaw. No tie, just a wrinkled suit jacket slung over his shoulder, belted khaki slacks with no crease, and a powder blue oxford-cloth shirt, sleeves rolled. His face had the frantic look of someone who had just fallen into a deep hole in unfamiliar surroundings, far from home and bereft of allies—a blend of panic, incredulity, and impotent rage. The perfect setup, in other words, for the move Sharaf was about to make, provided Keller hadn't gone and done something unforgivable.

Fortunately, the only impediment for the moment was Sergeant Habash, a classic Palestinian striver who was always looking for any way possible to get himself promoted out of this noisy little chamber where his bosses could literally peek over his shoulder.

"Habash!"

The sergeant stopped typing with a flinch, as if expecting a rebuke. He looked back at Sharaf with the wary eyes of a puppy that has been swatted once too often.

Habash was always volunteering for any chore that might win him extra credit, even when he was woefully unqualified. Recently he had begun writing the English versions of the "Case of the Week" summaries for the department's Web site. Habash's English was practically nonexistent, and Sharaf suspected the fellow was relying on some sort of clunky translation software, a suspicion that seemed confirmed when he came across a recent posting touting the department's arrest of a Bangladeshi burglar:

> All his illegal motives just towards the easy and shortly gain, ignoring
> the theorem of being either his legitimate or illicit rights. But no
> longer, he had fallen under Criminal Investigation grasps.

Habash's ambition made him susceptible to the least bit of supervisory pressure, and Sharaf had mastered the art of exploiting him. Having Habash posted just outside his door was like having a handy tool within easy reach.

"I'll take care of this one, Habash." Sharaf handed the man a five-dirham note. "Go get a cup of tea. He's more trouble than he's worth, anyway."

It was far more generous treatment than Habash was used to, but he resisted anyway.

"But, I can't, sir. I—"

"Habash, are you really going to be so ungrateful?"

"No, sir. It's just that Lieutenant Assad said that I, personally, was to—"

"I'll deal with Lieutenant Assad. By now he will have already forgotten your name. The only decision you need to worry about in the next half hour is milk or sugar. Hand me the paperwork. All of it, please."

"You can't have the complaint!" Habash bent protectively over his typewriter. "I'm still writing it up."

Even ambitious flunkies had their limits, and Sharaf knew better than to risk further ill will.

"The affidavit, then. It looks finished."

He snatched it from the desk before Habash could protest. Better than nothing, he supposed.

Habash looked doleful, as if he knew this would only lead to trouble. He nonetheless took Sharaf's money and bolted for the door, hoping perhaps that everything would turn out okay if he fled quickly enough from the scene of the crime. His departure set off a fresh round of groans from the waiting area, where everyone was quick to note that only two of the six desks were now manned.

"This way," Sharaf said to Keller.

The American looked like he didn't know whether to be relieved or upset. Not having read the charges, Sharaf couldn't yet say which reaction was more appropriate. He shut the door to his office. Keller took the only other chair, facing directly across the desk.

"I should have known you were behind this," Keller said.

"Sergeant Habash seems to think it was Lieutenant Assad's idea."

"Oh, I see. Good cop, bad cop. Which one are you?"

"I'm the ignorant cop, looking for an education."

"On a stupid trumped-up sex charge?"

"*Sex* charge? Assad is charging you for what happened at the York?"

"No. For what happened last night at the hotel. Or didn't happen. It's a complete misunderstanding, and if you'd just phone Ms. Weaver . . ."

"Please. Allow me to examine the paperwork. I might actually be able to help."

The affidavit had been filed by the hotel security staff. Apparently someone had observed bawdy behavior on a hallway surveillance camera. Hardly the first time Sharaf had seen such a charge, but it was fairly astonishing at a high-ticket spot like the Shangri-La, where Westerners were generally allowed to cavort as much as they pleased, as long as it was behind closed doors. Perhaps the security man was new. Or maybe Assad had indeed played a role, seeking something in return.

"So they arrested you at your hotel room?"

"Woke me up. I was alone, of course, not that anyone cared. The whole thing's ridiculous. All they need to do is contact Ms. Weaver. She'd clear it up in about ten seconds. By now she's probably wondering where the hell I am. If this is your way of pressuring me for more information, you're wasting your time. I'm more than willing to cooperate. This will only get a lot of people upset over nothing."

Obviously the fellow had no idea what he was up against. But Keller wouldn't be at all useful to him in this agitated state unless Sharaf could first develop some leverage.

"So you think this charge is *nothing*? Are you aware of the penalties in my country for this kind of behavior, Mr. Keller? I have seen men brought in on suspicion of prostitution simply for occupying the backseat of a taxi with an unmarried woman. Another poor fellow got three years—three *years*, sir—for disrobing on the beach at night with his girlfriend."

Sharaf watched, satisfied, as Keller's eyes widened.

"We are a young country, Mr. Keller. Young and wealthy. And like any young and wealthy individual, we can famously act on a whim, with a spirited temper to match. So, whatever you do, do not underestimate the grave potential of the charge facing you."

Keller swallowed hard. Sharaf placed a freshly opened bottle of water before him, and the man dutifully drank some. When Keller next spoke, his voice was subdued, chastened.

"But I really did do nothing. Ms. Weaver will back me up."

"Don't worry, I will contact her shortly. We at least owe you that much. Yet what am I to make of this affidavit? The hotel staff cites the indisputable evidence of video footage in which you are very clearly seen entering the room of a female guest late last night. In an obvious state of intoxication, I might add."

Keller reddened, then seemed to recover some of his previous spirit, and he sat up a little straighter. Sharaf was relieved to see it. In order for his plan—still hazy, still forming—to stand any chance of success, the American would first have to show some potential for tenacity, even rebelliousness.

"Look. Yes, I went in her room. Guilty as charged. But it was for business. I was delivering a . . ."

He paused, seeming to stumble as he reddened slightly. "I was delivering a business item that Ms. Weaver had requested. And if they check the time signature of the video they'll no doubt see I was only there a few minutes."

Sharaf wondered what sort of "business item" could have made him blush, but that was a subject for later.

"A lot can happen in a few minutes between a man and a woman, Mr. Keller, as you and I well know. But even the possibility of an illicit sexual congress could be overlooked if you hadn't entered her room so forcefully."

"Forcefully? She invited me in."

"Apparently that's not what the tape shows. I'll read from the affidavit: 'Subject then forced his way through doorway, despite female's attempt to resist. Female pushed subject's chest, but subject continued forward and shut door behind him.' "

"But that's crazy. I—"

Keller stopped abruptly, and his frown disappeared.

"Okay," he said, brightening. "I think I know what happened. She dropped her key card and nudged me back so she could stoop to pick it up. All the video probably shows is her hand coming out through the doorway to push me. Someone in security must have overreacted. That's all. Just call her. She'll clear it up."

"As I said, I plan to. Because I am quite certain this charge will prove to be spurious."

"You believe me?"

Relief and gratitude showed in Keller's eyes. And they were good eyes, Sharaf saw. Even in their weariness they conveyed a dogged reliability, a trustworthy competence, the very sort of eyes his wife, Amina, was always drawn to whenever she sought an honest merchant or a reputable doctor.

"Yes, I believe you," Sharaf said. For the moment, at least, he had an ally. "That is why I am prepared to let you make that phone call. Provided, of course, that you are prepared to help me in return, if only for a few hours."

Most self-serving scoundrels would have agreed right away. Keller, to his credit, didn't.

"That depends on what kind of help you want."

Sharaf was impressed. The question now was how to best put the young man to use without exposing them both to peril—and without the Minister finding out.

His desk phone rang.

Sharaf held up a hand in abeyance. He lifted the receiver to hear a voice from his past, a source from the bare hinterlands, an acquaintance from boyhood days of rabbit hunts and falconry, of royal encampments in empty sands. The man had news, and it was instantly intriguing.

"Where?" Sharaf asked, switching to Arabic.

He noted the location in a rapid scrawl.

"I will come immediately. And thank you, Daoud. As always, your good word and fine service are exceeded only by your generous hospitality. I am in your debt."

He hung up, and addressed Keller in English.

"It appears I will need your help sooner than expected." He rose from the desk. "Let's go, before anyone thinks to reclaim you."

"Where?"

"To identify a body."

"But Charlie has been—"

"Not him. A woman. Caucasian, in a blue sequin dress. Sound familiar?"

Keller nodded, speechless. He stood uncertainly. Sharaf then led the way back through the hubbub of the booking area toward the main exit. Fortunately, Sergeant Habash hadn't returned, and everyone else was bent over their paperwork. The last thing he needed was someone remembering that the two of them had left the building together. They crossed the parking lot to his Camry, which looked very lonely in its far, empty corner.

Then, without a further word between them, Keller and he climbed aboard and headed out onto the busy roadway, where Sharaf pointed his car toward the desert.

8

A Bedouin stood watch over the body, knee-deep in a depression of sand some thirty yards off the empty highway. His face reminded Sam of one of those nineteenth-century lithographs of Apache warriors—weathered skin, perpetual squint, a latent fierceness held in abeyance by a taut frown. His hair was long and black, and he wore a traditional white headdress that he had looped into place with a black *egal*. A red Toyota Land Cruiser, presumably his, was parked on the shoulder.

Even with Sharaf pushing the Camry to the limit, it had taken nearly two hours to get there. As they braked to a halt, Sam saw that the body was barely visible from the road.

"How did he ever see it?"

"You or I wouldn't have," Sharaf said, his hand on the door latch. "The lazy people who dumped it wouldn't have, either. That's why they thought it was a suitable spot. But the Bedu always notice, and Daoud has an especially keen eye."

"You know him?"

"Many years."

Daoud approached the car. The two men greeted each other with a ritual of hugs and of hands placed on hearts. Daoud spoke while Sharaf listened. Sam didn't understand a word.

Sharaf nodded and uttered a brief reply. Then Daoud led them to the body, where flies buzzed in a frenzy. Sam, bringing up the rear, saw immediately that it was the woman from the York.

She lay curled on her side, like she had gone to sleep, but there was a huge hole in the back of her head, gaping black and brown from dried blood and brain. The blue sequins of her dress shimmered in the late-morning sun, except across the front, where they were stained by blood. The dress was hiked up high on her thighs. Her hose were torn, and the end of a gun barrel poked from beneath her waist.

Sharaf stooped for a closer look, focusing first on her legs. They were bent at the knees, and her ankles were bound tightly to her thighs by a stiff white cord.

"To keep her from kicking while they had her in the trunk," he said. "They didn't shoot her until they got here, so they wouldn't make a mess in the vehicle."

Sam kept his distance, nauseous at the sight of the flies coming and going from her mouth, her nostrils, and the ragged cavity at the base of her skull. Sharaf continued with his observations.

"After they shot her, they tossed the gun into the depression and dropped her on top. Wiped all the prints first, no doubt. A Makarov nine-millimeter."

"You can tell just from the barrel?"

"I saw the shells at the York. The rest is guesswork. We'll soon know for sure."

Daoud directed their attention to a nearby set of tire tracks. Sharaf straightened, watching carefully as the Bedouin crouched and ran his fingertips across the imprint. Daoud then gazed back toward the highway, scanning the vehicle's looping path. He spoke for a few seconds.

"He says it was an SUV, a BMW X5. Two passengers besides the woman. They arrived a few hours before dawn, and they were in no particular hurry."

"All that from the tire tracks? Do you believe him?"

"When Daoud was a boy, his father could look at a set of camel prints and tell you how many riders had passed, how recently, their tribes, what quarter of the desert they had come from, and whether any of the animals were stolen. The means of transportation have changed, but the Bedu can still read the signs of any passing traveler in the sand. Normally for even half that information you would need an entire crew from the crime lab, with markers and plaster casts. But why waste valuable resources when Daoud can offer an instant reading free of charge, simply out of friendship and honor."

Sam looked at Daoud and nodded appreciatively.

"Salaam aleikum," he offered, expending half his supply of Arabic.

"Aleikum salaam," Daoud replied, nodding solemnly.

"He also found a set of footprints," Sharaf said. "New shoes, heavy-set male. Had to be reasonably brawny to have unloaded the body by himself while his partner sat in the car."

Daoud began to babble again, this time in a more animated tone. Sharaf turned abruptly and gazed back down the long, straight black-top toward the city. A quivering black dot was barely visible in the shimmer of the horizon.

"They're coming," Sharaf said. He set out briskly for the Camry. "You need to get out of sight. Open the door on the opposite side and lie down on the floor in the back. Quickly."

"Who's coming?"

"Police. Two cars. Our friend Lieutenant Assad, would be my guess. Fortunately Daoud can see them long before they see us. But hurry."

Sam wavered for a second, wondering which cop offered a better chance for freedom. Maybe the arrest was just Assad's way of applying pressure. Further involvement with Sharaf might lead to anything.

"Now!" Sharaf said. "Any closer and it won't take a Bedouin to spot you standing there like a fool."

Sam obeyed, although it was all he could do to bend himself into position and pull the door shut from the floor. He heard Daoud speak.

"What's he saying now?"

"There are three people in the lead car. Meaning Assad has rein-forcements. The second vehicle is a meat wagon, for the body. Not another word from you until I say so."

Sam obliged him by not answering.

A few minutes later he heard the whine of the approaching en-gines, then the sizzle of gravel in the wheel wells as they turned onto the shoulder and stopped. Doors slammed. There was a clatter of something metallic. A stretcher for the body, perhaps. Then a voice—Lieutenant Assad's, followed by Sharaf's. They spoke in Arabic, unfor-tunately, so he had no idea what they were saying. But the tone of mutual disdain was unmistakable. He imagined them squared off on the pavement. All that Sharaf had on his side was a silent Bedouin, a dead woman, and a hiding American. Not very promising. Sam stayed low to the floor, sweaty and uncomfortable, and hoped for the best.

"So," Assad began, "you poach my murder scene, steal my main witness, and now this. It's all very annoying, Sharaf, mostly because it creates the distinct impression of a pattern of deliberate interference. Care to explain?"

"I stole no one. Just needed to chat with him a moment, so I borrowed him from Habash. Then I gave him right back."

"Well, he's gone."

"Who? Habash?"

"You know who I mean."

"He couldn't have gone far. He didn't strike me as the resourceful type. In fact, he didn't strike me as a Lothario, either, which made me wonder about your morals charge."

"A Lo-*what*? Some character from one of your Russian novels, I suppose."

"A ladies' man. A seducer. And it's from a play by an Englishman."

Sharaf didn't usually show off like that, but with the likes of Assad the temptation was too great.

"Whatever. Why did you even need a chat?"

"Paperwork from my needless visit to the York. Can't claim the overtime unless I justify my presence."

"Paperwork for that travesty? I'd very much like to see any report you file from that."

"Likewise with yours. We'll trade and call it even."

Assad scowled and looked around. Sharaf hoped Keller was keeping his head down. He had to restrain himself from looking at the Camry. Fortunately neither Assad nor his two assistants made a move in that direction. Assad instead stepped toward the body.

"Who is she, anyway?" Assad asked.

"I was hoping you'd know."

"Russian, I'm guessing. Not my kind of people. You're the one who speaks their language."

"Money and power is their language. I've heard you're fluent."

"You never did say what you're doing here."

"Daoud is an old friend. He found the body. You'll have to forgive him for playing favorites. Obviously someone else must have phoned it in as well. But I'm happy to leave the matter in your hands. There's a Makarov beneath her, by the way. Please make sure it finds its way to the evidence room. And whenever you're interested in trading reports, my offer stands."

Assad scowled and didn't reply. Sharaf crossed the highway to the Camry and climbed in, taking care not to open the door too widely. As he started the engine he hissed a warning to Keller, locking his lips like a ventriloquist.

"Stay down. The lieutenant has his eye on me."

And a baleful eye it was, making Sharaf wonder yet again what he was getting into, sinking deeper by the minute into choppy waters. He eased the car into a slow, looping turn to head back toward the city. Fluency in money and power, indeed. Sharaf shook his head. It was a stupid thing to have said.

He waited a full mile before he spoke again.

"Maybe you had better stay down for the whole ride. It would not do either of us any good to be seen together."

"Where are you taking me?"

"Excellent question. For the moment I have no answer. They will have the hotel staked out, of course, so that's not a possibility. Do you have your passport?"

"Yes. But not my phone or my BlackBerry. They're at the hotel. Wouldn't it be safer if you just took me to the U.S. Consulate?"

"Maybe. They might even decide to fly you home, possibly as soon as tonight."

"Sounds good."

"Not to me. I cannot afford to have them put you beyond my reach. Remember our deal? I help you, you help me?"

"I don't remember agreeing. And I'm not sure I'd call this helping."

"Getting in the car with me and hiding from Assad was just as good as an answer, wouldn't you say so? You are in this now whether you like it or not."

"You did promise to let me call Ms. Weaver."

"And so I shall. The timing is another matter. Why put her in jeopardy with knowledge of your whereabouts until we've decided upon a secure location?"

"But maybe she could—"

"Please. I will judge when it is best."

"But if I—"

"Quiet, sir. I need to think."

He also needed to calm down. Having Keller in the car was like driving a load of stolen goods. He kept expecting Assad's car to come roaring up from behind, headlights flashing. But as the miles passed with nothing but the whine of the tires and the whoosh of passing trucks, Sharaf relaxed, and his mind drifted into memories that had been stirred by the sight of his old friend Daoud.

As a young boy Sharaf had considered the Bedouins to be foolish, living in their goat-smelling tents far from the comforts of the city when, like him, they could have dwelled along a tidal creek, with its cool breezes and fine homes. Then, at age eleven, he met Daoud. It happened when his father, flexing the muscle of sudden wealth and new connections, purchased four hunting falcons and got himself invited on a royal hunt.

His father had bought the birds at a dear price from a desert trader. He gave one to Sharaf, who was supposed to keep the bird with him morning, noon, and night, in order to properly feed and train it. Sharaf's tutors were delighted. Sharaf wasn't. Going to sleep with a bird of prey in your bedroom was downright creepy. It preened and fretted, and its little leather hood made it look like it was awaiting execution.

When the time came for the royal hunt, Sharaf accompanied his father and their four birds. They rode in the back of a Range Rover, one of three vehicles in a royal procession packed with two dozen men and boys. They drove for hours, deep into the desert. That evening Sharaf watched in fascination as Sheikh Rashid's men set up the encampment—an oval of tents with a surrounding screen of palm fronds, to keep out the wind, the snakes, and the scorpions. They put a fire ring in the middle, along with a giant kettle.

Sharaf slept in a tent with two of Sheikh Rashid's younger sons and their friends. They were welcoming enough, but were several years older, and he would have felt lost if not for Daoud, who was his own age and also an outlier of sorts. Daoud's father was the hunting party's Bedouin tracker and guide.

In the morning, after prayers and breakfast, everyone stood at the ready, birds on their arms. Sharaf remembered his father looking particularly proud, although he had already heard some of the other men making fun of the names his father had given their birds. Sharaf had expected nonstop action, but the hunt evolved slowly as the sun climbed above the dunes. It was a painstaking process of stalking and waiting while Daoud's father searched the sand for fresh footprints of the elusive houbara.

After a fruitless few hours, Sharaf's father, thinking he knew better, released all four of their birds anyway to go search for prey on their own. Sharaf was surprised to feel a tug of sorrow as he watched his own bird disappear over the horizon. Half an hour later, Daoud's father found a promising set of tracks, and sent the rest of the birds off in the opposite direction from the Sharaf falcons. Even then, success wasn't guaranteed. In all, the hunters released more than forty birds, and by day's end nine hadn't returned, including one of Sheikh Rashid's. It was apparently common for some of the falcons to lose their way over the vastness of the desert.

But no one fared as poorly as the Sharafs, who lost all four birds. For the moment at least, tact prevailed, and no one else remarked on it. His father brooded nonetheless, especially as some of the falcons returned with a dozen houbara for the cook fire. To make sure Sheikh Rashid's guests had plenty to eat, the cook had also bargained with a passing herdsman for a pair of goats. The meal was outstanding after the long and tiring day, and Sharaf began to hope that the evening might pass without further humiliation.

Then the coffee was brewed, the smoking pipes came out, and tongues began to loosen. The fireside circle enjoyed much hearty laughter, and increasingly the levity came at his father's expense. Sharaf wasn't sure what was more horrifying—having his father be the butt of everyone's jokes or watching the man's anger build to a combustible level behind a stoical mask of gathering scorn. Among the boys, only Daoud managed to subdue his laughter, a display of solidarity that won Sharaf's loyalty forever.

Events reached a climax when one of the men unwisely asked, "What will you hunt with tomorrow, Mahmoud Sharaf, your son? Will you fling him into the sky on a string?"

His father stood amid the fresh gale of laughter. Sharaf braced for the worst.

"Actually, I will not hunt at all tomorrow. My plan is to leave this party altogether at first light, as soon as prayers are over. Even if it means I have to walk every step of the way, with no coffee and no breakfast."

The declaration was a colossal insult to the hospitality of their royal host. Some of the men gasped. The rest were silent, and many looked away. No one dared glance at Sheikh Rashid, but everyone was waiting for his reaction.

The sheikh did not lash out. He did not even rise from his seat. He instead handled the situation as only as a natural leader of many peoples and tribes could have managed. Sharaf couldn't recall Rashid's exact words, only that he began by making an offhand remark that made light of the entire proceeding. It signaled that he was not offended, and that he was willing to dismiss the intemperate outburst as a harmless release of steam.

This still left hanging the question of what his father would do the following morning. Would he stand around, birdless and humiliated? Or would he stalk away in a huff, as threatened? Sheikh Rashid solved that problem, too.

"You know," he said, "my driver came out here tonight, as I always require, to bring me the daily news from the city." Indeed, everyone straggling back from the hunt had noticed his vintage car parked by the tents.

"Well, as it happens, I am told that prices in the souk have begun to rise quite a bit in our absence. It has made me feel very guilty on behalf of the two merchants in our party. For that reason, I am begging them both to accept an offer of transportation in my car back to the city in the morning, so that they may safely attend to their business interests without missing out on the bountiful opportunity of the moment."

It not only gave Sharaf's father a graceful way out, it softened the landing by including a second man among the departures, a noted tea merchant. Sharaf remembered that Daoud nodded to him from across the campfire, as if to say, yes, this is how a great man should operate, not in vengeance but in reconciliation.

From the floor in the back of the Camry, Sam Keller spoke up after a long silence. His voice came up through the driver's seat like that of a hidden radio, which only added to the sense that the fellow had been reading Sharaf's mind:

"How did you get to know Daoud?"

Sharaf, momentarily startled, said nothing at first. He saw by the dashboard clock that nearly half an hour had passed.

"From an old hunting party," he said at last. "Our encampment was not very far from where the body was found. It was long ago."

A pause, several beats.

"A hunting party?" Keller prompted.

"With falcons. It is a complicated story."

Sharaf's cheeks burned with embarrassment at the mere thought of telling it to Keller. He had felt similarly embarrassed during the long ride back to town in Sheikh Rashid's car. The lone benefit of the hunting trip was that he saw Daoud several more times that year, when the boy accompanied his father to town to sell firewood.

They remained friends, and when Sharaf became a policeman he stayed in touch by relaying advance warnings of any coming decrees or edicts that might affect life in the hinterlands. Daoud reciprocated with news of interest to a detective, just as he had done that morning. If the body had been the victim of some tribal dispute or Bedouin feud, Sharaf doubted Daoud ever would have called. But a foreign victim had clearly been the result of some bad business in the city.

Traffic was picking up. As they neared the huge ten-lane beltway on the outskirts of the city, the desert highway widened to four lanes, then six. It was then that Sharaf came up with the solution to their predicament.

"I have decided your destination," he announced. "You will stay at my house. Under the circumstances, it is the only practical choice. But I must ask you to remain out of sight until we have reached it."

"Your house?" Keller's tone was uncertain.

"I can assure your complete comfort there. I have a family. And it will only be temporary. Perhaps only a single night."

"And after that?"

"We will figure something out."

Keller's silence told him the American wasn't sold on the idea. Sharaf wasn't either. Amina certainly wouldn't be. Only Laleh would like it, if only because she would have someone roughly her own age to talk to. Not that Sharaf would let that happen. In fact, the whole idea of it almost made him change his mind. But there was no alternative, short of driving Keller back out into the desert to hide him among the Bedouin.

He continued driving in contemplative silence until they ran into the usual nightmarish traffic. Finally, with a weary sigh, Sharaf turned in at the open gate to the family compound and coasted into the shaded carport.

"Okay," he said, setting the hand brake. "I suppose it is safe to issue the all clear."

Before Sam could answer, Sharaf looked in his rearview mirror and reacted immediately.

"Shit!" he said. "Exactly what I didn't need."

"What?" Keller asked, as he struggled to sit up. "The police?" If so, he was doomed.

"Worse," Sharaf said. "My son Salim. And it's obvious that he wants something."

9

Sam, still catching his breath after the false alarm, stood in the foyer of Sharaf's house while the detective rushed back outside to deal with his son. A family crisis, by the sound of it. The two men were shouting in Arabic, each interrupting the other.

A young woman appeared suddenly from the next room.

"What's all the commotion? And who are you?"

She was roughly his age, and quite attractive—Sharaf's daughter? Her intense brown eyes threw him off balance. So did her clothes, a smart and sexy skirt-and-blouse ensemble that she might have picked up yesterday in Manhattan. Hardly what he would have guessed an Emirati female to be wearing.

He also hadn't expected Sharaf, a mere police lieutenant, to be living in this kind of style and comfort. What he had already seen of the house was well maintained and tastefully appointed. And part of a family compound, no less, a prosperous-looking assemblage of four manicured lots behind a high stucco wall. Salim's house, if anything, had looked grander than this one.

"Well, what are you staring at?"

"Sorry. I didn't know anyone was home."

"Who are you? Did my father bring you?"

"He did. I'm Sam. Sam Keller."

"I am Laleh."

He held out his hand for a shake and immediately realized it was probably taboo for her to touch him. Unfazed, she took his hand any-way, a warm, fleeting grip. Her eyes conveyed the rest of the greeting. They were full of questions, and his inclination was to answer them all, come what may.

She had emerged from just around the corner, as if she had been waiting there since hearing the arrival of her father's car. She'd proba-bly heard the door shut when he went back out, and Sam's impression was of a careful—even sneaky—listener, someone accustomed to oper-ating on the edges of propriety. Already she had glanced twice toward the door, as if prepared to vanish the moment Sharaf reappeared.

Sam wondered what she must make of him in his current disheveled state—sweaty and unshaven, shirttail out, suit coat slung over his shoulder. His clothes were dusty from his long spell on the floor of the Camry. She probably thought he was some disreputable source from the world of crime.

"Come have a seat," she said. "There's no telling how long they'll go on like that. And my father isn't much for social graces. Or are you not a social caller?"

He wasn't sure what Sharaf would want him to say.

"Strictly business, I guess. But your dad is putting me up for the night."

"Here?"

She seemed astonished. She even backed away a bit, as if he had said something unbalanced.

"You should ask your father. It's complicated."

"His work usually is."

She led him into a sort of parlor, where he sat on a long, deep couch while she remained standing. There was an awkward lull before an idea occurred to him.

"Would you mind if I used the telephone?"

"Until I know what my father has in mind for you, it's probably best if you didn't."

So she was loyal, too, in her way, even though her initial manner had seemed dismissive of household authority. Or perhaps, being the daughter of a policeman, she was instinctively wary of seemingly inno-cent requests. He wondered if she actually lived here. Surely at her age she was only visiting.

"But I know he wouldn't mind if I got you something to eat and drink," she continued. "Would you care for tea? Coffee? What's your preference?"

"Water would be fine."

"Very well." She turned toward the kitchen.

"Actually—"

"Yes?"

"Coffee would be great. I haven't had a cup all day, and I'm getting a headache."

She nodded and disappeared. Sam heard a cabinet open, then water rushing from the tap. Outside, the shouting continued, although the volume had dropped and there were fewer interruptions. A few moments later a coffeemaker began to hiss. He called out to Laleh from the parlor.

"Do they always go on like that?"

"My father and Salim? Oh, yes. Except when my mother is here. Then my father doesn't feel quite as free to let go. That was Salim's first mistake. Not waiting for ground support. He's never known the right way to deal with my father."

"And what is the right way?"

"Obviously I haven't discovered it, or I wouldn't still be living at home at the age of twenty-four. I run my own company, you know. Did my father tell you that?"

"He hasn't told me much of anything."

"He can be like that. Is filter coffee okay?"

"Sure. So who else lives here?" He realized it was a nosy question. "Sorry. That was a little, well . . ."

"Blunt? Intrusive?" She appeared at the doorway, tray in hand.

"Yes."

She set the tray on a small table and sat across from him, then watched as he took a sip. The coffee was strong, exactly what he needed. A moment ago he had been exhausted and out of sorts. Now he felt tuned to a perfect pitch, alert to every word and gesture. Her graceful movements were like a tonic.

"It's all right," she said. "I am accustomed to blunt. Everyone I work with is blunt. Englishmen mostly. Or Europeans. Media and public relations types who still act like boys and want to get rich in a hurry. Blunt is the only way they know how to be."

"Oh."

It was chastening to be lumped with a bunch of cads, but he was disarmed by her ease with his way of speaking. It wasn't just that her English was good. She had the right mannerisms and cadences, too, even the offhand tone. Her father, for all the breadth of his vocabulary and flawless grammar, didn't have that facility.

"Do you want milk? Sugar?"

"Black is fine."

"My business is in Media City. Have you been there?"

"No. I'm in pharmaceuticals. Pfluger Klaxon. What kind of company do you own?"

"A marketing firm, specializing in visuals. Graphic design and so on. Although we're capable of handling the copy end as well. I still live with my parents because my mother and father wouldn't allow it any other way. Even in the business world, women here must do things the old way. If you are not married, you must live with your parents."

He wasn't sure how to react to all that. He was charmed, but he also found himself thinking of her as a bit of a spoiled rich girl. She was smart and bored, so Daddy put up the money for a business start-up, which helped get her out of the house. Strange, he supposed, but hardly the strangest thing he'd seen in Dubai. It reminded him anew of how little he knew about most of the places he visited; all those doings that percolated just beneath the surface.

"You know," she said, "Pfluger Klaxon would be far better off with a larger public presence here. In marketing and supplying their products, I mean. It really wouldn't take much, considering the poor state of medicine in this country."

Sam stopped in mid-sip, astonished. It was exactly what he had been thinking before the trip. Because for all of Dubai's wealth and boomtown feel, it was known as a place where even wealthy expats didn't find it easy to get the best pharmaceuticals. The company could have easily built more goodwill simply by making its products more readily available.

"You're right. Exactly right."

"Well, if your people ever decide on that course, I can advise them on the best way to handle it, with maximum publicity benefit." She handed him a business card.

A born salesman, then. Already she had wedged her foot in the door, and she had managed it in a manner that made him smile. Maybe she was no dilettante after all.

"I'm sure you could. Thank you."

Sam slipped her card into the lapel pocket of his suit coat, and took a fresh look at his surroundings. He was again impressed. The furniture and fixtures were stylish but comfortable, in complementary earth tones. Someone in the family had a good eye for these things, and enough money to pull it off.

"You seem surprised by our house," she said.

"I am. In America you wouldn't generally find this much good taste and, well, prosperity, in the home of a police detective."

"And why is this?"

"Well, police salaries in America are pretty lousy."

"They are here, too. Practically a beggar's wages."

"Oh. Then how . . ." His voice trailed off.

"How do we afford all this?"

He wasn't sure he wanted to know, now that he had pinned his hopes to Sharaf. But he nodded anyway.

"The land and the house were free. Every citizen gets one. The rest comes from the businesses he owns, of course."

"Businesses? Your father?"

"The Punjabis and Iranians who come here to open shops and restaurants must have someone to sign the documents, to stand in as a local owner. So my father has done that for maybe twelve of them. On paper, he is the owner. In reality, the Punjabi is, or the Iranian. The foreigner, of course, does all of the work. But out of gratitude he sends my father a check every month."

"They all do? All twelve of them?"

"Of course. Many Emiratis do this, in all walks of life. You look as if you disapprove."

"Well, it's just that, for a policeman . . ."

"What?"

"It could appear to be . . ."

"A conflict of interests?"

"Yes."

She smiled, the same smile you offer children who believe in Santa.

"You sound like everyone who works in my building. They are more interested in appearances than in reality. Maybe it is because of what they do for a living—managing spin, molding perception—whether they are in PR, like me, or work for CNN. To me, either you are honest or you're not. If you are, no amount of money can compromise you. If you're not, then even the best appearances don't mean you can be trusted."

"And your father?"

"Not the easiest man to live with. But he is honest. Always."

The front door slammed shut. Laleh's expression changed dramatically, and with the deftness of a magician she pulled out a white head scarf seemingly from nowhere and quickly wrapped it around her head, covering her hair in an instant. Heavy footsteps sounded in the foyer. Sharaf appeared in the doorway and warily surveyed the scene. He was still breathing heavily from the encounter on the lawn.

"Laleh! What are you doing in this part of the house unaccompanied when there is a male visitor? And without your abaya! What would your mother say?"

"That I'm being hospitable?"

"You probably weren't even covering your head until I came in."

Her blush told him all he needed to know.

"Yes, I thought so." He turned on Sam. "You weren't speaking with her, I hope?"

"I just—"

"He hardly said a word. I did most of the talking."

"Not surprising. Well, I'm here now, so he'll get all the hospitality he needs."

"Nice to have met you," Sam said, feeling he should help deflect blame. "Thanks for the coffee."

"That will be quite enough, Mr. Keller."

"I have a ten o'clock curfew, if you can believe it." Laleh was halfway out the door. She now sounded more like a teenager than a confident young businesswoman.

"That will be all from you as well."

Sharaf stared until she had retreated out of sight. Sam heard a television switch on, a channel in English playing just the sort of music that Sharaf probably despised. The volume went up a notch. Sharaf stepped across the room, shut the door, and then turned back toward Sam.

"Does she really have a curfew?" Sam asked.

"Is that any of your business?"

"No. But I'm not really any of your business, either, according to Lieutenant Assad. So maybe you owe me an explanation before things go any farther. Or maybe you could just let me use the phone."

"I wonder if Laleh always has this effect on men, making them too bold for their own good. Has it occurred to you, Mr. Keller, that Lieutenant Assad might actually have been doing you a favor by having you arrested this morning?"

"What do you mean?"

"By moving you out of harm's way. Especially considering what has become of the only other reliable witness to those men who killed your friend."

"You mean—?"

"Yes. I mean it is probably not safe for you to be wandering around on your own. Even if you were free to do so."

"Then why didn't you leave me at the police station?"

"Because it is also possible that Lieutenant Assad wants to put you somewhere secure, like a jail, not to protect you but so that an accident can easily befall you. Which do I think is the likeliest? I have no idea. And that is one reason I want you here. With your help I might be able to find out the answer, to that question and to others."

"So you're not going to let me use the phone."

"Not for the moment. But I will reexamine the question tomorrow."

"What will I do about clothes? And money. A toothbrush, my razor."

"Yes, I see what you mean."

Sharaf sized him up, then nodded.

"You are about Rahim's size. He lives between us and Salim. Not that I wish to see either of them again anytime soon. But I will do what I can. Stay here."

Sharaf disappeared into the kitchen, then headed out the door. Sam immediately went to use the phone. But when he got to the kitchen he saw that the cradle was empty. Sharaf had taken the handset with him.

He went back to the couch, where he sat listening to Laleh's music from down the hall over the muffled sounds of shouting from next door. He half expected her to come creeping back now that her father had gone, but he supposed that for the moment she had expended her supply of boldness. He was sorry for that. With only himself for company he felt his worries return. He was even kind of homesick.

On the other hand, he definitely wasn't bored. Given what he had already seen of the household dynamics, the evening ahead promised to be interesting. After all those times he'd yearned for adventure, or an insider's view, he was finally getting his wish—stretching himself, as Charlie might have said.

Of course, that was before armed Russians and vengeful policemen had entered the mix. Simply staying alive sounded like a pretty good option, too.

10

Sharaf slunk down the hallway before dawn, a prowler in his own home. He paused by Laleh's door to listen for suspicious activity before proceeding to the guest room. Keller was still asleep, thank goodness. So was everyone else.

It had been a restless night. Amina had returned home from grocery shopping to be scandalized by the unannounced presence of an unfamiliar male. She viewed Keller's installation as a workplace incursion into her domestic fiefdom. She nonetheless rose to the demands of hospitality by preparing a huge dinner and making strained conversation for a few hours. But just when the mood had started to loosen, Keller had put things back on edge by asking, "So tell me about the living arrangements in your compound. Who lives in the other three houses?"

That was sometimes the problem with Western guests, particularly Americans. Show them a little warmth and they assumed an awkward familiarity. They were always wanting you to "open up," as if candor equaled friendship.

To make matters worse, Laleh proceeded to answer with unnecessary frankness.

"Well, Salim lives in one. He's the one you saw arguing with Father. He's the eldest, with two wives and four children. My brother Rahim has the smallest house, which is just as well, since he is twenty-nine and lives by himself. My two other brothers are both still students, living abroad."

Not noticing her mother's chilly glare or her father's doomed look of woe, Laleh rattled on like a runaway train. Perhaps the American's appreciative smile was leading her into peril. Amina undoubtedly noticed that as well.

"The third house is the most interesting. It belongs to my aunt and my cousins. My father invited them to build there because he felt sorry for them. His brother shocked everyone by dying without a penny to his name."

The airing of the last point was especially awkward. Sharaf's decision had always been a sore point with Amina. Accommodating a fourth house meant the other three had to be smaller, and Amina had never liked Sharaf's elderly aunt. He understood his wife's resentment, but there were deeper and more secretive reasons for his generosity, ones that he never intended to share with anyone.

Shortly after Laleh's soliloquy, Amina stiffly offered her regrets and marched off to bed, leaving the cleanup to her loose-lipped daughter.

Sharaf had braced for the worst when he finally headed for the bedroom.

"I know, I know, I know," he said preemptively as he joined his wife. He hadn't even bothered to pour a glass of camel's milk, knowing it would settle poorly after the beating he was about to take. "Having the American here is an imposition, and I apologize. I'll have him out of here as soon as possible. Don't worry, I'll make sure that Laleh doesn't say another word to him."

Amina said nothing in reply. She offered only a glare over her shoulder as she dressed for sleep. When she settled into the mattress she rolled onto her side, turning her back to him. Her matronly hips curved beneath the sheets like a distant, imposing bluff, snowy and insurmountable. Her continuing silence was unnerving. It was like bedding down next to a volcano. Eventually there would be an eruption, and the longer she remained inactive, the more violent the eventual explosion would be. Sharaf decided to vent some steam.

"If it's any comfort, no one outside our family knows about this. There will be no hint of scandal with regard to Laleh. So if anyone from my office calls, for whatever reason, don't mention a word."

"So what you're doing is also illegal? Is that what you're telling me?"

"Of course not."

"Wonderful. What crime has this man committed? Fornication? Rape, even?"

"Please, Amina. I can assure you he has committed no crime at all."

"Which is why no one can know he is here, because he is so pure and innocent. Yes, you're making perfect sense. Good night, Anwar. Trouble me no more, please."

Great. He had made her even angrier. Meaning he didn't dare reveal his own worries, which would have upset her more. Because to Sharaf's mind, Keller's presence imperiled far more than social propriety. If word leaked out, he could imagine armed intruders scaling the wall of the family compound to pry open doors and windows in the dead of night. Rogue policemen, or worse, would be at their doorstep.

He tried to relax by reading Dostoevsky, but every line about guilt and torment only reminded him of his predicament, so he soon turned out the light. When he awoke shortly before five he knew it was useless to try to get back to sleep before prayers. So he rose, washed his hands and face, and then retreated to the parlor, where he knelt to pray. First he completed the late prayer from the night before, having forgotten it amid the turmoil of the evening. Then, a few minutes ahead of schedule, he offered the morning prayer, followed by a hasty version of the midday prayer. These three-for-one sessions weren't exactly by the book, but he had learned to appreciate their economy on the pearling boat. Sharaf doubted God minded a few shortcuts. It was like dealing with any authority figure, he supposed. Show some respect and you'd generally be left to your own devices.

He brewed a pot of coffee and took a steaming cup to his office at the center of the house, where he shut the door, opened his cell phone, and punched in the number for the Minister, another early riser.

"Sharaf?"

"Just checking in."

"Early, but I'm glad you called. I have something for you. Straight from the heart of the matter."

"Our Slavic friends?"

"Word from the Tsar himself. Via my contacts, of course."

The Minister claimed to have sources in all sorts of unlikely places. Sharaf didn't know whether to be impressed or alarmed.

"Big doings tonight. A rare summit conference with the Persians. Eight o'clock."

"I thought we called them Iranians now. What's the location?"

"Neutral territory, out in the open. The mall at the Burjuman. Beyond that, my source couldn't be more specific, but I'm sure you'll manage to find them."

"Probably one of the restaurants in the upper courtyard. What's the agenda?"

"That's what I want you to find out."

"Hard to see how, unless they invite me to join them."

"Oh, come on. You're a resourceful man."

"Who tells you these things?"

"About you or the Russians? And what does it matter, as long as it's correct? By the way, about that American."

Sharaf tensed. He wondered what the Minister had heard.

"The dead one?"

"The live one. The witness. I'm told he has disappeared."

"I heard the same thing."

"You know nothing more?"

"Why should I?"

"Because you were interested in him. You told me so yourself."

"And you said to steer clear."

"Come on, Sharaf. I know how you operate. Where do you think he's gone?"

"To the embassy in Abu Dhabi, if he has any brains."

"Seeking asylum? Do you really think they would smuggle him out?"

"His employer certainly has the clout. You're the one with the connections. You tell me."

Silence. Sharaf suspected the Minister was smiling knowingly, having guessed the truth but trusting Sharaf not to screw things up. Or maybe that was wishful thinking.

"Don't make trouble for us, Sharaf. Don't get reckless on me."

"Of course not."

"And keep me posted on tonight's events."

That went without saying.

A few moments later, the dawn call to prayer sounded from the neighborhood mosque, with its signature line, "Prayer is better than sleep." He heard Laleh groan in disagreement from her bed as he trooped to the kitchen for more coffee. Still not a peep out of Keller.

He expected Amina to appear in her robe to make breakfast, as was her custom. When she didn't he sighed and made it himself, setting out fruit, bread, and yogurt on the table. Then he unfolded the morning's fresh copy of *Gulf News*, his daily means of keeping up with the English-speaking world.

The front page was the usual silliness, bright colors and bold head-lines splashed on extravagantly glossy paper: An Israeli war game was in progress, drawing the typically hysterical reaction. Six new lanes had opened on Emirates Road, bringing it to twelve in all. Atop the page was a headline announcing that Sheikh Mohammed had been named the UAE's "Distinguished Personality of the Year." Now there was a surprise. He was indeed a great man, but this daily pandering was annoying.

Sharaf flipped the page. The agency handling car registrations was planning to auction the rights to more license tags with single-digit numbers. It seemed like a pretty good idea, seeing as how someone had paid $15 million for a tag with the number 1. He turned another page. Three killed in horrendous crash. Local college girl arrested for smok-ing hashish. Did Laleh know her?

There was nothing about a woman's body being found in the desert, not that he had expected any coverage. Nothing yet about Charlie Hatcher, either. He had heard that the news would be released this afternoon, which would produce a brief onslaught of foreign press inquiries. He was happy to let Lieutenant Assad handle them.

Down at the bottom of page five was a brief about a missing tourist. Sharaf scanned it and moved on to sports, but something about the story set a hook deep in his mind. Flipping back a page, he reread the item carefully. A few moments later he rose from the table, walked qui-etly down the hall, and slipped into the guest bedroom. Taking care to make as little noise as possible, he lifted Keller's trousers from the back of a chair, checked the back pockets, found the man's wallet and pass-port, left them both in place, and then folded the trousers over his arm. He picked up Keller's belt, shirt, undershorts, socks, and shoes from a small, neat pile at the foot of the bed. Clutching the bundle tightly to his chest, he tiptoed back into the hallway and gently nudged the door shut behind him. Fortunately, Laleh and Amina were still in their rooms. He exited the rear of the house and walked to the carport, where the Camry was parked next to Amina's and Laleh's BMWs.

The birds were in full morning song, and the first rays of sunlight were golden in the pale leaves of an olive tree. He opened the door of a small shed at the rear of the carport and stepped inside, where it smelled like potting soil and motor oil. Sharaf dropped Keller's belongings onto the concrete floor. Then he leaned beneath a workbench and, grunting with effort, tugged out an old washtub of corrugated steel, and put Keller's belongings inside. Turning to go, he decided to first check Keller's wallet.

The contents were about what he expected: cash in two currencies, American driver's license, credit cards, and a sheaf of dated receipts, including one from the York Club from the night of Charlie Hatcher's murder. The only surprise was a folded sheet of hotel stationery from the Shangri-La. Someone had written down three names and phone numbers. The numbers were local, and two were vaguely familiar, although he couldn't place them. Below was "Monday, 4/14!" underlined twice, followed by a scribbled sequence of letters and numbers that made no sense at all.

Was it connected to the case? Possibly. What could be so important about April 14, which was only six days away? It made him wonder what else Keller was holding back. He would delve into it later.

He held on to the paper but put the wallet back into the pocket and returned the trousers to the tub, while making a mental note to round up the rest of the necessary supplies later in the day. But to really make this plan work he would first have to phone his old friend Mansour, who, like Ali, had been a fellow diver on his pearl boat during that long ago summer.

Sharaf congratulated himself on his idea as he relocked the shed. A little unorthodox, perhaps, but it just might succeed. It would also serve the dual purpose of keeping the American from running away. You couldn't very well leave the country without a passport.

He reentered the house to find that Keller was up and about, having dressed in some baggy clothes of Rahim's. He did still have his suit coat, which seemed to be the only item that fit properly, but he wasn't taking matters well at all.

"What the hell did you do with my wallet and passport? Not to mention my clothes?"

"No profanities in my household, if you please. I've taken those items into custody for evidentiary purposes. I assure you they're quite safe."

"Evidence of what?"

"Please. We will discuss these matters later. For now, it is time for breakfast."

"At least the damn shoes fit," he muttered. "Pardon my French."

He seemed on the verge of protesting more, but held his tongue. Sharaf was guessing the young man didn't want to make a fuss in front of Laleh, who had just appeared. She wore an abaya, praise God, although she had showered and dressed in record time.

Amina joined them seconds later, lips drawn. Her demeanor cast a pall on the table, and for a while the only sounds were of chewing and sipping. Sharaf broke the silence just before his last swallow of coffee.

"There are some serious matters we need to deal with," he said to Keller.

"I should say so," Amina chimed in.

Laleh bent forward to her bowl of fruit and yogurt. Was she suppressing a laugh? Keller kept his head down, seemingly wary of the family dynamics. Sharaf decided that the young man and he had better evacuate the premises before there was further trouble. He escorted Keller to his windowless hideaway and settled him onto the couch.

"I have a busy schedule planned for you later today, but first I have to keep up appearances by going into the office. While I'm gone I'm afraid you will have to remain locked in this room."

Keller opened his mouth to protest. Sharaf raised a hand.

"Let me finish. I know this is a trial, but you must be patient awhile longer. Even if you managed to leave the house, without your passport you would not be much use to anyone except the people who want to throw you in jail, or worse. And don't worry. When we have concluded our chores, I'll let you make that phone call. I promise."

That must have been what Keller wanted to hear. He shut his mouth, adopted a resigned frown, and sagged back onto the couch.

"What am I supposed to do all day?"

"There are some books in English here." Sharaf gestured toward oak shelves along a far wall. "You are welcome to read them. I shouldn't be more than a few hours."

"And what are these chores you're talking about?"

"We will discuss it later."

Sharaf wasn't ready to tell Keller they would be attending a Mafia powwow. He hadn't yet figured out how they would pull it off, and it would only scare the poor fellow. Understandably so. Because if

Sharaf's hunch was correct, Charlie Hatcher's killers would be among the participants. Now all he had to do was figure out how to let Keller make an identification of the guilty parties without anyone—the Minister included—finding out. It would be a tricky business in the wide-open spaces of the Burjuman Mall. The mere thought of it made his stomach churn and growl. At this rate, he wouldn't be drinking camel's milk for days.

11

Just a few more hours max, Sam thought, and he would be out of this mess. But for the moment he was back on the floor of the Camry, listening to the sounds of stalled Dubai traffic through Sharaf's open window.

It was just after 8 p.m., well after rush hour, yet they were at a standstill. A cloud of greasy smoke told him they were idling near a kebab shop. He heard sidewalk chatter in three languages. A man and a woman were the loudest, arguing passionately in some Slavic tongue and getting rougher by the moment.

"What's going on?" he asked from the floor.

"A prostitute and her pimp. The subject is money. She's Asian; her Russian is terrible. His accent is Georgian, like Stalin's. Oh, dear."

"What happened?"

The shouting gave way to the sound of a scuffle.

"He slapped her. Now he's forcing her into his car."

"Shouldn't you do something?"

"I'm not even in uniform. And the last thing we want is attention, especially when the people we are going to see are probably his bosses. In fact, you can sit up now. We are almost there."

"Russians?" Sam struggled up from the floor and brushed himself off. "You're taking me to some *Mafia* thing?"

Traffic was moving again. No Asian woman or Russian man was in sight.

"I was hoping you might recognize a few of them from the other night at the York."

"Are you crazy?"

"My wife thinks so. But only because I brought you into the house, a viper to steal her daughter's virtue. Do not worry, we will stay well out of sight."

"You said we were just going to a mall."

"We are. To observe a *strelka* of rival factions, Russians and Iranians."

"A what?"

"A meeting. A conclave. These fellows have taught me all sorts of Russian that my tutors never dreamed of. A *strelka* is a meeting of rival thugs."

"They meet at malls?"

"Out in the open, where they know they can trust each other, and neither side has a natural advantage. They'll probably stake out part of a restaurant. We'll watch from a safe distance."

Sam saw they were only a few blocks from the York Club.

"I didn't know there were any malls in this part of town."

"It's Dubai. There are malls in every part of town. And don't let the look of the district fool you. The Burjuman is very upscale, although I cannot say it is one of my favorites."

"You have favorite malls?"

It came out harsher than he intended. Sharaf turned in his seat.

"Tell me, Mr. Keller, have you ever been in Dubai in July?"

"No."

"You would not ask that question if you had. In the summer the malls are our Great Outdoors. Everyone has their favorites. Everyone. Because of this, each mall has acquired its own personality, its own clientele. And the Burjuman, well, it is not to my liking, even though I can certainly appreciate its strengths as well as its drawbacks."

"Which are?"

"You are an observant man. I am sure you will see."

Looming just ahead was a sleek glass tower, maybe thirty stories tall, with curving walls that tapered to a sharp point, making the structure a giant wedge. Perched atop it was a huge fan of perforated steel, like the sail of a capsized windsurfer.

"Is that it?"

"The mall is on the lower floors. We will park underneath it."

They swerved into an underground garage. Sharaf snatched a ticket as the gate swung clear. The Camry was a humble addition to rows of gleaming SUVs and luxury sedans.

"So we're going to walk up to these guys, just like that?" Sam asked.

"Patience."

There were plenty of empty spaces, but Sharaf drove to the lowest level. In the middle of the vast deck was a glass-walled chamber with an escalator that climbed past a roaring man-made waterfall cascading from the overhead floors where, presumably, all the shops were. They ignored that entrance, and walked instead to unmarked elevator doors in a far corner of the parking deck. Sharaf punched in a numeric code to open the doors and they rode up a few floors. The rear door opened onto a nondescript hallway leading to unmarked steel doors at the far end. Sharaf knocked. A buzzer sounded and they entered a gray vestibule rimmed in chrome.

A fellow in a security uniform emerged from around the corner. Sharaf, wearing gray Western slacks and a black long-sleeved shirt, flashed an ID, and the man wordlessly escorted them to the next room. Sam had no idea what a mall security center was supposed to look like, but he suspected that, as with so many other things in Dubai, this one was lavish and excessive.

A massive three-panel bank of video monitors fanned out around a semicircle of black Formica-topped desks. Each panel had more than a hundred screens, all of them in full color and crystal clear. The desks were covered with telephones and laptops. A uniformed man sat in front of each panel, watching intently. All three of them wore head-phones, so apparently they could listen as well as observe.

"Looks like the control room of a nuclear power plant," Sam said.

"Except here the stakes are higher," Sharaf said, with no hint of irony. "Just a few months ago at the Wafi Mall a gang of Serbian thieves drove two Audis through the entrance and smashed their way into a Graff jewelry store. In ninety seconds they stole thirteen million dollars' worth of loot, then drove back out, right past the fake Egyptian temple and all the shoppers eating ice cream. Here at the Burjuman there are forty different merchants selling high-end jewelry, including Tiffany and Cartier. Extravagant goods call for extravagant protection."

Sam scanned the screens. Impressive names leaped out from the storefronts—Saks. Chanel. Dior. Versace. Dunkin' Donuts?

The shoppers were nothing special. Shorts and beach clothes, plenty of blue jeans. Only rarely did he glimpse someone in traditional local dress—the men in white *kandouras*, the women draped head to toe in black.

"Weird," he said, the word slipping out.

"What is?"

"There are hardly any Emiratis. They almost look out of place."

"Now you see why it is not one of my favorites. That is why I wore these Western clothes. To fit in, if I have to. I feel like a tourist here. That, plus all the damned Russians, the mob types in particular."

"This is their hangout?"

"One of Anatoly Rybakov's, anyway. A local chieftain. People call him the Tsar."

"I'd have thought he'd prefer Emirates Mall, the one with the ski slope."

"Russians who come to Dubai have had quite enough of snow and ice. If Rybakov gets homesick he can always turn up the air conditioner and drink a liter of vodka. But it's mostly their wives and daughters who come here. There. Screen twelve. Look at her. Zoom in, please."

The security man nodded, typed a command on his laptop, and maneuvered a joystick. The image closed in on a sturdy Russian woman, middle-aged, with rouged cheeks. She stood outside Louis Vuitton. Her bleached hair was piled into a bun, which served as a perch for jeweled designer sunglasses. Tight slacks, fire-engine red, were matched by a bulging spandex top, which was draped by a clingy white cardigan she had buttoned to just below her massive cleavage. She puffed forcefully on a cigarette, inhaling greedily, as if she stood to win a million rubles if she could finish within a minute.

Alongside her was a formidable old babushka in a scarf and peasant garb, strictly Old Country, and shaped like one of those Matroyshka nesting dolls—the big one that all the little ones would fit into. Maybe they were in there now, squirming to get out.

"The younger one is Rybakov's wife," Sharaf said. "I am guessing that's one reason he chose this place. Give her a night of shopping while he takes care of business."

"So the Russians picked the place?"

"They usually do."

"And the Iranians don't mind?"

"They are outnumbered here. Or outgunned, anyway. The Indian mob, now that would be another matter. As for the Iranians, when your people have been here for four hundred years as traders and smugglers, you don't get too worked up about little things like who picks the meeting place, as long as you are still making money."

The woman on screen 12 was on the move.

"Follow her," Sharaf said. The security man nodded and moved the joystick. The camera panned left, tracking her progress, which was hobbled somewhat by the slow-moving babushka.

"She'll appear next on thirteen," the security man said.

They followed her across three more screens until she approached a man sitting on a bench. She opened her Louis Vuitton bag to show him the fruits of her labors. He nodded, neither smiling nor frowning. Then he stood. He was compact and deeply tanned, with bristly gray hair trimmed close to the scalp. Black jacket, black slacks, shiny black shirt, with the top two buttons undone to reveal silver chest hair and a thin gold chain. Two younger, bigger men reared up behind him, peeking over his shoulder into the shopping bag as if it might be carrying a bomb.

"That's Anatoly Rybakov. Recognize any of the muscle?"

"No. Sorry."

"Do you have sound?"

The security man nodded and clicked a mouse. A garble of Russian and ambient noise burst from a nearby speaker, muffled by the rain-drop crackle of a fountain.

"Will the audio be clearer in a restaurant?"

The security man nodded firmly, a man certain in his judgments.

The wife and the babushka headed off for more shopping, while Rybakov chatted with his bodyguards.

"Is this how he always operates?" Sam asked. " 'Hi, I'm a Russian thug, let's chat?' "

"Officially he is the regional executive for RusSiberian Metals and Investment. Their specialties are Russian commodities and real estate development."

"Is any of it legit?"

"The commodities were all looted at subsidy prices. The real estate is for laundering money. Yet another reason you see so much construction here."

Rybakov and his bodyguards began walking. They stepped aboard a rising escalator.

"Stay with him," Sharaf said.

"He'll be coming up next on one-thirty-seven," the security man said. "Center panel."

Sharaf and Sam eased behind the next fellow with headphones, watching over his shoulder. They followed Rybakov's progress across four more screens to the uppermost of the mall's four levels, where he entered a restaurant called Bella Donna. The view of level four, offered panoramically if you scanned enough screens at once, was fairly spectacular. It was a darkened area of subdued lighting. The mall's arched glass ceiling was underlaid by teak framing and a spaghetti of blue neon, which cast an eerie glow on the restaurant's rooftop tables, where Rybakov was now taking a seat with his bodyguards. They were the only customers up there. Two minutes later more Russians arrived. Four more beefy fellows, nearly indistinguishable in dress and demeanor.

"That's him!" Sam exclaimed, hardly believing his eyes. "Second from the left. One of the guys from the York."

"In the gray jacket?"

"Yes. I'm sure of it."

"Yuri Arzhanov. One of the Tsar's lieutenants. A real *vory-v-zakonye* type of enforcer, which is another word my tutors never taught me. A leadership title he would have earned in prison. And you're positive he's the one you saw at the York?"

"Absolutely. He stared right at me."

"Interesting. People of his rank don't normally dirty their hands with blood errands. Recognize anyone else?"

Sam watched the group fill a second table. Two chairs across from Rybakov were still empty. Presumably they were reserved for the top Iranians.

"The one on the far right. I think that might be the second guy, but I'm not as certain."

"He is not familiar to me. Probably one of Arzhanov's minions. Could we have some sound, please?"

It still wasn't optimum. Voices overlapped and were disrupted by the clatter of cutlery and glasses, the thumping beat of music. But definitely better than before.

The Iranians arrived, a contingent of seven. The one in the middle stepped forward to address Rybakov, a handshake that turned into an awkward bear hug. The Iranian seemed to resist before finally submitting with an expression of irritation, as if he realized he had already been put at a disadvantage.

"Mohsen Hedayat," Sharaf said. "The other six, I haven't a clue."

Everyone sat. Hedayat and an underling took seats with Rybakov and the two Russian bodyguards. The other Russians sat at the second table, while the extra Iranians claimed a third on the opposite side. A waiter materialized, stating his name and rattling off the specials just as he would have done with a party of British housewives. Everyone ordered drinks and settled into their seats. A few even put napkins in their laps. The two bosses began talking, a tentative exchange that soon grew fairly animated.

"What are they saying?" Sam asked.

"Rybakov is apologizing. Not exactly with grace, but an apology nonetheless. He is doing it in Persian, probably out of deference. His grammar is terrible, but at least he is going slow enough for me to follow."

A pause, then more.

"Hedayat talks too fast for me to decipher. I don't think Rybakov can understand him, either, because someone is translating for him, and now he has gone back to Russian. All I can tell for sure is that Hedayat is unhappy about something, and is demanding satisfaction."

"What was the apology for?"

"I am not sure. But I think I have an idea."

"What, then?"

"Quiet. I am trying to listen."

More talk. Sharaf leaned forward in concentration, and Sam didn't interrupt. The conversation went on for another five minutes, continuing even as the drinks arrived. The bosses gestured toward their contingents, and several men from both factions stood, the Russians a bit uncertainly.

"Well, now. This is interesting."

"What?"

"Rybakov is ordering your two boys to accompany four of the Iranians. To make some sort of pickup, apparently. Arzhanov doesn't look happy about the arrangement, but he is not in a position to refuse. There they go."

The six men departed the restaurant, the two Russians flanked on all sides by the four Iranians, like a parade formation as they strolled back into the open spaces of the mall.

"Moving to two-forty-nine," the security man said. "They're bypassing the escalators and heading for the rear elevator."

"The one we used?" Sam asked. Were they coming here? Had he been set up?

"No," Sharaf said. "Opposite side."

The men moved briskly. The Iranians were still grouped around the Russians like bodyguards. They boarded the elevator and the doors closed.

"What's the next screen?" Sharaf asked.

"The down arrow is lit," the security man said. "They will exit either on three-twenty-two, two-thirteen, or seventy-six. Those are on three separate panels."

Sam and Sharaf feverishly scanned back and forth.

"There!" Sam shouted. "Seventy-six!"

"That's the lower level," Sharaf said, "down where we parked."

"There's a blind spot," the security man said. "Two cameras on that level are out."

"Since when?" Sharaf asked.

"An hour ago."

"Shit! What quadrant?"

"Southeast corner."

"Let's go!" Sharaf said.

Sam followed him as they rushed out of the room and back down the corridor to the elevator, where Sharaf cursed as he fumbled with the key code.

"You see? These people have extended their influence everywhere. I would bet any amount of money that someone from mall security was bribed to disable those two cameras."

"Why?"

"Can't you guess?"

He could. And it was the last thing he wanted to be rushing to see. The elevator opened, and they headed toward the glass cubicle in the middle of the deck.

"There they are, way on the other side," Sharaf said. A black Toyota Prado SUV eased into view from the upper ramp, tires squealing as it headed toward the Mafia men in the far corner. Sharaf and Sam had just reached the glass walls of the escalator cube.

"Stay back!" Sharaf said. "We'll watch from here."

The car stopped next to the men, maybe a hundred yards from where Sharaf and Sam stood, trying to watch through the glass walls.

"Should we be out in the open like this?" Sam whispered even though the nearby fountain was roaring like a waterfall. His question was answered in rapid succession by two muffled pops, sharp but wheezy barks that echoed dully off the low concrete ceiling. The two Russians dropped out of sight, and the Prado's rear hatch swung open. The torsos of the four Iranians stooped downward, then moved toward the Prado. The hatch slammed shut and the Iranians climbed in through the front doors. It all happened within seconds.

"Jesus! Did they just—?"

"Get inside!" Sharaf hissed. "Try to get up the escalators before we're seen!"

Sam did as he was told, weak in the knees. He didn't dare look below, but he heard the tires of the Prado squealing as the roaring SUV headed back in their direction. Sharaf clambered up the rising steps, and Sam followed. Just before they moved out of sight he glimpsed a flash of black metal as the Prado raced past below, toward the exit ramp. When they stepped off on the next floor, Sharaf was panting loudly. A Japanese family, overloaded with shopping bags, bumped past them with a stream of apologies in halting English. Sam tugged Sharaf aside.

"Where to now?" he asked.

"We wait five minutes for everyone to clear out, then we do the same."

"What about Rybakov? Won't he be waiting for his men?"

Sharaf shook his head.

"His business here is complete."

"But—?"

"It was an arrangement. Part of his apology. Arzhanov must have done something very wrong. By killing your friend, most likely. What doesn't make sense is why that would have upset the Iranians. They don't control prostitution. The Russians do."

"Could Charlie have been working for them?"

"The Iranians? Do you really think so?"

"No. But I didn't know him very well." And it certainly fit with Nanette's theory that Charlie was involved with unsavory dealings. He wondered if she had suspected as much even earlier. It would better explain why she had wanted him to track Charlie's movements. "What will you do now? Arrest them?"

"Those men in the Prado? As far as I'm concerned this never happened."

Sam was amazed.

"You're not reporting it?"

"What is there to report? We saw two men drop from sight and heard popping noises that could have been cars backfiring. The whole time, the security cameras were blind as bats. There are no bodies to be found, and never will be, unless Daoud finds them for us. More to the point, if I report this the first question will be, 'What were you doing following Anatoly Rybakov, and why was the American with you?' "

"Yes, but—"

"Around my office, Mr. Keller, the prevailing view is that as long as these people settle their own affairs without involving the rest of us, then who are we to interfere? Why do you think our crime rate is so low? It is the same reason there are so few fatal accidents at construction sites. All that matters is how you do the counting."

Sam supposed he shouldn't have been surprised. But if all that were true, then why was Sharaf so interested in this case? Was he the only cop who cared, or was he, too, part of the problem?

"What do we do now?" Sam asked.

"We go to our final stop, just around the corner. Then you can make your phone call."

That was a relief to hear, although Sam was shaken by what he'd just seen. What he really wanted was a stiff drink, but Sharaf was already bustling toward the exit. A few minutes later they emerged on the street and strolled past the Burjuman's ground-level shops. Road workers were tearing up the median at 9 p.m. to add an extra lane. Across the way a construction crew was building a high-rise. This place never rested.

Sharaf pushed through a revolving door into a sushi bar, where a long conveyor belt carried food past diners along a three-sided counter. The policeman led them to a pair of seats away from the window.

"Who are we meeting?" Sam whispered.

"No one. I'm hungry. Rybakov's little rendezvous made me miss dinner."

"I don't have much of an appetite."

"Then don't eat. Any policeman who went off his feed after an episode like that wouldn't live very long."

Sharaf plucked a purple plate from the conveyor belt. A colorful menu card told Sam it was a dragon roll, with eel, crab, avocado, and spicy rice.

"I wouldn't have guessed you for sushi."

"You also wouldn't have guessed a CEO would have a curfew. Yet she does."

Sam said nothing.

"She lives in our house by choice, you know. It's not me or her mother making her do it, even though she likes to say so. The reality is, a single Emirati woman can't rent her own apartment, even if her parents let her."

"It's illegal?"

"No. But there isn't a landlord in Dubai who would do it. And as long as she lives in my house, she lives by my rules. One rule is that she doesn't talk to unfamiliar men who happen to be there on her father's business."

"Sorry."

"You're forgiven. She knew better. And if, while my back was turned, she gave you one of her business cards, I would like you to please return it now."

Sharaf held out a hand.

"She didn't," Sam lied. "We never made it that far."

The wording made it sound like they had been caught making out on the couch, and Sam blushed. His reaction drew a fleeting grin. It was the first time he had seen Sharaf smile, and Sam was surprised by how much it pleased him. In spite of everything, he was beginning to like the man. Maybe it was the fatherly gruffness, which for all its testiness was sort of comforting. He did still wonder what Sharaf's real motives were, but he sensed a basic honesty. Or maybe he had been swayed by Laleh.

Sharaf made quick work of the first plate and reached for a tuna roll on an orange saucer. He spritzed soy sauce into a bowl, stirred in a lump of wasabi, then swaddled a piece of the roll with a slice of pickled ginger before dipping it in the sauce. He downed it in a single bite, wincing as the wasabi exploded in his sinuses. Then he flagged down a waitress and ordered tea.

"And you, sir?" she asked Sam. "Something from the hot menu, maybe?"

In spite of himself, he was now hungry.

"Shrimp tempura. And I'll have a tuna roll from the belt."

"To drink?"

"Do you have beer?"

She frowned. So did Sharaf. Sam then remembered that alcohol was nonexistent once you strayed beyond a hotel. Even the bar at the ski slope had been affiliated with an adjoining hotel. So had all the discos he and Charlie visited.

"Mineral water, then."

"Tell me," Sharaf said after the waitress departed. "And this is not out of piety, I am only curious. Why do you Americans need to consume alcohol with every meal? Is it for digestion? Or is it from some compulsion to chemically relax?"

"With beer I like the taste. Especially with the wasabi. The tang of the hops. The yeastiness."

"Tell me about beer. Gin I can smell from across the room. Whiskey, too. Vodka, as far as I can determine, might as well be odorless rocket fuel, mined straight from an iceberg. I suppose that is why the Russians like it. But with beer you mentioned the yeastiness. Does it taste at all like kvass? Because a Russian I once knew told me that kvass tasted like liquid bread. I tried some once—it has no alcohol, you see—and he was right. Is beer the same?"

"Liquid bread? Maybe a little. But I've never had kvass, so I can't really compare."

He had seen it, though, served by street vendors in Kiev. On a summer day it had looked refreshing enough to make him curious. But he hadn't tried it, mostly because the vendor was using the same glass for every customer, wiping it between swallows with a soggy towel. Such worries seemed foolish after what he had been through in Dubai. And now here he was in a sushi bar, of all places, seated next to an Arab cop while hiding in plain view from mobsters and, for all he knew, the rest of the police force.

But now he could comfort himself with the thought that in a few minutes he would be speaking to Nanette—a familiar voice from saner times, calm and efficient. She would arrange for his safe passage to New York. He heaved a great sigh of relief.

"What's wrong?" Sharaf asked.

"I'd like to make that phone call now, if you don't mind."

Sharaf assumed a grave expression and gingerly placed his cell phone on the counter.

"I keep my promises, and you are welcome to telephone whoever you wish. But there is something I need to show you first. Here."

He pulled a folded paper from his jacket.

"Your arrest report. I obtained it this afternoon, despite Lieutenant Assad's best efforts to hide it. Read it carefully, please."

Most of it was a rehash of what he already knew—the images from the security camera, the erroneous police spin on why Nanette had nudged him at the door, and so on.

"I told you. It's a misunderstanding."

"Please. All the way to the end. There at the bottom. See?"

There was a box containing information about the filer of the complaint. Inside it was a crisp signature with bold loops and slashing verticals, handwriting that was the very model of brisk efficiency. Nanette Weaver, his would-be savior, had filed the charge.

"*She* did this?"

"First thing that morning. Before you were even awake."

"*Why?*"

"The charitable interpretation would be that she wanted you to be moved out of harm's way under police protection. Considering all that has happened since, I'm not inclined toward charity, are you?"

"No."

Sam shook his head. He felt lost, confused, and then angry.

"It doesn't make sense. Yesterday she couldn't wait to get me out of the country. And now—"

"Now she wishes to not only keep you here, but also to make sure you are unseen and unheard, and unavailable to answer any more questions from people like me."

"But I don't know anything. Or nothing more than what I've already told her."

"She obviously thinks you do. Or maybe she is convinced you have wronged her in some way. Have you?"

"Not enough to deserve this."

"But something, yes?"

Sam shrugged. They had reached uncomfortable territory, items that so far he had hidden from the police.

"Maybe."

"You'd better tell me."

So he did—the whole story of how he had been roped in to keeping tabs on Charlie Hatcher, only to become so charmed that he let his guard down and Charlie was killed.

"I was sure she was going to fire me. Instead she was completely sympathetic. Or seemed to be. She even, well, don't take this wrong because of the arrest report, but I'd swear that for a while she was sort of coming on to me. I was drunk, yes. But I'm not stupid, and as soon as she shut things down I left right away. You have to believe me."

"I believe you. She was setting you up. That little trick of hers in the doorway—dropping her key card, then nudging your chest. A very clever performance for the security camera."

"You're right. It must have been. But why? That's what I still can't figure."

"I suspect that she and Lieutenant Assad have worked together before. He used to be with the customs police, and was in charge of cracking down on the transshipment of counterfeit pharmaceuticals, which I know is of great interest to Pfluger Klaxon. Beyond that? Perhaps you said something that raised an alarm. Something that seemed meaningless to you, but was significant to her."

Sam shook his head.

"I was doing whatever I could to help find out who killed Charlie. I even—"

He realized he was about to incriminate himself.

"You even what?"

Sam hesitated.

"Please, Mr. Keller. In case you haven't noticed, I am all you have left."

He took the plunge.

"When I first called her from the York, right after Charlie was killed, she told me to take his BlackBerry."

"Before the police arrived?"

"Yes."

"Did you?"

"It wasn't there. It turned up later when they searched his room. But he did have a datebook. So I took it."

"Did you give it to Lieutenant Assad?"

"No. I gave it to Nanette."

Sharaf frowned.

"Then her actions make no sense. Unless . . . Did you look inside it? More to the point, did you tell Miss Weaver that you looked inside it?"

Sam frowned in concentration.

"I did. I mentioned he'd written a few names and numbers. That was right before she invited me to her room. I was delivering the datebook when she dropped her key card."

"Meaning she began her charade *after* she learned you had seen the contents. In that case, it is very important to know what you saw."

"Like I said, a few names and numbers. None of it made much sense. But I wrote it all down on some hotel stationery."

Sharaf brightened. "The piece of paper in your wallet?"

"You searched my wallet?"

"Of course. I am a policeman. But one more question, a very important one. When you wrote these things down did you summarize, or use shorthand?"

"No. It's verbatim. I'm an auditor. We don't take shortcuts."

Sharaf beamed a fatherly smile, as if Sam had just brought home a perfect report card.

"That, at least, gives us a starting point. I will begin calling those numbers as soon as we're home. Perhaps I will even pay a visit or two before the night is over."

"I'll go with you," Sam said.

The words were out before he had time to think. It was partly because his anger with Nanette was coming to a boil. He was also realizing that simply hiding was no longer an option. He needed to fight back, and he had to do it here. Even if he made it safely back to New York, Nanette had probably spread enough poison to get him fired, or even jailed.

Sharaf was having none of it.

"I cannot allow it," the policeman said. "Not with what you are up against. And I don't just mean the Russians. I saw your Miss Weaver in action this afternoon."

"Where?"

"CID headquarters. I was upstairs for a briefing. She was coming out of Assad's office, and she looked me right in the eye, like she knew exactly what I was up to."

"She can have that effect. What did you say?"

"Nothing of substance. We exchanged the customary pleasantries and she was on her way."

In truth they'd said more, but Sharaf didn't want to elaborate, partly because their exchange had unsettled him more than he cared to admit. Her directness took him by surprise. Most males in her position would have offered a fake smile and an oily hint of a bribe, or, if they wanted to be threatening, a vague allusion to all the local clout at their disposal. None of that for Nanette. She got straight to the point.

"Assad tells me you're responsible for letting our Sam Keller go on the lam."

"You've been misinformed. The booking sergeant was in charge of his custody."

"Well, just so you know the gravity of the matter, Sam Keller stood idly by while a fellow associate got himself killed. And for all either of us knows, he was a participant in the affair. For good measure he then crossed the line sexually with a female superior, probably in an attempt to find out what I know. The sooner he is back in hand, the better for all of us, wouldn't you agree?"

With a lesser adversary Sharaf would have continued to play dumb. Using that approach with her seemed foolhardy, even dangerous. It wasn't just that she represented a powerful corporation (although he knew that would have been sufficient grounds for the Minister), it was that he detected in her a keen and watchful intelligence, plus the patience to deploy it to maximum effect. What's more, she seemed willing to use it toward any end, an advantage he would never enjoy.

In addition, her manner was so convincing that for a moment he even entertained the thought that she might be telling the truth. After all, how much did he actually know about Sam Keller? Could the young man really be trusted? Maybe he *had* attacked this woman. Maybe he *had* cooperated with the men who'd killed Charlie Hatcher. Perhaps Nanette Weaver had information that could help him.

But by then, Nanette Weaver had already turned on her heel and was heading for the door. Sharaf was on the verge of flagging her down when he noticed Assad watching eagerly from his office, and that was when he came to his senses. Assad's stupid, leering grin gave away the whole sham, and Sharaf realized he had nearly been duped. A compliment to her talents, he supposed.

"So you've seen firsthand what she's like," Sam said. "All the more reason you need my help."

"I cannot allow it," Sharaf repeated. "If I put you at further risk we will both be in trouble. You are neither trained in this kind of work nor accustomed to its dangers."

"But I'm stuck here. With nowhere to go and no one to help me."

The remark cut deeply. There was no way Sam could have known it, but it was a direct echo from Sharaf's bedtime reading of *Crime and Punishment* the night before, calling to mind a line uttered by a desperate drunk named Marmeladov:

"Do you understand, sir, do you understand what it means when you have absolutely nowhere to turn?"

As if sensing an opening, Sam pressed his case.

"You're forgetting that I'm an auditor. I'm trained to look for things that don't fit. Outliers, anomalies. Particularly on the corporate side, which is Nanette's strength."

"Maybe so," Sharaf said. "But first we must find you safer quarters. For my sake as well as yours. Fortunately I know the very man who can help, and I am due to see him in the morning."

"Good enough," Sam said. "Count me in."

"Then we had better get going, before one of us changes his mind."

12

By the time Sharaf arrived at his favorite old haunt, Ali al-Futtaim had already selected seven dominoes and placed them in his wooden rack, ready for action. But Sharaf was in no mood for a game.

"Leave your tiles in the boneyard, Ali. No time for that this morning. A life is at stake."

"Someone in your family?"

"Someone under my protection. A foreigner."

Ali showed his disapproval by taking a domino from the rack and slapping it into play, a double-six that clicked loudly on the cool ceramic floor.

"No foreigner takes precedence over our game," he said. "Especially when you now trail me by three hundred dirhams. Choose your bones and make a move."

"Two hundred ninety dirhams, to be exact," Sharaf said. He placed a forefinger on the lonely tile and shoved it toward Ali, like a tugboat nudging a premature departure back into the docks. He sipped the muddy coffee that had just been delivered by a young waiter, the boy knowing without asking that Sharaf liked his medium with a single sugar.

"Seriously, Ali. There are urgent matters to discuss. I need your wisdom."

"My connections, you mean?"

"Is there a difference?"

Both men smiled, as they always did at such remarks. Ali motioned to the boy for tea, and he didn't put his tile back into play.

They were seated cross-legged on the floor at their usual spot at the Seaman's Majlis, or meeting place, which was located in a once fine home with thick plastered walls, a rooftop parapet, and a crumbling wind tower along the banks of Dubai Creek. It was just around the bend from the wharf where, as boys, Ali and Sharaf had put to sea for pearling and smuggling. Like everyone there, they came for fellowship and conversation, removing their shoes at the door and hunkering down on rugs and cushions for card games and dominoes, while waiters delivered tea and coffee on trays of hammered brass.

It was not a young crowd. Retirees, mostly. Old men whose skin had been stropped to leathery darkness by salt and sun. Sharaf's single year of seagoing experience only marginally qualified him for admission, although no one would have begrudged the presence of a policeman. The warmth of his welcome had far more to do with the status of his friend. Ali had spent seven years on the water, commanding a smuggler's boat during his final season—a big twin-engine *sanbouk* of varnished teak, owned by Sharaf's father—back in the day when an illicit load of gold hidden in a cargo of dates turned a handsome profit in the port of Bombay. Sure, you might get caught by the Indian authorities, but as long as your own ruler viewed smuggling as business as usual, the only danger on the home front was that some waterfront snitch would report your departure to an Indian spy. That was how Ali, as a seventeen-year-old deckhand, once ended up having to swim ashore in Bombay after his ship was boarded by customs police. He then spent a week making his way cross-country and into Pakistan, where he finally boarded a cargo flight home from Karachi.

Such resourcefulness was perfect training for his current job as manager of the Dubai Land Office. When he first joined up, the land office was a sleepy outpost where locals went to mark off plots for homes or dispute neighbors' claims to a few scraggly date palms. Now it was the bustling nexus of Dubai's most lucrative commerce. Builders, developers, financiers, and con artists of all nations flocked there to stake claims on the latest slice of boomtown wealth.

The work obviously agreed with him. Ali was trim and relaxed, looking younger than Sharaf even though he was two years older. He carried himself elegantly in a long white *kandoura*, which made Sharaf feel frumpier than usual in his police greens. As if to soften the contrast, Sharaf always removed his beret when he met Ali at the majlis. It was also a signal to everyone in attendance that the cop was off duty, no matter what anyone there might say or do. What happened at the majlis stayed at the majlis.

They met there once a week. Ali had always preferred this location over the better-known Fisherman's Majlis on the beach in Umm Suqeim. For one thing, no one minded that he and Sharaf made taboo wagers on their dominoes. It was a carryover from deckhand days, when Ali taught Sharaf how to gamble against gold runners three times their age.

Their meetings were often occasions for swapping favors in the local tradition of *wasta*. Ali sometimes needed help tidying up minor police matters for his moneyed contacts. To keep his own hands relatively clean, Sharaf always referred Ali to one of the Syrian or Egyptian cops with a reputation for reasonable prices. He had the good sense never to ask later about results, and Ali had the manners never to mention them.

In return, Sharaf sometimes availed himself of aid or information from Ali's vast network of developers, bankers, and builders. And at the moment he needed Ali's help in keeping Sam Keller out of harm's way. So he described his predicament, and even mentioned his recent secret correspondences with the Minister, whom Ali had also assisted on a few occasions.

"And the Minister?" Ali said. "You say he does not know you are hiding this fugitive?"

"Please. Don't say 'fugitive.' I'm on shaky enough ground as it is."

"This 'falsely accused individual,' then. Does that make you feel better? Ah, Anwar. Only you would take a case like this, and it is because you are just like a Bedouin."

"A Bedouin? How so?"

"In the most important way of all. Tell me, do you know why the Bedouin move around so much?"

"For the grazing. That's what they would tell you."

Ali waved his hand dismissively.

"A convenient pretext. The real reason is because they are too lazy to clean up after themselves, even though they are masters at making a mess. The moment they find some new place and pitch their tents, they begin to soil it, them and their stinking animals. When it finally becomes too filthy and clotted with goat shit even for them, they strike the tents and move on. And that is what you do. You make a mess by stirring up a lot of the wrong people, then you strike your tent and move on to the next case, because you are never willing or able to clean up behind yourself. The problem, Anwar, is that the desert is huge, practically limitless, but your department isn't. Soon there will be nowhere left to pitch your tent."

"I never knew you were such a snob about the Bedouin."

"You're ignoring my point."

"Where do you get these stupid theories, Ali? From the Egyptian you pay to change court dates, or the Palestinian who fixes your friends' speeding tickets? I don't make messes, I clean them up. Can you help me with this young man or not?"

Ali grinned and slid his double-six back into the starting position.

"Of course I can. Don't worry. I will discreetly find someplace where he can stay awhile. We'll have him resettled by sundown. But tell me—not until after you've selected your seven dominoes from the boneyard, of course—what level of camouflage does he require? Because some of the more secure places I have in mind, well, I am not so sure he would find them much more to his liking than a jail cell."

Sharaf obliged Ali by selecting seven tiles. He placed them on a small wooden rack that kept Ali from seeing them, then chose a three-six combination and positioned it endwise to the middle of Ali's double-six.

"For now it doesn't need to be so extreme," Sharaf said.

"In that case I can probably have a place lined up by . . ." Ali checked his watch, a massive Breguet with a jeweled rim. "Let us say three o'clock. I will send a driver to fetch him. A sedan with smoked windows, so he can relax and not be seen. Plenty of places to choose from. In fact, there are all sorts of new apartments lying vacant right now. Some of them don't even have an assigned address yet, that's how fast things are moving. Far *too* fast, if you ask me."

"You are worried?"

"When properties are turning over fourteen times before a single tenant moves in, I begin to get indigestion. Or maybe it is from all the truffles and caviar the developers feed me at their groundbreakings. If

I were you, Sharaf, I would not buy a new house anytime soon, no matter what Amina wants. That goes double for your sons."

"My sons," Sharaf said, rolling his eyes, although he already felt better now that the matter of Sam Keller was resolved. He had been preoccupied by worry all morning, especially after what he and Keller had learned the night before.

They had returned home from the Burjuman to huddle in Sharaf's sanctum, where they pored over the information from Charlie Hatcher's datebook. The enigmatic scribbles below the underlined reference to "Monday, 4/14!" had intrigued Sharaf the most, although neither Keller nor he had any idea what they meant.

"He talked about the fourteenth like it was some kind of deadline," Sam said. "He said he was canceling his flight to Hong Kong and was going to stay in Dubai."

"Maybe one of these people will know," Sharaf said, gesturing toward the three names. "Let's give it a try."

Sharaf quickly discovered why two of the phone numbers seemed familiar. The first one connected him to the front desk of the Palace Hotel at the Royal Mirage resort. Sharaf had visited there twice on police business—a jewel theft, and a robbery on the hotel's private beach. He asked for the name Charlie had written.

"Rajpal Patel, please."

The cordial male voice at the other end turned officious. "Who is calling?"

"Does it matter? I'm a friend."

"Then maybe you can tell me why Rajpal hasn't bothered to show up for the past three nights, or why he won't answer his phone."

"Three nights?"

"Three very inconvenient nights, yes. Who is this?"

Sharaf hung up and turned to Keller.

"Did you and Charlie Hatcher visit the Palace Hotel at the Royal Mirage?"

Keller told Sharaf the story of the hotel staffer in the garish uniform who had met Charlie in the lobby.

"If he was dressed like that, then he was probably one of the bouncers at their exclusive little club, the Kasbar. It is a known gathering place for people like the ones we were observing tonight. Did you mention this meeting to Lieutenant Assad?"

"Yes. He seemed pretty interested."

"In that case, my Bedouin friend Daoud will probably find Rajpal before we do."

"You mean—?"

"That was the front desk at the Palace just now. Rajpal Patel has been missing for three days. Just like the woman from the York who Daoud found, who I am guessing is Tatiana Tereshkova, the second name on the list. It's a mobile number. I'm betting there won't be an answer."

He tried it anyway. On the third ring a recording announced that the number was no longer in service. Whoever paid Tatiana's phone bill had been very efficient about closing her account.

The third number was the other one that had looked familiar, although the listed name—"Basma," but nothing more—hadn't.

A woman answered. "Beacon of Light."

"Of course," Sharaf said.

"Pardon?"

"I'm sorry. This is Detective Sharaf with Dubai Police. I would like to speak with Basma, please."

The woman seemed to gasp. Then she paused just long enough to arouse his suspicion before saying, "There is no one here by that name."

"Not even for a policeman to speak to?"

"No."

"Then is your director, Mrs. Halami, in?"

"Not this evening."

"Please have her call me, then. On my mobile. And give her a message. Ask if she is familiar with an American named Charles Hatcher, of the Pfluger Klaxon company. I need to know if he has made contact with Basma or anyone else at the shelter."

"I will tell her." The woman's tone was stiff, tense. Sharaf couldn't tell if Charlie's name had made an additional impression. It was the mention of Basma that had set her off. "And your mobile number, please?"

"She has it."

"Thank you. She will be back tomorrow, probably around midday."

"You know them?" Sam asked after Sharaf hung up.

"It is a shelter for abused women. Housewives, mostly, although it has also become a place of refuge for prostitutes who manage to escape their pimps. So it is not very well liked by the people we were observing this evening. Some of my police colleagues are not crazy about the place, either."

"Why not?"

"They believe disagreements between husbands and wives are personal matters, not issues for law enforcement."

"Even if he beats her? Do *you* believe that?"

"I do not beat my wife, so it is irrelevant what I believe. Please, you are beginning to sounding like Laleh, who has already spent far too much time among those women. That is why I recognized the number. She donates her money, handles their PR account for free, that kind of thing. She is quite the friend to them. I probably would have gotten further by mentioning her name instead of mine."

"Maybe Charlie was a donor, too. Out of guilt, considering his track record. He did say something about atonement."

"Or maybe this Basma was a favorite of his from a past visit, and he was tracking her down. The Tatiana woman could have been his contact. I can see how that might have upset the wrong people, especially if he was helping Basma stay free. Sending her money or something."

"You really think that's what happened?"

"That, or a hundred other possibilities. Whores are not the only women who end up at the Beacon of Light, or even wives. They take in housekeepers, maids, nannies. Which in Dubai are just milder forms of prostitution. Shady companies import them by the thousands on *hali-wali* visas."

"What's 'hali-wali'?"

"A 'who cares' visa. Obtained from some dupe in a government office."

"You mean like those fake ownership papers for Punjabi shopkeepers?"

Sharaf supposed the remark was intended to get a rise out of him.

"I'm guessing Laleh told you about that. But at least you are beginning to grasp the way things work here. Now if you could just tell me what these other scribbles in the datebook mean, you'd actually be contributing something worthy. Otherwise, all we have learned this evening is that, of the three names he listed, one is missing, one is dead, and one may or may not be staying at a place where women sometimes hide from their Mafia pimps. And the message of all that would seem to be pretty clear: If you are a friend of Charlie Hatcher's, Dubai is not a very safe place."

That was the thought Sharaf took to bed with him, and the one he awakened with as well. It was why he was now so relieved by Ali's assurances of Sam Keller's safety, which left him free to enjoy his coffee and their game of dominoes, while venting about his wayward sons.

"My sons," he continued to Ali, "wouldn't know how to handle a real estate transaction unless I did it for them. To them it's a major crisis if their iPods crash. When those Internet service cables were severed on the ocean floor last summer I thought they were going to cry. You would have thought a ten-day sandstorm had just blown into town, followed by a plague of locusts."

"Locusts," Ali said. "Now there's a memory. Remember that old man in the souk who used to fry them in a big kettle whenever a bunch of them blew in from the desert?"

"Yes. Very tasty. Until that year the British sprayed them all with poison, then went round the neighborhood with a bullhorn, telling us they were unsafe to eat."

"The visitors always end up ruining things," Ali said. "And if this speculation market ever comes to ruin, well, at least this time they'll be burned even more than the locals. Because we will still have our salaries and our homes, while all their precious new buildings stand empty, collecting nothing but desert dust. By the way, Sharaf, did you happen to invite some of your police colleagues to come and visit us here this morning?"

Ali was looking toward the door, and Sharaf realized that the place had suddenly gone quiet. Old faces all around them were looking up from their card games toward the entrance. Sharaf turned to see what was happening as his last swallow of coffee settled into a muddy lump at the base of his stomach.

Three rank-and-file policemen stood just inside the doorway, led by a Sudanese sergeant in lettuce green—the very fellow who had handled a favor for Ali a few years back, even though he was known to have a steep asking price. The moment they spotted Sharaf they began moving in his direction, not even bothering to remove their shoes. A low murmur went up from the regulars. The scurrying waiters halted in their tracks.

Sharaf sat still, but his mind moved quickly. By now, Keller would be alone in the house, assuming the police hadn't already picked him up. Laleh was at her office. Amina was visiting friends, and probably wouldn't turn on her mobile phone until after lunch. He could tell Ali to phone the house, but Sam Keller might not have the nerve to answer.

"Call Laleh at her office," he said under his breath. "Tell her what has happened. Find any way you can to get Keller out of the house immediately. And you'd better take him to one of those tougher locations you had in mind."

"What about you?"

"Contact the Minister," Sharaf said. "But unless you want to get me into even bigger trouble, don't mention the American."

The policemen arrived at his side. One gripped Sharaf's right arm, another took his left, and they raised him to his feet. The sergeant spoke loudly enough for all to hear.

"You will hand over your phone, your keys, and your wallet and come with us, Lieutenant Sharaf. You are under arrest."

"On what charge? Under whose orders?"

They said nothing in reply. Sharaf didn't resist as they escorted him to the door.

A police car was outside, with a detention van idling behind it. Already a crowd was forming. A show of force like this was for more than just an arrest. It was designed to humiliate him. Even Lieutenant Assad probably couldn't have rigged up this big of a display, and that suggested involvement at a higher level. This train of thought led Sharaf to the most chilling possibility of all—that the Minister himself, for whatever reason, was behind this.

An officer shoved Sharaf toward the van. He looked back toward the majlis and saw Ali standing at the entrance, grim faced.

"I'll do what I can," Ali called out.

Normally, such words from Ali meant the deed was as good as done. This time, to judge from his deepening frown, they both realized that the odds were against them.

As if to drive home the point, the officer produced a blindfold and roughly tied it into place. He then gripped Sharaf by the shoulders and shoved him through the van's open panel doors, barking Sharaf's shins on the rear bumper in the process. The doors slammed shut, and the agonized Sharaf was in darkness. The driver revved the engine once, then they careened away in a clatter of spraying gravel. Sharaf took a deep breath and held it until the pain in his shins subsided.

Between that and the darkness, it reminded him a little of diving for pearls in deep waters. Stay calm, he told himself. Relax and keep your eyes open. If further dangers arise, revel in them. Embrace them. But he had better keep holding his breath. He had a feeling he wouldn't be coming up for air for quite a while.

1 3

Earlier that morning, Sam Keller awoke to an empty house. All was quiet. The window shades were drawn against the sunlight.

Sam had been dreaming of his father, and as he opened his eyes he still heard the voice from some of his earliest memories; the old man telling him to live a little, to give it a try, to go ahead and see what happened and let the chips fall where they may.

Flipping back the blinds onto a view of a scorched courtyard, Sam tried to pin down exactly when he had stopped heeding that advice. Or maybe he had never paid it much attention to begin with. Such words—on the surface, at least—had always seemed pat, even trite, the sort of pep talk that any father might offer.

But now, after having been in the workforce for five years, he recalled the gray face of resignation his dad had always worn when he came through the kitchen door every evening at six—or more often at nine during tax season—looking frayed at the edges as he cracked open an ice tray to mix the ritual daily pitcher of gimlets to be shared with Sam's mom. Paul Keller had hated his job, Sam realized, now that he could recognize the symptoms. Accountancy had paid the bills and then some, and the technical side had probably come easily enough for a man with such a mathematical mind. But what stood out now was all of the little ways in which his father had tried to steer Sam in other directions, not least by teaching him to sail at the earliest possible age under all conceivable conditions, even when the wind was up and skies were aboil. As if, by seducing the boy with a few thrills, he might guide him toward a more exciting vocation.

"You're a good man in a storm," his father always insisted, whenever the boy held the tiller firm against a fresh gust. But it was really the old accountant who had needed to get out on the waves, Sam realized, if only for a way to unbend his mind and let it play among the angles of wind and water, pushing the boat to its limits. More math, when you got right down to it, but calculated on the fly, with a face to the breeze, tiller in hand, the hull's trammeled force straining beneath his grip with the quiver of a saddled horse.

Of course, when Sam's aptitude had emerged along similar lines as his father's—a head for numbers, a knack for analysis—the boy had inevitably begun tacking the same general course. His father had nodded stoically at the news that Sam would seek his MBA at that eggheads' paradise, the University of Chicago. But the man hadn't been able to bite his tongue when, on graduation day, Sam announced he had accepted an auditor's position at Pfluger Klaxon.

To Sam the job had sounded exciting—loads of travel, an apartment in Chelsea. Wasn't that bohemian enough? But perhaps his father had foreseen where that course would really chart, and Sam now recalled with sudden clarity a long forgotten conversation. They had just emerged from a downtown tavern after sharing beers with his two best pals from grad school and their dads. His father turned to him in the afternoon glare on a busy sidewalk and said quite solemnly, "Promise me one thing, Sam."

"Yes?"

"That if this position doesn't suit you or, worse, if it's starting to confine you, that you won't be afraid to give it up, or even start over."

"Dad, I'll be traveling all over the world."

"I know. But still." He shrugged, ammunition spent. Or perhaps what his posture was really saying was, "Hasn't my own life taught you anything? Haven't you been paying the least bit of attention?"

But Sam hadn't been able to read those signs just yet, so all he said in reply was, "Any job is taking a chance these days."

"True enough."

Now he understood, of course, because look at what all his careful behavior and painstaking work had gotten him—a reputation for dullness and rigidity, even as he slipped into a world of trouble, out here on the sharp glass edge of a barren land.

So why not start over, indeed, just as his father had advised? Except instead of taking a new job he would be assuming a new role geared strictly for self-preservation, the good man in a storm facing the stiffest winds yet. He would have asked his father for advice, but that was no longer an option. The old man had died three years ago, killed on the highway that he had taken to and from the office every day for more than forty years—all his safest calculations failing to beat the averages, after all. Sam's mother had followed six months later, succumbing to a cancer that had seemed to come from nowhere, an actuarial anomaly given her family history.

But if Sam's job had taught him one valuable thing, it was that he truly was a quick study, a whiz at problem solving. And that was where he would begin focusing his efforts this morning. With or without Sharaf's blessing, it was time to take action.

The policeman had left a note for him just inside the bedroom door.

"I decided there was no need to lock you in my study today," Sharaf wrote. The handwriting was neat, with European penmanship. "You must realize how foolish it would be to wander off on your own. By my accounting you are now being sought by the police, your employers, your embassy, and the criminal elite of two nations."

"True enough," Sam answered aloud. Even if he could show his face, he wouldn't get very far without a wallet and a passport. Finding them was one of his priorities.

"You will be pleased to know," the note continued, "that I am meeting someone this morning who should be able to find you more secure accommodations. Then we can start thinking about how to get you safely back home. I hope that you have slept well. There is coffee, bread, and yogurt for you in the kitchen. I should be returning for you by noon."

Sam checked his watch. It was a little after 10 a.m. The extra sleep had done him a world of good.

Sharaf must have told his prickly wife that he was giving Sam the run of the house, because she had disappeared. He smiled, wondering what the conversation had been like around the breakfast table. Both of the elder Sharafs probably made damn sure that Laleh was safely off to her office before they dared to leave.

If Sam was to make himself at all useful in this investigation, he knew where he needed to begin, and having Sharaf's house at his disposal was a plus. Would the Internet be available? Possibly. There was no computer in Sharaf's hideaway, but Sam was betting Laleh had one. That would allow him to begin pursuing the questions uppermost in his mind, most of which involved Nanette.

Who was she working with? Liffey, obviously, and Lieutenant Assad. But was the policeman a full partner or just an errand boy? What had brought the threesome together? Did she have an alliance with the Russians? The Iranians? Both? Neither? And if the mobsters had decided that shooting Charlie was an error meriting the death penalty, did that mean they had wanted to let Charlie run free? Had Nanette wanted that, too, so that Sam's surveillance could have led her—or all of them—to a more interesting destination than the York Club? To this woman named Basma, perhaps?

The nature of Nanette's job meant that it would be difficult to find out much about her. People who made it their business to pry into the affairs of others were often skilled at keeping their own lives a secret. It was the age-old conundrum of espionage and detection: Who watched the watchers? Surely her work at Pfluger Klaxon was subject to an annual audit. The question was who had access to the information. The Internet offered a starting point. Pfluger Klaxon's Web site had password-only portals for its globe-trotting employees, to allow constant access to encrypted information. And Sam, being an auditor, rated a fairly high security clearance.

He finished his coffee and went on the prowl. Laleh's door was locked. No surprise, but no problem. He easily sprang the lock with the thin, flat edge of a kitchen spatula.

The room was a revelation, a museum of arrested development that clearly displayed her status as a businesswoman still confined by the rules of girlhood. In the far corner by the window were the relics of her recent past. The wall was plastered with torn-out magazine photos of pop stars and film idols. A set of shelves was crammed with books— English editions of all seven Harry Potter titles were lined up in a row—along with music CDs and loads of silly knickknacks, the kind that a girl might get as party favors at her best friend's Sweet Sixteen. An iPod was docked in a set of Bose speakers next to a small television, the one he had heard blaring the other day. It was of modest size, but had an LCD flat screen.

The princess trappings grew sparser the farther you moved from the window, and the decor was correspondingly more mature—two prints of Matisse cutouts, professionally framed; an artsy color photo of a desert bluff at sunrise. The open door of her bathroom seemed to emanate her scent on a cloud of herbal shampoo and body lotion. Just inside the door, a blue towel was curled on the tile floor next to a shower cap and a loofah sponge. He tried not to dwell on how she must have looked when she dropped the towel to the floor.

By the time the view reached her desk, the transformation was complete. Here she was all business, having stacked and shelved thick hardback textbooks on marketing, accounting, and other entrepreneurial topics. A calendar that doubled as a blotter was marked with the month's morning appointments. There were issues of *The Economist* and *The Week*, plus a few tattered pink sections from the *Financial Times*. Off to one side was a glossy page torn from *UAE Business*, a local magazine devoted to puff pieces on the region's start-ups and commercial superstars. The story, only a few months old, profiled Laleh's marketing firm, and the photo took his breath away. She was covered nearly head to toe in a black abaya, but it was her face that really got his attention—an ultra-sober expression nearly as stern as her mother's had been at the breakfast table. She could have passed for thirty, and looked utterly, prudently competent. You would have trusted her with your last million.

Beneath the picture was a lengthy quote from her, highlighted in boldface type: **"All of the wealth is very heady, but I sometimes wonder if in our rush to prosperity our elders haven't embraced the new ways of doing business a little too readily. There is a certain sense of recklessness to the whole enterprise, which I think makes it a very good time to stay low to the ground."**

He wondered how dear old dad must have reacted to that—an implicit generational slam, yet a seeming endorsement of his more traditional values. An oddly appealing mix, he thought, especially from someone who looked so good in a short skirt. But he still couldn't shake the sense that she must be something of a dabbler, a rich girl who had talked Daddy into forking over some start-up capital to give her an excuse to get out of the house.

Sam reminded himself he was there for business, not pleasure, and he turned his attention to Laleh's desktop computer, a powerful HP with a liquid crystal monitor that flashed to life when he nudged the mouse. Viewing the desktop icons, he knew he was in luck. She had one of those broadband connections that was always active. When he clicked on her Internet icon, a Google homepage flashed to life.

At the same moment, an instant-messaging box popped up in the screen's upper right corner, with remnants of an IM conversation from only a few hours ago. The screen names had been trading girl gossip. He guessed that "LaSha" was Laleh's, and he blushed as he read her parting dispatch, a gloomy emoticon of a cartoon frown followed by "He may be leaving today."

Both her friends frowned back, then everyone declared "GTG," got to go.

Sam was surprised by how much it pleased him. He also experienced a pang of sympathy for Laleh, realizing what a departure from the norm his visit must represent in such a cloistered life. He X'ed out the messaging box, drew a deep breath, and refocused, typing and clicking his way to the Pfluger Klaxon homepage and its drop-down menu for cleared employees. A prompt asked for his password, and he obliged.

Access denied. Password invalid.

He tried it twice more, slowly, in case he had mistyped.

No luck.

Nanette had moved quickly. Discouraging, but also intriguing. He knew from auditing experience that whenever barricades began to appear there was usually something worth finding out farther down the road. She wouldn't have blocked him otherwise. And there were other passwords out there, some with even better access than his. The question was how to get one.

It was time to use the telephone. A call to Manhattan from Sharaf's house would be risky, especially if Nanette had sounded the alarm on him to Pfluger Klaxon. A transatlantic call could easily be traced through phone records. But that would be a minor problem as long as Sharaf found him a safer location by day's end.

Who to call, then? Any supervisor would be too chancy. So would friends from other departments, who probably couldn't help much anyway. That left his six fellow auditors. He quickly ruled out Ansen and Greenberg, who toed the company line even when it meant taking shortcuts with their work. Paar and Lukins were at the other extreme, but their reckless cowboy tendencies might do him more harm than good. Gupta, the newest hire, was the least known. With only two months' experience he would probably be reluctant to stick his neck out for anyone, much less an official pariah. That left only Stu Plevy. An up-and-comer. A conniver even, with a reputation for playing every angle. His talents were such that he could hold a conversation with two people at odds with each other, and both would came away convinced that Stu agreed with them. Plevy would be looking out for himself, meaning he would almost certainly report any call. But if Sam could dangle the possibility of some kind of benefit, Plevy might also help, in his own sneaky fashion. Better still, it was 2 a.m. in Manhattan, meaning Sam could phone Plevy at home, where the line wouldn't be monitored. Even if Plevy blabbed, Pfluger Klaxon wouldn't learn of the call for another seven hours. By then Sam would be in a new location.

A brief Internet search turned up a home number at an address on the upper East Side. Sam moved to the phone in the kitchen to punch in the numbers. After two rings the receiver clattered as if someone had knocked it loose in the dark.

"Hello?" The voice was scratchy.

"Plevy? Sorry to wake you, but this is urgent. It's Sam Keller, calling from Dubai."

"Keller? What time is it?"

"Around two your time. Ten in the morning here."

"Aren't you in some kind of trouble?" Plevy already sounded eager and alert. Sam heard a drawer open, as if Plevy was retrieving something to write with. "Heard about the thing with Charlie. Terrible. There were also rumblings of some kind of sexual assault involving No No Nanette. By you, even? What's up with that?"

So she had indeed poisoned the well. To hook Plevy he would have to lace the bait with some embellishments of his own.

"I was a dupe on the thing with Charlie. The assault charge is a frame-up to keep me quiet. From what I can tell, Nanette has some connections to a local hood. Between you and me, that's what I was sent here to check out."

"By Gary?" Their boss.

"Gary's out of the loop. This goes higher. Meaning it won't exactly hurt your career if you can help."

"Sounds like you've already got plenty of backing. Why not just go to your sugar daddy?"

"Because this isn't official, and we didn't plan for this kind of contingency. So you can understand if I'm in a bit of a bind."

Plevy paused, then said, "Especially if you're blowing smoke out your ass. Even if you're not, the whole setup sounds toxic. Where are you now?"

Fat chance he'd answer that.

"Working with some undercover people. Locals. I don't need much, Plevy."

"I heard some scuttlebutt about the babysitting assignment Nanette gave you. But I guess that could explain why they'd have picked you for an undercover job."

"Very good. But keep it to yourself."

"Did she give you one of her special phones?"

"How'd you know that?"

"She's done it before, keeping tabs on naughty boys like Charlie. No disrespect to the dead, of course. They've got GPS tracking and she receives the signal, so she always knows where you are. Remember that veep she busted in Africa? Same deal. So if you're still carrying, better ditch it."

No wonder she got so upset when Sam switched off the phone. And when he switched it back on, the Russian thugs had closed in on the York within minutes. Fortunately, the phone was still back at the Shangri-La.

"Keller?"

"I'm here. Don't worry, I ditched the phone."

"Not that I don't believe you, but you do realize that helping you isn't exactly a risk-free proposition?"

"Go ahead and report this call, Plevy. I'd do the same. Cover your ass all you need. All I want is a Web site password. Mine's blocked."

"Whoa, now. You think I'm stupid enough to report you but let you go snooping around the database under my name?"

"Yeah, well . . ."

Sam didn't have an easy answer, and his hopes faded. There was a pause of a few seconds with nothing but static, which Sam supposed was better than a flat refusal. Unless, of course, Plevy had grabbed his cell phone and was punching in the home number for one of Nanette's assistants.

"You don't need my password," Plevy said at last. "I'll give you Ansen's."

"How do you know Ansen's?"

"I know yours, too. The whole department's. Dumb-ass Gary left them up on his screen about a week ago. Seemed like the sort of thing a good auditor ought to file away for future reference. Not that it would do me much good, since we change them every month."

"If I need anything more . . ."

"No, no, Keller."

"Just as a hypothetical."

Plevy paused, still calculating. "What kind of hypothetical?"

"I don't know. Someone I could send up a flare to, if all else fails."

"If you have to, shoot a message to my personal address. Better still, send it to my sister's. Hold on, I'll get it."

Plevy returned a few seconds later and spelled out an AOL e-mail address.

"Put my name in the subject line, she'll know not to look. Which means she'll look anyway, so be as vague as possible."

Like brother, like sister, Sam supposed.

"Thanks, Plevy."

"Don't says thanks. I was no help at all, officially and otherwise. Unless you turn out to be right, of course."

Ansen's password worked fine. The first thing he found was Nanette's corporate bio.

She had been with Pfluger Klaxon for four years, having come to the job after six years with the Bureau of Diplomatic Security of the U.S. Foreign Service. Before that she had spent two years as a risk-assessment manager with Intermax, a global security consultant, right after graduating with honors from Brown.

Sam checked her Foreign Service postings. The first one was to Paris. The second was far more interesting: three years in Moscow.

The corporate bio was predictably glowing. Three particular programs were cited. The most intriguing was a 2007 project in Dubai in which Pfluger Klaxon, "in close cooperation with customs officials and local police," had financed the formation of a special squad at the port of Jebel Ali to ferret out the shipments of counterfeits. Probably when she met Lieutenant Assad, just as Sharaf had guessed.

Sam scrolled back through archived press releases until he found the retirement notice for her predecessor. It mentioned that a search had commenced for his replacement, and a boilerplate job description noted, "Pfluger Klaxon's chief of corporate security is a vice presidential position subject to an internal audit every four years by an outside consultant, reporting to the Chairman of the Board. Additionally, the vice president for security must file quarterly reports to the audit committee of the Board, with copies to the corporate legal officer, ethics officer, and audit officer."

The audit officer was Sam's boss, Gary Grimshaw. If Gary was lax enough to leave departmental passwords up on his screen, then a smooth operator like Plevy could probably easily find Gary's copies of Nanette's most recent quarterly reports.

Sam called up his personal account on Gmail and dashed off a message to the AOL address for Plevy's sister, keeping it as vague as possible:

"Need N's last five quarterly reports, copies filed to G."

That would cover her time on the Jebel Ali project. He pecked around awhile longer on the off chance the audits were available online, but to no avail.

He then searched a State Department Web site for the U.S. Embassy in Moscow. Press releases were archived for the previous six years, long enough to include Nanette's last two years on the job. Three stood out.

The first was an announcement of a meritorious honor award Nanette had won for "sustained excellence as a whistle-blower in identifying fraud and waste." There were no specifics, but Sam knew from his own experience that this brand of "excellence" more often resulted in embarrassment than advancement. Sure enough, six months later she showed up in a press release outlining changes among the embassy's Bureau of Diplomatic Security staff, when she was reassigned from investigations to consular affairs. Probably no pay cut involved, but her status and responsibility were certainly diminished. It made Sam recall a remark she'd made the other night. Even while she was taking pains to entrap him on the bogus sex charge, she hadn't been able to resist an offhand complaint about her occasional lack of support from the board of directors. He wondered if being thwarted by higher-ups was a recurring theme in her role as a security cop. If so, resentment might have compelled her to take a few liberties of her own.

The third press release, toward the end of her tenure, was the most intriguing. It was an announcement of an import-export seminar for visiting American executives, organized by commercial attaché Hal Liffey. Five Russian companies had pitched in as local sponsors. One was RusSiberian Metals and Investment, the firm that was now providing business cover in Dubai for crime boss Anatoly Rybakov. The press release helpfully instructed anyone interested in participating to contact staff security officer Nanette Weaver, who was handling visa questions and security clearances. So there they were, comrades in commerce for the betterment of East-West relations. And now here they were in Dubai, perhaps continuing their fruitful cooperation. But to what end?

He checked the Web site for the U.S. Embassy in the United Arab Emirates and found a thumbnail bio of Liffey. His photo showed him smiling in front of an American flag. Liffey had been posted to the UAE two years ago. His previous postings overlapped with Nanette's in Paris and Moscow. A long, productive friendship, no doubt.

All of it was promising, but it proved nothing. His last order of business on the desktop was to erase his Internet footprints from Laleh's computer. Then he went looking for his wallet and passport. He searched the house room by room—every drawer, closet, and box, plus the pockets of Sharaf's shirts, jackets, trousers, and *kandouras*, which were hanging all in a row like choir robes. An hour later, still unsuccessful, he even tried the refrigerator, unwrapping foil parcels in the freezer just to make sure. No luck.

He searched Laleh's room last, then logged back onto her computer just long enough to check his Gmail account, on the off chance that Plevy had already sent a message. No luck there, either.

Sam then went to the kitchen, poured a tall glass of water and downed it at the sink while pondering where to look next. Perhaps Sharaf had taken the items with him. Glancing out the back window, he spotted another possibility—a storage shed at the rear of the carport.

Just then the phone rang, loud and jarring in the silence of the empty kitchen. He stared at the receiver, debating whether to pick it up. He supposed it could be Sharaf with new marching orders. But if someone in New York had already traced the phone call, it could also be Nanette, or the police, trying to verify his location.

He swallowed the last of the water and headed out the door while the phone continued to ring. Outside it was sunny and the temperature was already in the mid-eighties.

The shed was locked, so he circled to the back, where a small mullioned window offered a view into a dim chamber. As his eyes adjusted to the darkness he saw that it was mostly a repository for gardening equipment and discarded household items such as an old television. Then he saw a corrugated aluminum tub, filled with water. Were those his trousers, for God's sake? They were. His shirt was there, too, sopping wet, and if his passport and wallet were still in his pants pockets, they also would be sodden.

Now what was the point of this outrage, other than sheer maliciousness? His first instinct was to smash in a pane, unlock the window, and climb in. But he didn't want to risk cutting himself, so he ran back to the house, his anger building, and grabbed the damp blue towel from the floor of Laleh's bathroom. He returned to the rear of the shed, balled up his fist inside the towel, and took aim at the pane just above the window lock.

That's when he heard the cars come roaring up the drive. He lowered his fist and peeped around the corner. Blue bubble lights flashed atop a police cruiser, followed closely by the same black BMW SUV that Assad had driven into the desert. Doors opened on the cruiser and four cops in khaki uniforms piled out. Two headed for the front door of the house, and two for the back. A fifth shouted orders from the driver's seat. The door of the BMW opened, and Lieutenant Assad stepped into the drive, hands on his hips as he watched the search unfold.

It was a raid, plain and simple, and Sam was the quarry. He dropped the towel to the ground and backed away, using the shed for cover. Then he turned and ran for the rear wall of the family compound. It was about eight feet high. The first time he jumped, his hands slid off the top. The second time they held, and he grunted and pulled until he was in position to awkwardly sling a leg across the top. The baggy borrowed clothes hampered his movements, but the shouts of the policemen kept him going. Fortunately he was still screened from view by the shed. He dropped heavily to the grass on the other side of the wall, and found himself in an almost identical compound. It, too, had a wrought iron gate at the end of a driveway. Sam easily climbed over it onto a sidewalk that ran alongside a busy four-lane road. The median was a narrow strip of grass with an iron fence, and there was no opening in the fence for several blocks in either direction.

Traffic was light, so Sam darted across the first two lanes and scaled the fence as a passing driver slowed down to stare. He then bounded across the last two lanes to the far sidewalk and took stock of his surroundings.

He knew the police would soon realize he wasn't in the house, and would probably begin patrolling the neighborhood. He was vulnerable out here in the open, and he was already sweating enough to soak his clothes. It was too hot to be wearing his suit jacket, but as the only item of apparel that fit properly it made him look a bit less ridiculous.

He had to find shelter. Looking east he saw nothing but more houses. A few blocks to the west there were some commercial buildings. Even if they were offices he could duck inside, so he took off for them at a dead run. After a block he thought better of it, figuring he was more likely to attract attention by running. Sweat was pouring down his face.

When he reached the buildings he was relieved to spot a sidewalk cutting between two of them to an inner brick courtyard. Inside was a small shopping plaza, tucked well out of sight of the road. A restaurant was to his right, a kitchen boutique was straight ahead, and a Coffee Bean café was to his left. He ducked through the smoked-glass doors of the café and took a seat at a corner table with his back to the wall. Sweat dripped onto the tabletop. The five seated customers—three teenage girls in one group, two women in Western business suits in another—stopped in mid-conversation and eyed him with a touch of apprehension. So did the two young men behind the counter. Sam smiled wanly and pretended to study the chalkboard menu as he wiped his face dry with a napkin.

In a few seconds conversation returned to normal. He glanced nervously toward the door, but no one was in pursuit.

For the moment he was safe. But where could he go next? He had no money, no phone, no charge cards, and no passport. For a few moments he verged on panic. Then he calmed himself and glanced again at the menu, if only for the benefit of the other customers. It was then that he remembered the one item he did have, tucked in the inner pocket of his suit jacket.

He reached inside and retrieved Laleh Sharaf's business card.

Sam turned toward the two businesswomen, who were speaking English in British accents. He smiled in a way that he hoped was neither maniacal nor threatening, and launched his cover story.

"Excuse me. I just arrived this morning after an overnight flight from the States. They lost my luggage, which is why I'm wearing these ridiculous clothes, and now I'm afraid I've missed an appointment with a friend who was supposed to meet me here. I'd call him, but my cell phone is dead and the charger is in my luggage, and, well, I was just wondering if I might borrow one of your phones to make one quick call?"

"Certainly," one of the women answered, although her eyes said she was anything but certain about Sam. She handed over the phone without leaning toward him an inch more than necessary.

"Thanks."

He turned in the other direction and punched in the number. A receptionist answered in English, which he supposed was the language of commerce in Media City. He reluctantly offered his name, and she put him through to Laleh without a moment's delay.

"Are you safe?" She sounded almost frantic, and he wondered why.

"Sort of. I'm at a café a few blocks from your house. The police came when I was out back, so I ran for it."

"My father's been arrested. I've been calling and calling the house, trying to reach you."

"Arrested?" He glanced toward the door, already losing hope. The woman who had loaned him the phone narrowed her eyes. Maybe she was eavesdropping.

"My father's friend Ali is making arrangements for you as we speak. Where did you say you were?"

"Some café—the Coffee Bean."

"It must be the one off Jumeirah Road. Don't move. I'll be there in twenty minutes."

She hung up. He wiped his sweat from the phone and returned it, feeling more like a fugitive than ever. The countermen seemed edgy again, and he didn't have a single dirham to buy a coffee.

"I'm meeting a friend," he said to one of them. He cleared his throat self-consciously and stared out the glass walls. Fifteen minutes later—she must have driven especially fast—Laleh strode briskly into the sunny courtyard. Sam was shocked to see that she wasn't wearing her abaya. He stood quickly and met her just as she was coming through the door. They both looked around nervously, and neither spoke until they reached her car.

Already she was a different young woman from the one he had met at her house. She was neither the flirtatious girl on her home turf nor the confident young businesswoman in the magazine. You could tell she was uncertain in this new role, yet a little excited by it as well.

"I've spoken with Ali," she said. "I'm driving you to Media City. One of my creative people is out on a call. You can wait in his office until Ali is ready to move you. You really should do something about those clothes, you know."

"Speaking of clothes—"

Laleh blushed. "You're not to say a word of this to my mother or father."

"Wouldn't dream of it. And I'd be dressed better myself if your dad hadn't put my clothes in a tub of water."

"He what?"

She looked at him like he had lost his mind, so he didn't belabor the point. Laleh pressed her key to pop the locks of the BMW. Then she paused, as if she wasn't quite sure where to put him. He supposed she almost never rode anywhere with a male her age, not without an escort.

"Should I lie down in the back? It's what your father had me do."

"Yes." She seemed relieved by the suggestion. "It's probably best for you to stay out of sight."

At least her car had plenty of floor space. There was even room to sit up. He wondered if this was going to be his mode of transportation from now on in Dubai.

When she turned the key in the ignition, music blared from the speakers. There was flustered movement up front as she switched off the radio.

"Sorry."

"No problem. You can play it if you want."

"That's all right. Are you comfortable?"

"I'm fine. Thanks for coming to get me."

She put the car in gear and eased away from the curb, heading west.

"Ali told me my father was desperate for someone to get you out of there, although I doubt it was me he would have preferred for the job, especially if it means spending time alone with you. Well, not really alone, but . . .”

“I know what you mean. Why was he arrested? Because of me?”

“Ali wasn’t sure. He just said they took him away in a meat wagon, the van they use for common criminals. It was clear they wanted to make a spectacle of it.”

“That doesn’t sound good.”

“No, it doesn’t.”

A few minutes of stop-and-go driving passed in silence while Sam caught his breath. She had rolled up the windows and switched on the air conditioner. His sweaty clothes were clammy, but it felt good to be out of harm’s way. Laleh pulled onto a big, smooth highway—Sheikh Zayed Road, Sam guessed—and the BMW kicked into high gear.

In a few miles the silence grew uncomfortable. It was awkward enough trying to strike up a conversation from down on the floor, and he wasn’t sure what to say to a young woman who was probably just as nervous. He decided to break the ice with family talk.

“Your dad seems like a pretty reasonable guy. Except maybe where you’re concerned.”

“He’s come a long way even there, considering where he started. You should hear him talk about what things were like when he was a boy. A woman my age couldn’t even leave the house unescorted, unless she was married.”

“Wasn’t Dubai mostly desert then?”

“Yes, but he lived on the creek. When he was smaller his family lived in a shack built of palm fronds. Lots of people did. Then his father struck it rich and built a big house with a wind tower. Even then they only had electricity six hours a day, with one lightbulb per room. They had a well in their house, but it was salt water, only good for doing the dishes. Sweet water had to be hauled in by donkey, all the way from Hamriya, and it had worms. You had to wait until they set-tled to the bottom.”

“How’d his dad make his fortune?”

“Pearling, I think. And smuggling gold to India. Apparently pretty much everyone was doing it. Sort of like real estate today. My dad worked on his father’s boats one summer, but he never really talks much about that part of his life, except with old friends like Ali.”

“What made him want to be a policeman?”

"There is a story he tells from when he was a boy. A doctor they knew was the first man in the neighborhood with a TV, so everyone used to go there to watch while the electricity was on. There was only one station, run by the Americans at the Aramco oil company in Saudi Arabia. So the picture would come and go, and most of the programs were in English. Of course, my dad had already learned a lot of English from his tutors, so he would translate for everyone, especially during their favorite, the *Perry Mason* show."

"I've heard of it. About a lawyer, I think."

"Yes, a lawyer who always won. My father said he always felt like he was taking part in the victory, a partner of this man who solved every crime. I think he would have gone to law school if his father would have sent him overseas. But he didn't, so . . ."

"Being a policeman was the next best thing."

"Yes."

"Good story."

"If it's true."

"You don't believe him?"

"I believe him. I just think there was something more. Something that he doesn't talk about. His sense of justice is far too strong. He is adamant about it, even when it hurts his career. I don't think you get to be that way just by watching a TV show."

"Maybe not."

Her remarks reminded him of something Charlie had said on the night he died, something about how easily people fell into predatory behavior. "Don't you fall into that trap, old son," he had warned. "Once you do, atonement is damned near impossible."

He considered the implications of those words as the wheels hummed on the pavement. Soon afterward they exited the highway, and within moments Laleh had pulled into a parking lot.

"This is my building. We shouldn't be seen entering together, so I want you to stay here while I go inside. Wait five minutes and then follow. Here are my keys." She reached back across the seat. "My offices are on the fifth floor, suite 516. The receptionist will be expecting you. Give her my keys and keep going to the first office on your right. The door will be unlocked, and it will be empty. You might have to wait a few hours, but I'll come and get you when Ali arrives."

She got out and shut the door behind her. He listened as the sound of her footsteps faded. It was a trusting, even naive gesture. He could have easily driven back to the Sharafs' house to see if the coast was clear, and then grabbed his soggy passport and credit cards for a trip to the airport. Buying a ticket would have been no problem, but he wasn't sure he could have sneaked past the border authorities onto a flight home, especially if Assad had put his name on some sort of watch list.

But even if he had been inclined to try, he wouldn't have felt right taking advantage of Laleh's trust. Or of her father's trust, either, now that Sharaf was apparently in trouble on his behalf.

So after five minutes he squirmed up onto the backseat, opened the rear door, and hopped out before locking the car. Only later, when he found out what a terrible destination Ali had arranged for him, would he regret the decision.

14

"I've sold you into slavery," said the grinning man whom Laleh had just introduced as Ali al-Futtaim. "Not really, of course, but that's what it's going to feel like."

Sam looked to Laleh for further explanation, or some hint of a smile to indicate this was Ali's idea of a joke. He noticed she had put on an abaya for Ali's benefit. She shrugged and shook her head, seemingly as befuddled as he was.

The three of them stood in Laleh's office with the door closed. It was dusk, and everyone else had gone home. Her work space contained none of the ambiguity of her bedroom. White walls, gray trim, all the furniture upholstered in red. Nothing frilly or frivolous, but there were plenty of designs and mock-ups for proposed advertisements and marketing campaigns, posted on walls and easels, and spread across the broad white expanse of her desk. The desk itself resembled a command post—three-sided, with two phones, a PC, and a Mac. The Mac had a flat-screen monitor bigger than the television in her bedroom.

The view through her smoked-glass window looked out across Jumeirah Beach Road toward the palms of the Royal Mirage resort and beyond, across the emerald waters of the Persian Gulf. Off to the right, you could see the glittery archipelago of the huge Palm development, with its beehive of new villas and hotels.

From his hiding place in the office next door, Sam had listened for more than seven hours as phones rang and people came and went in the corridor. Some were her employees, others were clients. All sought her advice, and everyone spoke English. Once or twice he overheard animated discussions in which Laleh's point of view sometimes yielded ground but always prevailed. Not by fiat, but by persuasion. The prevailing attitude among her employees seemed to be that Laleh Sharaf knew what she was doing, and you had better as well if you wanted to keep working there. Not once in those seven hours had Sam heard the call to prayer. Either no one had yet built a mosque out this way or the nearest muezzin wasn't amplified enough to overcome the insulated walls and the constant sigh of air-conditioning.

Sam realized he had judged Laleh unfairly from all the trappings in her bedroom. No matter how she'd come up with the money to start her business, this was no dabbler or hobbyist. She was a young woman with a plan, a dedicated professional.

The question now was what to make of this fellow Ali, who frankly seemed a touch too slick to be a confidant of a rumpled old pro like Sharaf. His white *kandoura* was pressed and spotless, which made it seem as if he was gliding with every step. He wore a spicy scent and had an enormous watch and three rings on his fingers. From his smooth English and his familiar and comfortable manner it was clear he was accustomed to dealing with people of every nationality from all walks of life. Maybe that was why Sharaf and he were a match—Sharaf supplying the spit, and Ali the polish; the cop keeping his own counsel while his pal played the bluff extrovert, forever ready to make a deal. Or so Sam hoped, now that he was about to entrust the man with his life.

"My apologies for taking so long to arrive," Ali said. "But your father's arrest necessitated stronger measures and more careful preparation. I thank you, Laleh, for keeping Mr. Keller safe in the meantime. I know that your father would thank you as well, even though he would blanch at the whole idea of your involvement."

"Is he all right?" Laleh asked.

"All I have been able to find out is that he has been arrested. I know he is not being held at police headquarters, and he is not at the courthouse. That troubles me."

It troubled Sam, too. He hoped Sharaf didn't become Daoud's latest find.

"Let us go, then, before they find you as well," Ali said. "I will drive you myself."

"I'm coming, too," Laleh announced.

"Really, my child, there is no need. And you know that your father would not permit it."

"But my father is not here. And although you're his friend, I am still acting on his behalf."

Ali seemed genuinely affronted.

"Do you not trust me? Can you not do that on your father's behalf as well?"

"Of course I trust you. But don't you think it's safer if more than one of us knows where Mr. Keller is being taken? What if something happens to you?"

Ali examined her carefully. He slowly shook his head, and with a measure of apparent affection said, "You are too much like your father. He, too, believes that everything will fall apart unless he is there to personally supervise. So on his behalf I will indulge you."

"Where am I going?" Sam asked.

"We're taking you off the grid. Not just Dubai's. The world's."

Sam envisioned some Bedouin encampment deep in the dunes, a shadeless purgatory among goats and sand fleas.

"The desert?" he asked.

"What, to live with the Bedouin?" Ali laughed, a bit too heartily under the circumstances, Sam thought. "I would not even consider entrusting you to them. I could pay one of them to protect you, of course. But the moment another one learned you were being hidden he would turn you in for a bounty. And it is far easier to find one isolated man in all that emptiness than here in the city. Safety in numbers is better. You will be hiding among a hundred and fifty thousand people, at the Sonapur Labor Camp."

Laleh put a hand to her mouth.

"Labor camp?" Sam said. "Like a prison?"

"Worse, I'm afraid. In prison, your confinement has a limit. Serve your sentence and go free. At Sonapur everyone is supposedly free from the moment he arrives. But in practical terms it is a life sentence. All those men you see in hard hats, building everything? There are half a million of them in Dubai, and they are all living in camps like Sonapur. Entire cities without a single woman. They rise before the sun and return after nightfall. And when they die, no one even bothers to count them sometimes. So you see? It is the perfect place for you to be lost for a while, and you will be one of the lucky few with a prospect for departure. A speedy one, I hope."

"Will I have to work?"

"Of course. All the better for keeping you camouflaged. You will be high up on some new tower, where the only way someone can reach you is by industrial elevator or by climbing onto the arm of a crane."

Sam felt queasy thinking about it. He may have been a daredevil on the water, but he had never been comfortable with heights. Ali slapped him companionably on the back.

"Come. Best to get you settled before dark."

They piled into Ali's roomy Mercedes with tinted windows. Sam sat up front next to Ali, with Laleh in the back. They headed south and east, and soon were driving through industrial parks and freshly graded tracts awaiting development. The traffic was heavy, with a preponderance of dump trucks, cement mixers, and flatbeds carrying backhoes and bulldozers. Sam also noticed battered buses filled with men in hard hats. He saw Laleh watching them as well.

"Won't there be people at Sonapur who would want to turn him in?" she asked.

"Not likely," Ali said, glancing at her reflection in the mirror. "They're too busy and too tired. And none of them are local. They're from India, Pakistan, Bangladesh. Besides, Mr. Keller will have far more to worry about than exposure, I am sorry to say."

"They aren't big on safety rules, huh?" Sam asked.

"Just be glad it is not summer, when a building slab is like a skillet. Still, on balance it is much safer than leaving you at the mercy of Lieutenant Assad."

Ali exited onto a potholed two-lane road clogged with trucks and buses. They made their way slowly toward a smudge of low-slung buildings on the near horizon and turned onto a rutted dirt lane. A thunderstorm had recently passed, one of those cloudbursts that never seemed to reach Dubai's coastline. Craters as big as compact cars were filled with water, and the whole area stank of mud and raw sewage.

They were surrounded now by complexes of grimy buildings, two and three stories high. Each looked like a cheap motel, with rows of doorways along breezeways. Brightly colored laundry hung from the railings. Some rooms had windows, and most were mounted with air-conditioning units. Other rooms had neither. The complexes were separated by iron fencing and low plaster walls. Each had an entrance gate that displayed the name of a contracting firm. Buses were unloading workers from the day shift. Weary-looking men in jumpsuits shuffled toward their dormitories. The only other vehicles in sight were the lumbering "honey wagons," tanker trucks that worked around the clock to pump out septic tanks.

Sam could already tell from the preponderance of dark faces that he wasn't exactly going to blend in with the crowd.

"I'm going to stick out like a sore thumb."

"In here, yes. Although at least you're on the darker side of Caucasian. That will help. So will a beard. But the more important thing is that the moment you put on your uniform and leave these gates you will become invisible. In Dubai these workers are everywhere and nowhere. No one sees them, because no one *wants* to. You must trust me on this. It has worked before, even with someone whiter than you. What is it they say in your country? 'Hidden in plain sight.' Here we are."

Ali parked the car next to a whitewashed plaster wall, which was spattered a rusty brown by hundreds of spittings of *paan*, the local chewing tobacco. A cinder-block hut sat next to an entrance gate, where a security man stood guard with a holstered weapon. The sign out front said the site belonged to the Al Mumtaz Engineering Co.

"Free room and board?" Sam asked.

"Rooms, yes, but the meals will be up to you. Laleh, give him the envelope."

She handed it across the seat.

"Three hundred dirhams," Ali said. About eighty bucks. "Keep it with you at all times. If you need more, tell the foreman. His name is Zafar. You will meet him shortly. He is your link to me. He will always know how to reach me, but don't mention my name around the others. It is best if you do not contact me at all. As soon as it is safe for you on the outside, I will come for you myself. Don't leave with anyone else. Understand?"

"Yes."

Ali turned toward Laleh.

"I am taking him inside. You must not leave the car under any circumstances, and you must not open the window. Even in an abaya, your presence here would be a provocation."

He turned back toward Sam.

"Come with me to the blockhouse. There will be some papers to sign."

"Good-bye, Sam," Laleh said.

"Good-bye," he said, glancing back at her. Just as Ali was climbing out the door she furtively thrust forward her right hand with a small square of folded paper. She nodded quickly, as if to say, "Please, take it before he sees us." So Sam snatched it away and nodded in reply. More forbidden behavior, he supposed, which made the gesture all the more touching. He stuck the paper in his pocket so Ali wouldn't see it, and then opened his door to follow.

"Good luck," she whispered.

Ali led the way through the front door of the blockhouse. The white billow of his *kandoura* looked out of place among the mud and the disheveled, wiry laborers, a white bloom of prosperity in a scrap yard of weeds.

Inside, another armed security man eyed them suspiciously. A dark middle-aged man in a wrinkled gray shirt stood up from behind a steel desk littered with paperwork.

"Ali."

It was a professional greeting. No smiles, handshakes, or hands on the heart. Ali nodded in return and said, "This is Zafar, the foreman. He will look after you."

Zafar didn't seem like the type who looked after anyone, except to ensure they gave him a full day of labor. He walked over from the desk, sizing up Sam from head to toe. Spreading a thumb and forefinger like calipers, he clamped them around Sam's jaw, turning his head one way and then another.

"It is good you not shave," Zafar said, releasing Sam's bristly jaw. "Black hair. Brown eyes. These good also. Grow beard. Right now, too white. Too many will stare. Speak only when you must. Only few on your crew speak English."

"How will I know what they're telling me to do?"

"You watch. Do what others do. Very easy. You will see."

He returned to his desk, where he motioned Ali toward a small pile of documents on a front corner. Ali handed a pen to Sam. All the writing was in Arabic.

"Sign them both," Ali said.

"What are they?"

"One is an employment agreement. The other is a receipt for your uniform, your hard hat, and your boots. They are company property, so you must take care of them."

Sam obliged, although for all he knew he was selling himself into slavery, just as Ali had joked.

"How much will I be paid?" he asked, trying to make light of it.

Zafar's answer was businesslike.

"Seven hundred fifty dirhams, one month."

Roughly two hundred dollars, Sam calculated. Less than a buck an hour.

"We hold first two months' pay for cost of equipment, housing, medical helpings. I cannot change this because I already make special change for not having passport. Two changes not possible."

Sam was less worried about pay than the implication that he might be here for months. He turned for reassurance to Ali, who placed a hand on his shoulder. But the man was no longer smiling. Perhaps he, too, was just realizing the gravity of the situation. Or maybe his earlier offhand attitude had been an act, to keep up Sam's spirits.

"The good news," Ali said, "is that this is not a Muslim crew. They're Hindu Bengalis, so perhaps you will not be resented so much. Of course, that means you will also be expected to work on Fridays, the Muslim holy day. Be strong, Mr. Keller. I will do what I can to make sure that your stay here is a short one."

He turned to go. Sam watched through the doorway as Ali climbed back into the big Mercedes and eased it down the rutted lane. Neither Laleh nor Ali was visible through the tinted windows, and the car was soon swallowed by the crowds. It felt as if his previous life had just disappeared along with the car, so he reached into his pocket for Laleh's note. Even with that in hand, he hadn't felt this abandoned since being dropped off for his freshman year in college. And then at least his father had eased the shock by reminding him of what a great adventure he was about to have.

"Now for the fun part," his father had said, grinning through a surprising flush of tears. "Always look before you leap, son. But don't ever forget to leap."

Good advice now, Sam supposed, as long as none of the leaps came from fifty stories up. For a brief moment his thoughts seemed to scatter, and he couldn't pin one down. It was a feeling almost like panic. Then he drew a deep breath and exhaled slowly, steadying himself.

"Here is your uniform," Zafar said in his flat tone. "Hat and boots, too."

The canvas jumpsuit was the bright blue of surgical scrubs. It smelled sour, as if it hadn't been properly laundered. The helmet was blue and scuffed, and the boots looked small. He wondered if anything would fit. Most of the other workers were shorter.

"You must buy food. Store that way." Zafar pointed vaguely left, beyond the compound. "First Charbak take you to room. You sleep with seven more."

Eight to a room. Cozy.

Charbak, some sort of sub-foreman, wordlessly led the way into the narrow mud courtyard, which was bordered on either side by long two-story dormitories with rows of open doors. Drying laundry was draped on every rail. There were fifteen doors per floor on each side. Sam added it up. At eight workers per room, about five hundred men were living here in a complex roughly the size of one of those chain motels you found along interstate highways. Down at the far end, backed by a high fence topped with razor wire, was a cinder-block room with the showers and bathrooms. Men were coming and going in towels and rubber slippers.

Along the lower breezeway to the right was a row of propane canisters attached to stovetop burners. Men stood at the blue flames with giant skillets, frying chopped eggplant and some sort of stringy meat. Nearby shelves held blackened pots and pans. The smell of hot grease masked the stench of sewage, but at the moment Sam had no appetite.

Charbak led him to a door at the right end of the first level, where they entered a nine-by-twelve-foot room crammed with four steel bunk beds. Three men squatted on the floor in a narrow space between the bunks, eating with their hands from a steaming bowl of stir-fried greens and meat. A fourth fellow watched in silence from a lower bunk that had been stripped of its bedding. Every other mattress had sheets and pillows.

Charbak barked an order in a language Sam didn't understand. The fellow sitting on the bare mattress looked up sullenly but didn't move. Charbak spoke again, louder. The man jumped to his feet with a sudden roar and came straight toward them, eyes wild with anger. Sam braced for impact, and before he knew it the man had grabbed his lapels and was shoving him against the door, shouting all the while. His warm breath smelled like onions. Charbak piled onto the fellow's shoulders from behind, while two of the men on the floor grabbed the madman's legs. The scrum tottered, then collapsed, sending the bowl of food clattering beneath a bunk. Sam, who nearly had the wind knocked out of him, disengaged from the pile as the others subdued the attacker and slung him back onto a bunk. Judging from their shouts, his name was Ramesh.

"He wants that you not take bed," Charbak explained.

"If he'd like to switch, tell him that's fine."

"No. He wants *no one* being there."

"Why?"

Charbak shrugged.

"He is crazy man. You take bed." He pointed to it.

"But if—"

"You take bed!"

Now Charbak was angry. Sam held up his hands in a gesture of surrender. Then he shrugged toward the men on the floor, as if to explain he had no choice. Figuring he had better mark his new territory, he removed his suit jacket and tossed it onto the bare mattress. That drew a snarl from Ramesh, who was still muttering darkly from the opposite bunk. One of the men eating dinner turned and snarled back at him, and for a moment Ramesh looked genuinely chastened. He then curled into a ball and rolled onto his side, facing away from the others, toward the wall. Thank goodness that was settled, at least for now.

Sam still had no appetite, but figured he had better buy supplies and cook something if he was going to have any energy the following day. Charbak had already departed, so he offered his question to the room at large.

"Can someone tell me where the food store is?"

One of the men on the floor eyed him carefully, then nodded.

"Go left from the blockhouse," he said quietly. His English was perfect. "Four hundred meters. The Al Madina market. You will see it."

"Thank you."

The man resumed eating without another word.

The Al Madina was tiny and crowded, every aisle jammed with men. To Sam's surprise there was an abundance of fresh fruit and vegetables. He didn't know if the prices were decent or not. He piled eggplant, green peppers, bananas, oranges, flatbread, and cooking oil into a basket, along with a two-kilogram bag of rice. Fresh meat was for sale, but at seemingly outrageous rates, so he turned to the freezer. He avoided the frozen carp and some buffalo product labeled as "Bobby Veal," settling instead on chicken parts. Then he bought soap, a towel, a toothbrush, and a set of sheets. The only ones for sale had a wildly colorful pattern of bright green palm trees against an orange beach.

To his surprise, there were a few other shops as well—a small pharmacy, a narrow restaurant selling rotisserie chicken and kebabs, a jeweler, a cell phone dealer, and a small photography store where you could develop film or buy a disposable camera. He supposed there must be a market for sending pictures home, especially for family members who had been away for years. There was also a lottery kiosk that seemed to be doing a brisk business—the great, faint hope of the world's dispossessed.

When he returned to the room, Ramesh was still sulking with his back to the others. Sam tried to make as little fuss as possible while making his bed. He put his perishables into one of several small refrigerators set on the floor between the beds. No one had labeled anything, so he supposed there was an honor system.

He took a few pieces of chicken and one of the peppers and chopped them on a table outside. He had to wait half an hour for one of the burners to become available, and it gave him time to work up an appetite. It was only when he was almost finished cooking that he realized he had no plate or utensils. That's when he noticed the fellow from his room who spoke English hovering nearby.

"Here," the young man said, handing over the large bowl he had just washed, along with a clean spoon.

"Thanks," Sam said.

"The bed you are in. It belonged to Ramesh's friend, Sanjay. They came here together, from the same village. That is why he is angry."

"Tell him that Sanjay can have his bed back, as long as I have somewhere else to sleep."

"Sanjay is dead. He fell last week from the twenty-seventh story. He was standing at the edge, and the wind came."

"I'm sorry."

"Ramesh has been a little crazy since then. He believes that a demon was responsible. When he saw your white face taking Sanjay's bed, he said you were the demon, and had come to disturb his soul. Ramesh has been here eleven years. Too long."

"Sounds like it. How long have you been here?"

"Three years. It is only this year that I no longer owe money to the people who brought me."

"How long will you stay, then?"

The young man shook his head, as if those sorts of questions weren't even remotely answerable.

"I'm Sam, by the way."

"Vikram." He didn't offer a last name. Sam had yet to hear anyone mention one.

"You should hurry," Vikram said. "Lights-out in a few minutes."

"Thanks."

"And take care around Ramesh. When you are working, I mean. If he thinks you are a demon, well . . ."

"Yes. I'll keep that in mind."

"So why do you come here?"

He considered offering his own demons as an excuse, but figured the sarcasm would be misunderstood, perhaps even resented. So he offered what he hoped was a safe approximation of the truth.

"I have been having troubles in the city. A friend thought this would be a good place for me to stay until things are better. What time will they wake us in the morning?"

"Five. Before the sun. You must be waiting for the bus at five twenty, or it will leave without you, and you will not be paid."

Vikram turned to go before Sam could ask more. He ate hastily and washed out the bowl and spoon at an outdoor spigot. There wasn't time to shower, so he scrubbed his hands and face, and brushed his teeth at the same spigot. When he returned to the room all the other bunks were occupied. A few men were reading magazines or newspapers. Two were playing cards. Vikram was writing a letter. Four snapshots of children were arrayed beside him on the bed. Ramesh was still facing the wall, either asleep or brooding. Someone had switched on the air conditioner, which droned and rattled, and gave off a whiff of mildew.

It was then that he remembered Laleh's note. He retrieved it from his pocket as he was undressing for bed, stripping down to his briefs. Then he lay on his side in the dim light and opened the folded paper, while hoping that no one would be able to read it over his shoulder.

Dear Mr. Keller . . .

The handwriting was neat and proper, although not the least bit girlish. The salutation was certainly more formal than he would have preferred, but it struck a tone she maintained throughout, as if she wasn't at all accustomed to engaging in this sort of correspondence. But a certain warmth also came through.

> *Thank you for entrusting yourself into Ali's care. Even though I know you must have reservations, I can assure you that he will only do what he deems to be in your best interests. Nonetheless, I hope that you will also consider me to be an important part of your support network. Ali obviously has valuable connections, but I do as well, and among them are people who neither he nor my father are aware of (or, in my father's case, would even want to be aware of, as you probably well understand!).*
>
> *In other words, please do not think of me as helpless or overly dependent in these matters, as so many men here would be inclined to do. Should an urgent situation arise, do not hesitate to contact me for assistance. I remain at your service, both as my father's representative, and, I hope, as your friend.*
>
> *With best regards,*
> *Laleh Sharaf*

He smiled to contemplate how her father would have regarded such a note. It made him hope anew that Sharaf was okay, although the news had sounded grim. With any luck maybe they would both survive long enough for him to see the policeman's reaction to Laleh's new-found autonomy. Whatever happened, the old fellow was going to find a changed daughter on his return. The nature of fatherhood, he supposed, thinking fondly of his own dad.

He folded the note and put it back in the pocket of his trousers. Seconds later, without warning, the lights went out. Conversation halted, and he heard the rattle of paper as men put aside their things. Bed frames creaked as everyone settled in. Soon the cramped little room was silent.

A few minutes later the evening call to prayer sounded from a small mosque Sam had seen near the market. No one stirred among the Hindus. It was such a lonely sound, like a voice calling out from across the ocean.

By now, Sam figured, Nanette was probably enjoying a lavish dinner on Pfluger Klaxon's tab, or watching a pay-per-view movie on her hotel room's HD screen, bare legs curled beneath her on the large, comfy bed. Or maybe she was huddled at the consulate with Hal Liffey, planning what to do once Sam was finally flushed from cover.

Well, he wouldn't give them the satisfaction. He would wait them out, and then dodge whoever they left in their wake. He would stay in this work camp for days—even weeks if necessary.

But what if even then no one came to retrieve him? He supposed that at some point he might simply have to walk away from this building, back toward the highway, where he would hitchhike to Media City. If all else failed, Laleh would take him in. Odd to think of her as his closest ally now, but that was certainly what her note was encouraging him to do, and he liked the idea. Was it mostly because her father was a cop? Or was it more because he was attracted to her, and sensed that the feeling was mutual?

Above him, the mattress creaked. In another bunk a man began to snore. The sounds of deep, heavy breathing seemed to come from all directions. They must have been exhausted, and he supposed that by this time tomorrow he would be, too. He wondered if he would be able to meet the demands of the workday.

Sam reached toward the foot of the bed, groping in the dark for his jacket. He folded it to use as a pillow, then closed his eyes and tried to relax.

Just as he was drifting off he heard bare feet hit the floor, like the sound of a small animal dropping from a tree. Something gripped his bed frame, making it quiver, and he heard quickened breathing. He smelled onions. Ramesh. He tensed, ready to defend himself. There was a low mutter, like an incantation, and sudden movement to his left. The smell of onions was stronger, and when Ramesh spoke next his mouth was only a few inches from his face.

The words were rushed, emphatic, and incomprehensible, some Bengali curse or imprecation. Then the man was gone, the bed trembling as he released his grip. Sam let out a deep breath and unclenched his fists. Now what had that been? A warning? A threat? Some sort of superstitious spell, to ward off Sam's influence? Whatever it was, it certainly hadn't sounded like an apology.

There was a creak of springs from across the room as Ramesh climbed back into his bunk, and the room was again at peace. But for the next half hour Sam didn't close his eyes. He kept wondering whether Ramesh would pay him another visit, this time with more violent intent. The air conditioner droned on, changing in tone from time to time like a truck shifting gears on an uphill grade. Gradually, without realizing it, Sam slipped from wakefulness. And just as quickly, it seemed, he was being jostled awake.

He opened his eyes and felt the bed shake as the man in the overhead bunk jumped to the floor. All around him in the dimness men were rising, pulling on jumpsuits and boots, the scene lit by a lantern in the courtyard that shone through the room's open door. The air conditioner was off.

"Hurry, or you will not have time to eat," Vikram said, bending to his side, then quickly rising back out of sight. Sam wrenched himself upright and swung his feet onto the floor. He was groggy, ravenous, and thirsty all at once, and he was already worrying about how high he would have to climb on whatever site the bus took them to.

The workday had begun.

15

Waking up in the Dubai Central Jail wasn't how Anwar Sharaf had hoped to begin his day, especially when he opened his eyes to see a cockroach eating crumbs from the beard of the inmate in the opposite bunk.

Sharaf reached across the narrow aisle to flick at the big brown bug. It scurried away. With four other cellmates to choose from, the roach had plenty of options for breakfast.

Already Sharaf missed the comforts of nuzzling Amina's back, his usual harbor on a drowsy morning. He had grown accustomed to her welcoming shift and sigh as he glided against her, hand on her shoulder while his waist bumped her soft curves below. Except, of course, on mornings like the previous one, when she had still been angry from the night before.

Even with only one wife, Sharaf reflected, marriage was complicated. As he slumbered on the jailhouse bunk he recalled their early years, when she hadn't yet trusted his stated intention to never take a second wife. She'd been convinced that his monogamy was merely a phase, fueled by a desire for rebellion that would fade over time, and she had always said so at the end of every argument.

"When you are done pissing off your father, you will want another wife, and then another after that," she said. "I am sure of it."

But when three years passed after his father's death and Sharaf still made no move in that direction, Amina had at last believed him. She had even accepted the basis of his explanation—that she was more than enough woman for him, not only in bed, but also in the artful ways she ran their home.

Sharaf was wise enough to keep the real reason to himself: He simply never could have endured the extra aggravation, complication, and political finesse that would have been required to maintain peace and sanity in a household of multiple spouses. From early in boyhood he had known that when he sailed into middle age and beyond, he wanted to do so on a tidy ship with clean lines, an uncluttered deck, and all hands pulling together. And that would be possible only with one captain and one mate. The crew of children could mutiny all it wanted as long as the hands at the wheel remained steady.

Yet, here in jail, awakening among hundreds in shared misery, he realized in a moment of morning clarity that thirty-four years of marriage had produced something quite unexpected. The words of his long-uttered rationale had actually come to pass. Amina really *was* all the woman he needed, and he missed her terribly.

A loud fart from across the room jolted him further awake. Then the call to prayer sounded over the intercom. Even the muezzin sounded institutional, as blandly uninspired as the food. On the bunk just behind him, an inmate that Sharaf already despised sat up quickly and announced to the cell, "It is time for everyone to rise and wash so that we may pray, inshallah. Prayer is better than sleep, inshallah."

The man was apparently incapable of speaking without tacking the word "inshallah"—God willing—onto every phrase, a verbal tic of piety as maddening as a dripping faucet. Sharaf had noticed this tendency in other devout locals of late, as if invoking God's name at every turn might help ward off the growing erosion of morals by the incoming tide from the West. But he had never heard anyone as persistent as this fellow.

Sharaf wasn't the only person irritated by the repetition. The fellow with crumbs in his beard sat up and said loudly, "Can you please shut up, *inshallah*? Or will we be forced to pin you to the floor, *inshallah*, so that we can all drop our drawers and pee into your Godly little mouth, *inshallah*."

There were snickers from every bunk but one. Sharaf turned his face toward the wall to hide his smile. No sense making an enemy in a place where someone could attack you while you slept. Especially when the man in question wore a red stripe across his white tunic and down the legs of his drawstring pants. The color signified that he was a lifer, meaning he had probably committed a crime of unspeakable violence.

The markings were for the benefit of the guards. It made it easier for them to know who to keep an eye on. A yellow stripe meant a sentence of up to six years. Blue was for up to two. Green was for the lightest sentences of a few months. Sharaf's uniform was the only one with no stripes at all. Just plain white, as if everything about him was yet to be determined. Appropriate enough, he supposed, since he hadn't yet been charged with any crime, much less tried and sentenced. For all anyone knew, he wasn't even here.

"You speak blasphemies only to mock me," the offended fellow said, ironically forgetting to add "inshallah" now that he was angry. "That is even more sinful than uttering a blasphemy in complete sincerity. Did you know that your soul is in peril?"

"Oh, go fuck yourself. Inshallah."

After Sharaf's arrest the day before, his blindfolded ride in the windowless van had lasted for nearly an hour. His hips and shoulders were still bruised from all the bumping. When the blindfold finally came off, he was facing Lieutenant Assad in a dingy room of whitewashed cinder blocks, lit by a bare bulb that dangled from a frayed wire. The room, like the van, had no windows. He had never seen the place, meaning it wasn't at police headquarters. And he knew enough about the Interior Ministry's new offices to know that he wasn't there, either. They wouldn't have tolerated such dirty walls, or the gritty floor with its crumbling tiles, stinking of cat urine and spilled motor oil. Maybe they were in some sort of garage. Judging from the length of the ride in the van—assuming they hadn't driven him around in circles—he was either far to the east of the city, out past Jebel Ali along the road to Abu Dhabi, or well to the south, somewhere in the desert.

The latter possibility reminded him uncomfortably of the woman in blue sequins, but he quickly dismissed the idea that he might meet a similar fate, if only because it was probably what Assad wanted him to think. Sowing fear and doubt were among the best possible ways to lubricate an interrogation. Establishing trust was even more effective, of course, but Assad must have known that was out of the question.

Assad, dressed impeccably as always, waited more than a minute before speaking. Sharaf figured it was supposed to make him lose his cool. Instead he used the time to marshal his defenses.

"We know you're hiding him," Assad finally began. It was the first of many small tricks he would attempt. A quick denial would have been an admission of guilt.

"Hiding who?"

Sharaf wrinkled his brow in what he hoped was convincing bewilderment.

"Oh, come on. The American. You were the last officer seen with him."

"Ah, so that is why I'm here. You still haven't found him, and you need a scapegoat to explain his escape. There must be pressure from upstairs. Have they threatened a suspension? I don't envy you, Assad. Who is it you're trying to impress? Someone in the cabinet?"

"We searched your house. The guest bedroom had been slept in."

Meaning they hadn't found Keller. A pleasant surprise. He wondered how the young man had gotten away. Assad's choice of words also told him they hadn't found Keller's clothes, passport, and wallet out in the washtub in the shed. He supposed he might have overlooked those items as well, because who in their right mind would have placed such things in a tub of water, leaving them to soak? Dumb luck on his part, although he certainly had his reasons.

"My son Salim has been sleeping in the guest room. Would you like me to enumerate his embarrassing marital difficulties for you, or must you trouble the rest of my family with prying questions as well?"

Even if Assad checked the story with Salim, a contradiction wouldn't necessarily be damning. There wasn't an Emirati male alive who would admit to being kicked out of the marital bed—or, in Salim's case, both of them.

"Seriously, go and check. You'll even find some of Salim's clothes hanging in the guest room closet. Unless he has already moved back home, of course."

The search must have found the clothes—the very ones Sharaf had taken from Salim's house for Keller to borrow—with their non-American look and their local store labels, because now Assad didn't seem so sure of himself. It convinced Sharaf that the lieutenant had nothing more on that front.

"Our search also determined that the American had recently been in your daughter's bedroom. Ah, I see from your face that this is a surprise to you, and no doubt an unpleasant one."

Sharaf inwardly cursed himself for betraying his emotions. Had he raised an eyebrow? Drawn a sudden breath? Damn that Laleh. What had she been doing after hours? And God only knows what she would be doing in his absence, especially if Ali had recruited her help in keeping Keller out of harm's way. Or was Assad bluffing, by probing his best-known weak spot? Sharaf bit his tongue and stared back, trying to look as impassive as possible.

"Yes, he was in her bedroom," Assad continued. "Her computer had been used not long before we arrived. The screen saver had not even had time to come back on. Keller was familiar with your daughter, wasn't he? What is her name? Laleh, that's it. I've heard things about her. Her social carelessness, for lack of a better term."

Sharaf hoped the color wasn't rising in his cheeks. He wasn't sure who was upsetting him more—Assad, with this line of inquiry, or Laleh, for providing such a handy tool to lever his emotions.

"I'll wager you weren't very pleased by their behavior together. And under your own roof, no less. So save yourself a future ulcer, Sharaf, not to mention lots of embarrassing stories that would be needlessly spread around the city. Just tell me where you've stashed this hopelessly uncouth American. Leave him to my team, and this whole affair will be closed cleanly and quickly, with minimal embarrassment and upset to all those parties whom we least want to embarrass and upset. Even his own people wish for this outcome. His embassy is quite up in arms about his disappearance. Or were you not aware of that?"

Another little trap, which he quickly sidestepped.

"Can't a young lady's older brother visit his sister's room without some sort of rumor being attached? Especially an older brother who is currently not welcome in his own home? I'm sure Laleh wouldn't begrudge Salim a few minutes' use of her desktop computer, even if he didn't bother to ask her permission."

"Very well, Sharaf. Stick with that story for as long as you like."

Assad surprised him by not pressing the point. Nor did he follow up with brutality or deprivation. He didn't even shout. When Sharaf asked to use the bathroom, Assad let him, albeit with a police escort. And when Sharaf returned to the room a bottle of cool water and a clean glass were waiting on the floor by his chair. After a half hour more of desultory questioning, Assad ordered him back into the van, this time not bothering with the blindfold. When the panel doors opened an hour later, Sharaf had found himself here, out in the desert at the Dubai Central Jail in Al Aweer. The message seemed clear enough: This was where Sharaf would remain until he decided to talk.

Everything about his arrival at the prison had been unorthodox. Most inmates came on big buses, and were unloaded in an underground garage at the entrance to a holding cell in the intake area. The new arrivals then stood in various lines where their paperwork was processed while guards constantly shouted at them. Each of them got a strip search and a color-coded uniform.

Sharaf was processed upstairs with no waiting and no paperwork, but he did get a strip search. Some goon probed his buttocks with the cool smooth end of a varnished black baton. A guard then handed him the strange white uniform and a pair of slippers before marching him to his cell. On this day, at least, the guards seemed to be dividing the newcomers by nationality. The Indians and Pakistanis went one way, the Westerners another. All the fellow newbies in Sharaf's cell seemed to be Emiratis.

Sharaf had been freezing cold since his arrival, thanks to the prison's relentless air-conditioning. He had no underwear and no socks, and on his bunk there was only a top sheet and a thin wool blanket. The way they cranked cold air into the place you'd have thought it was a dairy. Cold or not, it was time to rise. He threw off the flimsy blanket, shivering as he swung his slippered feet onto the chilly floor.

The prison was practically new. As with much of Dubai's recent construction, no expense had been spared. The rulers had insisted on the best penitentiary money could buy, and at first glance they seemed to have gotten their wish. The bright lights, the stainless steel, the acres of whitewashed concrete, and the glassed-in security hub, with long cellblocks extending from it like the legs of an octopus, made the Central Jail seem like the very model of spotless efficiency.

Look closer, however, and the underlying shoddiness of quick-buck construction was already in evidence. Cracked linoleum. Crumbling concrete. Balky electrical locks that refused to open on demand. Often the intercom failed. When it did, a fellow patrolled the wings with a bullhorn to announce the next mealtime or prayer. The place seemed clean enough, but there was that cockroach Sharaf had spotted, plus a steady stream of ants. And any way you looked at it, it was still a prison, with the usual pecking order of such places—the bullying and the savvy at the top, the timid and the weak at the bottom. Fortunately none of Sharaf's cellmates seemed to know he was a cop. And on his one visit to the dining hall he had kept his head down, lest any old adversaries spot him.

He was relieved to have made it through the first night. The guards here had a reputation for roughness, and they supposedly earned it in the wee hours. Beatings and searches were said to be routine. Foreigners sometimes complained, but that usually resulted in a longer stay, and few pursued it. Sharaf supposed that if Lieutenant Assad could engineer his incarceration, then he might also be able to arrange for a few blows to the head after midnight.

"You are not praying!"

It was the pious asshole, standing to his left.

"Why are you not washing so that you may pray?"

Sharaf avoided the man's gaze and pushed through narrow saloon doors into the bathroom at the rear of the cell. He stood in line to wash his hands, and by the time he was done the fellow had zeroed in on another laggard. Sharaf dropped to his knees and asked God for strength and patience, and for any possible help in making sense of things. No answers were forthcoming, and he wasn't surprised. He wondered idly if there was a library here, and whether he would have access.

"So you are also a newcomer? I am Nabil."

It was the fellow with the beard. He looked to be in his mid-thirties. Unlike most Emirati men of that age, he had the weathered look of someone who still made a living with his hands.

"I am Anwar," Sharaf said. He decided not to mention the cockroach. "I think we're all new except for the one in the red stripe. Maybe they're trying to intimidate us."

"His name is Obaid. I made the mistake of talking to him last night at dinner. He told me he threw a prostitute out a window. She was a temptress, of course." Sharaf glanced uneasily toward Obaid, who was kneeling with his forehead pressed to the floor. "Don't worry. You could set off a bomb while he's praying and he wouldn't flinch."

The lock buzzed and the cell door opened. A guard appeared and immediately began shouting in Arabic with a street accent from Cairo.

"Form a line for breakfast! Form a line! Single file to breakfast!"

Everyone lined up but Obaid. The guard was about to shout again when he saw the red stripe. Or maybe he was acquainted with the fellow's violent brand of piety. Whatever the case, he waited until the praying was done before he shouted again.

"Form a line! Form a line for breakfast!"

They shuffled down the corridor with more than a hundred other men. A clock high on a wall said it was 5:30 a.m.

Breakfast was a smear of bean paste and bread, served on a partitioned tray of stainless steel, along with a cup of weak, sugary tea. Sharaf learned that Nabil was from Deira, just across the creek from where he had grown up. Nabil repaired boats, a dying art, especially among locals. The rest of his family owned shops in the souk, although most of their money came from real estate speculation. Nabil complained that his old neighborhood was now dominated by Indians and Palestinians. His father had decided years ago that he didn't want to move to some new villa out to the west, and now all the better locations had been taken.

Sharaf warily scanned the other tables. A face a few rows over stirred vague memories of a botched robbery followed by an awkward arrest, the man spread-eagled on a sidewalk in front of his family. Sharaf looked away. He was sure there would be more. Damned Assad. How long would this go on?

"Tell me why they brought you here," Nabil said. "Why don't you have a stripe?"

Sharaf gave the man a closer look. Could he be a plant or informant? He certainly didn't look the type. Even if he was, the questions were harmless enough.

"I don't know. A policeman wanted me to tell him something that I couldn't. The next thing I knew, he brought me here. No crime, just punishment."

"It is the same with me! They were looking for a family friend. I truly didn't know where he was, so I told them. So did my cousin, Khalifa. Now both of us are here, like you. Except that I have this green stripe."

"What charge?"

"Public profanity. I guess it was the first thing that popped into the policeman's head. So of course the judge, some ignoramus from Syria, accepted his word as if it were God's. He listened to me for five seconds and sentenced me to four months, just like that."

"And your cousin?"

"The same. They put him in another cellblock. So we wouldn't be able to keep our stories straight, they said. I don't even see him at meals, or in the yard."

"Sounds like they think one of you really knows something. Your cousin, maybe?"

Nabil was silent. Sharaf realized his remark had made him sound like a cop. Old habits were hard to break. But Nabil soon resumed his patter.

"Actually, I think Khalifa *does* know where our friend has gone. But that is his business. The missing fellow is from India, and his family runs Khalifa's shops in the Gold Souk. I guess he is worried they would all be deported, which would ruin him."

"Deported? The fellow must have done something pretty bad."

"The police didn't say. But he works at the Palace Hotel, so you can imagine. Even if it was only stealing, you know how the government is about crimes against tourists, especially wealthy ones."

"The Palace?" Sharaf tried to keep the eagerness out of his voice. "The hotel at the Royal Mirage?"

"Yes. He is some sort of doorman."

The one from Charlie Hatcher's datebook, probably, the fellow named Rajpal Patel. Up to now Sharaf had assumed the man was missing because Lieutenant Assad—or some Mafia ally—had spirited him away. Instead it sounded as if Patel had gotten wind of his pursuers and bolted. Much like Sam Keller, wherever he was.

Stumbling onto one of Patel's neighbors was enough of a coincidence to rekindle Sharaf's suspicion. Maybe Nabil *was* a plant.

But he knew from experience that no more than a dozen or so new inmates were admitted each day to the Central Jail, and of those only a handful were Emiratis. Furthermore, the new arrivals tended to be grouped by nationality. The timing of his arrest meant the odds had actually favored just this sort of meeting. The pity was that Nabil's cousin wasn't his cellmate, since Khalifa was apparently the one who knew the whereabouts of the doorman.

Sharaf wanted to ask more, but Nabil was already gossiping about two fellows he had spotted across the room. Apparently they were also from his neighborhood. They had been arrested for buggery several months earlier and were now sharing a table, all smiles.

"I wonder if they also share a bunk," Nabil said with a leer. "Now *that's* where they should put our friend Obaid. Give him an education in sin he would never forget."

Sharaf decided not to ask again about the doorman, lest he raise suspicion. There would be plenty of time later for that. Far too much of it, probably.

After breakfast the guards led them outdoors onto a thirty-by-thirty-meter slab of concrete—the so-called exercise yard. As if by rote, everyone began walking counterclockwise in a crowded parade around the perimeter. Sharaf joined in. Those who merely wanted to talk retreated to the corners. One or two Europeans tried to jog, weaving clumsily through the crowd. He wished it were warmer, but the sun wasn't yet high enough to reach over the walls.

Amina and Laleh must be up and about by now, he supposed. He wondered if they knew where he was, and, if so, if they would be allowed to visit. Did the Minister know? More to the point, was he doing anything about it?

The rest of the day was more of the same. Two more meals. Two more trips to the yard, with plenty of time for worrying as each hour passed without word from the outside. And the next day was virtually identical to his first. Maybe Assad was counting on the boredom to break him. Sharaf didn't have a single dirham, but fortunately the kindly Nabil let him borrow enough credit from his account at the prison store to buy socks and underwear. He also picked up an American paperback from the woeful offerings in the prison library, where most of the books in Arabic were religious texts and there was nothing in Russian. Nabil made no further mention of his cousin, and Obaid continued to punctuate every remark with "inshallah."

Not long after dinner on the second day, when everyone had been locked down for the night, Sharaf settled into his bunk to read. The book was the worst sort of pulp, a high-action thriller that described weapons more lovingly than people. But it must have passed the time, because the next thing Sharaf knew he was awakening in the dark to strange noises overhead.

The bunks in his cell were silent, but the ceiling trembled as if cattle were stampeding on the floor above. Thundering footsteps receded, only to be replaced by a frantic howl, and then another. The distant noise of barking dogs chilled him enough to want to pull the blanket tighter. Then came more footsteps, a hoot of laughter, and silence.

Someone in the next bunk moaned and rolled over in his sleep. The cell door buzzed ominously. The lock clicked loudly and the door swung free, as if opened by a spirit. Sharaf quickly pulled on his slippers and slid from the bunk. Already he heard the mutter of voices from the unseen end of the corridor, low and conspiratorial, people up to no good.

He leaned forward for a glance. The first thing he saw was the clock—4 a.m. Then he saw the guards, maybe fifteen of them. Or he supposed they were guards, because they weren't clad in their usual forest green. These fellows were dressed like burglars—black T-shirts, black pants, black balaclavas with holes for their mouths and eyes, and long black batons, like the one that had probed him during the strip search.

Sharaf pulled the door shut, but the lock wouldn't catch. The guards began to shout. The men in black were rousting prisoners from their beds in the cells at the far end.

"Wake up!" Sharaf said. "They're coming!"

"Shit!" Nabil said, rubbing sleep from his eyes. "I've heard about these raids. Not good."

Obaid must have, too. He was already kneeling on the floor, offering a plaintive prayer of fear and woe.

"Deliver us, inshallah, most holy God our protector!"

"Out of your beds and into the hall!" It was a guard. His mouth, visible through the hole in his balaclava, moved like a pink sea creature. The inmates complied, but for good measure he whacked each passing man on the rump with his baton.

"Faster!" he shouted. "Unless you want more of that. Faster!"

Only Obaid remained in the cell, still kneeling. In a spasm of rage, the guard elbowed quickly through the doorway and struck a savage blow to the back of his bowed head. It resounded almost musically, as if the baton had struck hollowed wood. Sharaf cringed. Obaid went silent, and slumped sideways, still in a kneeling position. Blood trickled from his nostrils.

"That's what the rest of you will get if you don't move when I say. I don't care what colors you're wearing. Down the hallway, now!"

The men stepped briskly. No one said a word. Every other cell was in similar chaos—cries of pain and anguish mixed with the thumps of batons, although none were as gruesome as the blow to Obaid's head.

Doors opened at the end of the corridor. Waiting on the other side was a receiving line of perhaps a dozen more men in black, except each held a German shepherd straining at a leash.

"Run!" their escort shouted. "Run past them if you can, all the way to the yard!"

A man ahead of Sharaf tripped. The nearest guard released his dog, which pounced as if someone had just flung a steak to the floor. The poor fellow shouted in terror and covered his head with his hands. Nabil, just ahead, nearly lost his balance as he slowed to dodge the fallen man. Sharaf grabbed his tunic in the nick of time and shoved him forward. A dog's snout flashed out from the right, teeth snapping. Sharaf veered left and ran hard, finally reaching the far door just behind Nabil. They spilled into the yard, nearly collapsing onto the others who had already reached safety. No one had turned on the outdoor lighting, and it was eerily dark beneath the pale glow of a half-moon. From cellblocks all over the prison you could hear shouts and screams, and lots of barking. Sharaf's tunic was soaked with sweat, and he was heaving for breath.

"My cousin, Khalifa!" he heard Nabil say. "There he is!"

Indeed, nearly every cellblock on their side of the prison was emptying into the yard. The space was filling rapidly. There must have already been two hundred men there, and more were coming every second from doors at both ends. Some were bleeding. Others were doubled over in pain. No guards seemed to be among them. Looking back through a large window on the side, Sharaf saw several of the prison's ranking officers in khaki uniforms with gaudy stripes and epaulets. They were laughing uproariously and taking flash photos with their cell phones.

When Sharaf turned back around, Nabil had disappeared. Sharaf finally spotted him in a far corner chatting rapidly with a man who must be Khalifa. As shaken as he was, Sharaf realized this might be his one chance to ask about the doorman Patel. The problem was that he still needed to play it cool, even though he was buzzing with adrenaline, and the cousin would be as well.

He shoved his way through the crowd. Fortunately Nabil saw him coming.

"There he is!" Nabil said loudly, pointing at Sharaf. The earlier stunned silence of most of the prisoners had given way to relieved yammering and shouting, a collective release of emotions. "This is the fellow Anwar I was telling you about. He's here for the same reason, except they didn't even bother to charge him. Anwar, this is my cousin, Khalifa."

Figuring time was limited, Sharaf got to the point.

"I think I know the policeman who is looking for your friend, Rajpal Patel," Sharaf said. "I also believe I know why they are after him. And I know this because I am a policeman myself. If you will tell me where to find him, then I may even be able to help him, if and when I get out of here. My name is Sharaf, Anwar Sharaf, and I give you my word as an honorable man."

Sharaf knew immediately he had miscalculated. Khalifa backed away and gave Nabil a puzzled look.

"Why have you told him about Rajpal?"

Nabil's answer was swallowed by the cries of the mob. Guards were pouring in from both doors, some with dogs, others with raised batons. The men howled and shoved toward the center of the yard, raising their hands to their heads as the guards threshed their way through as if harvesting crops.

Sharaf held his ground as the guards moved closer. Nabil and his cousin did the same. One reared up a few feet away, raising his baton and then swinging it down like a saber toward Sharaf's right shoulder. He was just able to deflect the baton with his right hand, knuckles smarting as the wood struck them in a glancing blow. He staggered back into Nabil and the second blow came too fast to avoid, smashing into his collarbone. As he lost his balance the baton then struck his head, a thump near the hairline that sent him to his knees as Nabil cried out in protest.

The last thing Sharaf felt was a boot pressing into his back as he collapsed forward, and then a ringing blow to the back of his head, which reverberated like a bell through every bone in his body.

After that, nothing. Nothing at all.

16

Just as Nanette expected, Sam Keller had sent up a flare. As soon as she had all the details, the hunt would begin in earnest. It was 10:12 p.m. in Dubai, and Gary Grimshaw had just phoned from Manhattan with the news.

"Damned if you weren't right," Gary said. "He went looking for help, just like you said."

Nanette wasn't interested in compliments. She wanted information, and right away.

"Who did he call?"

"One of my people. Stu Plevy, a coworker. Bit of a weasel, but I've gotta hand it to him, he reported it first thing this morning. Played it right by the book."

"This *morning*? It's what, two in the afternoon there now?"

"Well, I had to clear everything with my division head. And by the time he was back in pocket I was chairing a lunch meeting, so—"

"So I've already lost nearly six hours. And I'm betting from the timing of Plevy's report that he took the call at home the night before. Correct?"

"Well, yeah. But—"

"Didn't you give your department instructions for immediate notification?"

"I told you, he reported it first thing in the morning. How much more immediate do you want?"

Idiots. Like half the people she was working with here in Dubai. In Nanette's experience, both in government and in the corporate world, you could easily fire about half the workforce and maintain the same level of productivity. If it wasn't laziness, it was sheer stupidity, and Gary Grimshaw was amply supplied with both.

"Never mind. What time did Plevy take the call?"

"Uh, let's see . . ." Nanette bit her lower lip as Gary shuffled papers. "Around two in the morning."

"So 10 a.m. my time, meaning twelve hours ago. Christ, Gary, that's half a day!"

"Sorry."

"Did he leave a number, or any hint of a location?"

"No."

Of course not. All the stupid ones were on her side.

"What did Plevy tell him?"

"Nothing. Just that everyone had heard he'd fucked up. He said Keller asked for help, but Plevy didn't give him any."

"Keller was probably angling for a way to access the system. Did Plevy say anything about a password?"

"He said Keller hung up as soon as it was clear Plevy wasn't going to help. Like I said, he played it by the book. I was very clear on that with all my people."

"Here's what I want you to do."

She thought fast, already assembling a checklist in her head. Fortunately she hadn't swallowed a drop of alcohol since the moment she'd heard Keller was missing, and this was the very reason why—so her head would be clear when it was time to act. Two hours ago she had worked out on the treadmill in the Shangri-La's fitness center, and now she was at peak energy following a shower and a room service salad with iced herbal tea. Add a fresh pot of coffee and she would be energized until 3 a.m. if necessary. By then all the pieces would be in place for what she wanted to accomplish next. She had no doubt that Keller would eventually be run to ground. Preferably sooner rather than later.

"First, change all of our system access codes and passwords. Company-wide, all branches and regions. Nelson in tech support will know what to do. Just tell him the order came directly from me. Do it as soon as we hang up, understand?"

"Sure."

"Scratch that. I'll call him myself."

"It's okay. I can—"

"Second, cut off all access for this Plevy fellow, effective immediately."

"But he blew the whistle."

"You said yourself he's a bit of a weasel. We have no idea what actually passed between them. It's the one door Keller has tried, so we may as well nail it shut."

"Plevy won't be able to do his job without access."

"Then suspend him until this matter is concluded."

"Without *pay*?"

"It's your budget, Gary. Make an executive decision. Or do you need a meeting first?"

Another whistle-blower dumped on, which was regrettable. But she'd certainly experienced that kind of backlash herself more than a few times. It was a vital part of her education on the way up the food chain. No good deed went unpunished, so why keep doing them?

She telephoned Nelson in tech support, reaching him immediately, as she had known she would. His two predecessors had discovered that you made yourself available to Nanette Weaver at all hours or you wound up in the unemployment line.

First she explained the immediate need for everyone to be issued new passwords, except, of course, Plevy.

"Consider it done," Nelson replied, his mouth full of something wet and sloppy.

She appreciated Nelson, even though he never washed his hair and always stared at her legs. Not only did he do as he was told, but he also occasionally suggested tweaks and improvements, and he never second-guessed.

"Then I want some sort of lock or trap set up to capture the particulars of any attempt to log on to our internal system via any server in the UAE, even if the attempt is made with an incorrect password. Can you arrange that?"

"No problem."

"How soon?"

"One hour, two at the most."

Meaning that by midnight, Sam Keller would have no way in, yet would still snag his trousers in the doorway. And once that happened, they would have a fix on his approximate location within a few hours, solving the last of her potential problems now that the renegade policeman Sharaf had been neutralized. Assad, like Gary, had his faults, but he had finally bought her idea that they were badly underestimating the frumpy Sharaf.

Nanette sighed in relief after hanging up. She wouldn't need coffee, after all, and could instead focus on getting a full night's rest. The idea of a nightcap was tempting, but she decided against it, knowing she would regret it if the phone rang a few hours later with news of a fresh emergency, or another signal from Keller.

In the morning she would send her assistant, Stanley Woodard, home on the first available flight. Time to clear the decks for action, and he would only be in the way. Because soon enough it would be time for battle, and to judge from all the recent complications, she was now certain that victory would be possible only by leaving no survivors. By the close of business on Monday the 14th, no opponents would remain standing.

Now that was a good thought to sleep on, even without a drink to celebrate.

17

By his second day on the job, Sam Keller could finally step to the edge of the thirty-first floor—no guardrail, no safety harness—without going weak in the knees, although his blood still rushed to his fingertips. Toward midmorning he even dared a glance at the ground. Blue helmets moved to and fro like jittery pixels on a video display. It made him dizzy, so he quickly looked away.

Sam hadn't experienced these sensations since he was eleven, when he got stuck on the Swamp Fox roller coaster in Myrtle Beach, S.C., during a power failure that stranded him at the top for four hours. Rising fumes of corn dogs and cotton candy had turned a mild case of vertigo into a queasy ordeal that lasted past midnight. He remembered the rapt upward stares of the people below, openmouthed with anticipation, as if awaiting the next *Hindenburg* disaster. Here, at least, everyone was too busy to pay attention to his misery, so he went about his duties in silence, still drained and disoriented from the chain of events that had led him to this edge of existence.

The job site was in the Marina district, an entire cityscape rising from nothing. From his lofty vantage point Sam counted nearly two hundred high-rises under construction, laid out along canals and channels that snaked from a huge man-made inlet of the Persian Gulf. Cranes clung parasitically to the sides of buildings and were perched atop others. The newly paved streets were quiet, except for the occasional truck hauling in more supplies.

Out along the beach, a recently opened hotel held the area's only current overnight inhabitants, tourists who seemed bemused to be vacationing at a construction site. One had gaped at Sam's white face when he stepped off the bus with the other workers, pointing in amazement as if he'd spotted an albino in a stampede of wildebeests. But none of the man's friends had seemed to notice. It was just like Ali had said. To the rest of Dubai, Sam was now invisible.

He had followed the long stream of men in dust masks and helmets to their work site several blocks away, where he boarded a steel-cage elevator that clanked its way up the side of the skeletal building. The view, while disconcerting, was spectacular. Ocean and sky. Desert and golf courses. And everywhere, more construction in vast housing developments and sprawling business parks. Yellow cranes bloomed like flowers in the wake of a sudden rain.

Where were the millions of people who would live and work here? Sam had no idea, although signs along the approaching roadway still boasted of quick sales—SOLD OUT IN 6 HOURS! SOLD OUT IN 4 HOURS! SOLD OUT IN AN HOUR! or, his favorite, SOLD OUT AT PRE-LAUNCH! It was the giddiness of a pyramid scheme nearing its pinnacle. And up here, where you got a better feel for the scale, he sensed an unsteadiness at the base, a Jell-O quiver beneath the weight of high-yield expectations. Or maybe he was just trembling from his fear of heights.

He was sore, blistered, and sunburned from his first day of labor. Up on the thirty-first floor, any exposed skin was soon burned and chapped from sunlight and the gritty wind. His first job was carrying hods of concrete. But Sam couldn't keep pace with his stronger and more experienced coworkers, so today the foreman had assigned him to operate a freight elevator to haul up blocks and mortar from a landing five stories below. Workers down there filled the platform, then Sam raised it to stops on the intervening floors.

Like everything else at the job site, the elevator's diesel motor and cable pulley were jerry-rigged, braced by a framework of scaffolding. Sam had to look down the side of the building to make sure the platform stopped at the right levels, which meant he had to lean out into thin air. He crooked his left arm around the scaffolding for support while operating a lever with his right hand. Not the greatest feeling, but he soon got the hang of it, and was no longer convinced he was about to fall to his death. He even grew accustomed to the gusting desert wind, which made everything groan and wobble. Probably the very sort of blast that had killed Ramesh's friend, Sanjay.

Fortunately, the elevator job kept Sam far removed from Ramesh. But Vikram had told him of new trouble on that front. Ramesh had apparently convinced other workers from his home village of Sam's guilt in Sanjay's demise. This clique was now referring to Sam as the white *jambuka*, or jackal, an animal that feasted on the dead. For today at least, the foreman had assigned Ramesh and his pals to jobs on lower levels.

It was soon time for lunch. There was a jug of water handy, so Sam decided to eat right there. Everyone else, Vikram included, took their food to ground level. Some of the men liked to walk out to the beach in hopes of spotting Western women in bikinis. It was another reason the photography store sold so many disposable cameras. In the barracks Sam had seen revealing snapshots taped to walls and pinned to over-head bunks—fantasy photos that allowed the men to imagine the pleasures of an Angelika from Düsseldorf, an Astrid from Stockholm.

He ate quickly, enjoying the solitude while the sweat cooled on his back. He now felt comfortable enough to swing his feet off the side of the ledge. Looking toward the coast, he saw the distant banners of the government development firms—Nakheel, Emaar, and Tameer—flag after flag snapping in the breeze. Nakheel's were the last ones you saw before exiting into the Marina district. From his seat on the bus the company slogan had seemed like a taunt: NAKHEEL: WHERE VISION INSPIRES HUMANITY.

Turning east he saw the chockablock shimmer of Media City. He tried without success to pick out Laleh's building. Thinking back on the day in her office, he realized what a privilege it had been to listen in on her comings and goings as a boss, a planner, a thinker. Even her parents didn't have that kind of access to the young woman she had become, and Sam believed it had given him an edge, a secret knowl-edge that might help bridge the gap between their backgrounds. She had hinted as much herself, telling him with a complicit smile, "Don't ever mention a word about all this to my father." By "all this" it was clear she meant not just her workplace habits or manner of dress, but also her air of relative freedom in a world that was more like Sam's than the one her parents knew.

He wondered if she had yet replied to his e-mail message from the night before. He had sent it by paying a few dirhams to use the Internet on the camera store's desktop computer. The store's dial-up modem was maddeningly slow, but it had also allowed him to do some further online sleuthing.

Two messages from Plevy had been waiting on his Gmail account.

"See first 2 attachments," the first one said. "N has been quite the traveler. Also note third one. You have officially attained pariah status."

Sam frowned and clicked his way through the items. The first was the most recent audit of Nanette Weaver. The second was a compilation of her three most recent quarterly reports. Few things leaped out except, as Plevy had hinted, her extensive travels—most notably several trips to Dubai plus another to her old diplomatic stomping grounds in Moscow. He filed away the dates for future reference.

One oddity was a commendation for a project she had worked on nearly a year ago with none other than Charlie Hatcher, although further details revealed it to be nothing more than an effort to streamline and secure shipping routes from the Far East.

Plevy's third attachment was a company memo announcing that auditor Samuel Keller had gone AWOL in Dubai following "a criminal complaint alleging an attempted sexual assault on a coworker," which it said was part of "a pattern of reckless personal conduct that may have led to the death of a valued associate, Charles Hatcher."

Outrageous, but the fuse for an explosion refused to light. Too damp from weariness and despair. Sam was in exile in a prison of dust and sewage, stranded among thousands of overworked men of other nations and tongues.

"Shit!" he shouted, more in despair than in fury. His curse drew the attention of the Punjabi shopkeeper, who checked his watch and exclaimed, "Your time is run out! Ten more dirhams, or vacate the premises!"

Sam was about to sign off when he remembered he hadn't opened Plevy's second e-mail, which had arrived only a few hours later. It was a shock.

"What did you do, asshole? I'm suspended w/o pay, so fuck off! You better hope N finds you first."

So much for a lifeline. It probably also meant Ansen's password was no longer operable. He thought about trying it, but his instincts told him to lay low for now.

"Ten dirhams!" the shopkeeper shouted. "Ten dirhams or you must go now!"

It was then that Sam thought of Laleh, the only person he could still expect any sympathy from. So, he paid another ten dirhams from his precious supply, pulled out her business card for her e-mail address, and told her about his first day on the job. He kept the location vague, figuring that by now someone might be monitoring his Gmail account. He probably shouldn't have sent the message at all, but he told himself he was doing it because Laleh was a more reliable link to Ali than Zafar. The real reason was that he felt better just typing her name. He imagined her reading the message in her bedroom, with the teen queen posters at one end and the all-business stuff at her desk. He smiled and clicked SEND. Then the owner chased him out of the shop.

Sam was finishing lunch when he heard the lurch of the personnel elevator. A bit surprising for anyone to be returning this soon. Glancing toward the ground, he saw that no blue helmets were yet streaming back to the building. Maybe Vikram had come to keep him company. He heard the door clank shut and looked over his shoulder to see Ramesh briskly moving toward him, fists clenched.

Sam carefully swung his legs off the ledge and stood slowly, all too aware of being within inches of a four-hundred-foot drop. He sidled left and crooked an arm around the scaffolding of the freight elevator.

Ramesh stopped about ten feet away, breathing fast and watching him carefully, as if planning his next move. A gritty burst of wind gusted in from the desert, and the framework swayed and groaned. Sweat beaded down Sam's back like the stroke of a fingernail. Ramesh broke into a grin and stepped closer. He was huge. If he got a firm hold, it would be only a matter of seconds before either Sam lost his grip or the shaky framework collapsed, so Sam let go and moved quickly to his right, staying on the balls of his feet in a slight crouch. The vague memory of a basketball coach telling him to slide fast and stay low flashed across his mind. Ramesh would reach him in another two steps.

Sam faked left, then dodged right as Ramesh lunged toward him. By the time the big man had recovered, Sam was on safer footing, away from the precipice. If he could beat Ramesh to the other elevator, he might be able to jump aboard and throw the switch. But Ramesh blocked his path and lunged again. He was agile for his size, and got a hand on a sleeve before Sam was able to twist free. They were both panting now. The wind gusted again, the grit stinging Sam's eyes.

Ramesh, still grinning, now straightened to full height, arms akimbo. Then he muttered, "Jambuka"—jackal—just as a clanking sound announced that the personnel elevator was in motion, retreating from the thirty-first floor. Someone must have summoned it from below, cutting off Sam's only escape route. Ramesh now knew he had mere minutes before others would be joining them. His grin disappeared and he lowered into a crouch, a wrestler ready to spring. Looking around him, he grabbed something from the floor—a crowbar, which he raised like a bludgeon.

He faked left, and before Sam could recover, Ramesh swung the crowbar in a wild arc. Sam raised an arm to fend off the blow as the hooked steel end tore through his jumpsuit and raked the meat of his upper arm, throwing him off balance. Ramesh's charge took them both down in a violent tackle. The big man locked his arms around Sam's knees as the crowbar clanged to the concrete.

Sam kicked for all he was worth. A boot heel connected with Ramesh's chin, and there was a sharp *clack* like a dog snapping its teeth. Ramesh instinctively grabbed for his chin and Sam rolled free. Enraged, the big man bellowed as he sprang back to his feet. Sam ran toward the middle of the building. He then remembered belatedly that at the center there was an empty shaft for the elevators that had yet to be installed. He skidded to a halt, only managing to turn halfway before Ramesh plowed into him. They fell in a heap, the wind knocked out of Sam as Ramesh's shoulder slammed his chest to the concrete slab. He heard the clank of the personnel elevator as Ramesh tightened his grip and rolled them over—once, then twice, a bear hug with a crushing weight against Sam's chest and spine. He saw only a blur of concrete and of sky. They were headed for the empty shaft, and Ramesh seemed determined to take them both over the edge.

Sam flailed his arms, clutching for anything that might slow their progress. He felt sudden emptiness beneath his shoulders, then a sickening moment of weightlessness as excited shouts called out from behind. Someone grabbed his boots just as his upper body tumbled downward. His legs were hinged at the knees, with the dangling Ramesh still clinging to his torso, a millstone.

They were upside down now, the blood rushing to his head as Ramesh grunted and cried out, as if unable to comprehend why they weren't falling free. Sam saw his helmet tumbling toward the ground like a rock down a well, then heard its faint clatter far below. Several people now held tightly to his ankles and boots on the floor above, although his legs were still bent at the knees, which ached as if at any moment they might come loose under the load of Ramesh, who was now screaming in rage.

Sam felt a steel rod rake his chest. Someone had taken a rebar and was poking from above, trying to pry apart the entwined bodies. Ramesh and he were like a pair of doomed acrobats, suspended from the precipice. Ramesh bellowed and flailed for the rebar with his right hand, but in gripping it his left hand slipped from Sam's waist. Whoever was holding the rebar up above must have then let go, and Ramesh fell free with a great roar. Sam watched him drop like a giant from a beanstalk, the man still crying out in anger all the way to the bottom. The sound of his impact was like that of a huge, heavy sack, punctuated by the pop of his skull.

Sam looked upward, but all the faces gathered at the rim of the shaft were gazing past him to the bottom. Thank God no one had let go in all the excitement. They hauled him back up to the concrete floor.

Other workers were rushing forward, mouths open, just like all those people in Myrtle Beach when he was eleven. Except this time they indeed had a disaster on their hands, and you could see the horror in their eyes.

Vikram was one of the men with a death grip around his ankles.

"Come," Vikram said. "You must come away from here. Some of his friends may still be around. We must take you to the ground. The slow way, my friend. By elevator."

He stood on quivering legs, and after a few steps he stopped and heaved up his lunch onto the pale gray floor, a hot, chunky stream that stank of bile and fear. Vikram gently guided him to the elevator. Sam couldn't bear to look out the side until they had reached the bottom. Nor did he look off to his right, where a handful of men with large flat shovels were wordlessly collecting what remained of Ramesh.

Someone with a depleted first-aid kit hastily cleaned and bandaged the slash across his arm. The foreman glanced at the torn sleeve and reminded Sam that he would have to pay if he wanted a new uniform.

Back at the camp that night a friend of Vikram's undid the bandage and applied a wet cotton rag with a warm poultice of salt, turmeric, and lemon juice. Vikram assured him that this was the best possible remedy. The cut was painful but superficial.

"You should not shower tonight," Vikram added.

"To keep the bandage dry?"

Vikram shook his head.

"Ramesh's friends. They will be waiting. To their minds you have now killed two of them. Your legend as the white jackal will only grow. You should talk to Zafar. Perhaps he can move you to another camp."

But Zafar was not in the blockhouse. Apparently he was out for the entire evening, and the sullen Charbak, whose English wasn't good to begin with, didn't seem the slightest bit concerned when Sam explained his situation.

"It is for Zafar to decide," he said quietly, turning the page of a newspaper.

Sam washed up as well as he could at the outdoor spigot, escorted by several men from his room, who had taken up his cause after seeing firsthand the madness of Ramesh. Throughout it he was aware of a huddle of large fellows eyeing him from the entrance to the showers.

"This cannot continue," Vikram muttered.

"I need to send a message after dinner," Sam said. "Maybe some of you could walk with me to the camera store so I can use the Internet."

He pooled his food with Vikram and two other men, and they shared a dinner of fish and okra, stir-fried in a large skillet. One of the others added some spices. It was his best meal in days.

"Let us go now to the camera store," Vikram said. "We should not return until just before lights-out."

There were no further messages from Plevy—not that Sam expected any—but he was thrilled to find a reply from Laleh, sweet in its concern. It made him vaguely hopeful, although for exactly what he couldn't have said. He answered by briefly describing the day's events and his current predicament.

"Please tell Ali," he wrote, "Zafar is no help."

He wondered if Nanette had posted any new alerts. Ansen's password offered the only possibility of finding out, but he wasn't at all surprised by the response.

Access denied. Password invalid.

What *was* surprising was that he was then unable to exit the page. Either the dial-up connection was getting even slower or something else was happening. He tried various escapes, but nothing worked.

Only a reboot would do the trick, and even that seemed slow in coming. He had to press the OFF button for several seconds before the machine finally gasped and the screen went blank. This, of course, sent the shopkeeper into a rage.

"No turn off! No turn off! You pay ten dirhams, please, for losing connection."

He paid it, scowling, and left the store, but couldn't shake the sense that he'd blundered. And even with his impromptu bodyguards, he felt like a marked man.

They got to the room with only a few minutes to spare. All was quiet. To no one's surprise except Sam's, Ramesh's empty bed had already been filled by a replacement worker, who was tucking in the corners on a fresh set of sheets. Maybe the angry Bengalis would come up with a conspiracy theory for him as well.

Everyone settled in for the night. Vikram nodded reassuringly from his bunk. Then the lights went out. Sam lay awake for a while, startled by every noise and creak. He kept expecting the door to fly open, and Ramesh's friends to barge in with belts and kitchen knives, or whatever else they used around here. But he was so exhausted that he soon gave way to the rhythms of the night, and was sleeping soundly. Not even the mice and the bugs that scampered across his legs in the dark could rouse him.

He came awake only when a strong hand clamped firmly and moistly onto his mouth. He kicked out with both legs, and struggled to raise himself, or cry out, but to no avail. From a rush of night air he knew that someone had opened the door, and in the distance he heard the sound of police sirens, moving closer. Some sort of scuffle was in progress around him, and there were angry voices. He kicked again in an absolute panic, and wrenched a hand free.

Then a rag came down across his nostrils, smelling strongly yet sweetly of chemicals, and within seconds he was fading from consciousness just as more hands were lifting him into the air. Next came a dreamlike sensation of falling, the air so thick that it arrested the speed of his plunge. The concrete floors of the building in the Marina area flashed past him, one by one. He tried to grab at them, but the fumes kept pushing him downward, with a host of shadows in pursuit.

His last thought was to wonder if he would ever reach the bottom.

18

The first thing Sharaf saw was the Minister, bending over his face to place a cool washcloth against the lump on his forehead. It stung. Sharaf winced.

"You're conscious!"

"Where is everyone? What are you doing at the prison?"

"You're at my villa, free and safe. For now, anyway."

Sharaf tried to sit up but his head swam so he lay back on the pillow.

"I should phone the doctor, fetch him back here," the Minister said. "He predicted you might soon be up and about. He advised that you stay put for a while."

"How long have I been out?"

"Almost five hours." He checked his watch. "Yes, five."

The Minister wore an elegant and spotless *kandoura*. The room was like something in a top-notch hotel. Sharaf had never been in the man's house—in fact, their only face-to-face meeting had occurred in an anteroom of Zabeel Palace—but he had seen it from the outside. Just about everyone in Dubai had, either in person or in a photograph. The huge, modernistic three-story villa, with its curved walls of stone and reflecting glass, stood out even among the other ostentatious homes in Jumeirah's wealthiest corner.

Sharaf realized he was no longer wearing his prison garb. Someone had dressed him in a freshly laundered *kandoura*. The sheets were soft, lightly scented. He could easily have shut his eyes and slept all day, but too many questions were already on the prowl, and still more were lining up to join them as his life slowly regained focus.

"There was a riot," he said, remembering. "The guards went crazy. I found a potential witness in there."

"A riot? The warden only mentioned a small fight. You and some lifer with a red stripe."

"The warden's lying. He's covering for his thugs."

Sharaf gently removed the damp cloth from his forehead, then touched the tender lump at his hairline. It felt like a coconut was trying to force its way out of his skull. He again tried to sit up, and this time was able to prop against the headboard with minimal dizziness, although the lump throbbed violently.

"Easy, Sharaf. Easy."

"Why did you bring me here?"

The Minister shrugged.

"You know how our hospitals are. The best that money can buy, but somehow never quite good enough when something bad happens. Why else would the royal family always seek treatment overseas anytime one of them sneezes?"

"The Iranian hospital isn't so bad."

"It's first-rate. But considering some of the enemies you've made recently, well, I couldn't be sure of your safety."

"Ah, yes. Thank you."

"You see? Your powers of judgment are still clouded. My personal physician predicted it. He is a German, trained in Boston, and he advises you to go slow for a while. I agree, of course. But I also have some advice."

"And what would that be?"

"You must tell me where the American is. Assad is a lying fox, but I believe he knows something that you've been hiding from me."

Sharaf had no way of knowing what the Minister might have heard or learned while he was unconscious, but as the fog continued to lift he tried to gauge what he might say without tripping himself up. Evasiveness was one approach, and his injury offered possible cover.

"What do you mean, sir? You're confusing me."

"Well, obviously no one has found him yet. But I'm guessing you have known all along where he is."

"Look me in the eye, sir, because I am going to tell you the absolute truth." To his surprise, the Minister actually leaned forward over the bed, gazing intently. "I haven't the faintest idea where Mr. Keller might be. For all I know he might even have left the country."

The beauty of it was that Sharaf hadn't had to lie, not technically, which made his deception all the more convincing. He *didn't* know where Keller was, not at the moment. The Minister eyed him a few seconds longer, then pronounced his judgment.

"I believe you. Up to now, I'll admit, I wasn't so sure. But just now, looking you in the eye, man to man, I am convinced you are being honest with me. But where do you think he has gone? Surely you must have an opinion?"

"Honestly?"

"Of course."

"I believe he is dead. Or will be soon. Either by the hand of his own people, or Assad's."

"And where does that leave your case?"

"It complicates it, of course. That would mean five murders so far, counting the woman in the desert and the two Russian thugs. And I still don't know what the rest of them are up to."

Unfortunately, Sharaf believed his dire assessment of Keller's prospects might actually be true. Unless the young man had managed to cross the border or put to sea during the past few days, his hopes for survival were slim. It saddened him, because he liked the fellow. But perhaps Ali had been able to pull something together.

Thinking of Ali reminded Sharaf of all the work he needed to do—phone calls, contacts, follow-ups. Adding to his anxiety was the date Charlie Hatcher had scribbled into his black book, underlined twice—"Monday, 4/14!" It had taken on the feel of a deadline, a point of no return, and now it was Saturday the 12th. Only two days left.

A rough list of tasks began taking shape in his head, and Sharaf experienced a palpable sensation of his mind snapping back into place, like a dislocated shoulder into its socket. His head seemed to be clearing by the second. Or so he thought until he tried to get out of bed. Immediately wobbly, he sat on the edge while he waited for the skewed room to go level.

"Sharaf, please!"

The Minister reached out to steady him, although his touch was tentative, uncertain. You could sense he dreaded the idea of having to pick Sharaf up off the floor. As generous as the man had been so far, he obviously drew the line at physical contact. Maybe he saw Sharaf's ilk—a cop on a beat, when you got down to it—as beneath him. A sub-caste of manual laborer, practically untouchable. Or maybe Sharaf was just dizzy.

He collected his wits as best he could and turned his attention to immediate priorities. First he would call Amina and Laleh. Then Ali, for a discreet update on Keller, provided one was available.

"I need to use your phone."

"Your own phone is here." He gestured toward the nightstand. "The prison gave me your belongings. The police said your car has been returned to your home."

Sharaf's phone was in a tidy pile along with his keys and wallet. His police uniform, which he had been wearing when he was arrested at the Seaman's Majlis, was folded neatly on a console table at the foot of the bed. His boots were on the floor below.

He reached slowly for the phone, trying not to set off a new round of spinning. In doing so he realized that a folded sheet of paper was poking from the edge of his wallet. Someone had stuffed it in there with his cash. His curiosity got the best of him, and he took it out.

It was a handwritten note. He read it while the Minister watched with apparent interest.

"What is it, Sharaf?"

"A grocery list, from Amina. I'd forgotten it was there."

He waved it quickly so the Minister wouldn't see the writing, then folded it away before the lie became apparent. It was actually an address, scribbled in pencil. A location in Deira, just across the creek from where he had grown up. Below it was a message: "After we saw what happened to you, Khalifa and I decided you must be telling the truth. Good luck, inshallah. Nabil."

"Inshallah" was underlined twice, a parting joke from Nabil, who must have bribed a guard to put the note with his belongings. Now he knew where to find the elusive Rajpal Patel, assuming Assad hadn't beaten him to it.

"A grocery list?" the Minister said. "Are you sure that's all it was?"

"Unless you know some other coded meaning for bananas, bread, and coffee."

The Minister seemed on the verge of questioning him further when

Sharaf's cell phone bounded to the rescue, ringing loudly. Sharaf snatched it up so quickly that his head spun again. He paused to let things drop back into place before answering.

"Sharaf."

"You're up!"

It was Ali. Unfortunately the Minister didn't seem inclined to leave the room anytime soon. Sharaf would have to guard his words, not an easy task in his current state of mind.

"Yes. I am sitting here with the Minister."

"I see. But my news can't wait. I'm afraid something has happened to Keller."

"What, exactly?" Sharaf glanced at the Minister. He pointed at the phone and mouthed the name, "Ali al-Futtaim," then smiled quickly, as if to say everything was just fine. The Minister nodded, but didn't budge.

"Are you at liberty to talk about this now, Sharaf?"

"Maybe you'd better come and get me. I am at the Minister's house."

"Twenty minutes."

"Excellent."

He hung up, wondering what could have happened. Ali hadn't sounded happy.

"Surely you're not leaving?" the Minister said. "Not in your condition. It is imperative that my doctor must approve. He can be here in thirty minutes."

"I'll be gone in twenty." Sharaf reached for his clothes. He wasn't going to change back into uniform, not for the work he had in mind, but he would take it with him. "Have him phone me. You've got my number."

"Look at you, you're unsteady. It's too soon. Lie back down."

The Minister held out his hands, as if to insist, but he didn't touch Sharaf.

"Really, sir. I'm fine."

"Then in that case I suppose you're strong enough for new marching orders."

"New?"

" 'Amended' is probably a better word. Things have changed."

"Changed how? I thought you had backing from the palace?"

"I do." The Minister seemed mildly affronted that Sharaf had even questioned his clout. "But certain, well, *pressures* are being applied. From other quarters that can't be ignored. The American embassy, for one."

"What sort of pressures?"

"I want you to hold off on things for a while. At least until the whereabouts of this Keller fellow are established. You look awful, you know. Let me get you a glass of water."

The water helped. So did a wedge of bread smothered with honey. Maybe all Sharaf needed was food. Whatever the case, he was steadier by the time Ali's black Mercedes pulled up the curving stone drive, weaving among four liveried servants who were at work on the Minister's lawn.

"I still say you should wait here for my doctor."

"Look at it this way, Minister. The sooner I'm back at work, the sooner we'll find out something about the missing American, so that I can resume my investigation. And I thank you. You have been most generous and compassionate."

"It was the least I could offer, since you are working at my behest."

"I'm grateful you still see it that way. And as long as that's the case, could I ask one additional small favor?"

The Minister didn't look thrilled, but he didn't say no.

"There was an Emirati in my cell, a fellow named Nabil. He and his cousin Khalifa were jailed unjustly. Lieutenant Assad's doing, I suspect, so perhaps you could intervene on their behalf. Also, if you can quietly ensure that someone seizes the cellblock video surveillance recordings from last night, then I'm certain you and the rest of the royal cabinet will find the contents quite revealing. Let's just say that the prison is not being run in a manner worthy of Sheikh Mohammed. And with a few nimble moves you, not the ministers of justice or of interior, will be able to claim the privilege of being the one who set things aright."

This prospect seemed to brighten the Minister's mood, enough so that Sharaf was able to depart with his reluctant blessing.

Sharaf settled with gratitude into the leather upholstery of Ali's Mercedes. By the time they were pulling onto the street he was feeling almost normal, and for the first time in days he allowed himself a fleeting moment of optimism. Time was tight, but perhaps his enemies were growing rushed, careless. He might yet have a chance.

Then Ali told him what had happened to Keller, making Sharaf wished he had simply stayed in bed.

19

A few hours earlier, a Frenchman, a Belgian, and an Emirati in a white *kandoura* stood in an office frowning over the body of Sam Keller, a death watch of tame-looking strangers.

"What do you think?" the Emirati asked in English.

"I think you killed him," the Frenchman said.

"Don't say that! Besides, I'm not even sure it's possible."

"With halothane? Of course it's possible. How much did you use?" Laleh interrupted from across the room.

"Stop it! You're only making it worse. Have you checked his pulse lately?"

The Emirati, apparently designated to handle the medical side of whatever it was they were up to, lifted a wrist and glanced at his watch—a huge Audemars Piguet.

"Weak, but steady. Like before."

"How much longer, then?" the Frenchman asked.

"I told you, I'm not experienced with anesthetics. This is all guess-work."

"You've established that quite clearly, but—"

"Please!" Laleh said. "He did the best he could. And my friend is safe."

"Provided he ever wakes up. And if he does, will he walk and talk, or just lie there forever like a fallen tree?"

As if in reply, Keller's body twitched, a spasm across the torso. Then his right hand lifted slightly. The fingers fluttered as if playing a trill on an imaginary piano.

"It's alive!" the Belgian said, in his best Dr. Frankenstein.

The Frenchman giggled nervously. Laleh and her countryman held their tongues. All four watched intently for further signs of consciousness. Keller opened his eyes, and with a soft groan he slowly raised his head from the couch, sliding back his arms until he was propped on his elbows. He groggily scanned the room, seemingly as shocked as a newborn to suddenly find himself among the living. Time of rebirth: 4:47 a.m.

Laleh stepped nimbly between the Frenchman and the Belgian. She bent down and gently placed a hand to his cheek. Sam blinked slowly, then blinked again. Finally he spoke, his voice a croak.

"Where the hell am I?"

The others exhaled as one.

"My office," Laleh said. "Welcome back."

"I think now he will be okay," the Emirati said in apparent relief.

"In your expert medical opinion?" the Frenchman asked.

"That really will be enough, Jean," Laleh said. "And I can take over from here. Thank you. Thanks to all of you."

The three men nodded, glancing back at Sam as they departed without a further word. With the drama apparently over, weariness was now evident in their posture. It was still dark outside the big window. The building, bustling by day, was silent.

Sam felt as if he had just climbed out of a deep hole of drugged oblivion. Considering his flash of panic during his last previous moment of consciousness, he was vaguely pleased to have awakened at all. As far as he could tell, he was still in one piece. No apparent bruises or savage wounds, except for the poultice still taped around the cut on his arm.

"That smell," he said, remembering the hand clamping across his nose and mouth. "It was kind of sweet. What did they give me?"

"Halothane," Laleh said. "On a handkerchief. From a brown bottle Massoud took from the hospital. He's an orderly, not a doctor, but he thought it might come in handy. Then when he saw those men outside your room, I think he panicked. Plus the police were coming. Three cars that passed right by us on the way out of there. So I guess he decided it would be better if you came without a commotion. He probably used more than he should have."

"Those men? Which men?"

She described them—three beefy Bengalis, two with clubs and one with a knife. They had been gathered uncertainly by the door to Sam's room, as if awaiting a call to action. Fortunately they had been easily frightened off by the sudden appearance of Sam's rescue party, which had strolled toward them seemingly out of nowhere just before midnight.

"Ali called me late last night to say that he had found my father. He was going to pick him up at the Central Jail. In the morning he was going to get you as well. But when I saw your e-mail it sounded too dangerous to wait any longer, so I rounded up a few friends and did what I could. Do you think the police found out you were there? Or maybe someone saw the Bengalis and phoned for them."

"I'm not sure. With the Bengalis it was personal. Superstitions and grudges. The police? Who knows. Either way, it's a good thing you came."

Sam sat up straight, groggy but not in pain. He was on the couch in the foyer of Laleh's office, out by the receptionist desk with the big window behind it. He seemed to have his wits about him, but his motor senses were enveloped in a thin fog. There was a slowness to his movements that was almost pleasant, as if some higher authority had granted him dispensation to dial things down for a while. He looked up at Laleh and smiled, aware that it was probably a goofy expression, as idiotically faithful as a dog's. It seemed to please her, nonetheless, because she smiled back, and then sat beside him on the couch.

"Don't you have a curfew or something?"

Laleh's expression darkened.

"I thought my mother would strangle me on the way out of the house. She still doesn't know where I am. I've never done anything like this before. When my father comes back home . . ." Her voice trailed off with a shudder.

"You said he was in jail?"

"They beat him up. Out cold, like you. I'll call Ali after sunrise for an update. He said he was taking my father to the Minister's house, for safekeeping."

"So he's still in hiding?"

"So are you. I don't know where we'll put you next."

Laleh checked her watch and shook her head, frowning.

"What's wrong?"

"My mother. She really will kill me. One of my brothers chased me halfway down the driveway. I was lucky to get away at all. And I forgot to bring my abaya, of course. That was probably the first thing she noticed."

"Hey, calm down. I'll vouch for you."

In his relaxed state of mind he reached up and unthinkingly touched her chin to turn her face toward him. She didn't flinch, but her eyes widened, which made him realize exactly what he was doing. He dropped his hand, embarrassed.

"Not that me vouching for you will do you any good, I guess. The crazed foreigner, with his libertine ways from abroad."

She smiled.

"You're still feeling the effects, aren't you? You've never talked this way before. Not with me, anyway. You're so relaxed."

"Maybe halothane is good for me. Who were those guys?"

"I grew up with Massoud, the one from the hospital. He's a friend of my little brother Hassan. Jean works in the building, a cameraman for French television. He shoots freelance video for us. The Belgian, Paul, is a friend of Jean's. I think he works for Reuters."

"I'm guessing Jean and Paul have never met your parents."

"They're part of the network my parents know nothing about."

It wasn't a boast, or a put-down. It was merely a statement of fact, a casual affirmation of her competence in having rounded up the necessary manpower for a rescue mission on short notice, as if such business was all in a day's work. And maybe it was.

"What do we do now?" he asked.

"Wait for morning."

"Do you have coffee? Everything's fuzzy, but I don't want to go back to sleep."

"I'll brew a pot."

She left for a moment while he stared dumbly through the darkened window into the pre-dawn sky. He heard running water and, soon afterward, the pop and gurgle of a coffeemaker. It reminded him of his first visit to Sharaf's house, right before her father burst in on them, scolding and disapproving. She was right. Her parents would be furious. He smiled dopily.

Laleh returned with two steaming mugs. She again sat beside him on the couch—just as close as before, he was pleased to note. It was cozy, sipping coffee with her. Or maybe the anesthetic was still working its magic.

"So what will he do to you?" Sam asked.

"My father? Punish me, I suppose. The first thing he usually tries is to demand that I quit my job. When that doesn't work he changes my curfew for a while."

"Even earlier than ten?"

She shrugged.

"It's hard to blame him. Not that I won't. But I am so different from all the girls he grew up with. You really have no idea how far he has come."

"So you've said."

"Because it's true. And he is under a great deal of pressure in his work. Even before they threw him into prison I was worried for him."

"He tells you about his work?"

She laughed.

"He'd never tell me, or even my mother. But I hear things. I am a night owl, like him, and sometimes when he goes into his office, very late, I am still roaming the hallways like a ghost. So I hear him on his cell phone, plotting things out."

"You spy on him, is that what you're saying?"

She shrugged again.

"Maybe if I didn't have a curfew, I wouldn't be there to listen. So in that way he is getting what he deserves. But this case, the one about your friend, I think it is part of something much larger. He has even been to the palace to talk about it."

"About Charlie?"

"Long before that. A few months ago he went to Sheikh Mohammed's weekly majlis and asked for a personal audience."

"You can do that, just show up at the ruler's weekly audience?"

"Oh, yes. Hundreds of people do. They complain about everything. The lots the government gave them. The traffic in their neighborhood. And like a fool, Sheikh Mohammed actually listens."

"Did he listen to your father?"

"All I know is that a week later my father met with some cabinet minister, and has been chatting on the phone with him late at night ever since. It's about other policemen, I think. Bad ones, and the criminals they're working with. So I've been scared for him, and that's how I knew to be scared for you. And, well, it's not as if I had anything else to do this evening."

He was flattered, even honored, by her concern. It was wonderful. In fact, between his warm feelings about Laleh and the lingering effects of the halothane, Sam had achieved a floating bliss akin to mild drunkenness, leaving his inhibitions at a minimum. As he looked intently at Laleh's face, he knew exactly how her lips would taste, a moist blend of salt and lip gloss, soft underneath. If she had been any other young woman he would have kissed her then and there. But even in his altered state he remained aware of the distance between their ways of doing things. He never would have presumed to touch her, as he had done moments ago.

That made it all the more powerful when Laleh made the first move, by taking his hand into hers and enfolding their fingers. Her eyes told him she was aware she was crossing a chasm, with many perils below. He sensed this even as her face leaned close enough for him to smell her lipstick. The anti-Nanette, he thought. Someone I could happily be brave for.

Such thoughts made for a somewhat solemn first kiss, a little tentative, with passions held in check. The second one lasted longer and ranged further afield, stirring him at a level he was more accustomed to in these situations. She then retreated slightly, as if to take stock.

"I am afraid that the only practice I've had at this is from watching movies," she said softly. "Forgive my awkwardness."

"You're doing wonderfully."

He was touched by the thought of her watching movies from the end of her bed, studying a passionate scene from an American film as if it were a manual of love. And in a way, this was new for him as well. Never before had he kissed a woman who thought of him first and foremost as someone who had survived against all odds, a risk taker in a foreign land. With Laleh, he was someone altogether different from the careful young auditor.

They kissed again, the best one yet. His right hand found the open space at the bottom of her blouse at the small of her back, and he slid it up her spine. She followed suit, pressing closer, skin to skin, their sighs on identical wavelengths. Her left hand slid across his thigh, and then the telephone rang.

It was her cell. She primly disengaged and sat upright, blinking fast. She smoothed back her hair and drew a deep breath before answering.

"Hello. *Father?*" She blushed and switched to Arabic, but even through the indecipherable rush of words Sam could tell she was flustered and trying to improvise. After a minute or two she calmed down. Then she turned toward him, handing over the phone with a solemn expression.

"He wants to speak with you."

Sam took the phone, expecting the worst. He hadn't felt this way since he was seventeen, when he had walked shakily to the door to pick up his date for the senior prom. He cleared his throat.

"This is Keller."

"Please assure me, Mr. Keller, that nothing improper has happened between you and my daughter."

"Nothing improper has happened, I assure you."

"By your standards or mine?"

"By anyone's standards."

"Not anyone's, Mr. Keller. In some Muslim families she would already be a scarlet woman just by occupying the same room with you—uncovered, no less, and at this low hour of the night. It also disturbs me that you are beginning to lie almost as skillfully as my sons, especially when I have come to regard you as a decent and honest man. Perhaps I should simply stop asking questions for which I really do not want to know the answer."

"I, uh, don't know what to say to that."

"To business, then. Laleh told me what happened to you at the camp. I have not fared much better. So from now on we're going to have to operate differently. More like spies, or undercover men. We will stay low to the ground and keep our exposure to a minimum. I am not sure yet where we will be staying, but it will not be at my house. Can you handle that? Or shall I have Ali drive you to the airport and put you aboard a private jet for, say, Canada, or some other neutral location, to work things out for yourself?"

"I can handle it."

"Very well. Meet me later this morning, then, ten o'clock at Ibn Battuta Mall. It will not be safe for you to take a taxi, so unfortunately Laleh will have to bring you, much as I hate to involve her further. Ali will bring me, and we will meet inside the mall. It is the only way I will be able to tell if one of us is being followed."

"Won't it be too crowded for that?"

"Obviously you have never been to Ibn Battuta Mall. Beautiful place, but no one goes there."

"Ten o'clock, then."

"Park near the entrance to the Egyptian pavilion. Laleh will know. Bring her phone with you and tell her to wait in the car. Call me after you have entered the mall. I will be waiting inside. And Mr. Keller?"

"Yes?"

"I would like for you and Laleh to please leave her office building now. Drive around if you have to. Even eat breakfast if you must, but only if you are seated at separate tables. Do not risk any further temptations by remaining alone in an empty office. Understood?"

"Very clearly."

"Now if I may please speak to my daughter again."

"Of course."

The father-daughter conversation lasted a few moments longer. Her tone was no longer flustered, but by the time she hung up, the earlier spell between her and Sam was broken. She smoothed her clothes and cleared her throat.

"I told him you had only regained consciousness a few moments ago. I don't think he believed me, even though he wanted to. Apparently he's not in much better shape. He said someone had hit him on the head."

"Where is he?"

"On the way to Ali's house. Ali refuses to let him work until he has had more rest and something to eat. That's why he set your appointment for ten. I'm supposed to drive you there, but he didn't tell me where you were meeting."

"Some mall. Ibn Battuta."

She smiled.

"Of course. Malls are his touchstone, his home turf."

"I've noticed."

"Well, at least it's convenient. Only a few minutes away. That leaves us plenty of time for breakfast."

"He said we should eat at separate tables."

"He also said that I have a new curfew. Nine o'clock. Do you see me rushing home to obey it? I am going to pay dearly for all this, so I might as well get my money's worth. Meaning we will eat at the same table, side by side if you prefer. I know I do."

They took the elevator to the main lobby. Sam was surprised to see that it was light outside. A few early birds were already arriving in the parking lot for lonely Saturday shifts. They stepped through glass doors into the coolness of a fine morning. The mist of a nearby sprinkler made a small rainbow in the low sunlight.

"So does this mean we just spent the night together?" he said, trying to keep the tone light.

"I'm sure that's how my father sees it."

"Sorry. I shouldn't joke about it."

"No. It's funny, actually. Another new thing for him to get used to, poor man. But it's not like we removed any clothing."

"Well that's one thing to be glad for."

"I suppose."

She, too, maintained a lighter tone, and as they crossed the parking lot she reached across the gap between them and quickly squeezed his hand. Just as quickly she let go, and she didn't turn to face him, or slow down, or offer any other opening that he might have exploited for a kiss or even a sidelong hug. Demure and defiant, all at once, and very much in control. It restored his earlier good mood, and left him intrigued and aroused.

But as Sam turned to open the door he saw the stubble of the Marina district on the far horizon. Cranes were already swiveling into action. The blue helmets were too distant to spot, but he knew they were in motion as well, with a long day ahead. It was a reminder of the world he was about to reenter, a hide-and-seek frontier with no margin for error, where those who disappeared were easily forgotten. Sharaf had warned him that from here on they would have to operate like spies, trusting no one. Frowning, he checked their flanks. All clear for the moment. With a sigh, he eased into the front seat of the BMW, back on the job.

20

Ibn Battuta Mall looked more like a theme park than a place to shop—yet another Dubai monument to slapdash ostentation. Its vast and elaborate courtyards had been built to resemble the fourteenth-century glories of China, India, Persia, Egypt, Tunisia, and Andalusia—the onetime destinations of Ibn Battuta, the Arabic Marco Polo.

Sam pushed through the door and gazed at the painted-on skies, the massive colonnades, and the elaborate fountains. Disney or Vegas? Both, he decided. But the striking facades concealed pretty much the same retail offerings you'd find in Indianapolis—Borders, the Sunglass Hut, a twenty-one-screen multiplex, and so on.

He dialed up Sharaf on Laleh's phone.

"Look around you," Sharaf commanded. "Are you alone?"

"Far as I can tell. It's like you said. Hardly anybody here."

"Where are you now?"

"Somewhere in Tunisia."

"I am in China, at the Starbucks. Why don't you come and meet me. If anyone follows, I will be able to spot him."

"See you in a minute."

A Starbucks loomed around the next corner, but it was in Persia, situated beneath a huge dome painted in magnificent colors. It was like those splendid tiled ceilings you saw in the world's most beautiful mosques, although the aura of holiness was somewhat diminished by a lingerie shop, its window filled with mannequins dressed in gauzy items you never would have seen on the streets of Persia, ancient or modern.

Sam forged onward through India until he finally spied the China Starbucks near a massive replica of a shipwrecked junk with a split hull and red sails. The ship appeared to have run aground by the food court.

Sharaf lurked at a table near the back, watching carefully. Sam almost didn't recognize him at first because he was wearing gray slacks, a navy sport coat, and a button-down blue shirt, and everything was a few sizes too small. Not that Sam had room to criticize, since he was still wearing the oversized clothes borrowed from Sharaf's son.

"Interesting place," he remarked, taking a seat.

"Do not get comfortable. We will be heading straight back to Laleh's car, but by a different route. I just had to make sure there was no surveillance."

"Where'd you get the clothes?"

"They are Ali's."

"We make quite a pair. Good thing we're not worried about standing out."

"Would you have preferred I wore my police uniform?"

"It was a joke. Sorry."

"Jokes were not what I was hoping for when I agreed to let you help me."

"Then how about some information?"

"You have some?"

Sam told him first about what he had learned from his coworker Plevy about the phone Nanette had given him, with its GPS tracking device.

"Didn't you say you turned it off for a while?"

"Then I switched it back on, just before the Russians showed up at the York."

"No wonder Arzhanov panicked. He must have realized where you'd gone and felt like he had to act immediately. Anything else?"

He told Sharaf about how Nanette's and Liffey's careers had crossed paths in Moscow, and the press release that linked them both to RusSiberian Metals and Investment, the company providing cover for Rybakov in Dubai. He mentioned the dates of Nanette's most recent trips to Moscow and Dubai, and her cooperation with police on the anti-counterfeiting task force.

"Now if we just knew what was going to happen on the fourteenth," Sharaf said.

"What are Rybakov's rackets?"

"The usual. Drugs, gambling, money laundering. Through real estate, of course, or this wouldn't be Dubai. But being a former KGB man, his first love has always been porn and prostitution. The business of choice for ex-Soviet spies, or so I heard from an old hotel man in Bur Dubai. Years ago when there was still a Soviet Union, he did lots of business with Rybakov, renting him conference rooms for visiting Soviet commercial delegations. It was long before anyone had even heard of the words 'Russian Mafia.' "

"Conference rooms? I thought Rybakov was KGB?"

"There was very little here for those kinds of people to do back then. No one from the West to spy on but a few oilmen, or the occasional banker. So Rybakov would help out the commercial attaché in his spare time. Part of his cover, I suppose. And then, of course, the whole Soviet system collapsed. Poor fellows like the Tsar weren't even getting their paychecks on time. And that was when my hotel friend first caught him stepping out of bounds. Rybakov rented a suite of rooms, supposedly for some visiting oil and gas engineers. But when my friend happened to drop by to make sure everything was to the customer's satisfaction, he found a film crew and three naked women, with Rybakov directing."

"He was making a porn movie?"

"He'd been doing it for weeks, apparently, in hotels all over town. It was the only way he could get paid. So by the time all those construction workers began flying in, the Tsar must have seen them as a ready-made market for the naked women he was procuring."

"The perfect capitalist, adapting his product to the market."

Sharaf nodded. Then he slowly stood up from his chair, looking a bit wobbly.

"Where to?" Sam asked. They began walking, easing back through China toward Persia.

"Our first stop is an address in Deira, to see our doorman and bouncer from the Palace Hotel. I know a route that will allow us to elude anyone in pursuit. Next stop, the Beacon of Light women's center. The director returned my call while I was in prison. I finally reached her an hour ago, but when I asked about this Basma character from your friend's datebook she refused to say anything over the phone. I decided to take it as a promising sign, if only because nothing else seems very promising right now. In fact, we may run out of time even before we run out of leads."

"Monday the fourteenth, you mean?"

Sharaf nodded.

"It gives us less than forty-eight hours. And even that may be optimistic. The Minister, who has been backing me, is losing patience. I kept him from shutting me down only by convincing him that you are dead. Meaning we will have to hide from our friends as well as our enemies."

"Dead? Wasn't that a little extreme?"

"There were moments when I believed it. It is why I am pleased to see you in one piece, even if you did spend the night with my daughter."

"I was pretty much out of it the whole time."

"Yes, that was her story as well."

Sam didn't belabor the point, and neither man said a word as they exited the mall from a corridor in India.

The father-daughter reunion wasn't exactly warm and fuzzy. Sharaf called out gruffly to Laleh as he approached the car. She was seated at the wheel, her arm resting on the window frame.

"Here, take this and put it on."

It was an abaya he must have procured somewhere along the way. He was speaking English, as if to make sure Sam understood as well that he was restoring order to this world gone mad.

"Now hand me your keys. Mr. Keller and I need your car. I am going to drop you at the taxi stand, over there with the tourists. If you need transportation for the rest of the day you can use my Camry. Ali had it delivered to the house. But I suggest that first you had better make peace with your mother, assuming that is even possible after what you have done. Not that I don't appreciate the valuable service that you've rendered."

Laleh didn't budge.

"And good morning to you, too, sir." She, too, spoke pointedly in English. Sam felt awkwardly like he was witnessing a formal debate, and that he would soon be consulted for his judgment on the winner. "I'm gratified to see you're okay, but this is my car owned in my name, and I am driving. Please sit in the back. Or up front, unless it makes you uncomfortable sitting next to a woman driver."

"Laleh, this isn't a game." He glanced around the parking lot, as if nervous about remaining exposed. "I don't let women drive me around. Not your mother, and not you, especially not after your behavior last night. It's as simple as that."

"You do when it's not your car. Please, get in before someone sees you."

"I *paid* for this car, Laleh. And I'm losing patience."

He reached for the handle, but Laleh was quicker, shooting the lock and rolling up the window. Sam, trying to stay out of the line of fire, crossed to the opposite side and got into the back. He buckled up and braced for the collision.

Sharaf, cursing under his breath, walked stiffly around the front of the car. He slapped the hood sharply with his palm and made his way to the passenger door. Laleh unlatched it, and Sharaf threw it open. He paused briefly, as if deciding whether he could really endure this. Then his policeman's need for safety prevailed, and he slid into the seat, slammed the door, and gazed straight ahead, jaw rigid.

Interesting strategy, Sam thought. Apparently Laleh had concluded that the best defense was a good offense, and she had seized the initiative in the battle of wills. Whatever sanctions her parents had in mind, it was obvious that in Laleh's mind the game had changed forever, and henceforth she would press for every possible advantage. He was impressed.

"Buckle up, please," Laleh said. "You know how terrible the drivers are here."

Sam watched the skin above Sharaf's collar turn a deep red, but the man didn't say a word. Considering the trouble Laleh was already in, Sam wondered what her new curfew would be now. Sunset, probably, with no television and no Internet. Or maybe her father would simply dispatch her to some secluded finishing school for naughty young Islamic ladies.

"Where to?" Laleh asked, continuing to address her father in English.

Sharaf emitted a deep, guttural sigh but said nothing. He turned to gaze forlornly into the parking lot.

"All right, then," Laleh said brightly. "I'll head east, since there really isn't anything much to the west except Jebel Ali. Just grunt when you want me to turn."

The skin above Sharaf's collar was now livid.

Laleh pulled the BMW into the eastbound lanes of Sheikh Zayed Road and floored it, expressing her anger with the gas pedal as the acceleration pushed Sam deeper into his seat. When she hit 120 kilometers per hour—about 75 miles per hour—there was a loud, high *ping*, and then a mechanical voice spoke up from the dashboard: "You are speeding. Please slow down. *Ping*. You are speeding. Please slow down."

"Most people have that disconnected," Laleh said to Sam. "My father did in his car, and my mother did in hers. But of course in my car they would not permit me. So there you go. Just like in a taxi."

Her tone was controlled, but her foot pressed harder on the pedal, and the voice kept issuing its warning.

"Nice, isn't it?" she said brightly. "Especially when you're running late for an appointment and everybody else is flying past you anyway. Not that any of my appointments really matter."

Sam cleared his throat.

"All right," Sharaf said, breaking his silence. His voice was surprisingly under control. "You've made your point. But before I say anything more, you have to slow down. There is no hurry."

Laleh eased up immediately, having won the first round. Sam wouldn't have thought it was possible.

"But just what *is* your point, Laleh? That is one thing I would like to know. Are you simply trying to impress your friend here?"

"I'm doing it because, one, you need to see firsthand, here and now, that I am a thinking, resourceful person who, occasionally, can actually make judgments for herself. Two, that I'm scared for you, for both of you. And I figured the only way I'd have a chance to talk some sense into you was if I, well, sort of kidnapped you for a while, or at least got to drive you around. I've seen the precautions you're taking, the risks you're willing to endure, and the damage that both of you have already suffered. And, yes, Father, I've even heard you on the phone late at night, talking to the Minister about how terrible this might all be. If you want real privacy you should go outdoors, or better still, let *me* go outdoors. So I guess what I'm really saying after this awful and exhausting night is that I don't want you to risk your life over some stupid investigation. You're not just a detective, you're a father and a husband, and Sam here is a young man who, with any luck, will also be a father and a husband. So maybe you should both reconsider."

Sharaf seemed taken aback, but not in a bad way. The color of his neck had faded to medium rare.

"Laleh, you're only going eighty now. If you really are worried for my life, then please concentrate on your driving or we'll be rear-ended by some idiot doing two hundred."

Right on cue, a Mercedes whizzed past on the right, blaring its horn and blinking its brights. Laleh sheepishly eased to the right amid more honking, and brought their speed back up to a hundred.

Sharaf took a deep breath, which seemed to calm him further. Laleh had disarmed him as only a daughter can disarm a loving father—with her care and concern.

"All right," he said finally. "I see what you're doing. And because of how you feel I can almost excuse what you did earlier this morning. Almost. And, by the way, have you phoned your mother? Does she have any idea where you are?"

"I was going to do that later."

"You'll do it in the next five minutes, even if we have to pull off the highway. And that is not negotiable."

"Okay." Demure voice, ceding ground she knew she couldn't hold.

"Or maybe fifteen minutes would be better, because I can see now that it is going to be necessary for me to tell you a very old story. And to hear it you're going to have to take this next exit, because I won't tell it while you're driving."

She looked over at her father as if not quite believing him.

"Well, do you want to hear it or not?"

She took the exit, the one for Emirates Mall.

"Pull into the parking deck," Sharaf said. "A lower level, where we'll be out of sight."

She circled downward and squeezed into a space between two other BMWs. They sat in silence for a few seconds while the color of Sharaf's neck continued to fade down the spectrum. He turned toward Sam.

"This is a private story about my family. I am afraid I must tell it in Arabic so that only Laleh will understand it."

"Sure. Okay."

"No," Laleh said, employing her new favorite word. Sam figured she hadn't used it this much since the age of two. He braced for Sharaf's next explosion.

But the older man contained himself. Maybe he realized he was dealing with a strange new phenomenon of defiance, a force of nature every bit as unstoppable as a sandstorm, or a plague of locusts. Whatever the reason, he asked his next question in English, and in a tone that was calm and reasonable, if somewhat puzzled.

"Why do you say 'No' to me now, my daughter? Are you overly tired? Or is it because, as all of those ridiculous Western television programs designed for ladies like to say, that you are suddenly feeling 'empowered'?"

Laleh seemed to hold back a grin.

"My reason is more practical. If you really are about to explain why you can't possibly turn back, then doesn't Mr. Keller deserve to hear it as well? Now that your destinies are shared."

Sharaf considered her words a moment, then nodded, apparently relieved to find himself back in territory where he at least understood the logic.

"A valid point. Very well, then. If Mr. Keller has the patience, then he, too, may hear the story of our family's disgrace."

"Disgrace?" Her resolve seemed to waver.

"Yes. 'Disgrace' is exactly the right word, as you will see. It is the foundation upon which our wealth has always been based. Do you still wish for a stranger to learn why?"

There was a pause, followed by a small nod and a very quiet "yes."

"Then I will tell you. It is the very reason I became a policeman, or more to the point, an *honest* policeman."

"It wasn't because of that television show, *Percy Mason*?"

"No, my dear. And it's Perry, not Percy. Although that story is real enough. I really did feel like a shining knight of justice whenever I translated his triumphs for our neighbors. But that came later, when I had tutors and was learning English. By then my father could afford to pay for such things. The real reason came earlier, when I was twelve. It was summer, the year before Ali and I would put to sea. My family was not really poor, no more than anyone else. But our house was not as grand as it would become, and our pleasures were simple. One of mine was that on the night of every full moon I enjoyed sneaking down to the banks of the creek, because that was when the women and girls liked to swim. They went into the water in their dresses, of course, even after dark. But, well, you know what water does to dresses. It was the only way a boy of twelve could ever expect to see such things."

"I'm shocked," Laleh said. She was joking, but Sharaf hadn't even noticed. From his eyes Sam could see he was swept away on a current from his past.

"So there I was, lying in the reeds, swatting at mosquitoes and trying not to make noise, not that I had to worry about that because the girls were laughing so loud. Then I heard footsteps coming up on the path behind me. I froze. I was sure it was the father of one of those girls, who would swat my head and turn me over to an imam on Friday for a lesson in proper behavior.

"But no. Nothing like that. It was my own father, and he wasn't looking for me. Even in the moonlight you could see right away by the glitter of his eyes that he was a man on important business. Maybe that was why I decided to follow him. To see what was afoot."

"So even then you were a detective," Laleh said.

"Or maybe I just didn't trust him. I never had. He was always trying to swindle someone in the souk, or cheat a boat captain out of his cut. So I moved out of the reeds and tucked in behind him, walking as quietly as I could. He went a few hundred yards more until he stopped at a small walled lot behind the house that belonged to his brother, Abdullah. That seemed especially odd, because Uncle Abdullah had died only a week earlier, and the family was still in mourning. He climbed over the mud wall and moved toward a palm tree in the middle of the lot. Then he turned to face the creek—I had to duck behind the wall—and he took several careful steps straight toward me before stopping. He then turned directly to his right and made five more strides, counting them as he moved. Then he stopped again.

"I saw then that he was carrying something, one of those small folding shovels like the British soldiers used to have. He must have picked it up surplus, or maybe he stole it off one of their trucks. But he began to dig, right there by the light of the moon, and in only a minute or two he struck something. It sounded like metal hitting a clay pot, and at that moment I knew what he was doing, and what he had found, and I was scandalized."

"What was it?" Laleh said.

Sam, just as eager to find out, leaned forward from the backseat.

"Well, in those days, especially if you made your money from pearling, no one ever put their money into banks. You collected your savings in old silver coins called Maria Theresas. You'd put them into a big clay pot, stopper the top, and bury it somewhere handy, in a secret place that only you knew. And this pot my father had dug up must have belonged to Uncle Abdullah, because I had heard his wife at the funeral only days earlier, complaining to the other women that her husband had died before telling anyone where their fortune was buried. It wasn't an uncommon occurrence then, especially when men were lost at sea. Their families were left with nothing unless someone could find the pot. But apparently my father, whether by sneaking around, or threats, or whatever means, had known the location all along. And he had waited until the first full moon to go and dig it up.

"There must have been a lot of coins, because the pot was very heavy. He could barely carry it, especially with the little shovel tucked beneath his arm. But he made it home without anyone seeing him, and when he reached our garden he dumped the contents into a sack. He broke the pot into little pieces and took them out to the creek, where he scattered them on the water. Then he made a fire and put the coins into a cooking pot with water and dried lemons. People did that to remove the tarnish, because the dampness underground always made the coins turn green.

"The following week my father bought three new boats to add to the one small pearling boat he already owned. Then he bought new engines for all four. That summer he needed so many new crewmen that he had to put me to work, and he hired the two older boys who became my friends, Ali and Mansour. Two of the new boats were even seaworthy enough to make the crossing to India, so he was also able to enter the gold-smuggling trade as well, once the pearling season was over. It made his fortune. And of course his wealth was then passed down to me, and, in turn, to you and your brothers. All of it accomplished by an act of theft against his own brother's family.

"He took care of them in his way, buying them things from time to time, and making sure they were never wanting for necessities. And of course he let them think of him as a kind and magnanimous man. But I always knew the truth, and always hated him for it. And that is when I decided that I would do something in my life—as a lawyer, a policeman, whatever the world offered—to make sure that people like him would always be found out and punished."

"Is that all?" Laleh asked, as if expecting some further revelation.

"What do you mean, 'Is that all?' Is that not enough?"

"Well, yes, it's terrible. Inexcusable. But it was your father, not you."

"It was a matter of our family's *honor*, Laleh. Or its utter *dis*honor. Maybe some of those grasping people you work with would simply see it as the clever act of an opportunist, so why not make the best of it? But he stole from his own flesh and blood. It was a shame upon all of us, and by keeping his secret I became a part of that. With every tutor his money bought, I was tainted even more."

"Your father's right," Sam said before he could stop himself. "I understand completely."

Sam also understood that the age-old conflict between the values of the old and the young was playing out on the seat in front of him, here in a land where the new got newer by the minute. Not that Laleh wasn't appalled by her grandfather's actions. She simply didn't see it as a binding stain upon later generations, or even her father. And while Sharaf had undoubtedly spoken too harshly of the people she worked among in Media City, she probably had grown a bit jaded from the ambition so often on display in the workplace. Sam certainly had, even if he had realized that only during the past few days.

Laleh was silent for a few moments more. Then she nodded.

"All right, then," she said. "I understand why you have to continue. I also understand—finally—why you built our cousins a house on the family lot, so maybe you should tell Mom as well. But if, as you believe, our entire family shares this shame, then shouldn't I also share the burden of removing it, if only by driving you to your next destination, maybe? Or making inquiries in places where you or Mr. Keller would be recognized?"

Sharaf rapidly shook his head.

"You see?" he said to Sam. "This is the folly of revealing family secrets, even to those you love. Now she will always have a wedge to involve herself. And she—"

The phone rang before he could say more, and when Sharaf saw the number he answered immediately. The conversation was in Arabic, but Sam could tell from the tone that it was welcome news. By the time Sharaf hung up, his mood was transformed.

"Laleh, I have a bargain to offer you." He snapped the phone shut. "If I were to tell you that I know how to guarantee Mr. Keller's safety for the rest of his stay in Dubai, and that you could even play a role in this action, would you agree to let me take the wheel?"

She tilted her head, as if trying to determine if this was a trick.

"All right. I'll agree to that."

"Good. In forty minutes, my old friend Mansour from the Maritime Police will be stopping by our house. I will drop you off a few blocks away so that you can be there to meet him, because I cannot afford to be seen there myself. If you then follow my instructions, by this evening he will be able to announce to the world that Mr. Keller here has been found dead in the waters of Dubai Creek. Mansour will even have a body to prove it, complete with Mr. Keller's clothing and all the proper identification."

"But—"

"Just say that you agree."

"I agree."

Sam was dumbfounded. Then his auditor's brain began to assemble the pieces, and he smiled as they fell into place. Death, he decided, was going to be a pretty good thing.

2 1

"So that's why you were soaking my clothes in a tub," Sam said, after they dropped Laleh off. "And I'm guessing the tub is filled with, what, salt water?"

"Very good. But how did you know about the tub?"

"I saw it when Assad's men came for me. I was out back looking for my wallet and spotted it through the window of the shed. But won't you also need a body?"

"Mansour has one. It was found this morning. Some poor drunken unidentified tourist who fell off an *abra* into the creek five days ago. He was apparently traveling alone, with no friends and no next of kin. And now, as far as the government of Dubai is concerned, he is Sam Keller. I saw an item about him in the paper the first morning you were at our house. His body was still missing then. Witnesses had seen him slip into the water, but no one knew him and no one had come forward to report him missing. That's when I took your clothes, pulled out the tub, and phoned Mansour."

"And he agreed?"

"Spending a year together dodging sharks and the Indian coast guard tends to make you allies for life, just as with Ali. I knew Mansour would have jurisdiction whenever the creek finally decided to give back that poor fellow's body."

Sam shook his head, amazed by the audacity.

"It is called *wasta*, Mr. Keller, and it is how we do things here. I suppose to you it looks like corruption. To us it is a marketplace of favors and connections. Are things really so different in your world?"

"It's just that, well, it sounds like something your father might have dreamed up. No disrespect intended."

"None taken. I am quite aware of my inborn tendency for deviousness. That is why I am so committed to employing it for the greater good."

"I'm not complaining. So what will they do, dress the body in my clothes?"

"I am sure it is too bloated and nibbled for that." Sam winced. "Mansour's men will throw away the real clothes and put yours in the property bag, along with your soggy passport and wallet."

"What about dental records?"

"That will not be a concern until the American consulate ships the body home, which won't happen for days, maybe weeks."

"Hal Liffey will be the first one to see the paperwork. He and Nanette will probably have a drink to celebrate."

"You are the one who should celebrate. No more looking over your shoulder for a Russian with a Makarov. Which is more than I can say for the poor man we're about to visit. Rajpal Patel, the doorman from the Palace Hotel. He is hiding in Deira, on the far side of the creek."

"Then shouldn't we be heading south, to cross the bridge?"

Sharaf shook his head.

"By now Lieutenant Assad's men may be looking for this car as well. We'll park in the old quarter of Bastakiya, and make the crossing by *abra*."

"Just like the dead tourist."

"Only with better results, I hope."

The waterfront in Bastakiya, the oldest part of the city, swarmed with activity, making it the perfect place to blend in with the crowd. *Abras* came and went from the docks like a procession of airport taxis, jostling to and fro in the cloudy green chop as their big diesel engines popped and grumbled like Harleys. They were low-slung, narrow craft, built of thick wooden beams the size and color of railroad ties. Passengers sat on a two-sided bench that ran down the spine of the open deck, facing outward, ten to a side. You paid the mate a dirham and stepped aboard the rocking deck. As soon as every seat was filled, the skipper revved the engine in a billow of blue smoke and pulled away, bumping the scuffed hulls of other *abras* until he reached open water.

Sam made a move to hop aboard the newest arrival, but Sharaf put out a hand.

"I am looking for someone," he said. "Patience."

Three boats later, Sharaf muttered, "Okay," and they climbed aboard. This boat didn't look any different from the others, but the skipper nodded toward Sharaf as they eased into the channel. Glancing around him, Sam realized the obvious advantage of this form of transport. You got a good long look at every fellow passenger, meaning no one could follow without being noticed. It was clear that no Russians were aboard.

The *abra* headed downstream with the incoming tide, taking them alongside the bigger dhows that still carried spices and textiles across the gulf from Iran. They, too, had timbered hulls, with jutting bowsprits and flush transoms that lent a piratical air. Despite the new high-rises lining much of the opposite shore, it wasn't hard to imagine how the creek must have looked when Sharaf was a boy, barefoot and wiry. These waters ran straight from his heart, a key to everything about him, and Sam watched the man closely as they made the crossing.

When they reached the busy wharf in Deira, Sharaf again held out his arm in abeyance as the other passengers stepped ashore. The skipper nodded, and steered the *abra* back into the current. A few minutes later they pulled alongside a separate wharf that wasn't part of the usual taxi service.

"Thank you, my friend," Sharaf said as he and Sam climbed ashore. The captain merely revved his engine in reply, and headed upstream for a new load of return passengers.

"More *wasta*?" Sam asked.

"I have known his family since I was a child. He knows that in my work I prefer privacy."

"What does he get in return?"

"Please, Mr. Keller. You cannot be privy to all my secrets."

The moment they began walking, Sharaf stopped suddenly and grabbed Sam. He swayed for an instant like a stout palm in a stiff breeze.

"You all right?"

"A little dizzy. A little nauseous. I think it was the motion of the water, plus the lump on my head. I am fine now."

"Maybe it would feel better with a little halothane. We'll be just great if anyone comes after us."

They moved at a deliberate pace to accommodate Sharaf's wooziness, and found the address above a sagging jewelry store in a narrow cobbled alley, not far from Deira's Gold Souk. Being with Sharaf helped ward off the vendors who had swarmed him during his shopping trip the week before. Or maybe being unshaven and ridiculously attired made him look too impoverished to bother with.

They climbed a dim, fetid stairwell to an unmarked steel door. Sam was reminded anew that he hadn't shaved or showered in several days, which made it all the more amazing that Laleh had kissed him.

"Pay attention," Sharaf said. "You look like you're in one of those halothane dreams. This man may try to run when we announce ourselves. You need to be ready to move quickly."

They knocked twice before a girl's voice timidly called out in Hindi. Sharaf answered in kind. There was a click as she unlatched the lock. When she drew back the door, Sharaf jammed his foot in the opening and said in English, "We come as friends. We are here to see Rajpal Patel."

There was an immediate flurry of activity from inside—raised voices, the sound of a toppling chair, the groan of a window sash being raised. Sharaf, dizzy or not, burst inside, knocking the girl onto her rump. Sam followed him to a back room, where Sharaf grabbed a man's legs just as they were about to disappear over the windowsill. Two young boys ran to the fellow's rescue and began pounding Sharaf on the back with tiny fists. Sam tried to peel them away, only to have a third one race forward to swat his ankles with a broomstick. The girl screamed, loud enough for neighbors to hear. But Sharaf was winning his game of tug-of-war, and within seconds the squirming Patel fell back through the window as everyone collapsed in a heap on the floor.

"Please!" Sharaf shouted. He closed his eyes and put a hand to his forehead, as if to stop it from spinning. "We are here as friends of Khalifa, the owner of your family's shop. We are the enemy of your enemies, Mr. Patel!"

Patel, flat on his back, raised his hands in submission, which instantly calmed his corps of underage reinforcements.

"I was worried you were the police," he said, eyeing Sharaf

warily. He didn't seem sure what to make of Sam. "Do you really know Khalifa?"

"I met him in the Central Jail. I was released only this morning, and with any luck they will release him as well, along with Nabil. Don't worry, Khalifa has kept your secret from the authorities. But he gave me your address because he knows I can help."

"And who are you?"

"Someone who is investigating the policemen. This man with me is a friend of Mr. Hatcher's, the American who came to see you at the Palace Hotel. They were there together the other night, not long before Mr. Hatcher was killed."

Patel's eyes widened. He scrambled to his feet, as if ready to again bolt out the window.

"Mr. Hatcher was killed?"

"I am afraid so."

This set off a round of eye rolling and a few curses in Hindi. Patel brusquely ordered the children to leave the room, and gestured toward a sagging bed while he stood by the open window. Sharaf and Sam reluctantly took a seat.

"How do I know you are not here to kill me?"

"If that were true, Mr. Patel, you would be dead by now."

"Then who killed Mr. Hatcher?"

"A couple of Russians. And now those Russians are dead. We can only make the killings stop if you tell us why Mr. Hatcher paid you that night in the lobby."

Patel looked again at Sam, and the light of recognition dawned in his eyes.

"I remember you now. You were by the front desk, watching us. He said not to worry, that you were harmless."

"A little too harmless," Sam answered, "or I could have helped him. He gave you money, then he wrote something down. What was it you told him?"

Patel bit his lip, as if debating how much to reveal.

"I told him what was coming on April fourteenth, this Monday."

"We would like you to tell us as well," Sharaf said. "Provided you still remember."

"Of course, I remember. I had worked very hard to memorize it. I have a head for numbers, you see, so I am able to do such things."

Patel then tilted his head as if searching his memory. His next words emerged in a monotone, like a student reciting important dates in history.

"Payload of fifty, I-M-O, nine-zero-one-six-seven-four-two. Jebel Ali terminal two, gate six, lot seventeen, row four."

The recitation complete, Patel looked back at their faces.

"That is all. That is what I told him."

"Of course," Sharaf said. "An IMO number. They're assigned to container ships."

"And this one's arriving Monday at Jebel Ali," Sam said, "with a payload of fifty."

Finally, Charlie's scribbled numbers and letters made perfect sense. No code at all. Just a lot of shipping information in abbreviated form.

"But fifty what?" Sam asked. "Tons? Kilos? Weapons?"

"Women," Sharaf said. "For the flesh trade. Their new pipeline, now that the airport's under a crackdown."

"In ship containers?"

"Someone smuggled in a few boys that way for use as camel jockeys last year, back when the government was shutting down that trade. Maybe that's where they got the idea. The other numbers must be where the containers will be stored after unloading. In some freight lot at terminal two."

Sharaf turned back toward Patel.

"Thank you, Mr. Patel. But where did that information come from?"

"From the recording."

"What kind of recording?"

"The tape. Of those people who met in the Kasbar a month ago. I can explain, if you wish."

"Oh, yes. We wish."

So Patel told them all he could remember, which was considerable. His account dated back to a slow evening at the Kasbar three months earlier, when Charlie Hatcher had first appeared at the roped-off entrance. He had approached Patel with a conspiratorial grin and a folded hundred-dollar bill, and as Patel related the details Sam could almost hear his old colleague's voice supplying the dialogue along the way, right down to the offhand language Charlie would have used to pitch his diabolical offer:

"Name's Charlie Hatcher, old son. I'm with Pfluger Klaxon. Technically that allows me entry on our corporate membership, although I'm afraid you won't find my name in your big red book. So this token of my appreciation will have to do instead, provided you're free for a little conversation once I've settled in with a drink, yes?"

He handed over the bill. Patel pocketed the money and returned the smile.

"Of course, sir. As long as no one is needing my services for a few moments."

"Absolutely, old son. Wouldn't want to jeopardize your career in hospitality management."

By the time Patel slid into the booth, Charlie was ready with a proposition.

"First off, I have some photos for you."

He laid a sheet of paper faceup on the table with five Photostat images. Three were in color—one of a man with an American flag in the background, one of a woman with striking auburn hair, attractive in a stern sort of way, and one of a rather beefy man on a busy sidewalk. The other two, in black and white, seemed to have been copied from newspaper photos. One was captioned in Arabic, the other in the Cyrillic characters of Russian. Both were men, and one was a cop. No names had been typed in for any of the five.

"If it's not too much trouble, I'd like for you to keep an eye out for these people, and make a note of whenever one of them visits. What time, how many in their party, plus the name used to make the reservation. You'd be generously compensated, of course. In addition, next time you get a spare moment I'd appreciate it if you could look back through your reservation book for, oh, let's say six months, and let me know of any previous appointments made under the same name. Especially if that name matches one of these."

Charlie slid forward an index card. Five names were typed in a neat column.

Patel frowned and fidgeted. Customers occasionally asked for his help in acquiring the temporary services of women, and he was always ready with a few leads. In one or two lucky instances he had later received a small percentage from the beneficiary. But this request seemed more serious, and much riskier.

"I am very sorry, sir, but the privacy interests of our guests require that—"

"Please, old son. Hear me out. I'd very, *very* much like to make this arrangement work to your advantage." Charlie slipped a second hundred-dollar bill onto the table. "And this would only be the beginning—let's say, one-tenth of your total compensation package? So consider this a down payment on your loyalty. Besides, one of these people is even a coworker of mine. All you're really providing is a little enhanced corporate security. If you prefer, just think of yourself as a Pfluger Klaxon consultant."

Patel's frown deepened. He rubbed his palms on his knees and glanced toward the entrance to make sure no one was awaiting entry. Then he leaned across the table and lowered his voice.

"I see your point, sir. Perhaps it would not be such a serious breach of our policies if I was to, as you say, participate as a consultant."

"That's the spirit. One more item, then, and we're done."

Charlie produced the transaction's pièce de résistance from a briefcase. It was a small blue ceramic bowl, virtually identical to the ones the Kasbar's waitresses always brought to the table for their patrons, except Charlie's wasn't filled with the requisite helping of pistachios and smoked almonds. Moving as deftly as a magician, Charlie turned the bowl upside down just long enough to reveal a small silver item implanted in the bowl's recessed bottom.

"Did you happen to see that, old son?"

"What was it?"

"Digital recorder. Smaller than an iPod, but easier to operate. Keep this bowl of ours in some safe and handy place until you need it. Your locker, for instance, where you change into that fine-looking uniform. You have a locker here, don't you?"

"Yes. In the back. But—"

"Excellent. The next time any of these people walk in, all you have to do is retrieve this bowl, flip the switch, then slip a twenty to some waitress so she will deliver it to the table. Along with the usual refreshments, of course. Like so." He set the bowl down with a solid thunk, then took an almond from their own bowl and popped it in his mouth. "That's the real beauty of our arrangement, don't you see? Only one part of it is dicey, and a waitress handles that for you."

Patel knew by then that he was in over his head, but the idea of making a thousand dollars in only a few minutes of work had taken hold of his imagination. So he sighed and fretted, and again rubbed his hands on his knees. Then he nodded, as if to seal the deal, even though he never mustered enough courage to actually say yes.

"Very good. Of course, if the recorder comes back blank, your compensation will be adjusted accordingly. Results, old son. That's what you're being paid for, just as with any consultant. Understood?"

"Yes, sir."

"Until next time, then? Say, a month or two, or maybe even longer, when, if you have everything waiting for me, I'll pay you in full?"

"Yes, sir. A month or two. I will try to have your results."

Charlie stood up from the table and departed the Kasbar, not to return until the night he showed up with Sam Keller at his side.

"Those photos," Sharaf said, "and this list. Did you keep them?"

Patel nodded.

He reached into his pocket. They were creased and folded like old money. Sharaf took the page and the card and smoothed them out in his lap while Sam leaned closer. The color photos of Nanette Weaver and Hal Liffey seemed to have been printed straight from the Internet, from the State Department and Pfluger Klaxon Web sites. The color shot of Iranian mobster Mohsen Hedayat was clear enough, but looked as if it had been taken with a cell phone, on the sidewalk outside the Iranian Club, a thriving social club in the Oud Metha area of Dubai. The photos of Anatoly Rybakov and Lieutenant Hamad Assad had been copied from newspapers. All five of their names were typed on the crumpled index card.

Sam could tell Sharaf was trying to rein in his excitement.

"These people," Sharaf said, as calmly as if he were asking about Patel's family, "I take it that they all met at some point later, and you were able to tape them?"

Patel shook his head.

"No. Just one."

"One? How can only one person hold a meeting?"

Patel shrugged, as if that wasn't his concern.

"There were three people, but only one was from those pictures. His name was on the list. Mr. Hal Liffey."

"Who were the other two?"

Patel shrugged again.

"Mr. Liffey did not include their names with his reservation. All that was recorded in the book was that he had requested a table for three."

"So it might have been two of the others, then, but you're just not sure?"

"No. I am sure. It was not the woman, and it was not any of the other three."

"But you taped them anyway?"

"Just as Mr. Hatcher said, except I had to give the waitress a fifty. She said those people were too scary, especially the Russian."

"One of them was a Russian?"

"And one was Persian. The waitress said the Russian was Mafia, but she says that anytime a rich Russian comes here. But it made her scared. That is why I had to pay her a fifty, and when I began to think about it later I was scared, too. So I took the recorder home. I did not want to leave it anywhere around the hotel where it might be found, especially not in my locker. My only worry was what I would do when Mr. Hatcher came. He would expect delivery, and I knew I would not be paid unless he could be sure I had results."

"So that's why you memorized the information for April fourteenth, to assure him you had the goods?"

Patel nodded again.

"Why that part?"

"On the tape, it is the only time they are speaking English. The rest of the time they are only speaking Russian. I don't speak Russian."

"Is that why he paid you in the lobby, but took nothing in return?"

"Yes. Five hundred dollars. Half the total. At the moment I mentioned April fourteenth, he seemed very happy. He said he would pay me the rest when I gave him the recorder."

"No wonder he was short on cash when we got to the York," Sam said. "But he had already mentioned the date earlier that night, at the Alpine bar. That's when he called it the day of reckoning."

"So he knew it was important, but perhaps not why. Or not *exactly* why," Sharaf said. "This recording, sir, when did you deliver it?"

Patel shook his head.

"I took it to work with me the next afternoon. Mr. Hatcher was supposed to come pick it up. But when I reached my locker, the bouncer from the earlier shift told me a policeman was waiting for me at the rope. When I looked through the door I saw he was one of the men from the photos."

"Lieutenant Assad?" Sharaf said.

"Yes. I knew I was in trouble, so I left by the back. There was a police van with four more men in the main drive, so I crossed the hotel grounds to the beach and walked a mile along the water before cutting back to a bus stop on the main road. When I got home my family said the police had been there as well. That is when I came here, with Khalifa's help."

"Did you bring the recorder with you?"

Patel eyed them carefully. Sam held his breath.

"It is hidden," Patel said. "It is what cost me my job. And if you want it, you must pay the other five hundred dollars that was promised."

Patel folded his arms to indicate that his offer was final. Sharaf glanced at Sam.

"I've got a few hundred dirhams," Sam said, "but that's about it."

"Nonsense. We're not paying this little crook."

Sharaf stood suddenly, then caught himself, swaying as he had before, which only served to make him angrier. Steadying himself, he pointed a finger at Patel.

"Here is how it will work," he said evenly. Patel sat impassively, arms folded. "You will bring us the tape, here and now. In exchange, I will not tell Lieutenant Assad where you've gone. That is even more valuable than five hundred dollars, don't you think?"

Patel unlocked his arms and lashed out.

"But you promised Khalifa!"

"Yes. But I, too, am a policeman." Sharaf flashed his ID and flipped open his cell phone. "And with a single call, sir, I can summon an entire squadron to this doorstep within five minutes. So you will retrieve the recorder or else I will phone my colleagues. It is your choice."

Sharaf began punching in numbers, each beep sounding like a tiny alarm bell.

"Stop!" Patel rose from his chair. "All right, you will have it, then! I will get it for you now!"

"We will accompany you."

Patel flung up his hands in exasperation.

"As you wish, jackals!"

It was in the next room, stored behind a baseboard panel, which Patel loosened with a table knife. He sulkily handed it over.

Sharaf studied the buttons a moment, then pressed play. There was a rustling sound, then the clicking of footsteps, followed by a jarring thump as a woman's voice said in English, "Some refreshments for you. And your drinks, of course."

There were three light thunks on the table. Ice clinked in a glass as someone took a thirsty first sip.

"Thank you," a man said in English.

"Hal Liffey," Sam said. The mere sound of his voice made him angry.

The footsteps of the waitress receded, and Liffey got down to business.

"Two items, gentlemen. And I'd appreciate if both were reported promptly and precisely to your superiors. The first and most important is that our corporate sponsor informs me that the details are complete for the first major transaction, set for four-fourteen. No more dry runs, this one's for real. Ready for the particulars?"

There was a pause, followed by a muffled sound of movement and a few stray beeps.

"I don't believe it," Sam said. "They're getting out their Black-Berrys."

Liffey spoke clearly and slowly enough for everyone to log the details. He said exactly what Patel had repeated in his recitation:

"Payload of fifty, I-M-O, nine-zero-one-six-seven-four-two. Jebel Ali terminal two, gate six, lot seventeen, row four. Should I repeat that?"

Two muffled voices answered, "No," then Liffey spoke again.

"More people are coming into the bar. British, I think. Perhaps we should conduct the remainder of our business in Russian. Partly, of course, in deference to the man who helped bring us together. A toast, then, to the Tsar."

There was a clink of glasses. The next voice was an outburst of Russian from one of the others. Sharaf checked his watch, switched off the recorder, and popped it into his pants pocket.

"We will listen to the rest later, when I have time to translate. For now we're due at the Beacon of Light, where, if my guess is correct, we'll find out more about their payload."

"Fifty women," Sam said, "and they'll be arriving like livestock in two days. We better move fast."

22

Among the high-wattage villas of Dubai's Al Safa neighborhood, the Beacon of Light stood out more like a guttering candle—three stories of smudged stucco on a shaggy lawn, with a dented blue van at the curb.

The neighbors' bigger gripe was the procession of sullen men who regularly cruised past or, worse, parked in the rear alley, idling their engines with the windows up while waiting for runaway spouses to show their faces at the windows.

The shelter regularly employed a guard, but on this particular afternoon Sharaf was surprised to see two of them lurking beneath the drooping palms, and both were heavily armed. They shouldered automatic weapons like island defenders awaiting an amphibious assault. Sharaf heard the unmistakable click of a safety as Sam and he approached.

"Easy," Sharaf called out, showing his hands. "We're friends."

He seemed to be saying that everywhere lately.

"We're expected," Sam added.

A guard patted them down and escorted them up the steps. A woman of uncertain nationality answered their knock. Looming behind her was a third armed man.

"We have an appointment with Mrs. Halami," Sharaf said.

"Wait here."

On the way over from Deira, Sharaf had tried to prepare Sam for the local phenomenon known as Yvette Halami. She was a French-woman who had married an Emirati and moved to Dubai during the early years of the economic boom. A converted Muslim, she covered her head but never held her tongue, especially on the issue of how women were treated in Dubai.

She chain-smoked, knocked back espressos all day, conducted much of her business in English, and was forever answering a cell phone that rattled and rang like one long emergency. Her combative nature generated like-minded press coverage. Depending on which local paper you read, she was either a selfless advocate for the voiceless or a grandstanding loudmouth whose main goal was to embarrass men in general, and Emirati men in particular. Several of Sharaf's col-leagues couldn't utter her name without cursing.

Almost any native-born woman would have long ago faded into the background against that kind of opposition. She seemed to revel in it, which only infuriated her enemies more.

Sharaf had largely been won over to Yvette's cause by Laleh, and also by the assault victims he had interviewed over the years at the shel-ter. He had seen firsthand what happened when violent husbands, unpunished, were allowed to reclaim their wives from the law simply by signing a form promising they'd never do it again. He knew of one man who had done this eight times; he had seen all eight copies of the form—but no criminal convictions—stored neatly in the fellow's police file.

Sharaf was ambivalent about Halami herself. He believed she was one reason his daughter had become so rebellious. For every hour Laleh volunteered at the Beacon of Light—preparing meals, manning phones, directing media strategy—she seemed to emerge that much sharper around the edges.

Halami appeared from around a corner, cell phone in her left hand, cigarette in her right. Her greeting was typically abrupt. No names, no salutations, just a blunt question in a burst of cigarette smoke.

"Were you followed?"

"If we had been, we'd be in custody by now," Sharaf answered. "What's with all the security?"

"You wouldn't ask if you'd seen some of the goons who've been coming around. And I'm not talking about husbands. Pimps and their muscle. A very bad business."

"Does this have anything to do with—?"

"Please. Don't mention her name here. Follow me."

She led them past her office to a makeshift canteen, where one woman was reading and another was taking popcorn from a microwave. Halami spoke to them in Arabic, and they exited without a word. Then she lit a fresh cigarette and responded to a beep by checking a text on her phone.

"Some flunky from the Ministry of Health was in my office yesterday asking about the same girl. Immigration came the day before that. Same name. Basma, Basma, Basma." She moved her right hand like a yakking puppet. "For all I know, one or both of those fellows planted something near my desk to listen in, so I figured it was safer talking here. Any idea who's behind all this interest?"

The heads of both agencies were allies of Assad's, and rivals of the Minister, but Sharaf didn't want to get bogged down in politics.

"The same people who are making life miserable for us, I'd imagine."

"You know, it's a good thing you mentioned Charlie Hatcher, or I'd have suspected you were one of them." She gestured toward Sam. "Who's this one?"

Sam answered for himself.

"Sam Keller. I was a friend of Charlie's."

"I am sorry for your loss. Charlie was our friend. Why are you dressed like that?"

Sam looked to Sharaf for help.

"The same reason I'm out of uniform. Let's just say that we've had an interesting few days. Where is Basma?"

Halami's phone rang. She answered instantly, ignoring them.

"Yes? Of course, but where? Ethiopia is my guess. They're from villages on the brink of starvation. Someone puts up an Emirates Air poster with a nice photo of Dubai, and all you have to do is offer a plane ticket. An easy recruitment. Sure. Keep me posted."

No sooner had she hung up than the phone rang again.

"Yes? Where? Good, very good." She laughed with relish. "Another one bites the dust. We should have a party. Good. Later, then."

She hung up. Sharaf was getting annoyed.

"Could you maybe shut that damn thing off for a minute?"

"No. They are my clients, Anwar. You're just a cop, even though your daughter is one of the world's great human beings, spoiled or not."

"What can you tell me about Basma?"

"Our Jeanne d'Arc, you mean, if you will pardon the Christian metaphor. Sometimes I am more French than Muslim."

"I noticed. Why a martyr? Is she dead?"

"Alive, but only by her own wits. I will leave it to Basma to answer your other question. Where did you hear her name? I doubt Charlie would have told you."

Sam spoke up.

"It was in Charlie's datebook, with a number for this place. She was listed next to Tatiana Tereshkova."

"Another of our contacts from the trade. But I am worried about her, too. I can't seem to find her."

"Found, I'm afraid," Sharaf said. "Several days ago."

Halami lowered her cigarette.

"Dead?"

"She'd been shot. They dumped her in the desert."

He said it more harshly than necessary, the very stereotype of the uncaring cop, and he felt bad about it as soon as he saw Halami's reaction. She put a hand to her mouth and emitted a small cry, blinking twice. Her phone beeped, but she didn't even glance at it.

"It's where they take all of them," she said quietly. "They just throw them on the ground and leave them for the birds. Tatiana was one of the Russian originals, from those Aeroflot caravans in the early nineties. Worked her way up through the system, then got disgusted with it. She was the reason Basma got away, she and Charlie. I suppose someone found out."

"She was with Hatcher when he was shot."

"Oh, dear. I didn't know."

"Hardly anyone does. And I doubt you will read about her in the papers anytime soon, not if some of my colleagues have their way."

"Which is why I cannot trust you with the knowledge of Basma's whereabouts. Not if they are after you as well."

"Then I suppose we will never find out who killed Tatiana."

She eyed them carefully.

"Charlie was the only man Basma trusted. Ever since he was killed she has been certain she will be next. That's why we are hiding her. But she will not speak to any man. It's a fact. You will have to deal with it."

"We're operating under a deadline. Finding a suitable female officer will not be as easy as you think."

Halami smiled ruefully and flicked ashes into a Styrofoam cup.

"You know, Anwar, for such an intelligent man, you are sometimes a bumbling oaf. Because we both know of a woman who is not only suitable but is also readily available, and someone I trust."

Sharaf saw where she was headed, and moved to cut her off.

"That is not an option. Laleh does not participate in my business."

"More's the pity. She is brilliant and compassionate—the very combination necessary to induce Basma to tell her story. You say she is not an option? Sir, she is your *only* option. Like it or not, she is already a part of this business, simply by her role in ours."

Sharaf was exasperated. First Laleh, now Halami—both of them ordering him around, and taking events well beyond his control. Fine, let them. Why not just walk out of this place while his pride was intact? With the Minister's help, he might still organize a team to raid Monday's delivery at Jebel Ali.

The problem with that approach was that the scheme's principals— Assad, the mobsters, the American woman—would be able to scramble right out of the net. He only had Liffey on tape, and even what he had heard of that conversation was vague enough for Liffey to argue that he was talking about some other commodity altogether, and with another bribe it might even be convincing to a judge. Sharaf still needed to dive deeper.

The other problem, greater yet, was that Halami was right. It was midafternoon Saturday. Delivery was Monday. There was no time for other options. Laleh was the perfect choice. The cop in him knew this, even as the father continued to shut his eyes and shake his head.

He was jolted from thought by the sound of loud pounding on the shelter's front entrance. Halami moved to a window and flicked back a curtain, frowning. Then a woman poked her head into the canteen from the hallway.

"It's the police," she said. "A Lieutenant Assad. He says it is urgent."

Halami glanced at Sharaf in alarm, and with a hint of mistrust.

"What, you think I called him?" Sharaf said. "He's probably look-ing for Basma, just like me. But if he finds us, we're finished."

There was shouting from the entrance—Assad's voice ordering someone to search the house. They had to get moving, but Halami was blocking the way, still studying his face. Smoke curled from her ciga-rette like the signal of an impending decision, and for a moment Sharaf was convinced she would throw them to the wolves.

Then she yanked at his sleeve and shoved him into the hallway toward the rear of the house, while whispering harshly, "Take the stairs to the top floor. Then the ladder to the roof. Go!"

He ran, Sam followed. There was more shouting from the front room, and the house was in an uproar. Women were running out of their bedrooms, moaning and holding their hands to their faces. The commotion gave them the cover to make it up to the next floor before any police reached the stairwell. By the time they got to the third floor the chaos below was louder, with heavy thumps of moving furniture, and the indignant cries of the residents. When Sharaf reached the landing he doubled over, dizzy and out of breath. Sam tugged at his shoulder.

"We've got to keep going," Sam said. "It's over there."

A fire escape ladder was bolted to the wall at the end of a dim hallway, leading to a trapdoor in the ceiling. Sam climbed the first three rungs and flattened his palms against the door, wrenching it open with a metallic shriek while Sharaf watched from below. He threw it back like a hatch and burst into the sunlight, climbing onto a flat gravel roof. Then he thrust a hand back through the opening for Sharaf as he watched the big man struggle upward, hands sweaty on the rungs.

"Here," Sam called.

Sharaf reached higher as a shoe slipped. He took Sam's hand as footsteps echoed up the stairwell from the second floor. Sam pulled hard, boosting Sharaf past the last rung until he landed on the rooftop in a heap. They shut the trapdoor behind them.

"Stay low," Sharaf said. "We're too exposed."

They moved in a crouch to keep from being seen from the street, and headed for a massive air-conditioning unit that sat like a block-house in a far corner. Sharaf was breathing heavily. His swollen fore-head throbbed, and his head began to swim. He paused, and must have wobbled, because Sam was quickly at his side, coaxing him toward the far side of the blockhouse cube. They sagged onto the warm gravel behind the metal box, which sighed and grumbled as the big air-conditioning unit throbbed against the eighty-five-degree heat.

"Good thing we parked around the corner," Sam said.

"An even better thing that we didn't bring the Camry. In this neighborhood it would stand out like a rickshaw."

Ten minutes passed. They could hear little of the ruckus unfolding below, and after a while Sharaf began to hope that they could ride out the storm. He listened for voices from the yard, expecting that at any second the policemen would begin trooping back toward their vehicles.

Instead he heard the groan of the trapdoor as it opened on the far side of the roof.

"Shit!" Sam whispered.

Sharaf shifted uncomfortably, his rump sliding on the gravel. He supposed they could still try running. They could even jump, although the fall would probably knock him senseless, especially in his current condition. A weary part of him braced for surrender. Wasn't that bound to be their eventual fate, anyway?

Then he glanced at Sam, the young man unwittingly pulled into all this. He saw the look of eager desperation, the urgency of youth. And that made him think of Laleh, her concern, and her efforts to help. He rose into a crouch, settling on the balls of his feet.

Footsteps crunched slowly toward them across the gravel. A shadow slid into view on their left, followed by a khaki police uniform. The officer gasped. So did Sam. But Sharaf, to his own surprise, nearly laughed in relief.

It was Sergeant Habash, the ambitious young Palestinian and squad room grunt. Of all the policemen who could have discovered them, Habash was the luckiest possible choice, given the ease with which Sharaf had always manipulated him. Not that Sharaf had much leverage at the moment. Nor did he have much time to employ it.

"Hello, Sergeant. I assume you're looking for the same girl as we are."

"You'll do as a consolation prize," Habash said.

"So that's what you're opting for, then? A brief moment of glory on behalf of Lieutenant Assad, who will promptly claim all the credit for himself and forget about you? Unless I tell him how easily this fellow Keller got away from you last Monday."

"But that was your doing!"

"I doubt he'll see it that way. But there is an alternative, of course. What if I were to promise that, if you give me the chance, this fellow Keller will be dead by this evening, drowned in Dubai Creek? Don't worry, he doesn't speak a word of Arabic, so he has no idea what I'm saying."

"You would do that?"

"Of course. He is excess baggage, an embarrassment for us both. Killing him will solve your problem and mine. And the longer I'm away from the office, the less likely it is that I'll tell them how you let him escape, or how wretchedly bad your English is in all those press translations. Unless, of course, you're itching to be back on the street, walking your old beat in Deira."

Habash's conflicted expression told Sharaf he was making progress. But before the sergeant could answer, the trapdoor slammed again, and another voice called out.

"Sergeant, what are you doing over there?"

It was Lieutenant Assad. The air-conditioning cube still blocked Sam and Sharaf from view. For Habash, for all of them, it was the moment of truth.

"Did you hear me, Sergeant? What's taking so long? Is she up here or not?"

Sharaf smiled at the wording. Even a fellow as dim as Habash couldn't possibly have missed the opening Assad had just given him.

"No," Habash shouted back. "She's not up here."

"Then stop wasting my time! We're ready to leave."

"Yes, sir."

And, just like that, Habash turned and left, without even having to tell a lie.

The trapdoor slammed shut. The rooftop was silent. Sharaf sagged in relief against the air-conditioning unit, feeling its vibrations like a massage across his sweating back. A few minutes later they heard voices in the yard, followed by the slamming of car doors and the rev of engines. Two vehicles pulled away from the curb.

"Too close," Sam said. "What do we do now?"

Sharaf considered the question carefully, thinking only as a policeman, and he wasn't at all pleased with the answer that sprang to mind. He voiced it, all the same, as if merely testing its theoretical possibilities.

"We telephone my daughter, and put her to work. It is insane, it is outrageous, and, worst of all, it is exactly what she will want. But Halami is right. Right now, she is our only option."

23

An hour after the police departed, Sam and Sharaf were back in the Beacon of Light's canteen, staving off the jitters with snacks and soda. At dusk they watched through a slit in the curtains as a taxi arrived, the yellow Camry gleaming beneath the streetlamp. Laleh, wearing her abaya, stepped out from a rear door.

She had come straight from the office. Apparently she was more willing to brave the threat of surveillance than further doses of her mother's wrath. Or so Sam had concluded after listening in on a series of family phone calls. Even through the language barrier the urgency and anger were unmistakable.

Sharaf was wrapping up a call to Amina as Laleh came up the sidewalk. He sounded exasperated as he hung up.

"I will be paying off this debt for years," he moaned, snapping the phone shut. "The worst part is, I agree with her. Laleh is taking a great risk, even if only with her reputation. The way we are using her is unacceptable. I should bring this all to a halt, here and now."

"What happened to the greater good?" Sam said.

"Yes, the greater good. Stopping a shipment of prostitutes will probably only make the price go up. Then they'll send in another load. That is what passes for the greater good anymore in Dubai. All for the cost of a girl's standing in her community. You can't possibly understand how Laleh will be seen after this."

"Like a hero, maybe? That's how she'd be seen in most places."

"This isn't most places."

"But I bet she's all for it."

"Of course. From listening to people like you, who will come and go before she realizes the damage she's done."

"Did you ever consider she might be smart enough to overcome it?"

"Please. Don't lecture me on her intelligence. That's what makes it tragic."

Halami entered the canteen with Laleh in her wake. Tense excitement showed in the young woman's eyes.

Sharaf sighed. It was just too much. No matter how logical, he couldn't go through with this. He addressed her in English, so that everyone in the room would understand what he had to say, and why.

"I have decided this is not possible. It simply is not workable."

Laleh's mouth dropped open.

"I thought it was what you wanted?"

"What I want as a policeman is beside the point. As a detective I operate only on the basis of need, may God forgive me. As a father, I cannot agree to it."

"Then maybe I'd better talk to the policeman. Although I have to say, the father's behavior surprises me. Earlier he was so determined to remove his family's shame, no matter what it took."

Sharaf shot a sidelong glance at Halami, who was listening eagerly, and his next words emerged in an irritated tone.

"Please. Not in front of others."

"Fine. But I really would prefer to speak to the policeman. Provided he's still on duty."

Neither of them spoke for a moment. Sharaf's eyes flicked back and forth, as if somewhere inside he was engaged in a difficult argument. Finally he sighed and slapped a hand against the wall.

"Even as a policeman, I never let anyone act on my behalf unless they first understand all possible consequences."

"And you think I don't know them? Believe me, my entire upbringing makes me painfully aware of all that could follow. But what troubles me more is what will happen to both of us if we do nothing. I can live with disapproval from the outside. But from within? You should know better than anyone how unbearable that might become."

Sharaf sagged, defeated. Or maybe he was also relieved, now that Laleh had shown him a way he might proceed as both father and policeman, no matter how contrived.

"You are sure, then?"

"Yes, Lieutenant Sharaf, I am sure."

Her father smiled weakly and lightly placed a hand on her cheek.

"Then we had better get down to business before I change my mind."

He pulled his hand away and shook his head, as if trying to put the moment behind him. Then he sighed yet again, sounding tired and grumpy.

"Everyone be seated. We might as well stick to English, so Mr. Keller can assist us. The practical question is how you're going to handle this interview. These things are tricky, like sailing a dhow in a choppy sea. When the wind shifts, you had better shift with it, or you'll wind up dead in the water. But I do have confidence in your abilities, Laleh."

"I know. I have always known that, in spite of everything."

"Good." Sharaf nodded, a glimmer of pride in his eyes. The exchange was intimate enough to make Sam want to look away. Halami beamed at the old cop, her first sign of affection for him. She then left the room to let them carry out their business.

They worked quickly. Sharaf spoke for half an hour about what questions to ask, while Laleh took notes. Sam added a thought here and there. Then she was ready to go. A guard had been assigned to drive her, using not the battered blue van but a white Audi parked in the rear.

"We've checked the streets," Halami said. "No sign of surveillance."

"Not that you're qualified to make that judgment," Sharaf said.

"These men are. Trust me."

"But can we trust *them?*"

Halami stared him down and put a hand on her hip.

"Sharaf?"

"Yes?"

"Shut up and let me finish."

He said nothing in reply.

"It will take forty minutes, maybe longer, for Laleh to reach the secure location. The address is known only to the driver and two others of us here at the Beacon of Light."

"You're sure you've told no one else?"

"Only Charlie Hatcher. He visited her a little more than a week ago, on the night he arrived."

Sharaf turned to Sam.

"Did you know this?"

"No. I went to bed early that night. We were both exhausted from the flight, or so I thought. I guess Lieutenant Assad was right."

"*He* knew?"

"I don't think so. He just believed Charlie could have gone out after I went to bed. He practically scolded me for not staying up."

"Because he already knew you were working for Nanette, his business partner. You were their eyes and ears."

"Thanks for reminding me."

"Please, gentlemen," Halami said. "Do you want to hear the plan or not?"

"Continue," Sharaf said.

"Assuming that Basma is willing to talk, Laleh may be there an hour, even longer. The return trip will take another forty minutes. So maybe two and a half hours in all. In the meantime, you gentlemen are welcome to join us for dinner, but I suggest that you make other arrangements for sleeping."

"I'll call Ali," Sharaf said. "He is lining up accommodations."

"Safe Houses R Us," Sam said. "Hope it's better than the place he found for me."

Laleh stood to go. Sam expected a tearful farewell, but Sharaf seemed to deliberately avoid it by keeping his seat. He opened his phone in his lap and punched in Ali's number. From the intent look on his face, the policeman was working overtime to block the father's entry to the scene. Laleh smiled gamely, as if she understood. Then she mouthed a silent "good-bye" to Sam and was on her way. By the time she had disappeared down the hallway, Sharaf was talking to Ali as if nothing was out of the ordinary. Or maybe he was trying to drown out the sound of the shutting door.

Sam waited for the conversation to end, then spoke up.

"We should play the rest of Patel's recording," he said. "See what they said in Russian."

"Not here. Not anywhere in this house. Mrs. Halami might be right about her government visitors. Maybe they did plant a microphone somewhere."

"In which case we're dead anyway."

Sharaf frowned.

"Okay. Then I will tell you the real reason. I am too nervous. In my current state of mind I can only think in one language at a time. I would get half the translation wrong if I tried it now. Later, when we are at Ali's safe house."

"He found one?"

"Some golf course condo development where no one has moved in yet and, according to Ali, no one ever will. Four hundred empty units. Plus canals, of course. We will be sleeping in the furnished display model. Mansour's Maritime Police will provide security, front and back. Which reminds me. Sam Keller is now officially dead. Mansour released the news to the media only an hour ago. He told Ali that Hal Liffey was on the phone to him within minutes to arrange for transport of the body."

"Happy to do it, no doubt."

"And if Sergeant Habash was having second thoughts, he will realize now that he *has* to keep quiet about us, unless he wants to look like a fool."

They shared in the household's communal dinner, but to allow the women to feel at ease, the men ate in an alcove of the dining room, sealed off by a curtain. Neither of them ate much, and afterward they returned to the canteen to wait, flicking back the curtains every time a car passed out front. Three times the phone rang in the kitchen, jarring them to alertness. None of the calls were about Basma or Laleh, and none were from the police.

Finally, after two hours and forty-seven minutes, they heard a car come up the rear alley, followed by the opening and closing of the back door. Laleh walked up the hallway, fresh from her mission.

She was pale, subdued, and took a seat without a word. From her widened eyes, the set of her jaw, and the way she folded her hands, it was clear that something momentous had taken place. Her earlier signs of triumph and excitement had been replaced by something more sober and deliberate.

"So?" Sharaf asked, the policeman in him still just barely in charge. "What did you find out?"

"Far more than I wanted to. For the first time, I guess, I understand why you and Mom have always tried to shelter me."

She then placed her hands on her knees, as if to brace herself, and told them the story of Basma.

24

"She came from the war in Iraq, the last of her family. Everyone else died in some explosion. She didn't offer details, and I didn't ask for them. But that was how it started for her, as a war victim. She was fifteen and alone. Easy pickings. Some militiamen found her wandering in her village. They raped her, of course. Many times. And she *did* describe that, as if she still couldn't quite believe it had happened."

Laleh paused to sip her tea. Halami had presented the steaming mug like broth for an invalid. That's how shaken Laleh looked.

"For a week she was pretty much their slave, of course."

"Laleh, please stop saying 'of course,' " Sharaf said. "It's not as if such things are inevitable, even in wartime."

Halami stared him down like he was a dolt—a look Sharaf remembered from his tutors whenever he had mangled some obvious fact. Was this truly how the world worked when all control was removed? He'd certainly seen evidence to that effect before, but not to this degree, and he had hoped he would never have to. Too late now. He held his tongue. Laleh continued.

"They got tired of her after a while. She wound up near the border, then across it. She's still not sure how that happened. A lot of truck convoys and aid people were involved, and in all the confusion someone took her to a village in Iran. An older woman who ran a restaurant took care of her, got her some new identity papers, and promised to help. Another jackal, of course."

Sharaf cringed.

"This woman told her and the other girls that she knew people who could find them jobs in a beauty salon in Turkey, so all of them agreed. The next day they took the four girls away in a truck. Her memory of that part wasn't so good. Not enough food and water, and hardly any light. She wound up at some kind of port, big ships everywhere, and they put her and another of the women into a freight container that had been outfitted with a pair of cots, blankets, water and bread, and a pot to piss in. There were holes for air that let in some light, but that's all. She also remembers what else was in the container. Boxes marked with the name Pfluger Klaxon."

She glanced at Keller, not in an accusatory way but as if to say she now better understood why he was on the run. He nodded back, a kinship that Sharaf envied.

"They were seasick, of course, but they survived. The voyage took two days, maybe three, before their container was unloaded. Then it sat in a lot for another night while they wondered if they would ever get out. She thinks now it was one of the freight yards at Jebel Ali, based on what others have told her since. The next day the container was loaded onto a truck, and when it was finally opened they were in the back of the Rand Hotel in Bur Dubai. Russians and Uzbeks were standing in an alley, men with guns who took them upstairs where a woman, this Tatiana woman—"

"Tatiana Tereshkova?" Sharaf asked.

"Basma didn't know her last name. But yes, if that's the Tatiana that Charlie Hatcher knew. She was Basma's pimp, or at least some kind of boss, and she took the girls twelve stories up to a two-bedroom apartment. Fourteen other girls were living there, sleeping on mattresses, mostly Uzbeks and Tadjiks, and one or two others also from Iraq. One of the Iraqis had also come by container ship, only a month earlier.

"Tatiana got them cleaned up and fed, and gave them a place to sleep. Later she gave them dressy clothes, makeup, high heels and nylons, miniskirts, tights. The whole wardrobe they would need as whores, of course."

Sharaf felt shamed. Not just for Laleh, but for human beings in general, for his country, and for his own inability to do something about it, year after year. He couldn't look her in the eye as she continued.

"How long ago was this?" Keller asked, a question that should have occurred to Sharaf.

"Three months, maybe four. She couldn't be precise."

"Understandable. Sorry, go on."

"They kept the girls locked in the apartment all day. All they did was watch TV, eat, sleep, and do their hair. In the evenings they went out, always with pimps and bodyguards, someone to make sure that they got their work done and didn't run away. They were driven in vans to the York, or the Regal, or other places. They simply told her to start producing, as they put it. She was supposed to pick up men any way she could, for any kind of sex. Blow jobs, two-for-ones, whatever the men wanted."

Sharaf stared at the floor. Such an education he was giving her.

"After a week she was beaten because she had hardly made any money. Some man lectured her for an hour on how to be more aggressive—more appealing, as he put it. A few weeks later three more Iraqi girls arrived from Iran the same way Basma had come—inside a shipping container. Tatiana told her it was all part of a test, and that the shipment of three was the last one."

"A test?" Sharaf said, looking up, forcing himself back into the role of a cop.

"For the main event," Laleh said. "Those were Tatiana's words."

"Just like the space program," Keller said, shaking his head. "Mercury with one astronaut, Gemini with two, Apollo with three—working their way up to make sure they could handle the logistics of bigger loads. All of it practice for Monday. Payload of fifty."

"And if that works," Sharaf said, "who knows how many more will follow. It is just as I thought. The crackdown at the airport is taking a toll, so they're shifting to sea lanes."

Halami shook her head.

"Awful. Despicable. And right under your noses."

"Why do you think we are here?" Sharaf snapped. "Why do you think I am risking my daughter, and everything about her future?"

Laleh intervened.

"No one's blaming you, Father. I'm not, and I know Basma isn't. She is hoping it can be stopped."

"How did she get away?"

"With the help of Charlie Hatcher, and Tatiana. Charlie was one of her customers."

"A customer," Sam said, somewhat incredulous. "So I guess part of Nanette's cover story was true. No wonder he was talking about atonement."

Laleh shook her head.

"Not that kind of customer. He bought her for information, not sex. And when he came to the York he asked for her by name. That scared her at first, because she already knew what a 'special request' could mean. Usually something kinky, even dangerous."

Sharaf shook his head.

"But when they were alone, he didn't take off his clothes. He just sat on the bed and started asking questions. He said Tatiana had told him how she had arrived, and he wanted to know more about the boxes that were also in the container, the ones marked with the corporate name of Pfluger Klaxon."

Sharaf perked up.

"So even then he was already on their trail. I wonder how he found out?"

"He told Basma he had come across something in his work, something that made him believe he was partly responsible for what had happened to her."

"Responsible? That makes no sense."

"Unless . . ." Sam said, sitting up straighter than before.

"Yes?" Sharaf prompted. "Unless what?"

"The shipping routes. There was something in one of Nanette's quarterly reports about a project she'd worked on with Charlie. Boring logistical troubleshooting, or that's what I thought. But it had to do with securing and streamlining new shipping routes out of the Far East for a new line of imports, and I'm sure it mentioned some transshipment issues along the way."

"Meaning he had unwittingly helped her set up the whole operation," Sharaf said. "But how would he have found out?"

"Who knows? But once he did, he knew he couldn't report it to the corporate security officer."

"Or to law enforcement here," Sharaf said.

"So this was his atonement. His one-man show of morality."

They turned back toward Laleh.

"What else did Basma say about him?" Sharaf asked.

"He paid her triple the normal price and told her he was going to pay for her freedom, and put her somewhere safe, where he could talk to her some more. A week later Tatiana drugged one of the guards. Basma and an Uzbek girl got away. The Uzbek disappeared. Basma came to the Beacon of Light by prior arrangement. That was two weeks ago. A few nights later Charlie came to see her—last Friday. He told her everything was arranged. He was going to make sure they wouldn't be able to send any more girls the way they had sent her. He told her it was all planned for April fourteenth."

"Charlie's 'day of reckoning,' " Sam said. "No wonder they wanted me to follow him. He was their one big threat, and I was their homing beacon."

"And from Charlie's movements, they tracked down Tatiana and Patel."

"What will you do now?" Halami asked.

"Intercept their delivery, obviously," Sharaf said. "But that won't shut down their pipeline. The only way to do that is to round up the main players."

"Can't you just arrest them?" Sam asked.

"Only if they show up for pickup and delivery of the goods, which I very much doubt will happen. As long as Assad has ministerial support, they will remain untouchable unless we can establish a tangible link. You heard the recording, Mr. Keller. Even Liffey can probably wiggle out of it with a good lawyer. We need to catch the five of them in the act, preferably all at once."

"And how do we do that?"

Sharaf had been wondering the same thing all day.

"Obviously I don't know yet. We need time to think."

"Better think fast," Sam answered. "Charlie's day of reckoning begins in about three hours."

25

Sam had his doubts about their so-called safe house.

For one thing, it was the only apartment in the entire complex with any lights on. Even with the blinds drawn, it stood out like a neon tube in a tunnel of desert darkness. Then there were the two vans from the Maritime Police parked out front—the only vehicles on the newly paved grid of roads—plus the skiff in the canal out back, tethered to the wharf with its running lights burning. To Sam they were an open secret begging for further scrutiny, guaranteed to attract the curiosity of any passerby.

But as Sharaf and Ali had already pointed out, there weren't any passersby, and at this late hour the location was too remote to attract anyone but drag racers and vagabonds. Beat cops apparently never approached within a mile, and there were certainly no neighbors to raise an alarm.

Mansour had provided a bit of good news. Shipping records showed that the IMO number 9016742 belonged to a container ship called the *Global Star*. It was indeed due to arrive at Jebel Ali the next day, but not until 9 p.m., which bought them some extra time. Not that Sharaf had yet come up with any ideas. And for the moment he had other things on his mind as he opened the empty refrigerator in the model kitchen.

"I'm hungry," he said. "I should have packed some of Halami's free food in a bag while I was thinking."

Ali, who had just arrived from the city, smiled and placed a greasy paper bag on the kitchen counter. He unrolled the top and bowed grandly, like a headwaiter serving filet mignon. The aroma of grilled meat filled the kitchen.

"Lamb kebabs, Anwar. From the take-out window of Special Ostadi Restaurant in Bur Dubai, your favorite. And, no, I did not forget the yogurt sauce, the bread, or the spices. Maybe it will sharpen your thinking. Yours, too, of course, Mr. Keller."

Laleh had already gone to bed, heading off sleepily to the far end of the condo. The unit had been built with locals in mind, meaning its four bedrooms were divided between two wings to allow extra privacy for females.

Sharaf piled meat, yogurt, and greens onto a warm curl of flatbread. He was opening wide for his first sloppy bite when Ali produced a second surprise.

"Fresh clothes for all of you. I couldn't have done it without your wife's help, Anwar, especially now that the weasel Assad has placed a patrol car outside your compound. Amina told me to climb in over the back wall. She met me at the back door of Rahim's house. She had taken the whole load over there in steamer pots and casserole dishes, making it look like she was delivering him dinner. She is a clever woman, your Amina. But I have to say, Anwar, she is very angry with you. With all three of you."

" 'Hell to pay,' isn't that what Americans say?" Sharaf said, pausing gloomily between bites.

Sam sorted through the new wardrobe. A New York Knicks T-shirt, supposedly for him, plus baggy jeans, which, like the clothes in the previous batch, were a little too large. At least he still had his suit jacket, dirty or not. For Sharaf there was a freshly laundered *kandoura*, which looked as comfy as pajamas. Maybe it would be better to just go native.

Sharaf dug past his own clothes. He frowned as he reached the bottom of the pile.

"Look at this," he said disdainfully, holding aloft a flimsy pair of red spiked heels. He used only his fingertips, as if he had just tweezered something disgusting from a clogged drain.

"High heels?" Sam asked, wondering what all the fuss was about.

"Laleh's. The most scandalous pair she owns. Practically indecent.

Amina knows I hate them. *She* hates them. Sending these over here is a deliberate provocation."

"Hold your fire, Anwar. She told me to also give you this." Ali set down *Crime and Punishment* and a half-quart bottle of camel's milk, beaded with moisture. The wrinkles eased on Sharaf's troubled brow. Ali picked up the book for a second look.

"Some title," he said. "Maybe she *is* warning you."

"No," Sharaf said. "This is good. Her way of saying she might even forgive me. Or maybe she is just wishing us luck. God willing, we'll need it. Mr. Keller, where's that recorder? We had better listen to the rest of it while we eat. I'll translate."

They put it on the table and flipped the switch. To Sam it was all babble. Liffey and the two nameless Mafia lieutenants—he wondered if one of them might even be the unlucky Arzhanov—were speaking rapid-fire Russian. At first Sharaf didn't seem impressed.

"Generalities," he said, waving dismissively. "Everything vague and careful, all of it useless for our purposes. Your Mr. Liffey speaks very good Russian, I will say that. The Persian as well. Probably why he was chosen for this meeting, an act of deference to the Tsar."

The voices droned on, pausing only when the waitress stopped to take orders for a fresh round of drinks.

"Too bad Assad was not with them. I'd like to have heard if he would have ordered a vodka," Sharaf said. "Hypocritical infidel. Two-faced bastard."

"Tell me again about those pork ribs you ate as a boy, Anwar," Ali chimed in.

"Enough," Sharaf said. "Let me listen."

More Russian, more noncommittal grunts from Sharaf. Then he sat up straighter in his chair. He reached across the table to switch off the recorder, backed it up a bit, then listened again, eyes narrowed.

"What is it?" Sam asked.

"Some sort of alert on Charlie Hatcher, I'm guessing. Your Miss Weaver seems to have forwarded some instructions, which Liffey has duly repeated."

Sharaf played it back for a third time, translating as Liffey spoke.

" 'Your organizations should be advised that our corporate sponsor has reported a possible security breach. Here is a photo and a few particulars for internal distribution, although for now our corporate sponsor would prefer to handle this matter from her end, with possible assistance from our law enforcement element.' "

Sharaf paused the recording. "He means Assad, of course." He switched the recorder back on and resumed translation.

" 'She requests that your people be on standby for assistance. But she is adamant that there be no unilateral action by anyone. As she has previously indicated, she is well aware that your usual way of dealing with threats is immediate action. While that is bluntly effective, it is also inefficient. She points out that in the corporate world they first learn what they can from the source of the trouble—through briefings, interrogations, surveillance. In this way, potential debits can be turned into assets. Even then, liquidation occurs only after full consultation by all interested parties. She insists we proceed in a similar fashion. Any objections?' "

Both men grunted their assent. Sharaf again stopped the recording.

"Arzhanov's death warrant," he said. "He violated their security protocol. I suppose he panicked when he lost the GPS signal from your phone, especially when they saw where Mr. Hatcher had gone when you switched it back on."

"Meaning that if I hadn't switched it off, Charlie might still be alive."

"No, no. You heard her advice about eventual 'liquidation.' They still would have hauled him in, probably the moment you left for Hong Kong. He would have died, but only after a full and thorough interrogation, meaning Basma would probably be dead by now as well. Your Miss Weaver would have insisted."

"Maybe," Sam said, wishing he was as certain.

"Absolutely," Sharaf said. "You're just going to have to believe that."

"Why would a bunch of thugs let Nanette handle security?"

"I suspect she was a compromise choice. Neither the Tsar nor Hedayat would have trusted each other to provide it, not on a joint venture."

The recording continued for another ten minutes, followed by silence. Sharaf frowned and switched it off.

"Instructive," he said, "but still not helpful. Not for our immediate needs."

"Which means we have what," Sam asked, "about twenty-two hours?"

"Yes. We'll intercept the shipment, of course. Mansour's men can manage that."

"And then they'll be free and clear to rework their logistics and pick up where they left off."

"Probably. Unless some great idea strikes me like a lightning bolt while I sleep."

"Any clouds forming on the horizon?"

"Nothing but cobwebs. I am exhausted."

"Same here."

Both said little more before heading off to bed, discouraged. They left the recorder sitting in the middle of the kitchen table like an untapped secret. Sam showered, slid beneath the display coverlet onto a bare mattress, and was asleep within seconds.

Anwar Sharaf, however, couldn't relax. Maybe it was the bump on his head. It stung under the harsh stream of the shower, and throbbed afterward from the heat. He climbed into bed and flipped off the lights, but he could only toss and turn.

Why so restless? Despite the conundrum of the case, he had plenty of reasons to finally relax. Laleh was back under the same roof, even if it was someone else's. The American, Keller, was now safe, at least for the moment. And by this time tomorrow, fifty distraught young women would owe their salvation to his efforts.

Even the Minister would be mildly satisfied. The threads Sharaf had gathered might be too flimsy for a court of law, but in the right hands they could still be woven into enough dirty laundry to embarrass the Minister's top rivals for months to come.

He was also exhausted, and had a full stomach.

So why couldn't he sleep?

Sharaf sighed and threw back the covers. He switched the light on and trooped down the hallway to the kitchen, where he snatched the sweating bottle of camel's milk from the otherwise empty refrigerator. He intended to take only a swallow or two, but the cool, velvety taste felt so good going down his throat that by the time he set the bottle down there was nothing but white coating on the sides of the glass.

He licked his lips, then belched with satisfaction. Just what he needed. He picked up the copy of *Crime and Punishment* and took it back to the bedroom. Half an hour of reading and he would be sleeping like a baby. Thank God for Amina, knowing just what he needed, even as she must have cursed his name and his infernal job.

Sharaf propped two pillows against the creaky headboard and opened to his bookmark. Too bad Amina wasn't beside him, showing the curve of her back. He wouldn't even have minded hearing her complain about how he was leaving the light on too late and disturbing her sleep.

He began to read, while trying to recall where he had last left the story. The guilt-ridden Raskolnikov had committed two murders many pages ago and was still on the loose. The young man's fevered torment was growing tiresome, but at least now a detective of sorts had come onto the scene, an examining lawyer named Porfiry. Sharaf read with growing appreciation as Porfiry interrogated Raskolnikov, using an indirect approach that was clever and disarming—the very way Sharaf might have done it. This fellow Porfiry even looked like him, Sharaf thought, as he read Dostoevsky's description: " 'God has given me a figure that can awaken none but comic ideas in other people,' Porfiry said. 'A buffoon.' "

Perfect.

Sharaf began to relax. A few more pages ought to do the trick. Raskolnikov grew more agitated as the interrogation proceeded, especially when Porfiry began describing how he always lured guilty suspects to their doom, particularly the smart ones:

Have you seen a butterfly round a candle? That's how he will keep circling round me. . . . He'll begin to brood, he'll weave a tangle round himself, he'll worry himself to death! What's more he will provide me with a mathematical proof—if only I give him enough interval. . . . And he'll keep circling round me, getting nearer and nearer and then—flop! He'll fly straight into my mouth and I'll swallow him, and that will be very amusing, he-he-he!

Sharaf put the book down and looked up at the ceiling, suddenly giddy with insight.

He had it, his bolt of lighting, the tool they had been seeking, not only to stop the delivery but to bring its architects into the basket and up from the deep. With a little help, they would be able to pry loose the biggest pearl in the ocean, sharks be damned.

It was time to wake everyone in the house.

26

Laleh, Ali, and Keller sat before Sharaf at the kitchen table. They were in a grumpy stupor, and still wondering why he had awakened them so urgently at 1 a.m. The recorder remained at the center of the table—silent, waiting. It was to be the main prop in his presentation.

Waking Laleh had been the hardest part. Thinking like a cop, he had dashed to her bedroom first, knowing she would have to play one more role in this final move. But at her doorway he hesitated, overwhelmed by a burst of fatherly emotion. Light from the hallway cast a shadow across her face. He stepped to the bedside and brushed back her hair the way he had once done when waking her for grade school.

"Laleh?" he whispered. "Laleh?"

A flutter of eyelids.

"Yes?"

She was almost instantly alert. He then realized that for all the exertion and emotional strain, a part of her was immensely enjoying the cloak-and-dagger aspects of the past twenty-four hours. She was a player in the arena, out where decisions affected lives. He smiled in spite of his worry, admiring how easily she had taken to this new role, even though he still would have preferred to have kept her out of it.

"I need your help, one last time."

She sat up, propped on her elbows.

"What time is it?"

"After midnight. But this can't wait. We have to begin planning now, all of us. So get dressed and come to the kitchen."

She nodded, obedient. He went to wake the others. And now there they were, looking at him like he had lost his mind.

Sharaf began his spiel.

"Good news. Lightning has struck. We have found the candle to attract our butterfly. All five of our butterflies, in fact, if I'm reading things correctly."

"Butterflies?" Ali rubbed his eyes. "Anwar, what in God's name are you talking about?"

"Let's just say I know now how to bait the trap in a way that might well produce instantaneous results. Here, listen to this part of the recording again."

Sharaf hit the PLAY switch, and Hal Liffey's voice began speaking in Russian.

"He is saying that in the corporate world they first learn what they can from the source of the trouble—through briefings, interrogations, surveillance. In this way, potential debits are turned into assets. Even then, they only liquidate after full consultation by all interested parties."

He switched off the machine.

"So?" Ali said.

"Don't you see? Interrogation, debriefing, and full consultation. If we can present them with an immediate and serious threat to their operation, that's how they will respond. And given the timetable for delivery, I'm betting they'll respond right away."

"What kind of threat?" Keller said.

"Basma. At the first hour of business tomorrow she will telephone the police department and ask for their ranking authority on vice. She will of course be referred to Lieutenant Hamad Assad. She offers to share with him a most interesting tale of a human-trafficking operation using a new means to smuggle goods into the country. But she is worried, very worried, about her own safety, so she will only meet him on neutral ground, at a place of her choosing. Of course, that is the very sort of location Assad will prefer. The last thing he would want is to have her show up at the police station."

"And you think he'll rally the troops?" Keller said.

"Does he have any choice, seeing as how all the troops are here in town? Especially after what happened to the last fellow who decided to handle things on his own?"

Ali nodded.

"That part is plausible," he said. "Even at 1 a.m., with kebabs rolling around my stomach. But what will the location be?"

"I was thinking you could provide one. A place with actual neighbors, so the watchers can blend in with the scenery."

"Yes. I can arrange that."

"We'll have Mansour's men wire the place, and we will stake it out from every angle. Every possible entry and exit, fully covered. Then, when all the players have arrived and had time to fully implicate themselves in the course of their debriefing, we'll spring the trap."

The only one who hadn't spoken up yet was Laleh, and they turned to her now. She would have to play the most crucial role, and she didn't look pleased.

"I suppose you want me to talk her into this," she said.

"In the morning. After you've slept."

"Well, I can already tell you that she won't agree to it. Nor would I let her."

"Oh, so it is up to you to decide for her now?"

"No. But it is her life that will be at risk. It's one thing for you to do something stupid on your own. Quite another to ask someone else who won't even know the real danger."

"Oh, Laleh, come on. We're talking about one person helping hundreds, maybe thousands. The greater good, Laleh!"

"It's easy to say 'one versus thousands' unless you have to face the one."

Sharaf sighed and regrouped.

"Right now, Laleh, even as we sit here, fifty girls just like Basma are locked inside cramped steel containers on the pitching deck of a ship at sea, probably vomiting their brains out. And you're going to let that happen over and over again, just because the fate of a single young woman is in your hands? You're the one who wanted to participate, Laleh. Well, participation comes with a cost, and the cost is responsibility. For Basma, yes. But also for those fifty young women, and however many more will keep coming if we fail."

Laleh frowned and shook her head, almost a shudder. Sharaf hated pushing her, but it was a lesson she needed to learn. This was the hidden reality of the heady life in the arena. Remember this feeling well, my daughter, because the burden never lightens.

"I will ask her," Laleh said. "But I won't push. Write out your argument, and all your justifications. I will present it in your own words as you wish. But I won't be an advocate, only a messenger."

"Fair enough."

It was settled, then. They discussed a few other arrangements and then went back to bed, where Sharaf supposed he might finally be able to sleep.

But he couldn't, of course, not a wink, because now his plan seemed all too shaky, and riddled with holes. What if they didn't take the bait? What if everyone didn't show up? Or, worst of all, what if they simply sent an assassin to kill Basma? At this late date, who knew how they might really react, no matter what Liffey had said about contingencies?

Six hours later he was standing by the front window with a cup of coffee, stomach fluttering as he peeped through the blinds into the early-morning sunlight. Out by the curb, Laleh was climbing into a taxi. His girl, heading off on her mission to talk another poor girl into hers.

Shaky or not, it was all they had. The taxi pulled away from the curb. Their operation was under way.

27

Nanette Weaver lined up her supplies in front of the hotel mirror, a general preparing for battle. Arrayed before her were moisturizer, foundation, concealer, blush, shadow, eyeliner, and lipstick—all of it in demure little tubes, vials, and bottles, plus a chic mini-cube of molded Lucite.

Once, in a rare moment of budgetary curiosity, she had totted up the dollar value of this arsenal and had been mildly appalled by the result, especially once she added shampoos and conditioners. Despite the micro sizes necessary for travel, the damage had come to $271.

But excess in the defense of finesse was no vice, and today it was more important than ever that Nanette achieve just the right look. Because now was the time to take command, marshal the troops, set disarray back in order. Proper leadership was what they had been lacking, and at this crucial final hour she aimed to provide it.

A ruse lay in wait for them, of that she was certain. She had already foreseen its likely hazards, even when Assad hadn't, and she had adjusted their plans accordingly. If she continued to have her way, then by day's end the board might well be wiped clean of opposition.

As always, she would be relying more on wits, timing, and experience than on her makeup. But Nanette was the only woman in their dire little assembly. And her years of navigating the male channels of commerce had taught her that words and actions, no matter how compelling, were never enough. When a woman was presiding, men were just as likely to be swayed by a significant glance, a narrowed eye, even a flash of ankle. Or, in this part of the world, practically anything to do with hair, the very beacon of Islamic sexuality.

She applied moisturizer first. A dab and a swirl, then another. Clinique, as standard for the job as an AK-47 was for Third World insurrections. Next came the foundation, a pricey discovery from Saks called La Prairie Cellular Treatment. Imbued with sunblock, it was suited perfectly for Dubai, with shades calibrated by the number—3.4 for her. It even *felt* luxurious. At $70 an ounce, it had better.

Was the need for these preparations regrettable? Of course. But so was the need for going rogue, so to speak—meaning illegal in her case, when you got right down to it. Years ago she would have been appalled to even consider participating in such a scheme, much less designing it from top to bottom. But that was before she learned how little you accomplished playing by the rules. In government work they even demoted you for it. It was one reason she'd moved to the corporate world, where surely the meritocracy of the profit motive and the competitive ideal would finally reward her aboveboard way of doing things.

No, it hadn't. Not when she had gone after the wrong targets. And if well-placed, well-paid executives could squirm free to such obvious self-benefit, then why couldn't she? So she, too, crossed the line. Except she was the rare woman in a roomful of boys, meaning appearances still mattered.

Fitness, fashion, and grooming—that was the ridiculous state of play for a businesswoman with brains, the libidinous lie at the base of all corporate manners and mores. Glass ceiling? Certainly, but only so they could peek up your skirt once you climbed above it.

She opened a micro-bottle of concealer. Two light touches. For adding color she might have relied on her usual workout at the hotel fitness club. But any flush of genuine vitality always disappeared within an hour, so she opened the Lucite cube of blush—a cream, not a powder. Dior. A mere fifth of an ounce for $31.

Soon enough they would have the girl in hand, the stray named Basma who had eluded them for days. Then the muscle could go after Sharaf and his allies, whoever they might be. To succeed they needed to move carefully, deliberately, and she was the only one in the bunch with the necessary subtlety. But she still had to win the others over to her endgame. It was one reason she had insisted on this meeting, even at such a perilously belated moment.

Assad would be the toughest sell. And it wasn't just due to his geographic sense of entitlement, as the group's only true local. The bigger problem was cultural. At some level he would always regard her as a refined form of harlot and deal with her accordingly. Typical attitude in the Gulf States, so why not turn it to her advantage? Because men who dealt with women only as whores could be enticed to buy almost anything—in this case, her leadership.

It wasn't just an Arab dynamic. She had even detected a hint of it in clever young Sam Keller, the human calculator. Granted, he had been exhausted at the time, but she recalled with wistful amusement the look on his face once she had finally maneuvered him onto the couch in her hotel room—the avid eagerness of a swimmer curling his toes at the edge of the pool, crouching for the dive. His erection had been unmistakable, and he hadn't even tried to hide it. A symptom of his weariness, perhaps, because he had definitely been a smart one, and too curious by half. A worthy adversary.

Even at that, she had nearly tracked him down, barely missing him after narrowing the hunt to a computer terminal in a camera store in the Sonapur labor camp. Judging from the reports Assad's people brought back from the scene—wild tales of vengeful Bengalis, a dormitory scuffle, and a midnight abduction—Keller must have fallen in with the wrong people, and a day later he had washed up dead on the shores of Dubai Creek.

Then the long-sought Basma had finally surfaced as well, by making a phone call to the police. Assad had played back the recording in his office to Liffey and her. Nanette's Arabic was perfectly good, but Assad had insisted on translating anyway.

Basma: Is this Lieutenant Assad, of vice investigations?
Assad: Those are among my duties, yes.

He sounded hurried, disinterested, even careless. Nanette wasn't at all surprised.

Basma: I have a crime to report.
Assad: Then you should come down to CID, or contact our bureau of—
Basma: A smuggling crime, involving fifty girls. It is going to happen later today, on a container ship at Jebel Ali.

There was silence. Pages shuffled. It sounded as if Assad had shifted the receiver in his hand. All the signs of a man regrouping, reassessing. And Nanette understood why. The precision of Basma's information was shocking, unnerving.

Basma: Hello?
Assad: Fifty, you say? You know the exact number and location?
Basma: Yes, because I was also brought in this way, and managed to escape.

More silence. She had clearly thrown him for a loop.

Basma (timidly): Are you . . . still there?
Assad: I am. I am listening. You have my complete attention, Miss . . . Did you say your name? I am going to need a name to do this properly, you know, because this is a very serious charge you are making.
Basma: My name is Basma. I come from Iraq. That is all I can tell you until we meet.
Assad: Of course, Basma. Yes. I assure you that I take this matter just as seriously as you do. And if what you are saying is true—and I have no reason to disbelieve you—then we will need to meet, and very soon.

Good, Nanette thought. When push came to shove, Assad had followed her wishes to the letter.

Basma: Yes.
Assad: But not here. Not at the police station.

His voice lowered to a whisper. It sounded like he was cupping his hand over the mouthpiece.

It is not always such a secure location, my office. I am sorry to say that not everyone here can be trusted with your kind of information.
Basma: Yes. All right, then.
Assad: But I do know of places where we can meet. Safe locations where—

Basma: No. I know of a place, too. It will have to be there.
Assad: Well, perhaps. But time is short.

Damn him, Nanette thought. He gave in far too easily on the location.

Basma: Seven o'clock, then. Tonight.
Assad: Tonight? But that is so late. If these girls are arriving today, then why—
Basma: Seven o'clock. I will call you at six thirty with the address.
Assad: Wait, now. Just wait. Why can't you tell me now, or sometime sooner?
Basma: I am frightened. I am not safe. How do I know I can trust you? Especially if only you and I are meeting?
Assad: Don't worry. I will make sure you are safe. And I will bring others who can also help you. Safety in numbers, okay? That way you don't have to worry about trusting only me.
Basma: What others? Other policemen?
Assad: Better than that. Members of a . . . a special task force which . . . which only handles these sorts of cases. So you see? Already I have told you a very big secret. Already I am having to trust you before you must trust me. You will be in the very best hands. But can't we meet a little sooner?
Basma: Seven o'clock.
Assad: Very well. Seven. But you must do one thing for me so that I will know I can trust you. Because now I am the one in danger. So if you cannot tell me the location until half an hour before our meeting, then I must ask that we arrive at the same time, both of us entering together, right at seven. That way I will know this is not some sort of ambush, or some trick you are playing on the police. Understood?
Basma: I don't know.

The girl sounded flustered, as if she hadn't counted on this twist. Nanette wondered if she had been trying to consult with someone else in the room with her.

Assad: This is how it must be done, Basma. Understand? Seven o'clock at your location, that is fine, I agree. But no one arriving a second earlier, so that we will both be able to feel secure. Okay?

Basma: I guess.
Assad: You guess?
Basma: Okay.
Assad: Very good, then. I will speak with you again at six thirty.
    Correct?
Basma: Correct.
Assad: At this number?
Basma: Yes.
Assad: I will be waiting. And do not worry. You will be in safe hands
    from now on. I give you my personal assurance as an officer of the
    law.
Basma: Thank you.
Assad: Of course.

"Don't you find it suspicious that she phoned you?" Nanette asked.

"If she had requested me by name, yes. But I checked afterward with the switchboard. All she asked for was the man in charge of vice, so they connected her to me. And now she will be playing right into our hands."

"You're the one that's being played, Assad, don't you see? That's why she didn't tell you the meeting place. Waiting until the last minute is part of the setup."

He waved a hand dismissively.

"She's scared. She's only being careful, just as you'd expect."

"Well, I'm not going to your damn meeting, I can tell you that."

"I arranged that for you! You said it was what you wanted!"

"Only on my terms, not hers. Set foot in the door of whatever place she chooses and we'll be history, all of us."

"You are being unreasonable, a silly and stubborn woman who only wants things her way!"

"I am being prudent, Assad, but don't fret. Not yet. You can still take charge of this situation, you know, in a way that will please everyone and will still take her off the board."

Assad snorted. He seemed in no mood to listen further. But at this point Nanette crossed her legs and turned slightly in her chair, offering a view in profile that she knew Assad liked best, for the tightness of her blouse and the way her long skirt hugged her hips, and, never to be discounted, for its sidelong view of the fullness of her auburn hair.

It instantly made him receptive enough to at least hear out her idea, which, with Liffey's persuasive assistance, he eventually accepted as their plan of action.

And now, here she was, down to her finishing touches of eyeliner, mascara, and lipstick. In an hour they would set things in motion, and then she would convince the others to follow her remaining plans to the letter.

Would women be hurt as a result? She loathed how that question kept popping up in her mind, because the answer, of course, was yes. But women were always hurt, weren't they? Especially the ones without the brains or the guts to fend for themselves. Besides, what would really be more hurtful to a bunch of starving young rustics in Iraq—leaving them mired in the turmoil of war or removing them to the relative safety of steady hours and a steady income, even if they earned it on their backs? To her the answer was obvious. At least in Dubai they might have a future, a buyout, even advancement.

She stood, popping her lips and appraising herself in the mirror from several angles. She saw competence, seduction, a hint of menace, and even a touch of Yankee common sense. A woman most any man would believe he could rely on, even as he angled for a quick fuck.

Bring them on. Nanette Weaver was ready.

28

On a quiet residential street in Al Manara, Charlie Hatcher's hour of reckoning was nigh.

Mansour's surveillance teams were in place—two men in front, two in back. Inside the empty villa, recorders were ready to roll. Dusk approached like a veil of sand.

Two blocks away, Sharaf and Keller sat in Laleh's BMW, taking turns with a pair of borrowed binoculars. Sharaf, cell phone open in his lap, checked the display for any last-minute messages. None. From a few streets over, the muezzin of a neighborhood mosque began droning the sundown call to prayer—a few minutes late, truth be told. It felt as if God was signaling that the drama was about to commence.

"Shouldn't you be praying?" Keller asked.

"Now? I'd need to wash myself first. I'd have to get out of the car and put down a rug, kneeling and mumbling while Assad and his people came and went. Don't you think that might be a little conspicuous?"

"Sorry. Stupid question. I was just hoping for any kind of edge."

"You believe that God takes a hand in police matters?"

"Not really. I guess I figured it might make you feel more confident."

"Do I not seem confident already?"

"Not really. You haven't all day. It's like you know the whole thing is doomed."

"It is not a sense of doom, Mr. Keller. Just an abeyance of hope. My way of holding my breath until it is time to make our move. Then I will exhale."

Actually, he *had* been feeling doomed. The plan was a throw-together, a hasty improvisation. And what was worse, all of them knew it. But no one had come up with an alternative, and so momentum had carried the day. Ready or not, something was about to happen.

So far, at least, there was reason for cautious optimism, especially after Laleh's success in convincing Basma to participate. They had all listened together to the girl's phone call, which Laleh had taped on Patel's digital recorder.

"She did well," Sharaf remarked afterward. "Obviously you handled her perfectly."

Laleh seemed affronted by the idea she'd been manipulative. She frowned and folded her arms.

"I don't much like Assad's idea for simultaneous arrival," Sharaf said, "but I suppose there is no way around it. It will be best if Basma arrives by taxi."

"I'll need to be with her when she departs, of course," Laleh said.

"Not necessary. You can just phone her with the information."

"The phone there isn't secure. She was using my cell, and she will need it again to call Assad at six thirty. Then I will arrange the taxi and make sure she is safely on her way."

Sharaf didn't like this wrinkle, but there seemed to be little choice. His daughter was the only one of them who knew Basma's location. She had again painted him into a corner, which meant that her further involvement was indispensable.

Laleh left the room without another word. She didn't even glance at Sam, and the young man seemed crestfallen. Once she was gone, Sharaf was more candid about his concerns.

"Stop worrying, Anwar," Ali said. "Assad was planning this completely on the fly, even more than we are. We'll have every advantage."

"Maybe so. But I've made a career of being underestimated. And I worry that now we are underestimating them."

"Relax. Mansour and I have every possibility covered."

Ali placed a reassuring hand on Sharaf's back, then returned to the kitchen to continue preparations by telephone.

"Mr. Keller," Sharaf said, "I am afraid we will need your presence at our little affair."

"I wouldn't miss it."

"My preference would be to keep you out of harm's way. Killing you by proxy is bad enough. But it may be up to you and me to ensure that nothing happens to this poor girl, Basma. Laleh would never forgive me. Worse, she would never forgive herself."

"Won't Mansour's men be looking out for her?"

"They will be preoccupied with springing the trap. The death of a young Iraqi with no passport, I am sorry to say, would be of little official consequence. So that will be our job, to move her to safety as quickly as possible. Do you know how to use a gun?"

The question seemed to floor him.

"I, uh, took a class once. Courtesy of Nanette, in fact. She ran a bunch of us through an executive survival course, with lessons on escape and evasion, that kind of thing. Part of it was firearms instruction."

"Ali has procured these for our use."

Sharaf took a bag off the kitchen table. No kebabs, this time. Just a pair of Beretta handguns. He handed one to Sam. Sturdy and compact. But heavy—that's what never failed to surprise him about guns, no matter how often he handled them.

"Careful, it's loaded."

"I wasn't a very good shot."

"But you will at least have the element of surprise. To them you will be a ghost. Sam Keller, risen from the dead."

"An avenging angel. Sounds good."

It made them smile, until Sam again hefted the gun and nearly dropped it in the process. And now they were in place, watching the street from Laleh's BMW, waiting for the arrival of the last key players.

The phone rang.

"Sharaf."

"Anwar, I think it's working." It was Mansour.

"You see them?"

"Not yet. But the container ship, the *Global Star*, I'm told its arrival has been delayed. Engine trouble is the cover story. Not due until tomorrow now. They must already be resorting to contingency plans."

"Good. Basma's phone call spooked them. Keep me posted if you see anything."

He hung up and told Sam the news.

"If they're that scared, do you think they'll shoot her on sight?"

It was the same thought that had occurred to Sharaf far too many times already. But he offered the same answer he had kept giving himself.

"That would violate their own protocol. No, they won't shoot her on sight, not as long as your Miss Weaver has her way, and she is still in town. Room 408 of the Shangri-La as of this morning. She will insist on a full debriefing, and that is what will make our case."

"If you say so."

Sharaf wished Sam hadn't made that remark. Certainly the operation wasn't foolproof—no operation was—but with their manpower and positioning it seemed as airtight as possible. Why, then, did the coffee from an hour earlier keep sluicing through his plumbing like acid, bubbling and grumbling? He checked the dashboard clock. 6:50.

"Here comes Assad!" Sam said. "Police van, far end of the block."

"He's early, but that's hardly a surprise. Once Basma called with the location he must have left right away."

They watched the van slide into a curbside spot directly in front of the villa. Sam still held the binoculars.

"Is anyone with him?" Sharaf asked.

"Yes. There's a driver and a passenger up front. I'm assuming one of them is Assad. Hard to tell through the smoked glass."

Sharaf looked back over his shoulder, then again peered down the block toward the villa. No further traffic was in sight.

"Where are the others?" he asked.

"Back of the van, maybe?"

"Hard to imagine the Tsar and Hedayat agreeing to be hauled around like a sack of dates, or even your Miss Weaver."

"Maybe they're coming later, after Assad gives the all clear."

"Maybe."

Or maybe Sharaf was trying to convince himself that things were still going according to plan. The coffee now felt like it was on the verge of rushing back up his esophagus.

Nothing more happened for the next six minutes. The van simply sat there, while Sharaf watched the digital display of the dashboard clock as closely as if it were linked to the workings of the cosmos. No sooner had it switched to 6:56 than a taxi came up from behind them, headed toward the villa. A woman in a black abaya sat in the back.

"It's Basma," Sam said. "Here we go."

"Give me those," Sharaf said, fumbling for the binoculars with sweaty palms. The neck strap got caught on Sam's ears before Sharaf pulled it free. He adjusted the focus and tracked the taxi to the curb. He could make out Basma's form through the back window as she hunched forward to pay the driver.

"Merciful God. I hope Laleh gave her enough dirhams for the fare."

The door opened. Basma stepped out. Sharaf watched through the binoculars as she looked around uncertainly. Something was wrong, he thought. Terribly wrong. But he wasn't sure what until he noticed Basma's spiked heels. Red. Stylish. The very pair that he hated most. Then he noted the polished gait of her walk as she started off down the sidewalk, like that of a confident young businesswoman.

"It's Laleh!" he shouted. "My God, the stupid fool! It's my damned daughter out there!"

"Shit!" Sam gasped. He, too, saw it now.

Sharaf reached for the door handle, then thought better of it, his mind moving in five directions at once. A door opened on the police van, and a cop in a khaki uniform stepped onto the street. Not Assad, but Sergeant Habash, for God's sake. From around the corner at the far end of the block, an ambulance careened into view, red bubble flashing in time with Sharaf's heartbeat.

"This isn't right!" he shouted. "We can't let this happen!"

Sharaf unlatched the door just as Sergeant Habash grabbed Laleh and shoved her toward the braking ambulance. For a horrifying moment Sharaf was certain Habash was going to throw his daughter beneath the wheels. Instead there was a screech of tires. Habash reached down and punched something into Laleh's thigh. She went limp almost immediately.

Sharaf ran up the street as fast as he could, too winded to even shout her name. Rear doors swung open on the ambulance and Habash bundled Laleh aboard as arms reached out from the inside. The doors slammed shut. She had been swallowed whole. Sharaf was still in flight, footsteps heavy, head throbbing, like in a nightmare when you can barely move. Was this why he had felt so troubled all day? At some level had he known Laleh was planning this, but refused to acknowledge it? He could even imagine how she would have arranged it with Basma, and he was taunted by the sound of Laleh's voice in his head.

Let me do this for you, Basma. Just make the phone calls, and I'll do the rest.

And now the ambulance was speeding toward him, siren shrieking. All he could do was stop, staring and panting with his arms open wide, as if he might somehow enclose the whole thing with one grasping tackle and wrench his daughter free.

At the last second the ambulance swerved. The side mirror clipped his shoulder, spinning him to the ground, legs tangling as his rump struck the pavement. He let out a great sob. "Laleh!" Then the police van passed him, too.

Why were none of Mansour's vehicles in pursuit? Sharaf looked back toward the villa and saw that Sergeant Habash was manning an impromptu roadblock with a barrier that must have been dumped out of the police van. Two of Mansour's vehicles had emerged from their hiding places in garages farther down the street, but Habash blocked their way, gun at the ready.

Sharaf tried to stand, rising so quickly that his head swam. Fifty yards away he saw the BMW make a screeching U-turn to head off in pursuit of the ambulance—Sam Keller at the wheel, taking charge before they lost Laleh altogether. Thank God. Keller was already several blocks behind, but for the moment he was the only one with a chance to keep pace.

Sharaf reached for his phone, then remembered he had left it on the seat of the BMW. Keep driving, he thought. Stay with them. The young man was his daughter's only hope. God help us all. Tears of fear and anger streamed down his cheeks. God help us all.

29

At first Sam tracked the ambulance by ear, turning left-right-left, then flooring it down a major boulevard as he listened for the urgent wail of the siren. By the time whoever was driving had the gumption to shut off the siren and the flashing red lights, Sam had spotted both the ambulance and the police van. For the first time he felt the stirrings of hope. A shaky hope, granted, but maybe he could keep pace. And when they stopped he could call in their location on Sharaf's phone, which was there on the seat beside him.

It then occurred to him that he didn't know anyone's number—not Mansour's, not Ali's, not anyone's—and a charge of panic branched out through his body like a lightning strike, from the back of his throat to the tips of his fingers.

Then, sweet relief. The phone rang. His one chance for reinforcements. He snatched it open, swerving dangerously in his lane as a car horn blasted. The ambulance was several hundred yards ahead and turning right, the police van right on its bumper.

"Keller! Are you there?" It was Sharaf, sounding just as you'd expect a father to sound when his daughter was being wheeled away to destruction.

"I'm in pursuit!" What a stupid thing to say, like he was playing at cops. "They're heading for the expressway."

"Sheikh Zayed Road?"

"Interchange three. They're on the eastbound ramp toward the city."

"We are coming. I am with Mansour. Just keep the line open."

"Okay, but I've got to put the phone down."

"Of course. Keep driving. Don't lose them."

Sam pressed the speakerphone button and tossed the phone on the seat.

"Can you still hear me?"

"Yes. Good." Sharaf's voice was tinny and crackling, windblown. "Stay on them."

Sam floored the accelerator up the ramp, merging onto the expressway. In a few hundred yards the dashboard alarm began scolding him in its mechanical monotone:

"*Ping.* You are speeding. Please slow down. *Ping.* You are speeding. Please slow down."

He kept sight of the ambulance and van about a quarter mile ahead, gaining a little ground as they cruised past the next interchange. For a while he thought they might be heading for the Shangri-La, but they kept moving as the traffic got heavier, and within another mile Sam was at a standstill in a massive backup, maybe thirty car lengths behind. Heat shimmered from the stalled rooftops of the vehicles between them. The gold light of dusk had begun to fade. The ambulance put its flashers back on, and the sea of metal grudgingly parted as it slid forward, car by car. Sam still couldn't budge, and he pounded the steering wheel as he watched the ambulance easing into the clear.

"Shit!"

"What's happening?"

"Traffic jam. They're getting through by flashing their emergency lights."

"We see them. You're maybe a mile ahead of us now. Try to stay on them."

Sam popped the clutch and tapped the rear fender of the car just ahead, setting off an angry blast of its horn. The driver lurched the car forward, then thrust his head out the window to shout in a language Sam didn't understand. But Sam now had just enough room to slide into the right lane. He then squeezed over one more and finally onto the shoulder, where he floored it past a cement truck. This being Dubai, dozens of other drivers had already had the same idea, and Sam was soon locked into a hurtling caravan of Jaguars and Mercedes, surging forward on the shoulder within inches of a scarred Jersey wall. They skirted the smoking wreckage of the accident that had caused the backup, defying an angry cop who was trying to flag everyone down. Sam then eased into the clear as he searched the horizon for the ambulance.

He spotted it, well ahead. The van was still in its wake, and they were approaching the big traffic circle at the end of the expressway. Sam nearly collided with a dump truck, which blasted its air horn as he swerved in front.

"Where are you now?"

"Traffic circle, end of the line. It looks like they're going off to the right. Yes! I see them now, definitely turning right. I think they're heading for the Trade Centre. The U.S. Consulate, it's gotta be."

He immediately saw the logic of their choice. By being merely a consular office, and not an embassy, it offered a secure location after hours, meaning they'd have the place to themselves. But he also saw its limitations, and apparently so did Sharaf, who shouted back:

"If the Tsar's people are along, or Hedayat's, they won't be able to take their guns upstairs through security."

"What about Assad?"

"He'll be allowed, as long as he's in uniform."

But how would they slip an unconscious woman past security? On a stretcher, Sam supposed, straight out the back of the ambulance. Unorthodox, but possibly workable. By the time the security people in the downstairs lobby began questioning the logic of taking a medical patient *into* a building instead of *out* of it, the elevator would be halfway to its destination.

Sam wheeled into the lot. The ambulance was double-parked alongside the police van next to the building. Both looked empty, doors shut. Everyone must already be on their way upstairs.

"I'm there. I'm going in," Sam shouted. The Beretta bulged heavily in his pocket. Somehow he would have to get it through security.

"What floor?" Sharaf asked, voice strangled with desperation.

"Twenty-first. There's a punch code on the elevator. You'll need it for access."

"Do you know it?"

Sam remembered it easily. In his mind's eye he could still see Nanette punching in the number that evoked a national disaster, a date any American couldn't help but remember, which is probably why some lazy consular officer had chosen it.

"Nine-one-one. Two-thousand-one."

"You'd better wait for—no, never mind. Do what you can. We are a few minutes behind you. Good luck."

Sam figured Sharaf had been about to tell him to wait for backup, as any policeman would, especially with a civilian leading the charge. But it was Sharaf's daughter up there. Caution was a luxury, and so were the usual rules of engagement.

He ran to the glass doors and shoved through. The main lobby was empty, its café closed. At the far end, by the security station leading to the consular elevators, a bored man in uniform waited at the walk-through metal detector. Sam tried to play it cool, although he was soaked in sweat. Four other countries had consular offices upstairs, and he might plausibly be headed to any of them, but he wondered how many visitors arrived dressed like him, more like a skateboarder than an off-duty diplomat.

As Sam approached, two big fellows stood up from a bank of chairs along the wall—a pair of goons, one Russian, one Iranian. Fortunately they didn't seem to recognize him. The challenge now was to make it through to the elevators without giving up his gun. In a gray plastic tray by the security station were two ugly weapons that had been confiscated from the earlier arrivals.

Sam smiled and nodded at the security man like they were old pals. The fellow nodded back, keeping his seat as Sam breezed through the metal detector. The alarm blared shrilly. Sam shrugged and held up his cell phone with another smile, as if to explain away the alarm, but he didn't break stride.

"Sir, you'll have to put that in the tray and go back through. Sir!"

Sam kept smiling, nodded again, and kept on walking. He was five steps from a waiting elevator, doors open.

"Sir!"

The man stood, a newspaper sliding from his lap. There was a flurry of motion and metallic clicks as the two goons also leaped to their feet and plunged hands into their jackets. Sam leaped aboard as a deafening gunshot slammed the wall to the left of the UP button. Ducking out of harm's way, he punched the CLOSE DOORS button as two more shots bounced loudly around the lobby. Footsteps clattered toward him as the door slid shut. He fumbled for a second with the keypad, then jammed in the right numbers and hit the button for twenty-one. There was shouting from the other side of the door, followed by the muffled bangs of two more shots. His stomach lurched as the car shuddered and rose, gaining speed, leaving behind all the noise and bother.

He was on his way.

The door opened with a sharp *ping* onto a view of two clones of the fellows he had left behind downstairs. They stood by the closed door to the conference room. One was just pocketing his cell phone and already stepping toward the elevator. Both instinctively reached inside their jackets before they realized, with matching expressions of dismay, that their weapons were still downstairs. Sam pulled the Beretta from his pocket, heavy and cool, and held it forward at gut level. The first fellow kept coming anyway until Sam shouted.

"Stop or you're dead!"

His voice was high and tight, but for the moment it did the trick. The Russian was still eight feet away as Sam stepped off the elevator.

"Back up!"

They obliged. Terrified as he was, there was a certain giddiness to this brand of power. "Drop to the floor and give me fifty!" he felt like shouting, like one of his old gym teachers. But he knew that soon enough they would figure out he was clueless unless he came up with a way to get rid of them.

"Get on the elevator!" he said, in a burst of inspiration. He backed off to give them passage. "Now! Or I'll blow your fucking heads off!" An adrenaline punch in every word.

They obeyed, nodding carefully to the whacked-out novice, perhaps as fearful of his hair-trigger nerves as he was.

"Back up, into the corner!"

They complied. He reached inside just far enough to hit the button for the ground floor. The doors slid shut, and he listened to the cables groan as the car descended. Unless they knew the security code, which he doubted, they wouldn't bother him anytime soon.

Sam put his ear to the conference room door, but the oak was too thick and sturdy to make out anything but muffled voices. Just as well, or they would have heard all the commotion out here. Should he just burst in, gun raised? Or should he wait for help?

Then he remembered from the earlier meeting that there was a second entrance, a door at the opposite end, probably from the consul's office. Sam worked his way through a suite of offices, heading back around to the left until he saw that, sure enough, an entrance to the conference room was at the end and the door was open. From this vantage point he could see only the end of the long room. As he edged forward, the conference table came into view. Laleh was seated at the head of the table, slumped forward in a chair, her head resting on the oak surface. Three or four voices were conversing casually in Russian, as if everyone was waiting for the real business to begin. Or maybe they were just waiting for the guest of honor to come to her senses.

Lieutenant Assad's voice called out in English. "You said this would wear off quickly."

"Don't worry." It was Nanette, cool and commanding. "We have a little something to speed her along. When she gets a jolt of it, she'll be instantly alert. Then we'll get what we need and take care of her."

"Straight to the desert, with her pimp."

"I was hoping this time you might find a less conspicuous location."

Sam had to resist an urge to shout back. But at least now he knew he had some time to work with. And they still thought the woman in custody was Basma.

Another Mafia goon moved into view, holding a hypodermic needle in his raised right hand. Sam eased out of sight to the right of the door, but he was still able to see the needle jab Laleh's thigh, right through her abaya. The man paused a second, then moved away as Laleh's right hand twitched on the table. She raised her head, shook it slowly, side to side, then reflexively pulled her abaya off over her head, as if coming up for air.

She shook out her hair and opened her eyes, then gasped and put a hand to her mouth, seemingly astonished to find an audience.

Lieutenant Assad broke into laughter.

"I don't believe it!"

"What is it?" Nanette asked. "What's wrong?"

"We've been had! This isn't the whore. Although she's no better than one, the way she conducts herself. Except this time her own father is pimping her. This is Sharaf's daughter, Laleh."

"What do we do, then?"

"Cancel our delivery, of course. Instruct them not to even unload."

"But what about her?"

"Kill her, before she becomes an even bigger problem."

"Not here!" Liffey protested.

"All right, then. Choose some other place. But do it quickly. Sharaf will be looking for us for sure."

Sam tensed at the door. His grip on the gun was slippery with sweat. Should he keep waiting or go now? As if to answer the question for him, Sharaf's cell phone rang loudly in his pocket.

"Who's there?" Nanette called out from the conference room.

"Boris?" a Russian voice said.

Sam stepped through the doorway and turned his gun on the others as he sidled toward Laleh. Sharaf's prediction proved true. The Tsar, Hedayat, and the lone goon merely looked puzzled, even annoyed, but the other three—Liffey, Assad, and especially Nanette—stared in openmouthed shock. The dead man walked.

"*Sam?*" Nanette exclaimed. "But . . . ?"

Assad reached for his holster. Sam's nerve failed him just long enough for the man to pull the gun free, but he finally squeezed the trigger as Assad was leveling the weapon to fire. As he did, someone grabbed him from behind, and he felt them both tumbling backward as two blasts rang in his ear, deafening. He felt a powerful blow to the back of his head, as if someone had torn open the base of his skull, and his last fleeting thought was to wonder how Assad had managed to hit him at such a poor angle, and with such a devastating exit wound.

Then, for the second time in as many days, he was out, oblivious, erased from the moment.

30

Anwar Sharaf watched in agony as the numbered lights flickered in sequence, floor by floor, as the elevator rose to twenty-one.

"Stay behind me when the doors open," Mansour said to his left.

"Are you crazy? I'll be the first one in if I have to kill you."

The elevator slowed. Sharaf raised himself up on the balls of his feet. Just as the doors began sliding apart, two gunshots echoed sharply, and he cried out in anguish. He shoved through, banging his shoulders. The Tsar and Hedayat were stumbling toward him in an open doorway, looking confused and disoriented. Some goon was coming through in their wake. Sharaf didn't even pause. He ran past them, gun raised as he looked wildly about him, trying to take in the whole scene at once.

Laleh lay on her back to his right, her eyes open. Keller was on top of her, faceup, eyes also open but horribly fixed and glazed. Assad was sprawled across a chair at the far end, blood gouting onto the long wooden table. He groaned, clutching his chest. The redhead, Miss Weaver, stood next to Hal Liffey by the windows in a far corner. Their hands were raised. Mansour rushed around the table to detain them. Sharaf dropped to one knee and grabbed Laleh's hand.

"Laleh! Are you—?"

She pulled her hand free and struggled from beneath Keller, then raised herself onto her knees, gasping like an exhausted runner. Her clothes were bloody, but Sharaf realized joyously that the blood wasn't hers. Then his relief turned instantly to shame as he saw that the blood was Keller's. The young man still wasn't moving a muscle. Mouth slack, eyes locked. Sharaf dropped his gun, but Laleh was a step ahead of him as she checked the American's pulse.

"I think he's all right," she said.

"But he's—"

"Out cold. His head hit the table as I was pulling him down. Assad was about to shoot. He's been hit in the shoulder, but nowhere else. Call an ambulance."

"We can use the one downstairs. What could you possibly have been thinking, Laleh?"

They embraced on their knees, and he felt her relax into a sob.

"Brave girl," he whispered. "And a damned fool. If you think Assad was dangerous, wait until your mother sees you."

They shook together in laughter and relief. And that was the scene that Sam Keller opened his eyes to, seconds later. Looking up sideways from the floor, he saw the blur of father and daughter embracing, yet kneeling as if in prayer. At first he was groggy enough to believe it was a dream.

Then Sharaf looked down at him and smiled. The man looked exhausted, grateful. Or he did until Laleh reached down and gently stroked Sam's cheek, at which point the father frowned. Only then was Sam convinced that this must all be real.

31

It took one day of hospital treatment and two days of paperwork for Sam Keller to convince Hal Liffey's consular replacement that he wasn't really dead.

By then, Liffey, Nanette Weaver, and Lieutenant Assad had all begun pointing fingers at one another, while the mobsters kept their own counsel. The conspirators might well have maintained a united front of silence if not for the digital recorder that Laleh had been wearing on the evening they kidnapped her. But as soon as its contents became known, the accused began spouting a flurry of conflicting cover stories, too complicated for anyone but well-trained attorneys to puzzle out, at the rate of $500 an hour.

Still, the rogues were making progress of a sort. Of the ten people arrested that morning, only two of the hapless goons hadn't yet mustered enough money and connections to be released on bail.

Fifty young women from Iraq, meanwhile, had arrived dehydrated and seasick early Tuesday morning aboard the container ship *Global Star*. They were now resting comfortably on the government's tab at an airport hotel, awaiting repatriation to a more peaceful part of their home country.

You might say that Sam Keller was doing the same thing, albeit under more posh circumstances at the Shangri-La. His new passport had finally arrived only an hour earlier, delivered by courier along with a ticket for an Emirates nonstop to New York. Economy class, but he'd take it. The airport taxi was due in an hour.

As Sam sipped a gin and tonic in the lobby bar, luggage at his feet, he was already wondering who would prove to be more difficult—the consular officials who had grudgingly sorted out his details or his old employers at Pfluger Klaxon. Innocent or not, in the eyes of each group he had unpardonably damaged reputations by exposing the misdeeds of valued employees. He might need a lawyer as much as Nanette.

But at least two people remained indisputably on his side, and Sam watched as they approached him across the palatial lobby. They were quite a sight amid the gathered opulence and Western fashion—a slender young woman sheathed in a black abaya and a pudgy fifty-something cop, in uniform, with a droopy mustache and a stupid red beret. A few tables over, a trio of cosmopolitan-looking Euros had already drawn a bead on the pair, and one was snickering behind his drink.

Sam stood to catch their eye. He pulled out a pair of chairs and bowed theatrically.

Sharaf smiled. So did Laleh.

"Oh, my God, they're with *him*," someone muttered to his left.

Sharaf's smile broadened as they reached the table. He held out a fleshy hand, then pulled Sam into a firm embrace.

"Amina also sends her farewell," Sharaf said, "although I will not pretend she was eager to deliver the message personally."

"Can't blame her," Sam said. "She could've lost you both. Besides, I think I forgot to make the bed that last morning at your house."

When Sharaf released his grip, Laleh leaned forward and lightly touched his forearm. The gesture put a dent in Sharaf's smile.

"How is your shoulder?" she asked.

"Sore, but no lasting damage. I'll have the bandage off in a few weeks. What about you? Holding up okay under the glare?"

The Sharafs were still reeling a bit from all that had happened, especially with regard to its impact on Laleh and her reputation. The local newspapers had covered the events extensively, but their accuracy hadn't always matched their zeal. Laleh emerged as a hero but also as something of a libertine, and there had been loads of innuendo with regard to what must have gone on between her and the young American.

To help calm things down, Amina and Anwar had decided it would be best to send Laleh away for a while, by letting her take her long-desired trip to New York. Her brother Yousef would return from his own European travels to escort her, and she would be staying with protective aunts and uncles living in New Jersey. Sam wasn't yet supposed to know any of this, but Laleh had passed along the details in a series of surreptitious texts and e-mails. He had been wondering if Sharaf would dare mention it now.

Sam got his answer sooner than he expected. As soon as father and daughter had taken their seats, Sharaf waved away an approaching waiter and said, "Laleh, dear. I have some important business to discuss with Mr. Keller before we say good-bye. In private, if you don't mind."

She rolled her eyes and looked to Sam, who answered with a shrug.

"I'll go look at the postcards," she said. "But only a few."

Sharaf watched until she was out of earshot.

"You may already know this, Mr. Keller, but my daughter will soon be traveling to your own city of New York."

Sam tried to look surprised.

"Good for her," he said.

"Perhaps my relatives who will be taking care of her will invite you to their home in New Jersey one evening for dinner."

"If they do, I'll gladly accept."

Sharaf went on to describe the various layers of escorts and chaperones who would be surrounding Laleh at all times during her stay, generally making it sound as if getting time alone with her would be more difficult than wedging your car into a presidential motorcade.

Not that Sam was too concerned. If he could wind up alone with her in an empty office at daybreak in the heart of Dubai, then certainly he should be able to beat the odds on his home turf. Sharaf must have realized this as well, judging from his next words.

"All the same, Mr. Keller, I know firsthand that you are a resourceful young man. So I ask only that if and when you do see my daughter in America, that you act responsibly, and with the greatest of care for her feelings. Yes?"

"Of course. I wouldn't think of treating her in any other way."

Sharaf studied his face for a moment. Then he nodded, resigned if not entirely placated.

"I still cannot believe my wife thinks this trip is a good idea. But she feels it is the only way Laleh will ever regain her privacy. The worst of it is, that jackal Assad is spreading the foulest rumors. But try explaining that to one of these salivating fools from the *Gulf News*."

"So what will happen to you next?" Sam asked. "A promotion?"

Sharaf chuckled dismissively.

"Doubtful. The Minister, at least, is happy. I suppose that will always be worth something."

"*Wasta*?" Sam asked.

"Oh, major *wasta*. Perhaps a lifetime supply. As for the police, well, you never earn much credit by bringing down one of your own."

"Tell me about it."

"You, at least, can always go to work for the competition. Not an option for me, unless I want to end up like Assad. Ah, here comes Laleh." He scraped back his chair and stood. "I will say good-bye, then, and let her say her own farewell in private. She demanded that of me before we came, and you have seen how powerless I have become in refusing her demands. That is what always becomes of fatherhood, I suppose. Eventually no one pays any attention to you at all."

"If that means she has learned to think for herself, then you've raised her pretty well."

It wasn't clear from Sharaf's uncomfortable expression whether he considered that a compliment or not.

"So long," Sam said, holding out his right hand. Sharaf took it, and again turned it into a hug, and he whispered quickly into Sam's ear.

"I will forever think of you as I think of my oldest friends, those who dove the deepest waters with me."

Sam felt two meaty slaps across his back, then Sharaf released him and departed without a further word.

Laleh made her way past the other tables to his side. They remained standing. It was clear to Sam that she didn't plan to sit.

"I won't be able to hug you like him, you know. Not out here in the open."

"I know."

"So I guess all I can really do is say good-bye."

"You could say, 'See you in New York.' "

She smiled.

"My aunts and uncles will be watching me like hawks. So give me at least a week to make them feel secure. Then we'll see what we can arrange."

"I'm sure we'll think of something."

"We always have."

She fleetingly touched his hand, then turned to go. Over her shoulder, Sam saw Sharaf watching intently from beyond the tables, with a hint of a smile playing at his lips. The old policeman called out to him one last time.

"One more thing you should know about me, Mr. Keller. In addition to speaking five languages, I am also an expert at reading lips."

Sam couldn't help but laugh. Fortunately, Sharaf joined in.

ACKNOWLEDGMENTS

Like any city that has grown up fast and lives at top speed, yet still conceals a core of slower and more traditional culture, Dubai is not an easy place to get to know in a hurry. But during my visit there for a few weeks in the spring of 2008, many people were generous with their time, experience, and insight in helping me to at least make an attempt, and I would like to thank them.

At the top of the list is the courageous and irrepressible Sharla Musabih, founder of the City of Hope shelter for battered women. Ms. Musabih and her work are such irresistible forces that it was probably inevitable that she would inspire my portrayal of the fictional Yvette Halami, and her Beacon of Light shelter. Thanks also to City of Hope caseworker Yeshi Riske, for offering a wealth of anecdotes and information about the lives of imperiled women in Dubai.

Thanks also for the many observations on daily life—from both locals and expats—offered by Ahmed Al Attar, Zeyad Al Majed, Doug Cousino, Dhruv Dhawan, Elizabeth Drachman, Nancy Mahmoud, and several others.

For insights into Dubai's legal system, I'd like to thank Jack Greenwald and John Dragonetti, who also shared their observations on the sleepier way of life in pre-boom Dubai. The fascinating Dubai Museum also helped me shape portraits of the past. But I owe a special thank-you in this department to the invaluable *Telling Tales* (Dubai: Explorer Publishing, 2005), a fine collection of Dubai oral histories from all walks of life, compiled by journalist Julia Wheeler and photographer Paul Thuysbaert.

Building Towers, Cheating Workers, the exhaustive Human Rights Watch report on living conditions in Dubai's camps for construction workers, was quite helpful, as were the interviews I was able to conduct with workers living in the Al Qusais and Sonapur labor camps—that is, until I was chased out of both areas by image-conscious security personnel.

Thanks to the affable and interesting Bill Trundley, vice president of Corporate Security and Investigations for GlaxoSmithKline, for patiently explaining the duties and challenges of a security chief for a major pharmaceutical firm.

And thanks as well to Bert Tatham, the Canadian aid worker unjustly imprisoned in Dubai for several months in 2007, for offering his descriptions and observations on the sometimes harrowing living conditions inside the Dubai Central Jail in Al Aweer.

Last but not least, thanks to friend and colleague Sandy Banisky for advising me on how to best equip Nanette Weaver for battle, cosmetically speaking.

Dan Fesperman's travels as a writer have taken him to thirty countries and three war zones. *Lie in the Dark* won the Crime Writers' Association of Britain's John Creasey Memorial Dagger Award for best first crime novel, and *The Small Boat of Great Sorrows* won the association's Ian Fleming Steel Dagger Award for best thriller. *The Prisoner of Guantánamo* won the Dashiell Hammett Award from the International Association of Crime Writers. He lives in Baltimore.

A NOTE ON THE TYPE

This book was set in Janson, a typeface long thought to have been made by the Dutchman Anton Janson, who was a practicing type-founder in Leipzig during the years 1668–1687. However, it has been conclusively demonstrated that these types are actually the work of Nicholas Kis (1650–1702), a Hungarian, who most probably learned his trade from the master Dutch typefounder Dirk Voskens. The type is an excellent example of the influential and sturdy Dutch types that prevailed in England up to the time William Caslon (1692–1766) developed his own incomparable designs from them.

Composed by Creative Graphics,
Allentown, Pennsylvania
Printed and bound by Berryville Graphics,
Berryville, Virginia
Designed by Virginia Tan